FAIRY SWATTER
Stories

PETER MELILLO

Cover design by Linda Kosarin/The Art Department
Typeset by Raymond Luczak
Cover photo copyright of the author

Published by Querelle Independent, a division of Querelle Press LLC
2808 Broadway #4
New York, NY 10025

www.querellepress.com

ISBN: 978-0-9995177-2-7, paper edition
ISBN 978-0-9995177-3-4, e-book edition

Distributed by Ingram Content Group
Printed in the United States

First edition 2017

Published by Querelle Independent,
an author publishing service division of Querelle Press

For Huynh Luong

CONTENTS

PREFACE

The thrust of these six short stories is gay men interacting in a straight dominant world with murder in the mix. Usually same sex desire is how homosexuals are defined and the excuse for persecution. To avoid identity confusion, sex is present as a lesser element in these stories. It is hoped the positive depiction of homosexual coupling; bridging the physical, emotional, even spiritual experiences in this fiction will support same sex expression as normal in many guises. Of these six stories numbers two, three, four, and six are fiction, and any similarities to persons, places or events are coincidental.

From ancient times to the present most homosexual history has been overtly destroyed, or covertly deleted or hetero-sexualized by the majority heterosexual culture. However, traditionally small amounts of skewed homosexual history have been allowed; if the gay protagonist commits suicide or is queerbashed to death after having a pathetic life. Recent events have proven the myth that homosexuals must suicide or be killed wrong. Research data showing homosexual teenagers and children has gone from the highest number of suicides for their age groups to the lowest; since same sex marriage was legalized in the United States.

The first story in this collection is an example of an ignored then deleted gay historical civil rights action. It is a fictionalized version of an actual incident involving an ax labeled Fairy Swatter (photo included). The ax was prominently displayed in a now defunct heterosexual singles bar. Gay activists politely asked the bar's management to remove the homophobic symbol and implied implement of dismemberment, and were met with threats of violence. Follow-up letters, petitions and telephone messages respectfully asking for the removal of the offensive Fairy Swatter went unanswered. Left no recourse, Gay Activist zapped the bar; blowing shrieking whistles and loudly slapping fly swatters. Bar patrons fled the unexpected invasion of boisterous whistle blowing Fairies wheeling fly swatters. Then large numbers of police officers arrived and evicted the noisy faggots from the open to the public business establishment. The cops decided not to arrest any of the queers they physically strong-armed out of the hookup bar during the zap. The police feared their handcuffs would spark a riot similar to the Stonewall Inn Rebellion.

The bar's patrons were so traumatized by that night's events they never returned. Word travels fast among heterosexuals on the make, and alas that bar had to go out of business for lack of customers. This writer participated in that gay social action and can verify there was no gun play or beheadings at the nonfiction Fairy Swatter's zap. This "Fairy Swatter" story should be listed as historical fiction, but its history, like most gay history, was not found news worthy for the dominant culture. In any case this fiction tale is about a different "Fairy Swatter," a made-up oversize antique fireman's ax, but in coincidental historical circumstances to the original. Any similarities in this story to persons, places, antique axes, or events are fictitious. This short story does touch on loss, renewal, quitting cigarette smoking, being out of the closet, homophobia, Mexican drug lords, radical Muslim, teenagers, Turkish appetizers, and just a smidgeon about intergenerational gay relationships.

Most young Hip-hop fans have little if any knowledge of Rap Music's history glorifying: homophobia, misogyny, racism, gratuitous violence, and virulent antipolice hate. In "Rapper," the second story in this collection, a Rap artist tries to revive the bad old days of Hip Hop music. Caught in a catch-22 situation, he tries to coerce an award-winning documentary film artist into making a retrograde music video. This short story is not for the faint of heart, those with delicate sensibilities may want to skip it or stop reading at the first sign of discomfort. There are graphic threats of horrific torture, deaths by gun violence, and a somewhat explicit interracial gay sex scene.

Places like "Fort Gnats" still exist in the U.S. and other countries. This story is as much about place as about an escaped convict and two older Chinese-American male spouses at an impasse over a perceived moral imperative impacting their young ward. Most Southern Arizona days contain glaring-sun produced extreme heat, followed by freezing night temperature drops of more than forty degrees. The barren other worldly landscape can't hold the heat or the cold. Between the sunlight produced broiling hot of day and punishing cold of night are long spectacularly vibrant, dark colored cooling off sunsets, followed later by subtle pastel tinted warming sunrises. Set in an outer space like terrain, both sunsets and sunrises are beautiful to behold and mystical to feel for Arizonians open to see.

Males around the world are frequently socialized to believe their sex urges are spontaneous hormonal discharges so dangerous they must be denied or at least kept tightly constrained for fear of chaos, rather than naturally occurring physical appetites that require regular satiating. In "Matricide" Evan has figured out what he likes-needs sexually, and has the means to satisfy his esoteric appetites. Shlomo's path is constricted by family expectations, religion, and the traditions of a tightly controlled community. "In Psych-101 we learned about the Oedipal and Electra complexes. Evan, what is the name for the complex where your first lover's first lover was your father? I can't be the originator, can I?" Both men go through metamorphoses to arrive at a place neither had anticipated.

The fifth story in this collection, "Bebop Writers," is historical fiction based loosely on a true story of a murder committed by a nineteen-year-old Columbia

University student in 1944. Even though the actual people in "Bebop Writers" are dead, nevertheless their names were changed to protect descendants and descendants of descendants and anyone who might take offense to real names of famous authors used in fiction.

In 1944 many significant things happened at Columbia University, for example the A-bomb was developed, but that is not mentioned in this story. Four fledgling authors met there and refined their craft using New Vision Writing (no revising), that writing method is also not mentioned in this story. Mentioned here; Bebop music grew in popularity while the Second World War raged around four student writers. The war directly impacted these Columbia University English majors; with student deferments to avoid wartime conscription and domestic rationing of most consumables (except drinking alcohol) to support the war. Music was a distraction from the stresses of that worrisome time. In this story three student authors go on to notoriety and eventually celebrity status while the fourth and best Bebop writer goes to prison for murder. In prison, he consciously gives up his writer's gifts to survive and then attain a level of serenity. He passes his new-found consciousness on to keep his cellmate-protector safe from the electric chair.

The inspiration for "Recall" came late one afternoon while zoning out waiting for the doors to open on a Q subway train. A glance through the train door window revealed an exhibitionist standing inside. His private parts were exposed for all to see; unlike most exhibitionists he had a lot to show off. His challenges to public versus private propriety disturb the afternoon's reverie for only a very few subway riders. Most transit passengers didn't see, or when they obviously did, showed little if any reaction. In response to this puzzle, the situation here was inverted for one observer in the context of mass transit early rush-hour. "Recall" is about a profit driven serial killer with no modesty or scruples, real and pretend mental illness[1], and penis obsession. The story also touches on protecting the straight world from knowing a famous much-loved Russian music composer was homosexual, and no matter how sweet it was, the past can never be repeated.

---

[1] Natural same sex aspiration and practice was listed erroneously as a mental illness in the United States from the 1890s until 1973. Homosexuality before the late 1800s was considered natural and normal by sane people. In modern times being homosexual is a crime punishable by a horrible death in a few barbaric countries, and in the minds of individuals ruled by imaginary hate filled superstitions. The confusions between reality, supernatural fantasies, and defenses to cover psychological conflicts are often contributory symptom of mental illness, but not always indicative of disease.

FAIRY SWATTER

Luke and Nestor first met when they were assigned to work a patrol car together in the Tenth Precinct. Luke had graduated the police academy three years prior and Nestor one and a half years. From that first instant, they knew they would be more than just partners on the job. As their friendship grew in depth it took on a with benefits dimension when each revealed to the other being gay. Both men acknowledged a deep friendship but not romantic love, and yet at work would give up their life for the other without a thought. After work they were on the precincts softball team, bowling league, and went to various professional sporting events on days off. At the same time, they dated other people and occasionally helped each other out with friendship sex.

When Luke's name reached the top of the sergeants' promotion list, he was assigned a plain clothes unit in the Twenty-Fifth precinct. Rather than see each other less, Luke and Nestor decided to try being roommates. With both men sharing the same address the Police Department noticed. Odd man out in the Tenth, Nestor was assigned to undercover in the Sixth Precinct in the Gay Village. Nestor complained to his union he'd been *outed* by the department, and was reassigned to the rough and tumble fifty-second Precinct in the Bronx. Nestor thrived and he and Luke settled into a bachelorhood of domestic tranquility for two, two fisted cops.

The roommates were engaged in a close chess game when Nestor suddenly stood up. "Look at the time. I got to go."

"Where you going?"

"There's an emergency Zap tonight."

"What zap?"

"It looks like El Geordies is going under sooner than anyone expected."

"Good riddance."

"Just not today, we need a picture of the *Fairy Swatter*. Tonight could be our last chance."

"I said it, good riddance to El Geordies and the damn *Fairy Swatter*."

"No not yet, it's a chunk of gay persecution history. The young ones need to know where their elders came from and put up with."

"Okay, then I go too."

"No, you be a good boy and stay home, read your book, you're not invited."

"I go to lots of places I'm not invited. Give me one reason I can't crash this party?"

"You know how the media is always saying Gay Liberation is a middle class white boys' club? If I don't show my brown face with other rainbow faces tonight, the public might actually believe that crap."

"Un-hah, so this zap is minorities only? Do you guys have the Gay Liberation Steering Committee's blessing?"

"No, but if the zap went as planned for next weekend, it would be mostly middle class white guys with a few of us others sprinkled in for flavor. Anyway, word on the street is El Geordies will be locked and shuttered by then. There is no time for the steering committee's Robert's Rules of Order ad-nausea, and I got to get dressed. Now you behave."

Luke was fighting a lost cause, he paused before speaking. "Okay, but geez we'd have hundreds of libbers mobilized making a nonviolent statement against future El Geordies and their ugly homophobia."

"True but we want more than prevention. So much of our history has been destroyed or heterosexualized, the public needs to see the ugly *Fairy Swatter* and imagine the psychic damage it did to young people."

"You are discriminating against me."

"No, I'm not, this zap is short notice on a weeknight; it is proof men of color can mobilize and act fast. That gives us street-cred." Nestor quickly stripped down for a quick shower.

"And everyone on this emergency call out just happens to be Black, Brown, or Yellow?"

Drying off quickly Nestor showed Luke a serious face. "Don't leave out our Native-American or as they like to be called; Indigenous Brothers. We can handle this, relax water our houseplants while I'm out."

"Houseplants can die from over watering. So, if someone at El Geordies lets a punch fly you guys will throw-down, right?"

"We'll see?"

"I don't like it; I want to back you up."

"This will only be a photographic reconnaissance mission. Stop worrying, look at you even worrying over the house plants. If I need a baby sitter I'll call."

"How about a compromise, I'll drive you there and wait outside, and then drive you and your zappers home, how about that? I'll even spring for after zap snacks."

"First off you have an early tour tomorrow, and need some sleep for a change. This could turn into a late night developing film and photo editing."

"And?"

"Second it would be impossible for you to wait outside without calling some coworkers to keep you company, with M-4s locked and loaded. If the police need to be called, it will be El Geordies calling them on us for being too peaceful. We got this; you just relax and talk to our houseplants."

"Talk about what? At least take your off-duty piece."

"Ask them if they are thirsty. I won't need it."

"When are the photos due?"

"The *Fairy Swatter's* photo is expected for tomorrow's print deadline, 4:30 AM, promises were made space is held. It has to happen tonight."

Six foot four inch, hard muscled, two hundred twenty-five pounds of Luke van den Hoose easily picked up five foot eight inch, one hundred forty-pound tough as nails wiry Nestor Negron and gave him a friendly hug.

Nestor squirmed out of the hug and, quickly slipped on black bikini briefs and socks, pulled up freshly washed, well-worn jeans that fit just right. Then topped the ensemble with a new purple t-shirt with a big gold metallic lambda blazing its front, and finally black running shoes. Luke came over and patted Nestor down and a disappointed look clouded his face.

To please his roommate Nestor went to their gun safe and removed his S&W five shot .38 calibers off duty revolver in its black Velcro ankle holster. Luke took Nestor's bullet proof vest from the closet. But Nestor briskly shook his head no, while making a disapproving face as he secured the small weapon to his left ankle.

Pouting at the front door Luke finally relented and returned Nestor's see you later. "Be safe, I'll probably be asleep when you get back. Wake me if you need to talk."

After locking the front door and plopping on the coach, Luke couldn't get into the page turner action-adventure novel he'd been reading every free minute since starting it. Putting the book aside he flipped on the TV and channel surfed until he'd seen all the possibilities twice and none caught his attention. Flipping the TV off and the Radio on, he traveled up and down the dial trying to find something of interest. Bored out of his gourd trying to find a radio station with music he was in the mood for, Luke jumped when the telephone and doorbell went off almost simultaneously. Grabbing the phone and heading for the door he said, "Yeah, van den Hoose here."

His sister's voice tight with rage demanded, "Have you seen Dirk tonight?"

Looking through the front door's peep hole he saw his nephew, looking angry like only a teenage boy can. Luke thought *No, I refuse to get in between them for another of their coming of age battles.* Guardedly he said, "He's at my door, shall I let him in?"

"Do whatever you want. He and I are not speaking, I give up. He can stay at your place or he can sleep in some shelter for homeless teenagers for all I care. But he is not sleeping under my roof tonight."

"Shall I get both sides of the story before deciding not to get involved?" His sister slammed off the telephone connection without saying goodbye. So, Luke opened the door. "Hi Dirk, it's a little late for an unannounced social call, don't you think?"

"Uncle Luke may I stay with you and Uncle Nestor tonight? My Mom has totally wigged out this time. I'm never going back there, I need a little time to find a new place to live."

"Want a snack, a drink or what besides housing?"

"I don't want to talk about Mom going around the bend. She went off the rails at full speed this time. But a snack and cold drink would be awesome. Where's Uncle Nestor?"

Walking to the kitchen followed closely by Dirk, Luke nuked a bag of microwave popcorn and put ice in a glass then opened and poured in a can of cola. They only kept the soda pop on hand for Dirk's visits; the two lawmen didn't like sugary empty calorie drinks. Indicating with a gesture Dirk should sit, Luke placed the glass; can of pop and bowl of popcorn in front of the teenager. "Nestor is out on a gay liberation mission."

"Did you guys have a fight?"

"No, why?"

"How come you didn't go along? I've never seen you two apart."

"It's complicated. Are you shopping for a permanent new address or can your maternal relationship be salvaged?"

"If it's okay, I'd like to stay here for a few days until I find something permanent?"

"I'm okay with that, but you will need Nestor's permission, this is his home too."

"He'll say yes he likes me."

"Do you need mediation with your mother? I seldom get to use the mediation skills they taught us at the police academy. But if I practice on you two, you'll have to wear handcuffs, for my protection."

"No thanks, what I'd like is to eat this popcorn, go take a shower and then crash in front of your television. That okay?"

"Did you bring clean clothes?"

"Mom knows I always sleep naked, it's healthier your whole-body breathes. That's why *she is supposed to knock* before coming in my room. Tomorrow I'll get fresh clothes while she's at work."

"Nestor and I have a strict rule, we are the only ones allowed nude in our home. Guests must be dressed. You need to revise your plan you little cock tease."

"Then Uncle Luke do you have something I could sleep in?"

"What do you wear, size small? I'm extra-large, and Nestor is medium. Tell you what, I'll call the all-night pharmacy and have them deliver a package of small size adult diapers."

"No, no don't do that, I'll just turn my underpants and t-shirt inside out for tonight, okay?"

"Come to think of it Nestor has some t-shirts that shrunk to too tight for him. I think they are in our rag bag. I'll let you peruse them before your shower. But you're on your own to recycle whatever."

While Dirk was taking a shower, Luke brushed and flossed his teeth over the kitchen sink. Next, he opened the living room sofa into a bed and put in place sheets, a pillow, and comforter.

Dirk walked into the living room barefoot wearing one of Nestor's shrunk too tight old fashioned logo t-shirts. The small yellow stain in front showed he'd obviously turned his skimpy underpants inside out. His blond hair, still wet from the shower lay flat. His big dark blue eyes opened wider in surprise noticing the sofa bed made up for the night. "Are we going to bed this early?"

"Yes, I have an early tour and you have to figure out how to get to school *on time* by City Bus. Do you have money for the bus and lunch?"

"Yes, I'm all right. You aren't going to tell me about the fight you and Nestor had, are you?"

"I told you, Nestor and I didn't have a fight. But it looks like you and your mother had a big one; domestic discord must be weighing on you? You can talk to our plants they are in a receptive mood, or so I've been told."

"Aw come on, I'm all keyed up, not sleepy at all." Dirk flopped his 120 pounds of angular adolescence down in an easy chair and looked longingly at the turned off television.

"If you can't sleep; lay there and tell the house plants about it until it is time for school."

"You are so not cool."

"If you feel cold get another blanket from the hall closet. I sleep deeply, if there is an emergency shake me hard. Good night."

"You sleep like my Mom, and sometimes you even sound like her when you order me around, like just now."

Luke fought in a dream, tossing and turning, fists and kicks flying. Finally, his nephew's forceful insistent shaking and shouting forced Luke out of deep slumber's combat.

"Wake up, wake up! Uncle Luke get up, come on!"

"What … where's the fire?"

"In your living room, it's is full of cops."

Luke didn't think to hide his morning wood as he pushed down the rumpled bed covers, stood, stretched, and scratched his ass as he groggily rambled into the living room. His straight light sand colored hair was a bed head tangle. His hazel eyes looked dazed, heavy with sleep. "What's going on here?"

"I am Lt. Sean Gilhooley, Sergeant, who is this underage boy?"

After a big yawn, Luke said, "Dirk, show the nice Lieutenant your school ID and something with your birth date. Now what the hell brings you into my living room in the middle of the night?"

Dirk went to his school uniform's tan slacks and retrieved his wallet. "This is my high school photo ID, this is my student bus pass showing my birthday, and even though he might not admit it, that man is my uncle."

"Sergeant van den Hoose where were you between eleven and one tonight."

"Here asleep until you woke me. What time is it?"

"Three o'clock in the morning. Can anyone vouch for that?"

"My eighteen-year-old nephew who looks like you just woke. Now what is this about, or do I need to call my union rep before we talk further?"

Luke could see on Lt. Gilhooley's big red drinker's face, he was searching for words. It was common knowledge Gilhooley was a homophobe and a boozer, but Nestor liked him even though he regularly corrected his Lieutenant's politically incorrect, often even abhorrent speech. Nestor said he suspected most of his Lieutenant's hate speech was not genuine and just for show, so his consciousness raising might actually be working.

The Lieutenant turned to Officer Tim Mahoney standing at his elbow and the other three uniformed cops on the other side of the room and said, "Tim take these men outside and wait for me," then turning back to Luke. "You want to sit down."

"Just spit out what you have to say Lieutenant."

Dirk sat down on the disheveled sofa bed. His face showed he was about to tune out adult stuff and nonsense and concentrate on his own troubles.

"Officer Nestor Negron was killed tonight. I'm sorry to inform you, Sergeant."

"What! What happened?" Suddenly Luke couldn't have been more wide awake if in an out gunned gun fight.

Dirk's jaw dropped as his deep blue eyes grew to saucer size then tears spilled over and ran down his cheeks in rivulets.

"We don't have many details, but other cops, were also killed in El Geordies Bar. Four bar employees and a patron are also dead. The bar is a huge bloody mess. There are injured too, but nobody is talking."

"Oh no, this can't be."

"It will take some time before we know everything. This isn't my case, but I was called in because Nestor was one of my men. The other officer's Lieutenants were also called. Do you know what Nestor was doing there tonight?"

His head in his hands trying to digest what he didn't want to accept. Luke mumbled without looking up, "A group of gay activists went to El Geordies to photograph the *Fairy Swatter*. It's an old-fashioned fire ax wearing a sign that reads *Fairy Swatter*."

"Why didn't you go?"

"It was a nonwhite zap to take a photo. That's what I know … except I know letters and petitions were sent asking the ax be taken down. I heard follow-up telephone messages also went unanswered, so a social action was necessary."

"Like I said I'm sorry you lost your roommate tonight. He was one of my best men and a damn good cop by anyone's standards."

"Nestor wasn't just my roommate; we were best friends."

It was clear from his bloodshot eyes the little wheels inside Gilhooley's head were turning, finally after a long pause he said, "Like I said sorry for your loss Sergeant. He was a good man. I'll miss him." Then after another pause his tone went from conciliatory to full rank authority. "Don't do anything stupid. You didn't hear this from me, but narcotics have had that place under surveillance. It's possible one of the dead workers was an undercover cop. I got to go. You take some time off to mourn your loss, man. Whatever you do be careful and not stupid. Those older and wiser than you will make this right. You just stay out of our way."

Standing at the front door Gilhooley did something uncharacteristic for the much older beefy cop. He turned grabbed Luke in a hug, and gave him straight guy condolence back pats. Then he pushed them apart holding Luke's shoulders. "Nestor was one of my favorite officers. I get first crack at who did this, and trust me justice *will* be served." With that said he was out the door and the other cops waiting outside followed in his wake heading for their cars.

When Gilhooley said Nestor *was*, the reality hit Luke so hard his knees bent. Nestor was never coming home. Suddenly Luke wanted to howl and scream and hunt down and kill the bastard who took Nestor's life.

But he kept any outward sign of emotional turmoil in check, feeling Dirk's eyes on his back. He locked the front door behind their late-night callers and turned. "How much of that did you get?"

The teen was sitting cross legged among rumpled bedding. Luke was startled to see Dirk shamelessly crying, his usual open friendly face contorted by sobs. He sat down next to his weeping nephew and put an arm over his shoulders. Dirk slid an arm around Luke's waist, put his head against his uncle's chest and yowled with grief. Not intending to, Luke let the tears that he had held in check flow silently. Uncle and nephew wept holding each other until their tears ran dry, then desiccated with grief they fell back and slept arms still entwined.

Luke heard the alarm clock jangling from his bedroom got up turned it off and took a quick shower. He wondered *should I go to work today, I might get some clues about who killed Nestor, or I might say or do dumb things from grief. Wait, what kind of example will I set for Dirk if I don't go in?* Luke decided, after concentrated thought, what he wanted more than anything was to be alone, curl into a ball and morn out loud. But common sense told him sending Dirk back to his sister with their problem unresolved would make a bad situation worse. So, heading to his bedroom to get dressed he shouted to Dirk, "Get up and get dressed old pal we need breakfast."

Dirk made a big show of groaning awake, yawning and stretching. "I'm not hungry; I'd rather sleep some more, maybe for a week or even a month." With that said he rolled over turning his back to Luke.

"If I have to come over there you'll be sorry, hurry up put some clothes on, and let's go."

"Or what?"

"Or I'll pick you up and carry you to the restaurant wearing only your inside out underpants showing skid marks and Nestor's too big for your old T-shirt."

Dirk blushed, stood pulled off his inside out briefs, examined the seat and then blushed an even darker red and pulled on his school slacks without underpants. His face showed anger and embarrassment brewing into a big storm as he finished putting on his school uniform.

"Take it easy will yah, you weren't showing your ass until just now. Nobody saw except me and I'm family so I don't count." Luke had turned his face away from his nephew's furious undressing then redressing in embarrassment. His grieving resurfaced with a vengeance, but he forced it back down. "Dirk, don't forget to take your cell phone."

Neither man spoke leaving the small house, or driving to the eatery. Luke was lost in rapid fire scattered thoughts about mortality. Dirk was boiling shame and anger and the finality of death all mixed together into a bitter stew. The air between them was heavy with doom and gloom.

Seating themselves in a booth at the Twenty-Four-Hour Breakfast Spot Dirk said, "It would have been nice if you said something about my underpants last night. And now I expect you're going to make me go home to my mother, on top of everything."

"I'm sorry I embarrassed you this morning. As soon as the words left my lips I knew I was out of order. My brain is fogged up with Nestor's murder."

"And I overreacted because I love Nestor and don't want him dead." Dirk started sniffling then blew his nose.

"I know that. But I don't know what's up between you and my sister. Normally hearing both sides of the story would help me help. But right now, all I can think about is Nestor. You and your mother are on your own to fix what's broke between you."

"Since I grew pubic hair mom and I have a rule, she is supposed to knock and wait for permission before opening my bedroom door. Yesterday she came home early from work and walked in on me and my boyfriend doing you knows what. Let me tell you it got horrible fast. She and I said awful hateful things. We won't be getting over that anytime soon, I can guarantee it."

"I get it. I was a teenager once, hundreds of years ago. Having privacy was at a premium even back then, especially with your mother, my snooping sister always looking to get in my business."

"Then can I stay with you?"

"Yeah, I suppose, if you try to make peace with your mother."

"Cool."

"There is something I need you to understand, Nestor's murder is weighing on me. So, I may not act like myself or even anywhere close normal. You'll have to deal with that and not make my problems our problem or your problem, understand?"

Dirk visibly relaxed, accepting his uncle's qualified invitation; just then the food server came and took their order. Sliding back in the dark red plastic upholstered booth he said, "Even if mom and I weren't having differences right now I'd rather be with you during this time. I'll run the vacuum, take out the trash and do whatever I can to help. You know I really loved Nestor. Only in different ways than I love you?"

"I noticed. Truth be told, I was a little jealous of your relationship. You and I never got as close."

"You want to know why? I'll tell you why, because you act like my father and sound like my mother. My father died in the War, I'm not looking for a replacement and my mom is more than enough. Uncle Nestor was fair and I could talk to him about anything without being judged."

"Nestor is no longer with us and I am trying to figure out what to do about that. What do you say we have a fresh start? What can I do, that he used to do?"

"I'm running low on condoms. He usually bought me the biggest size box."

"What, Nestor gave you condoms? He never mentioned that."

"You always say, 'Be careful and play safe.' Uncle Nestor always asked, 'Do you have condoms to play safe with.' When I said no the first time, he got me a handful of different sizes, and said, 'Let me know what size fits best.'"

"So, you want me to buy you condoms?"

"If you care, I need the largest size they make. Right now, I'm finishing the fifth big box Uncle Nestor bought me."

"Dimmit Dirk, if you are old enough to use condoms you are old enough to buy them. Does your mother know?"

"See what I mean? You sound exactly like somebody's father. When Uncle Nestor had the talk with me about *how* to play safe, I was already doing the deed in middle school and didn't know much. The drug store wouldn't have sold me condoms at that age. Remember I was much shorter than the other boys in my class back then. Yes, now that I'm the tallest in my class I could buy my own rubbers, but that isn't the point anymore. It was something Uncle Nestor and I shared and it provided a place for me to ask him about other adult stuff without getting a lecture. You brought this up, but you aren't okay with my answer, see what I mean pops?"

The food server brought their breakfasts and the delicious aromas caused them to dig in with appetites they'd forgotten they had.

"Would you say I've been trying too hard to guide and protect and that's why you think I'm trying to replace your father?"

"Yes, I know you mean well. You just don't get how hard it is to be a teenager these days. I don't want to hurt your feelings, but more often than not you aren't helping. And right now, my only confidant is dead, and part of me feels like I died too. I don't know what to do with that."

"Yeah, well likewise for me on that one. In the meantime, I am driving you to school and then going to work. Here is cab money, afterschool go home and grab some clothes. I'll try to get back from work early and then we can talk and you can make suggestions on how I can be a better uncle, okay?"

"Can I have my boyfriend stop over after school? Oh, and I don't have a key to your house?"

"There is a spare key in the car, you can use it. No visitors without prior approval."

"Did you know Nestor used to give me motel money so I wouldn't do it in unsafe or public places?"

"No, he never mentioned that either. Okay, let me meet your boyfriend; have him bring photo ID proof of age. After I meet him, we'll see. What's his name?"

"Marco. Can I invite him to eat with us tonight, *dad*?"

"Fine."

2.

When he arrived at the police precinct there was a note from his Lieutenant. "See me before you sit down."

Lt. Schmidt wasn't in his office, so Luke dispatched his officers to street patrols with a promise to check in later, and they should call him if needed. He no sooner finished with them, then a pissed off looking Lt. Karl Schmidt literally grabbed him, pushed him into his office, and banged the door closed behind them.

Before Schmidt could start ranting, Luke spoke. "You weren't in your office, and my people needed to go on patrol. Your note said not to sit down, I haven't."

Anger cooled down a notch as Lt. Schmidt walked behind his desk but didn't sit. Instead he reached over the desk for a hand clasp. "I'm sorry for your loss Luke."

"Thank you, sir."

"You feeling okay, you don't look well?"

"I am fine, except my dearest friend was killed last night."

"Do you know what happened?"

"No, not exactly, I know a group of minority gay lib protestors' showed up at a straight pickup bar. So far there are no witnesses willing to talk."

"I hadn't heard about the Gay Lib part. You should take two or three weeks off to get your head straight?"

"My head is gay like the rest of me and I'd rather be at work than moping around the house."

"Then I am assigning you to desk duty. Doyle can supervise your people for now."

"What did I do?"

"You are not being punished. Officially you are on desk duty to catch-up on paperwork."

"You know my paperwork is always on time."

"Maybe you need to make funeral arrangements, notify folks, or go in the john to sulk. Or maybe even do what I ask for a change."

"All right, but I'd rather work."

"If you are working I want you close at hand in case somebody comes after you too. I'd like a clean shot at the son of a bitch."

"Boss what's going on, why you clipping my wings?"

"Strictly off the record, I just came from a meeting with the big muckety-mucks about all we don't know about last night's shootings. Before I bring you up to speed I need your promise to stay out of this muddle, unless I give you a green light, understand? Say yes."

"Yes sir, I hear you loud and clear. What happened last night?"

"I'd say it was a colossal screw-up caused by major failures to communicate by people who are trained to communicate. The investigation is now under the Feds jurisdiction, and we can expect sooner or later they will blame us for whatever went wrong."

"Oh no, not the Feds, I don't believe this."

"Yup we've been told hands off and back away. You and I know they are going to take a year to cover up their culpability, and make their findings about us fucking-up."

"Geez, how could this get any worse?"

"Homeland Security's DEA and their Antiterrorism Task Forces had been watching that bar without each other knowing. Can you believe that? They may or may not have had undercover operatives inside and outside when the shooting took place."

"Last night Lt. Gilhooley paid a Three A.M. condolence call and suggested we might have been watching the place too."

"True, our Narcotics people have had more than a passing interest in El Geordies of late. Naturally they didn't know of the Feds involvement, because that wasn't communicated."

"Dead cops, others dead, and we are told to back off. That's not acceptable, this is our City. Is it possible the Feds killed our guys not knowing who they were?"

"Anything is possible; none of our officers fired their weapons, so if it was friendly fire it wasn't us."

"Dammit with so many complications, you know I have to solve this."

"You can't. I know the timing sucks but you are in line for something important if you can keep your wits about you."

"I don't want to hear it. What more do you know about last night?"

"As near as I can figure there were too many mute moving parts. I suspect everyone had a whiff of something. But nobody got the full stink until last night."

"Okay, so what made it go hot?"

"That is the question?"

"Geez! Where do we start untangling?"

"What did I just say; back off, officially the Police Department will keep its hands off. The Feds say don't touch, they are the big dogs, know your place."

"Where I live have been reduced by fifty percent, I need to do something about that."

"You are hereby ordered to behave or face consequences you don't want to think about."

"Yeah, I heard you before, and if I do as told, there's a reward. Understood."

"Settle your ass down, off the record Gilhooley is taking Nestor's death personally; he can be like that with his officers. He has been on the job a long time, from when policing was done differently. He was eighteen when he joined the force, now he's well over retirement age. His don't give a shit attitude earned him large quantities of commendations and reprimands. In fact, he reminds me of you."

"Nestor said his methods are old school, but he gets the job done without a lot of bullshit. Yeah that reminds me of me too."

"Gilhooley is out for blood and the Feds be damned. My Captain asked me to watch the situation, I trust you, your desk duty will allow you to know what I know, if you follow orders. If I think it will help, you will let Gilhooley know what's happening, on the QT."

"Understood, we are not going after Islamist Terrorists or Mexican Drug Cartels as such, but we are going to take down those who killed Nestor and the others. Since the Feds say hands off, it has to be old school tactics. You want me for your information conduit to and from Lt. Gilhooley, right?"

"I will deny we had this conversation, other than you are restricted to desk duty until I say otherwise. Gilhooley is on board with you helping. Since we don't know what we're dealing with, I'm authorizing you to check an Uzi out of the armory. Take extra loaded magazines and keep them with you at all times. Just in case the bad guys come looking for you too and I can't get off some clean shots at them, dismissed sergeant."

Luke felt profoundly alone and forlorn slumped at his desk, while the squad room buzzed with frenetic energy around him. His eyes closed, head in hands, palpably mourning a loss, he acknowledged the splitting headache he'd been trying to ignore. After chewing three aspirins he felt himself drift into an emotionally and physically exhausted half-doze.

The jangling telephone at his elbow brought Luke to full consciousness. Quickly looking around the busy squad room nobody seemed to have noticed he had been half asleep. Checking his watch, he realized he had been desk sitting two hours, more unconscious than not. Picking up the black handset land line he said, "Sergeant van den Hoose."

"Is this Luke van den Hoose?"

"Yes, it is what can I do for you?"

"I'm Kwame Robinson; we met at a Gay Community Center's fund raiser years ago. The official word is you are the Police Department's gay liaison officer for last night's killings. I'd like to meet with you."

"Who said I was the gay liaison? That is news to me."

"I have it from the highest sources in the police department. Let me get right to the point, my spouse was killed last night so this request is personal."

"Sorry for your loss."

"Thank you. I want to talk with you, but not over the phone, would lunch or a drink work for you?"

"There hasn't been an official briefing yet, and by the looks of things it could be awhile before we get one. I don't know much."

"Can you recommend a place to meet?"

"Restaurants and bars are too noisy for talking, where are you?"

"I work downtown in the Federal Building; I don't want to meet here."

"My precinct is way uptown. How about we meet in the middle, there is a pocket park off Fifth on Fifty-third, it is usually underutilized. I get off at Two PM today, will that work?"

"I can make it work."

"Your meet, you bring the coffee; black no sugar, dark roast if they got it."

Luke noticed his headache was gone, and wondered *where do I know Kwame Robinson from?* Then the memory arrived. Speaking under his breath to himself, "Of course Kwame Robinson is a United States Attorney and his lover is-was a detective out of the Thirteenth precinct. What was his name …? Oh yeah, Jamal Lawler. Let's see Nestor and I met Lawler two years ago at that police conference at the Capitol. He was a nice guy." Sadness and rage started to build in Luke's gut until he capped it with a promise to himself he'd get retribution, bloody retribution, and as much as required.

There was still no briefing scheduled on the previous night's killings, just a perfunctory announcement. The atmosphere in the station house perceptively darkened as word of the killings spread. As the day progressed the atmosphere couldn't have gotten more morose if they'd covered the entire building in black bunting and played dirges on bagpipes. In that bleak atmosphere, Luke made the obligatory telephone calls notifying family and friends that Nestor passed. He postponed the call to his sister until later at home.

Kwame Robinson was standing behind a steel park bench when Luke arrived. He was holding two takeout containers of coffee and looked glum.

"I remembered your name but couldn't put a face with it until now. I'm sorry for your loss. My best friend and roommate got killed with Jamal and the others last night."

"I heard and am sorry for your loss as well. Here take this coffee and let's sit."

In the heavy silence that followed their greeting, Luke took stock of the man he'd met briefly years before. Kwame's dark amber eyes projected intense sadness from his dark coffee hued movie star handsome face. They were about the same height, taller than average. Kwame looked fit except for just a hint of middle aged paunch, was balding, and sprouted a big brush mustache on his long face. He had to be in his late forties, was dressed in an expensive looking three-piece suit, and a conservative neutral colored silk tie. Luke recalled Jamal, Kwame's lover as fifteen or twenty years younger, clean shaven, shorter and chunkier, also with dark complexion. He had been overflowing with energy and fun, closer to Nestor's age.

"Look, I don't want to waste your time, like I said on the phone we haven't had an official briefing. You probably know more than I do, you knew I was designated liaison to the gay community. I still haven't been told."

"Do you think there was a spy in the gay activist group that tipped off the bar a gay lib demonstration was coming?"

"To what point?"

"To warn them a gay Zap was coming."

"I doubt it, letters, petitions, and phone calls were made over months to get that damn thing removed. Anyway, if the *Fairy Swatter* was so precious they could have locked it up until after the zap, no reason to kill cops."

"But what would they tell their patrons who were used to seeing it hanging over the bar?"

"I don't know, 'it's out for cleaning or gilding or God knows whatever.' I doubt that clientele would buy less beer with the ax at the cleaner's. I'm not big on conspiracy theories, just give me facts."

"What is in your gym bag, it looks kind of empty?"

"Would you believe a submachine gun? My captain is paranoid."

"Do you think I should carry a gun?"

"Are you authorized to use lethal force?"

"No."

"I told Nestor if they got their precious photos in the media it could benefit El Geordies by bringing in more homophobes wanting to see the infamous *Fairy Swatter*."

"I told Jamal something similar; the gay libbers might actually save Geordie from bankruptcy by providing free publicity."

"I knew Jamal slightly, he was a nice guy."

"When all is said and done, what I want is revenge for his murder." This was said his clenched fists visibly shaking in barely contained rage.

"See that is where we differ, lawyers want revenge for society. I am a lowly cop who's only interested is public safety."

"Touché, always the hero, but I've heard about your unorthodox methods."

"Nobody should feel what I am feeling right now. If to protect the public from these feelings I have to use a little force, so be it, it's for the common good. When all the fancy words are spoken, for me it comes down to protecting the public."

"Your reputation precedes you Luke van den Hoose, apparently, what I heard about your style is true."

"I don't apologize for doing expedient police work."

"I understand, you don't know me or whether I can be trusted. So here is a proposition that could get me disbarred. I give it to you as a good faith gesture. If during your public safety campaign to avenge our men, you need an alibi, I'll provide it no questions asked."

"Now this is getting interesting, what would our cover story be your need for revenge?"

"No, we got together to burn black candles to curse the murders' of our friends. I know a scary Voodoo priestess who owes me big time; if I ask she'll gladly cover for us."

"I have been offered bribes before but yours; black candles and voodoo are new. Like I said I don't want to waste your time or mine, so thanks for the coffee, nice seeing you again and now I will be on my way."

"Don't waste times, give me something, and work with me."

"All right, what I am about to say you could easily find on your own. Your people have taken over; your dead lover and my friend is part of a Federal investigation that may have been complicit in their deaths. The police department has been ordered to step back, even though our own were murdered."

"Which agency, you can save me time having to work it out."

"Homeland Security's DEA and Anti-terrorism, and you didn't hear *that* from me."

"You're right; I'm in a position to learn things you couldn't, maybe even generate some heat if necessary. I still want your help."

"I'm listening."

"Local police, smaller less bureaucratic, might serve my intent and purpose better. Don't you guys have a code, if someone hurts one of yours, you *must* do pay back no matter what?"

"Something like that, we always collect our debts. The bad guys have to understand mess with us and we can be on both sides of the law. Now with the Feds taking over, we may need to use extra finesse, possibly extra, extra-legal measures to get payback. You really don't want to know about it."

"You're right; I need to get back to the office."

"Then at this point I think we have exposed each other's careers to enough risk, so I will again say thanks for the coffee, goodbye and good luck."

"Wait, what if I can get information for you?"

"If I agree, will you feel better?"

"I would actually, doing something is better than doing nothing. What about you?"

"How could I feel worse? The best part of my life is gone."

"Ditto here."

"What you see is a calm façade pasted over gut wrenching turmoil. You got a plan?"

"I'd rather people didn't know about our working together, so nothing written down, electronic, or telephone. Could we meet again face to face, here perhaps?"

"No that could get compromising fast. Tell you what, how about Wednesday evenings at the Gay Community Center?"

"What is your connection to the Center?"

"A gay teen discussion group; my best friend and I were the facilitators. With him gone we should have another adult present. It would be a perfect cover, once the kids get talking to each other we would have a little time for a private conversation outside the room. If you volunteer, we have a legitimate place to put our heads together."

"Huh, I don't usually like teenagers, are there any black ones."

"It's mutual the teens usually don't like adults all that much either. For the record, they come in black, brown, red, yellow and Caucasian. We help the kids stay off drugs and crime and give them a pressure release valve to manage whatever life has dealt them."

"Why do they need adults present, if they don't like us?"

"It took the Center's Legal Department a year to finally agree to the group. They freaked out over the idea of unsupervised minors using the facility."

"How did you bring them along?"

"Teens under eighteen have to return a signed parental consent letter, and sign their parents' signatures are genuine. Having two police officer facilitators also helped the lawyers sleep better at night and the insurance to stay in normal range."

"My being a Federal Attorney shouldn't hurt in a pinch."

"It would be good, if you can help."

"What's confusing is you don't look like the paternal type any more than I am. I hope you don't mind my saying that?"

"Very perceptive of you counselor, my nephew is gay and his mother has been less than supportive. Nestor and my nephew were instrumental starting the group for gay teenagers in his situation. I came along by association."

"Oh, I see."

"You read me right; I prefer to work with adults I usually know where I stand with them. Wednesday at seven thirty, the Gay Community Center, be there."

"See you then, hopefully with news to report."

As Kwame walked away, Luke took a second to look around the pocket park. A very young couple in one corner was holding hands; eyes locked together rhapsodizing in love. At the other end was an older couple, furtively kissing and touching. He imagined they were stealing a little extracurricular romance before going home to their less than loving spouses. Then out of the blue it hit Luke *this is the first time I've been alone since I heard of Nestor's death.* Then the flood gates opened and tears streaked down his cheeks and his shoulders shook with sobs. He covered his face with his hands and let the grief silently stream forth.

When cried out, he became aware of eyes intruding on his misery. Removing his hands and looking for the observer he spotted a young cop on foot patrol watching him. In the blink of an eye his grief turned to anger at the unwelcome intrusion. As the officer approached Luke stood and walked toward him his hands balled into hard fists.

The cop said, "You okay there, buddy?"

Luke sniffled, "Do I look okay?"

"Sorry to disturb you but your time in the park has expired. You have to move along." This was said with officious insincerity.

Luke was considering whether to slug the young cop on principle or just let it go and leave, when the patrolmen said, "It is okay to cry, that is allowed, but there is a half hour time limit for using the park."

"I didn't see any signs saying that."

"See over there and there. Tell you what fella; you can stay in the park as long as you need to cry. I won't give you a ticket this time."

Staring open mouth at the patrolman's patronizing recitation, and violation of park rules, after a couple of beats Luke said, "What are you some kind of social worker cop?"

"When my grandfather was on the force, calling a police officer a social worker was a grievous insult. Now they teach us Psycho-social assessment and other social work skills at the police academy," saying that as a rebuke the cop turned and strolled off, awkwardly trying to twirl his baton.

After a second to digest he'd just been put in his place by a rooky. Luke smiled, he knew the kid was right, and he'd spoken without thinking. "Wait up, lend me your baton, I'll show you how to twirl it properly."

The officer turned, walked back to Luke, his hand on his holstered pistol. "You want to what?"

"Take it easy, I'm slowly reaching for my ID. After you check my badge I'll show you how to twirl your baton so you don't look like an oaf." Luke thought *one good turn deserves another.*

3.

Luke returned home a little after five feeling lighter after his crying jag and then mind distracting baton twirl coaching. Upon opening his front door, he was struck by waves of delicious smells. Smiling he said, "What gastronomy is happening in here?"

Dirk came out of the kitchen followed by another teenager. "Hi, this is Marco Sandoval, I told you about him this morning. We made dinner."

"With what?"

"With what you had in your cupboards and the cab fare you gave me. I hope that was okay?"

"How did you get clean clothes if we're eating the cab fare?"

"Marco drove me. I hope you don't mind, I invited my mother to eat with us."

"I thought you weren't speaking?"

"I left her a note when I picked up my stuff, in case she hadn't heard. She hadn't and called after work; so I invited her to eat with us. She isn't as angry as last night."

"Actually, I'm glad you did that. But before Mary Ellen gets here maybe Marco and I can have a tête-à-tête?"

Smirking Dirk asked, "Shall I get out the rubber hose and flood light?"

"No, you are the only one who requires that treatment."

Marco pulled out his driver's license and Community College photo ID and handed them to Luke.

"Thank you. So how long do you two know each other?"

"We met Dirk's first year in high school. We both played trombone in the marching band."

"So, Marco, without my doing the math, how much older than Dirk are you, and how come I've never seen you around the Gay Community Center?"

"One year and two months older, I was a sophomore when he was a freshman. I've had to work in my family's business for as long as I can remember. Going to school and playing the trombone are my recreations."

"I hope you don't mind my questions. I've recently been told I'm overly protective of Dirk."

"That's okay; I love him and want him protected. Ask me anything sir, I have nothing to hide."

"Don't call me sir, I'm Luke."

"Okay Luke."

"Marco, I hope I'm not out of line by asking, but have you two been lovers all through high school?"

Dirk angrily jumped into the conversation raising his voice. "That's private and none of your business!"

Marco put a hand on Dirk's shoulder to calm him down. "I don't mind your question; it shows you are interested in his welfare as am I. I don't think it is a prurient question. It isn't, is it?"

"No, it is not, I just never heard about you before today."

"We have been best buds almost from when we met. Then last May when I graduated high school one thing led to another and we had sex without intending to, right Dirk?"

"Right, over the years Marco has held my hand and lent an ear through many of my failed attempts at romance. All the while he was saving himself for Mr. Right. Then it happened accidentally, at some point we decided not to stop making out, did the deed, and afterward realized our feelings went much deeper than just trombone buddies."

"After four years, sex could ruin a friendship, or turn it into something else I suppose."

"We talked the next day, Marco tried to apologize and I wanted more personal sex. See he isn't into casual sex, like I used to be. Now we are trying something different; to please each other with unconditional love."

"Explain that?"

"We are saving the most intimate sex act until our third anniversary. It will be proof of our love. Now I suppose you are going to tell us to wait even longer and grow up?"

"No, I sincerely wish you boys the best, you make an attractive couple. Here Marco, take my card in case you need a reference. I'll take my nephew's endorsement that you are of good character. So, what's for dinner I'm famished, I haven't eaten since breakfast?"

The doorbell sounded and Dirk started to move toward it, and then checked himself. "That's probably mom, want me to get it. *I know this is still your home.*"

"Let me get it." That said Luke opened his front door to find his sister Mary Ellen. She was holding a pink bakery box tied with white string in one hand, and a bottle of wine in the other. They buzzed each other on the cheek, an old family habit.

"I'm sorry to hear about Nestor's death. I'd give you a great big hug, but as you can see my hands are full. Wow something smells really good in here, Luke when did you learn to cook?"

Closing the door and following his sister into the living room Luke indicated with a head nod Dirk should relieved his mother of her packages. He did and gave her a peck on the cheek.

"Have you met Marco?"

"Not with his clothes on. Luke, you should see how big these boys get when they're sexually excited. It is positively astounding something so small can get that large. Hello Marco."

"Mary Ellen try and be nice, unless you need to get what's bothering you off your chest now, so we can all have a pleasant meal afterward?"

"Hello Ms. van den Hoose."

Dirk had returned and stood in the doorway to the kitchen, Marco took a seat near him.

"To Whom It May Concern, at my house there is a rule carved deeply in granite; no guests when I'm not home."

Hardly able to contain himself, Dirk shouted, "And you are not supposed to open my bedroom door without knocking first!"

"Listen, Buster. I came home early from work with a bad headache and heard strange noises coming from your room. I thought you were sick, or in pain, or God knows what was going on."

"You could have called out before opening the door!"

"It's my house, I pay the mortgage."

Luke moved to stand between feuding parent and child and using his authoritarian cop's voice said, "Okay, it happened now both of you get over it and apologize. We can discuss how to avoid future problems later."

Both Mary Ellen and Dirk, bodies ridged ready for combat, stared stilettos at each other. Marco stood and put his arm around Dirk's waist, and the boy's body instantly relaxed into the embrace. In a soothing voice, Marco said, "It must have been terrible for you to walk in on us like that, not knowing what to expect and fearing the worst. I'm so sorry it happened. I promise that will never happen again."

Mary Ellen's body language retreated from full battle readiness to maternal clout. "I will accept your apology Marco, it sounds sincere. I will accept it for both of you, since I know my son is an ingrate incapable of admitting mistakes."

Luke gave Dirk a look that propelled him to speak. "I'm sorry mom; I didn't mean to scare you. It won't happen again."

"Apologies accepted, both of you give me a hug." The boys surrounded Mary Ellen and the three had a warmhearted group clench.

"When do we eat?"

The atmosphere was noticeably brighter as hand in hand; Marco led Dirk into the kitchen. Dirk spoke over his shoulder. "As soon as the water is at full boil, I'll drop the pasta in, put the garlic bread in the oven to warm, and dish up the salad. We eat in ten minutes."

4.

Eight days after his spouse's murders, Kwame arrived at the Gay Community Center. He was twelve minutes early for his meeting. It was not usual for him to ever be early for anything. He consciously acknowledged it was a sign of his profound grieving for Jamal. His unconscious mind was a constant flow of thoughts about his beloved in spite of his effort to neutralize them with prayer.

To exacerbate his untypical behavior; Kwame was conflicted about giving Luke information and his own overpowering desire for vengeance. Being a snitch had been his idea, and was driven by revenge but didn't fit his self-image. He had to admit the big Dutch-American was intimidating too, but he didn't give off a racist or corrupt cop vibe.

To shake himself out of his scattered morose musings, Kwame carefully inspected the cleaning and brick pointing recently done on the surplus three story high school building in front of him. It had been built in the late 1800s. He had joined the finance committee when the City Council and Mayor decided to sell the worn-out vacant building to the gay community for one dollar.

He wondered if the gay community had known the costs of bringing the electricity up to code, the new efficient boiler and to say nothing of the renovations on top of renovations and then building on additions; would they have spent the dollar for the old white elephant. He shuddered remembering the exact amount the long overdue brick pointing and cleaning cost. They could easily have built a new modern green building for less than what was already spent on the old high school. Consciously calming himself he remembered being offered the building represented a new level of acceptance for lesbians, gay men, and transsexuals from a once actively homophobic local government. That had a value beyond money.

Kwame checked his watch, he was still early, thinking *what the hell,* and pushed through the entrance doors. Just inside the lobby he was surprised to see the atrium soaring up three floors to a big sky light in the new roof. He'd seen the architect's drawings but wasn't prepared for how lofty and grand it felt in real life. Like so much of the structure now, the atriums hadn't been part of the original building. The costs had been astronomical, but the result was impressive. Scrutinizing the lobby Kwame was pleased to see the latest renovations were subtly elegant yet practical. He thought *leave it to a bunch of Queers to turn an old worn out relic into something splendid and inviting.*

Just as he was beginning a more thorough scrutiny of the lobby, an orange haired teenager suddenly appeared in front of him, the boy's arrival seemed almost an apparition. The teen had an East Asian face, was about six feet tall, a thin 145 pounds, wearing skinny denim jeans, bright electric orange sneakers, and a flat black skull and crossbones on a metallic silver t-shirt. His orange hair was cropped short over medium brown penetrating eyes set in an open friendly face.

"Good evening sir, may I help you?"

"It's all right, I was just looking. Oh, but I have a question, where are the security guards? We pay quite a lot for security here."

"The Center has out of sight security. They see you but you don't see them except if necessary." Winking conspiratorially the teen said, "That is unless you know where to look. See the camera lens hidden in that cornice and over there?"

"That's interesting."

"May I inquire if your business is more than just enjoying the Center lobby?"

"I've come for the teen discussion group."

The orange haired young man's face registered disquiet, but he didn't verbally express it. Instead the question formed in his intelligent eyes regarding Kwame's age appropriateness for the group.

Kwame watched the teen's demeanor with interest. "Relax; I've been invited to be a substitute facilitator for the group."

"*Oh,* you are filling in for Nestor Negron. I'm David by the way. Are you a cop too?"

"Kwame Robinson, I'm an attorney with the federal government, nice to meet you David."

The two men chatted casually about the Center as David led Kwame to the receptionist located in a corner of the lobby. Then David said with mild authority, "You will have to sign in and get a name tag." Turning to the receptionist, "Jason, this is Kwame he is filling in for Nestor tonight."

Jason acknowledged Kwame with a smile. "Hi, welcome." Then he rotated a clipboard with the sign in sheet toward Kwame. "It is okay if you don't want to use your real name. We have closeted older folks walking around with name tags that say, 'Joe Frilly Jones, Mary Mack Truck, and even a Queen of Gay.' Don't worry, nobody checks IDs, we just need a head count in case of emergency."

Dramatically stiffening to full height and taking a step back puffing out his chest Kwame spoke with courtroom command, "I'll have you young people know I was out long before either of you were born, and it was my fundraising ability with affluent Afro-Americans that helped make this place what it has become."

Smiling David bowed his head and tented his hands in mock acquiescence, as Jason blushed and sputtered. "Sorry I didn't mean to offend you. It is only we deal with many older folks who are not out and it is my job to make everyone feel comfortable."

"Jason now that we have my sexuality and ancient age out of the way, do you want to try for national origin?"

"Really there was no offense intended, I'm sorry if I was too forward, sir."

Smiling candidly Kwame said, "Jason can't you tell when someone is putting you on? I'm a lawyer I trained for that. Hand me a name tag and I'll be on my way before the meeting begins without me." Turing to David, Kwame said, "Thank you for greeting me, you do it nicely."

"You are welcome, I'll see you at the meeting; I just have to go sign out at the security office." Then David was gone in the blink of an eye.

Turning to Jason Kwame asked, "Is David a security guard?"

"Not really, he works after school in the security office. I think he mostly does paperwork."

"What if I came here looking for trouble? He doesn't strike me as much of a deterrent."

"The security office is on the second floor for fast access to three or one; they monitor hidden cameras from a wall of video screens. If they suspected a problem they wouldn't send David. The Center's Security Department has some muscle gym bunnies no one in their right mind would want to tangle with."

"Thanks for the information, where am I going?"

"Your meeting is in Room 214 in the old wing, elevator around the corner or stairs there or there."

"Thank you, Jason, please forgive my putting you on."

Room 214 looked like it could have been a classroom in a previous life. It still had high ceilings and a wall of tall windows, but the other walls were refinished in faux textured soft autumn tones. The slate blackboards were gone, but the ceilings' and doors' old fashioned trim moldings stayed, finished in strong contrasting colors to the walls, the effect was striking and comfortable.

The chairs in the large room were arranged in a circle, and more than half were already occupied. Kwame spotted Luke seated facing the door and the two men nonverbally acknowledged each other. Luke indicated Kwame should sit next to him and he did. Just as Kwame was getting settled in his chair he saw David enter the room. "That orange haired boy greeted me at the front door, it was a nice gesture."

"David is a sweet kid." Luke stood and clapped his hands. "Let's get started. Are there any new people tonight?" Three hands went up, and Luke said, "Christie, Joey, and Doug take a new member aside and get a brief intro-bio while Jack reads the announcements." The three new members were taken out into the hall, while Jack read from an announcement sheet.

When Jack was done reading, Luke stood again and addressed the group. "Someone please bring in the new people." After a short pause while the hall people were seated Luke said, "Greetings everyone I am Luke one of your facilitators, let's go around the circle starting on my left and introduce ourselves, then the new folks will be introduced to us."

One by one each young woman or man spoke their first name. Then one by one the new people were introduced to the group. Kwame noticed Dirk from his close family resemblance to Luke. Kwame was beginning to feel left out as the introductions ended.

"David, please introduce Kwame." Luke made eye contact with David before speaking. An observer might surmise from the way the two men eyed each other Luke had counseled David in the past.

"Awesome, well hello everybody, it is my pleasure to introduce Kwame to you, this is his first time with us, obviously. He is a substitute facilitator for Nestor Negron. Kwame is a supervising United States Attorney with the Justice Department, and has worked for the government for twenty-two years. He has also been an important fund raiser for our Gay Center. Please welcome him, and treat him well."

Luke noticed Dirk's face scrunch up when David mentioned Nestor's name. But Dirk didn't show any other outward emotion.

"Thank you, David. Our agenda for tonight was to be part one of the Center's three parts coming out process. Yes, it's time for that again. But due to circumstances beyond anyone's control, coming out will have to be postponed. Dirk, are you able to tell the group why we changed the schedule?"

Dirk stood took a long deep breath, and looked slowly around the circle. He could see from making eye contact with each teen who knew and who didn't. "Nestor was killed last Tuesday. That's why last week's meeting was canceled. Since he was one of the founders of this group, my uncle Luke thought we might want to express our thoughts about losing one of our own unexpectedly."

It looked like a dark cloud suddenly passed over some of the bright faces and the mood of the whole group precipitously turned solemn. "Thank you, Dirk, one reason Kwame was invited tonight is his spouse Jamal, also a police officer, was murdered with Nestor."

Without raising his hand a teen spoke to the group. "So, is this meeting only going to be about death?"

"Not exactly, I am sure you all know the deal, if you get born you have to get dead, but at your age it may seem like you will live forever."

Smiling the boy said, "I do, I want to live forever."

"Good for you. But for the rest of us mere mortals we can only hope to live a long time and die in old age."

"So, then what is this meeting about?"

"If you came tonight only wanting to learn about coming out, you might want to leave, and we hope you come back next week when we will begin the coming out process." Two new members to the group got up and left.

"Each of us morn loss in our own way; some of you might want to share how you are feeling and handling Nestor's death. Try not to make this discussion all gloomy, we had happy times with Nestor too."

Standing again Dirk said, "If you want to speak, about my Uncle Nestor or what this group has meant to you, please raise your hands, then wait your turn to speak."

As the teens began speaking their thoughts, feelings and beliefs, Luke indicated Kwame should follow him and they quietly left the room and walked to a small unoccupied office nearby. Once they were seated Luke asked, "Any news?"

"I'm conflicted about being your snitch."

"Who said you were a snitch?"

"What do you call this?

"Two guys who lost someone important, commiserating?"

"Okay, that's what I'm doing here."

"That's it; you coming tonight make it special for the kids."

"Oh, I'm special am I, how come I don't feel special?"

"I don't know? For the record I don't feel special either, actually I feel like shit. Do you have any news about why I feel like feces?"

"More than I expected so soon. But remember you didn't hear any of it from me."

"We already covered that?"

"Yes, we did. Without going into all the machinations how I got what I have, I was able to talk to an undercover federal agent who was present during the killings."

"What happened?"

"She said things got out of control fast and were over faster."

"What did she see, just the facts?"

"Homeland has investigations ongoing, so nothing is official at this point. Only one undercover was present at the shooting."

"And?"

"The agent saw a group of gay activists run into the bar, take photos of the *Fairy Swatter,* and then were gone. One bouncer noticed camera flashes and told Rashid the manager. Rashid was high, but called an impromptu meeting of bouncers and bartenders and was berating them for allowing photographs to be taken in the bar, when the gay activist came back arguing. Then one of the activists tried to take the *Fairy Swatter* while others tried to stop him."

"That doesn't sound like Nestor. Why would he go back if they had the photo?"

"Or Jamal, he'd want to give the management a receipt and tell them where to redeem their confiscated property."

"Damn it, if he'd let me go I could have stopped that in fighting. What happened next?"

"Apparently, some insults were exchanged in Spanish with a Mexican bouncer, who then started fighting with a gay activist. The *Fairy Swatter* was caught in a tug of war. Rashid grabbed a gun from the office and came out blasting, the gay activists, the customers and staff all dove for cover."

"Just one gun killed five peace officers and the others?"

"I was told Rashid had an H&K MP7A1 with what looked like a forty-round magazine, and he fired twenty shots before one of his bouncers took the gun out of his hands. Do you know what kind of gun that is? I don't."

"Yeah it's a Heckler & Koch submachine gun. But why does a bar manager need such fire power in this City?"

"Is it better than what Jamal carries?"

"Bigger bullets; 4.6X30mm, and shoots lots of them fast. Where is that gun now?"

"I don't know, Rashid was apparently out of his head high, and one of his Arab bouncers took the weapon and shot some Mexican workers with it. Then Rashid and his two Muslim bouncers ran out of the backdoor with the gun, and the *Fairy Swatter.* Inside the bar was total chaos, our agent said she couldn't shoot without hitting bystanders."

"What happened next?"

"Patrons and workers called 911. When the police and EMS arrived, they found pandemonium among those who hadn't fled and blood everywhere."

"I heard it was a mess."

"The story the police got about what happened and who was there, is all mixed up and contradictory. Many patrons fled out the back exits as the police came bursting in the front. It is after all a pickup bar, many patrons probably hightailed it home to their wives and children."

"It sounds like bedlam."

"Now besides DEA and anti-terror, the FBI is onboard. The problem is the FBI, unlike the other two agencies, works independently. And this case has two different international links. The three federal agencies are having high level discussions to determine who is primary while dividing turf and bruising egos. It's a muddle."

"Rashid killed our men. What's his last name, got an address for the bastard?"

"Like I said I'm conflicted about what I'm doing by telling you."

"In for a penny in for a pound forty, tell me what you have so far."

"Here's the problem, if one of my attorneys catch this case how am I going to recues myself without disclosing I'm your snitch? Both of our careers could be in jeopardy."

"Chill out counselor, I had to promise Nestor's Lieutenant and mine I wouldn't take matters into my own hands. With three federal agencies fighting over turf, none of us, including the recently born, will live long enough to see this case go to trial. That is unless I locate Rashid and company first, and then going to trial is not a likely option either."

"Now it has gotten complicated, but I gave you what you wanted. Rashid killed our men and I want him dead as much as you do. But you made a promise to keep me out of it?"

"I keep my promises. I'm on this."

"Shouldn't we go back to see how the kids are doing?"

"Sure, by the way would you mind saying a few closing words to the group and if it doesn't offend your belief system to offer a closing prayer or meditation or moment of silence?"

"I don't mind. I'm happy to be with friendly faces during my troubles."

5.

The next morning Luke reported what he found out from Kwame to Lt. Schmidt. He credited the information from a third hand anonymous source that fled the State after the shooting. Then on his meal break Luke drove downtown looking for a Sergeant he had met briefly months earlier. She worked for the Police Department's small but dynamic anti-terror task force. He found her in her small back office at police headquarters. She was wearing a scowl typing away on a laptop computer.

Sticking his head in the door he waited for her to pause. "Hi remember me; we met at that seminar on advanced law enforcement technologies last April?"

"Hey, how's it going? Don't tell me, wait … Luke something Dutch, right?"

"Yeah, I am Luke van den Hoose, and you would be Amelia Youssef, still as beautiful as I remember. Hi."

"You know the usual bullshit. Listen flattery will get you almost everything with me. But oh wait, you're gay, right?"

"Gay doesn't mean I can't appreciate a beautiful woman when I see one."

"Flatterer."

"I hate to bother you but do you have any information about recent events at El Geordie's bar?"

"Now isn't that interesting, I'm just now checking on dotted I's and crossed T's in my unfinished investigation, not ever destined to *be* finished report on El Geordie singles bar. We've been ordered to stand down, the FBI and who the hell knows who all else are taking over and are going to paternally finish my investigation. And if you believe that crap I have a selection of bridges and underwater swamp land for sale cheap, cash only of course."

"My roommate Nestor and other police officer were killed in El Geordie's. I'm trying to find the last name and address for a Rashid the manager. I'm bothering you because rumor has it Jihadists might be mixed-up with that bar. Can you help me out with an address?"

"Now come on you know better, I can't talk to you about an ongoing secret investigation that is not even mine much longer. *Wait a minute Luke,* don't go yet."

"What? Sorry I disturbed you. I can see you're busy."

"Since you are here, and also a police sergeant, you can do me a big favor. I'm going downstairs and out back to smoke a cigarette or two, if you don't mind proof reading my report to check for grammatical errors and such, I'd appreciate it looking spiffy, nice and neat for Our Fathers the Feds. I've got to send the report post haste when I come back, so proof read fast, okay?"

"I'm always happy to oblige a fellow sergeant."

Luke discovered Amelia's team had been scrutinizing a radical Sunni Mosque located near El Geordie's Bar. The Mosque was a destination for returned American combat volunteers who fought in various Sunni-Shiite undeclared civil wars from hither and yon.

Rashid took over running the bar when its owner Mr. Hockawitz began drifting in and out of dementia after the new El Geordie's successful launch. *The Fairy Swatter* had been an advertised feature of Mr. Hockawitz's previous straight pickup joints for decades.

With Hockawitz's increasing dementia, Rashid began augmenting the bar's income dealing small amounts of drugs. Gradually, the bar's clientele changed from young up and coming hetero singles looking for uncomplicated casual sex, to older druggy types looking for hard drugs. The bar underwent a major metamorphic shift, ultimately becoming primarily an illicit drug market with the singles scene only a cover."

The Mexican Drug Cartel supplying Rashid with an ever-increasing supply of illegal substances began actions to take over El Geordie's bar for money laundering. When Rashid realized he was in over his head with drug suppliers, he hired combat veterans from the nearby Mosque to be bouncer-bodyguards. He wasn't into radical religious politics but knew about the Mosque from neighborhood gossip.

Amelia had a confidential informant working in the bar. But there was no mention of undercover operatives from Homeland Security or the police department's narcotics task force. Luke straightened up in the desk chair and rolled his head around on his shoulders listening to calcium deposits snap crackle and pop in his neck. There weren't three undercover operations going on, there were four with Amelia's, and now the FBI. He got what he came for; the last name and home address for Rashid.

Amelia returned, smelling like cigarettes. "Find any mistakes?"

"Just a second, I am changing your word order in this sentence so it reads clearer, see here?"

"Great, find anything else?"

"The phrase, 'one hand not knowing what the other is doing,' comes to mind. Oh, and I didn't know it was death to leave the Muslim religion."

"Oh yeah, every year in Saudi Arabia they lob off about forty heads; religious conversion is an enforced Capital crime in many Muslim countries. There is a lot to know, but tell you what? If you learn Arabic and Farsi I can teach you the rest and guarantee you an interesting if dangerous job."

"Thanks, but I think I'm too tall for your patch, I better stick to street crime. It's down and dirty but suits my personality. Do you have any idea where I can find Rashid and his two protectors if they aren't at home when I drop by?"

"Funny thing, your Lieutenant was asking me that very question about an hour before you showed up. Did Nestor work for Schmidt too?"

"No, Lieutenant Schmidt is my cross to bear, Nestor worked for Lieutenant Gilhooley, and Jamal worked for Lieutenant Leung. Those three are looking for blood, and Schmidt is trying to keep me out of it."

"I'd lay money Rashid's still in town, it's just a hunch. Where he is exactly is another matter. Why don't you let the brass handle this, it's too personal for you?"

"Thanks, I appreciate your concern. Here is my card in case you hear something. We should do lunch when this is over, I can tell you how I quit smoking, if you're interested?"

"Luke unofficially, my people have Rashid's residence under surveillance, he hasn't shown up since the shooting. We are quietly beating the bushes to find him. You don't kill cops and get away with it in my world."

"I like your style."

"I'm carefully trying to thread a needle; between what I'm paid to do and the Fed's need for me not to. Oh, that's my boss, call me and let's do a stop smoking lunch. See yah."

6.

Luke made a point to be home before Dirk returned from school. He was sorting a pile of mail when his nephew walked through the front door. "Hi, how was your day?"

"*You're home early*, I thought the place would be empty like usual. Are you checking up on me?"

"Do I need to check up on you?"

Sounding snarky Dirk snapped, "No, you don't dad." Then in a mollifying tone he spoke sweetly. "Whoops, sorry, I didn't mean to make you feel unwelcome in your own home. Just now I was trying to figure out what to make for dinner and still have time to cram for a surprise math quiz."

"What do you say to takeout for a change? Nestor liked Chinese or Thai. I prefer Mexican or pizza, but I'll eat almost anything that's not still moving, unless I'm really hungry."

"Ha ha, but I don't want to be a burden adding expenses."

"It's all the same to me, we have to eat whether buying groceries or ordering takeout. How about give the cook a night off and order in, plus we need to talk?"

"You're the boss, it's your home."

"At the expense of being redundant, how was your day nephew?"

"The usual, except I have a monster short notice math quiz tomorrow and I'm not ready. But if I study really hard tonight I might be all right. If Marco came over and helped, I'd ace the test; he's a math whiz and knows how to explain it so I understand. And how was your day Uncle?"

"Why don't you call Marco, see if he's up for tutoring? If he is, tell him we all need to talk something over."

Dirk pulled out his cell phone, hit speed dial and went out on the front porch. After a brief muffled conversation, Dirk was back. "Marco will be over in ten minutes. I'll go make us some green tea. You want another beer?"

"Sure, I'm separating my bills from junk mail."

When Marco arrived the three men settled on Chinese food. They ordered wonton soup for starters and four dishes to share; vegetarian egg-foo-young, spicy pork chow fan, duck lo main and sweet and sour shrimp. While they waited for the takeout delivery, Dirk and Marco set the table. Then Dirk showed Marco the math problems to be covered on the pop quiz.

When at last the food arrived, they consumed their soups with gusto. With that done, they eagerly opened the takeout food containers, filling the room with delicious aromas. Reaching over each other with snapping chop sticks they helped themselves to savory morsels placed on individual bowls of brown rice, and eagerly ate their fill.

The food was officially finished when the last fortune cookie was opened to proclaim double good luck. "Dirk your mother called me at work, your welfare and dental health are weighing on her mind and she needed to talk about it. But after a lot of verbiage, her only nonnegotiable and she was adamant, you must brush your teeth three times a day and no sex is allowed in her home for you forever. If you agree to those terms you can go home."

"No surprise there, she already told me that in several different ways."

"Sparing you the extraneous details why, I confided to her Nestor used to give you motel money."

"Not cool, how could you do that?"

"I don't know what my finances will look like without Nestor's half of expenses. So, I could only offer to split the cost of your monthly motel room with her. You know what she said?"

"Sure, she said absolutely positively no, No, NO, am I right?"

"She said okay, but only one weekend a month and she wants you to earn her contribution by house cleaning her place once a week. Our dad used to say there are no free lunches in life, your mom remembers and took his words to heart."

Dirk thought for a second then dolefully said, "Come on Uncle Luke once a month isn't enough. We are in love; I can't keep my hands off this handsome man. What does mom expect me to do the rest of the month? Wait, wait don't answer that."

"Once I get my expenses under control maybe I could spring for a second motel night a month, but no promises yet."

Marco said, "I might be able to work extra shifts at the garage to contribute money."

"No Marco you are working hard enough just for your tuition and books, you need time to study. Anyway, somehow it doesn't feel right having my mom pay for us to be intimate. There has to be a better plan. How about I get a job?"

"I'll have my EMT license in a year and then we can rent a small apartment and have a regular life."

"What do we do for a year?"

"We could call it our year of sacrifice for unconditional love?"

"A year sounds like a long time … sure if that's the best we can do."

Luke listened to the two young men's conversation with interest, while they cleared the table and he dished out pistachio ice cream. While the teens dug into dessert Luke asked, "Marco what's your parents take on your relationship with Dirk?"

"They like Dirk. His first time at our garage he pitched in and helped without being asked or worrying about getting dirty, my folks say they like his work ethic. But they don't like I'm queer; still they're slowly coming around to accepting us. I don't think they have extra money to give for motel rent if that's what you are driving at? And I share a bedroom with two brothers."

"That's okay, I wasn't asking about money. Dirk if you expect to get into a good nursing school you have to concentrate on your math and science, not your strongest subjects. No part-time jobs if you're serious about getting an RN."

"So, what do we do? We are young and in love, once a month is worse than not at all."

"Since you guys are sharing long term plans, I'd like to help. Here is my unasked for two cents; since your mother is setting rules and conditions, I think you should let her pay for half a motel room once a month. It will allow her to feel a part of your life without compromising her rules. That is if you have the time and inclination to do her housework to earn it."

"Uncle Luke I don't want mom in my head when I make love with Marco."

"I think Nestor turned you into a spoiled brat when I wasn't watching."

"Is there a cure for that?"

"No there isn't, how about a plan B smart ass. You are both of legal age for consensual sex, if I'm not here, and you cleanup any mess you make, it is out of sight out of mind with me. But I don't want to walk in on the two of you going at it in my bed."

"What if you come home early with a headache or something and walk in on us making love, will you totally freak out like mom?"

"Boy, you guys are tough, okay let's try for a plan C. Since my sister has an extra bedroom these days, I could suggest to her I spend one or two nights *a week* in your old room. She'd feel less lonely and I can sleep almost anywhere. Would that give you guys enough private time?"

As one, Dirk and Marco rushed over and hugged Luke just as he was raising his spoon of green ice cream to his mouth.

7.

The next morning when Luke arrived at work the sticky-note on his desk calendar was already two hours old. Straightaway he telephoned Kwame and said, "I just got your message. What's going on?"

"Any chance we can meet today? Say that pocket park again at two? But you bring the coffee this time, one sugar with a splash of milk."

"See you there."

The two men arrived concurrently, nodded in greeting, Luke handed Kwame a takeout coffee. "What's happening?"

"It's not what you think. A position just opened in our Washington bureau and I'm going to take it. Since Jamal's murder I've not been my best at work, and I'm a disaster at home. I can't read or even listen to music. Everywhere I turn I see him, the life we had and our dreams for the future. I have to get away and find myself. I've grown beyond wanting vengeance. I need to get a new life and start over, post Jamal."

"I'm happy you're through with revenge lust. That is not a healthy place. How soon are you leaving?"

"Right away, the movers are coming day after tomorrow to pack everything and take it to storage. I already met with a realtor to sell my place, and she will get me a small short term rental in Washington. If I like my coworkers and the city, I'll buy a place there after my residence here is sold."

"For what it is worth I found comfort commiserating in our short friendship. It is unusual for me to feel camaraderie with a lawyer, even briefly, you get points."

"I know what you mean, cops and I usually don't see eye to eye on much. Yet I felt a simpatico with you right from the first."

"Will you have time to say goodbye to the teen group?"

"I could, I wasn't planning to. Do you think it would be good for them to have another loss so soon?"

"Real life is about change. Your saying goodbye shows them respect and they have value. Queer kids don't get a lot of respect, and teens of all flavors often question their value in the big picture."

"I just didn't want to make it harder than it is."

"They are tougher than they look, especially the Nelly Ones."

"Okay I can say goodbye and what an honor it has been to meet them, it has. Thanks for the heads-up."

"There is another more delicate matter."

"What's that … tell me?"

"I suspect you haven't noticed, David the orange haired boy. Actually, he just lightened it to more of a light tangerine color; anyhow he seems enamored by you."

"*That isn't possible*; I'm more than twice his age."

"It is common for an older person to assume they made a mistake or misread cues when a much younger person comes on to them. The sad thing is when signals aren't received the younger person feels rejected for real or imagined self-identified deficits. It is an unnecessarily lose, lose situation for both parties."

"What makes you think David could possibly be interested in *me*?"

"Let's see, he's talking about changing his major to prelaw, rushes to greet you at the door of the Center, he moons over you whenever you are in the Center, and when he thinks nobody will notice, looks at you like you're an all-day sucker and he's desperate for a lick."

"You must be mistaken, he's so vibrant, and smart and good looking. What would he want with this old reprobate?"

"During the teen discussions, many young people of both genders express displeasure with their peers; finding them superficial and immature. They idealize and sexualize older successful role models who will teach them how to succeed to a good life. Remember a lot of our kids were discarded by their biological families for coming out. Role models are hard to find in our community thanks to the dominant heteros distorting or deleting our history."

"This is the first I'm hearing about intergenerational relations being common. Is it, common?"

"I don't know how common, but I've never found anything rational in affairs of the heart. Nestor was dark and I'm as light as they come, you and Jamal were both dark, my nephew and his boyfriend look very similar but come from different cultures and have different aspirations. Go figure?"

"But can you name me even one intergenerational gay couple I might have heard of?"

"The ancient Greeks considered gay sex superior to the obligation of straight sex to produce warriors and workers. It was the norm back then for an older man to court a younger one to guide him, with the approval of the boy's father of course."

"I knew that, anything more recent?"

"You've probably heard of the author Christopher Isherwood and his much younger life partner Don."

"I've read Isherwood's writings, sure."

"Lately I'm thinking about going for grief counseling over Nestor's murder. The shrink Harry Stack Sullivan was the main American Object Relations guy, founded the Journal Psychiatry and a famous New York psychiatric institute. Sullivan was out gay in the nineteen thirties and forties and took his much, much younger lover Jimmy everywhere with him, including to high government official gatherings. Like Isherwood, Sullivan mated for life with a considerably younger man. In their fields, they were both famous and their intergenerational relationships didn't diminish their success."

"I actually have herd of Sullivan, America's first out and proud gay psychiatrist. You'd be surprised how much psychology we use in the practice of law."

"Do me a favor, before you give your swansong to the teen discussion group, invite David out for coffee after the meeting and see if I'm not right. You can say that you heard from me he is considering lawyering as a career and did he have any questions."

"I could do that; I'd even like to do that."

"Oh, hey look at the time, sorry I got to run. Good luck in Washington, see you Wednesday night."

The two men stood, and shook hands. Kwame gave Luke a vacillating look of disbelief that went to acceptance, and finally comradely, and they turned and went their separate ways.

8.

Back at the precinct house Luke noticed Lt. Schmidt was still out. So there was no need to check back in since he'd not checked out. Being on desk duty meant working nine to five, Luke did not like being on that short leash. Sitting back at his desk there were four messages from Amelia Youssef. He phoned her office and was told she's in the field.

Calling her cell phone, he got an immediate response. "Luke, can you meet me at the morgue in a hurry? They may have your guy."

"I'm on my way, see yah." The morgue was close by Luke's precinct.

Amelia was leaning against her car smoking a cigarette when Luke drove up. They greeted each other with a wave.

"Let's get this over with. I hate the smell of the disinfectant they use," Amelia scrunched up her pretty face to show distaste.

"How did you hear about this? I thought the Feds took over everything?"

"I get the biggest budget for confidential informants, and you get what you pay for. And the police department is still open for business whether the feds like or not."

"It is and you obviously are, and thanks *be*."

"Nobody knows for sure who these stiffs are yet, so as far as I'm concerned jurisdiction is not officially assigned. Even if the feds think they own the world, they don't own my plot. How did you quit smoking?"

"Self-hypnosis and crumpling up cigarettes and will power helped a little."

"When we have time, you must elaborate, I'm definitely interested."

The Morgue's lobby notice board directed them to the auditorium; they arrived just after the formal post mortem grand rounds started. They had to stand against the back wall since all the seats held staff, students, and official looking spectators. The two cops had missed the introductions, preliminaries, and the list of cadavers to be discussed. The three bodies they were interested in were first. Much of what the lecturing pathologist said went over Luke's head or flat-out sounded like gibberish. Below the waists to above the knees portions of the three headless, handless, and footless cadavers were covered by sheets.

During the question and answer conclusion Amelia raised her hand and spoke up loudly before being called on. "When may we examine these corpses close-up, we are with the police department trying to determine identification for an open case?"

"See Maggie in autopsy room four, down the hall and to the right, in ten minutes. Tell her I sent you."

Autopsy room four was large, all gleaming stainless steel and overly bright white surfaces. It was very clean looking and smelled of the strong medicinal disinfectant Amelia had mentioned. Maggie was thin, medium height, with a low-pitched voice, possibly mixed race and could be a male to female transsexual.

"Hi, the pathologist giving the Grand Rounds sent us. We need a close-up look at your three headless horsemen, we are with the police." Amelia said this to Maggie while flashing her gold detective sergeant's badge.

Maggie scratched her head and looked puzzled. "Strange; the FBI is collecting these bodies ASAP. We didn't know how long today's Grand Rounds, so I haven't called them for pickup yet … I guess it is okay for you to have a quick peek. My boss likes to show off when we have something unusual." That said she pulled out three adjacent cadavers draws and pulled off the sheets covering the remains.

Luke had seen plenty of blood, gore, and guts as a street crimes cop. But he wasn't ready for three headless, handless, and footless male human bodies close-up. With their other distinguishing features removed their genitals became prominent. He was startled when a wave of nausea hit him and reflexively had to clench his fists to keep bile down.

Amelia leaned over each corpse and studied their wounds meticulously. "I'm ninety percent sure these are our guys and this one had to be Rashid; he was much older."

"Why are you so sure?"

"Their physiology is Arab, and they were cut like Muslin's circumcise. See absolutely no foreskin remnants; the surgery was between age six to ten. See here their heads came off while they were dying. I'd guess a large blade like a sword or machete."

"Could it be by an ax?"

"Maybe, except Arabs usually use a sword or long knife for beheading. But they would never take off hands and feet with decapitation. Huh, might be a Drug Cartel sending a message."

"So, this is more than us unable to identify these bodies."

"The hands and feet came off post mortem and it looks like a different tool was used." Crunching down and looking from different angles Amelia continued talking. "This was definitely done with a chain saw. Here look at the difference between the clean neck cut and the raggedy edged cuts at wrists and ankles. This is the work of a Mexican drug cartel, I'd bet my pension on it."

"Damn you're good, for the record I thought a cut cock was just a cut cock, period."

"No, there are clues left; age the cut occurred, cutting method, and quality of the results. Filipinos only make a dorsal slit and don't remove anything. They let atrophy causes the alteration."

"That's interesting."

Amelia started to speak, but Maggie had a perceptible mood change. She angrily cut Amelia off turning her back on her and spoke to Luke. "Your time has expired, I have work to do."

Reacting to Maggie's annoyed demeanor, Amelia became officious. "We need two complete sets of photos of the headless wonders, this is official police business. Here is my card; it has where to send to. If you want I'll do all the necessary paperwork right here in front of you, or not, your call? Come on Luke give her your card, and let's leave Maggie to call the feds. By the looks of it we bothered her enough for one day."

"Just go, you can skip the paperwork this time."

Outside the morgue lighting up a cigarette Amelia said, "With a drug cartel's trademarks on the bodies and no terrorists in sight, I'm off this unofficial case. So how exactly did you abuse packs of cigarettes to quit smoking?"

"If you are serious, I can give you the self-hypnosis tapes I used. Just be aware it took me a few failed attempts to muster the determination to quit once and for all. I've been three years without a smoke and can run longer and faster and hit harder than years ago."

"How's it work?"

"First you listen to the tape as you go to sleep each night, then make a list of each time you have a smoke. Then prioritize that list. The next time you buy a pack you remove the lowest priority cigarette and crumple it up and scratch it off the list. With the next pack take out two and crumple, scratch and so on and so on. Until you resent wasting a lot of money for only a few smokes from each whole new pack, got it?"

"Hmm, behavior modification, would you help if I try?"

"Sure, happy to. It's easier to resist temptation with a friend's support. Thank you for all your help on my non-case case. Now I can stop looking for Rashid and associates, they're not walking around anymore."

"If you ever need to talk or a hand or an extra gun slinger gives me a call. I like your style; laidback calm and hard as steel, just like me but not as arrogant. I can teach arrogance."

"I hope you don't take this the wrong way, but I find you more than just an attractive colleague, there is something else going on with me. Maybe it is chemistry or maybe grief has me out of my head, I don't know what?"

"In my travels, I call it mutual attraction. After you get through your grieving we should date to see how deep the attraction goes."

"You know I'm gay, right?"

"Is it like a strict religious thing, or can you get an excused absence to play for the other team?"

"It's been awhile for me with women, but I'd like to get to know *you* better."

The first chance to brief Lt. Schmidt the next morning came after eleven thirty, and the Lieutenant appeared out of sorts. When Luke pushed the gory glossy morgue photos fresh from his computer printer across the desk, his startled boss cringed back in his chair.

"What in hell are you trying to do; spoil my appetite for lunch? I *was* looking forward to a pleasant bland meal before this colored carnage appeared."

Luke emphatically pointed with one finger. "I have reason to believe this is the manager of El Geordies, the man who killed our men. ... What is going on with you? I restricted you to desk duty with specific instructions not to get involved. Was I not clear you big dumb Dutchman?"

"You were clear and I was at my desk except for meal breaks, and I don't appreciate being called names. In fact, I may file a complaint about your disrespect with my rep from the Sergeant's union."

"Why do we seem to be at cross purposes, Dutch? This is a Federal case that we are barred from working. If the big boys need your help I'm sure they'll ask. What none of us need right now is a loose screw undoing sub-rosa work, understand?"

"I understand, but you need to stop calling me names, and appreciate we are not working at cross purposes. What I've done so far, on my own time, is locate the killer." He spoke irritably jabbing his finger at Rashid's color photo.

"Okay, I appreciate your work, you royal pain in my ass. Now I need you to sit behind your desk shuffle paperwork and take complaints about lost pets and stolen bicycles. Don't make me suspend you without pay for insubordination. I'm removing temptations by hanging onto these photographs."

"Excuse me, I thought we were the police and solved crimes. I am not insubordinate, and you know I am not a desk jockey. You may not like my methods but my people clear more cases in this precinct than all your other plain clothes cops. Geez give me a break will yah?"

"Okay, now you are teetering right on the edge of insubordination. You're just about ready to lose your balance and fall into unpaid suspension for a month. Want to try for three months?"

"You're right, and I'm on the verge of slapping my badge and gun down on this desk and telling you where and how far to shove."

The Lieutenant shot his right arm straight out hand raised in the universal sign to stop. "Hold on Sergeant, we both need to take it down a notch. Take a big deep breath with me. Let's feel this stuffy dank office air fill our lungs."

"If you are expecting an apology, forget it."

"You may have noticed I've been out of the office a lot lately. I needed to know if the shit hit the fan while I'm out I have a good man here to take charge. That's you, when not otherwise engaged in unauthorized crime fighting."

"What, you goldbricking Lieutenant?"

"No, but maybe you need to know what is going on. Or maybe I even owe *you* an apology? After my speech the other day about communications, I don't seem to be doing a very good job controlling information with you."

"I'm listening; maybe this Dutchman isn't as dumb as you think?"

Tilting back in his swivel chair and tenting his fingers over his midsection a pensive Lt. Schmidt eyed Luke. "The reason I've been away from the precinct a lot, is I'm one of three names pulled off the Captains list. *You would not believe all the nonsense formalities and interviews they put us through.* I didn't tell anyone about it for fear of kyboshing my chances. At some point today I get final word; either I get that promotion or mine and another guy's name goes to the bottom of the test list. All three of us are over qualified for the open position. But I worked so damn hard to score highest on the exam; I don't want to be put on the bottom after all my effort. I should have told you sooner, only I've been anxious not to blow my chances blabbing about it."

"Hey good luck with that, you'd make a great captain. Even if your German genes hate Holland."

"Thank you for that, I don't hate the Dutch. But you keep being insubordinate and I could make an exception. I'm asking nice; please don't screw up my chances to be Captain. I know you are one of my best men and sometimes most worrisome."

"Thank you for that."

"I'm sorry if my self-interest took prescient over your grieving Nestor's murder. I liked him and you guys were a handsome couple. But by the book it is the Feds now. Let it go, headless bodies and all."

"Again, I wish you luck with the promotion. But after you get the results, no matter what, I want back on regular duty?"

"We'll see, I'm thinking acting Lieutenant for you, if my horse comes in. I'd like to leave this place in good hands, yours. Until then I want you behind your desk looking busy and keeping out of trouble."

9.

Sitting down at his desk, mulling over he'd almost just quit his job without another lined up. And incidentally did he really want to be acting lieutenant? Luke flinched when his desk phone jangled. Snatching up the handset he forced himself to pause, focus and then concentrate. "Sergeant van den Hoose?"

"Are you Dirk's uncle?"

"Yes, has something happened to Dirk?"

"No, this is Marco his boyfriend; we had dinner the other night at your house. I know I sound different on the telephone."

"Hi Marco, what's up?"

"My grandfather wants us to get guns. You gave me your card and said I should call if I needed help. Could you help us get some guns in a hurry?"

"Talk to me Marco. Why do you need guns?"

"A little while ago two men brought in a van to fix. My dad told them we had several big jobs ahead of them and it would be a few days before we could get to them. The boss guy said have it fixed by five o'clock today or else. My grandfather says both men have killer's eyes."

"What do you think, did they look like killers?"

"I don't know. What was strange is they didn't ask the price for repairs. The way the van sounds it's going to be expensive to fix. Grandfather thinks they are going to pay us with bullets and so that's why we need guns. Can you suggest where we can rent guns on short notice?"

"Marco, are the van men still there?"

"No, they left; my father and grandfather have to finish fixing a car on lift number one before they can move the van there."

"Did you get a look inside the van?"

"No."

"Do me a favor, take a look around inside. I'll stay on the line."

"I'm back; it's very dirty in there, a lot of greasy fast food wrappers and something sticky on the floor. In the very back by the rear doors, under piles of soiled plastic tarps there is a big old fashioned ax and a sixteen-inch gasoline chainsaw. The saw is a top brand, but not well maintained. What's weird is they both are dirty and smell like blood. Funny thing though, the ax is way too big for killing chickens. Anyway, where can we rent guns and what kind do you suggest? I've never seen my grandfather this upset."

"Can I call you right back at the number showing on my screen?"

"Yes, that's the repair shop's number. I'll be here; I'm working till closing."

"Who is working with you?""

"My mom is in the office, my older brother Astor and Cousin Jimmy are waiting for roadside assistance calls for their tow trucks, and my dad and grandfather are fixing cars. I order and receive parts, fix flats, and help around, why?"

"Did you see where the van men went?"

"There was an Escalade outside waiting for them; they got in the back, but the windows were all dark I couldn't see who was inside.

"Did you get license plate numbers?"

"They both have Arizona plates. I didn't see the entire Caddy number, but it started GBZ1, the van is GBZ468."

"Give me your address? Tell your grandfather not to worry. I'll bring people who know how to use guns. Tell him I said too many guns is often worse than not enough, see you soon."

When Luke ran the license plate GBZ468 through interstate police information, it belonged to an import-export business in Nogales Arizona, with headquarters in Nogales, Sonora, Mexico. Then using a reverse directory he found the business also owned an Escalade with license number GBZ194 registered to the same business in Arizona, but a different city and state address in Mexico. With a little digging then tunneling through layers of encryptions, he discovered the business was under Arizona and federal scrutiny for suspected money laundering, drugs import and firearms export.

Head in hands he considered options, if he ran off halfcocked he'd be suspended without pay for sure. If he asked for permission to go in the field, his Lieutenant would deny it. He could send others to protect Marco's family, but if it got ugly, that was his specialty and needed in it. *What to do, what to fucking do?* Then after several minutes pondering his hand reached out almost on its own, and dialed Amelia's cell number. When she said hello, he asked, "Is your gun slinging offer from yesterday still good?"

"What's ja-got-cowboy?"

"Maybe the van with a bloody *Fairy Swatter* and chain saw are in an auto repair shop, and some unsavory guys are coming to pick it up at five o'clock. Are you busy?"

"Mexicans right, not my turf."

"I know, just thought I'd ask, thanks anyway."

"I didn't say no, how many bad guys?"

"At least three, the van came with two men and there was a second vehicle. More people may be involved."

"What are you thinking?"

"If they pay their bill and leave, I'd like to follow them back to their lair. On the other hand, if they intend to slaughter the people at the repair shop, I would be violently opposed to that."

"Got it, you expect they might be packing heavy?"

"I'd like to be ready for any contingency."

"You got a plan?"

"If we can get there early enough I'd like to send the family that runs the place home and take over the shop. You and me inside, and whoever of my folks I can round up on short notice outside."

"Sounds okay, you got GPS tracking at your precinct house? Oh, and you cleared all this with supervision?"

"I'm working on supervision, GPS; we barely have running water up here."

"Let me talk to my guys, maybe I can find some off the clock volunteers. I'm thinking of two who wouldn't miss this for anything after seeing those morgue photos this morning. Give me the address; I'll be there at 4:30 unless you want to buy me lunch first?"

"Lunch sure, there's an excellent diner not far from that repair shop. The food is good, it's just after the Route 52 interchange; follow the billboards that say Eat at Ted's. How about 3:30?"

"See yah there, 3:30 sharp."

Luke no sooner disconnected from Amelia then he heard a sharp knock on his Lieutenant's door. Swiveling his chair around he saw Lt. Gilhooley's back enter Lt. Schmidt's office. He waited for a slow count of ten, then rapped his knuckles on the frosted glass door, without waiting for an invitation he entered to see the two lieutenants hunched over the morgue photos he had brought his boss earlier. Luke said, "Gentlemen can I invite you to lunch, my treat, and after lunch you can view the bloody tools that caused the injuries you are viewing?"

Lt. Schmidt was forming a less than polite rebuff, when Lt. Gilhooley jumped into the conversation, "Definitely, what's for lunch?"

"The best beer-batter fried clams, onion rings and crispy sweet potato fries, plus homemade coleslaw and delicious fresh baked on the premises desserts."

Preoccupied with his own concerns, worry deepening the lines on his face Lt. Schmidt made a shooing gesture with his hands. "You two go, I have had enough of Luke today."

"Would you like us to bring you a doggy bag Lieutenant?"

Shaking his head no to takeout food, Lt. Schmidt strode briskly around his desk. "Maybe another time, I'm too wired about the captain's job to eat anything. You two go and enjoy yourselves."

Lt. Gilhooley followed Luke to his desk, where Luke removed his holstered service weapon and the Uzi in a gym bag from his locked lower double draw. Gilhooley said, "Let's skip lunch, I only agreed because I knew Schmidt was holding you by the short hairs. Let's go check out those bloody implements."

"We can't sir; we need lunch first to plan. The bad guys are due back at five and I promised lunch to a colleague."

Not put off by Luke's counter command, spoken with authority he didn't possess. Lt. Gilhooley said, "Tell me something sergeant, why would these persons of interest hold on to incriminating bloody decapitation devices after the headless bodies have been taken into custody?"

"My guess is they aren't finished using them."

"Makes sense, you got a rough plan beyond munching lunch?"

Luke filled the Lieutenant in on what he'd learned from Marco and then said, "The official version of what is going down right now is I'm taking you and Amelia Youssef to lunch. We are going to stop at an Auto Repair shop afterward so I can price some new oversize tires for my muscle car. You guys are coming along to make sure I get the best deal."

"So, that's the story, is it? What blarney! Who'd believe that bullshit?"

"We are not, let me repeat myself, we are not sticking our noses in any Federal investigations. But we are the police and authorized to keep the peace."

"Nicely put boyo, except what is your motive of record van den Hoose. Why would a gay sergeant be buying a straight Lieutenant he doesn't work for lunch?"

"Interesting question, brown nosing is out I suppose? ... Oh, I know are you being considered for the open captain's position?"

"Are you kidding? With my reputation and I make no secret I'm retiring in a year or so, or later. Speaking of that, my driver Timmy Mahoney has taken it upon himself to be my personal bodyguard until I retire. He'll be wanting lunch too."

"Perfect, my motive of record is; we are going to have lunch for planning a party to celebrate Lt. Schmidt's promotion to Captain. Oh, I need to call my troops in from the field for lunch."

"No, you don't, if you bring the people you supervise it will look even more bogus than it already does, unless they are certified party planners?"

"They are good at the kind of party I'm planning."

"Then that is a definite no to your people coming."

"Then it's only four of us with Amelia. Do you think that's enough?"

"It might be enough; I can always get more if needed. And to authenticate your little farce, I will pick up the check. If I have the paperwork completed correctly, the Department should pay for our meal."

"Oh, I forgot Amelia might bring two or three officers with her. It's too late to call them back, they are on the road."

"No problem, six or seven is a good meeting size for all kinds of business."

Amelia and three of her officers were waiting in her unmarked car outside Ted's Diner. Luke instructed officer Mahoney to pull in next to her. The seven cops got out of their cars, scoping each other. "Save the introductions for inside."

In the Diner Luke spoke to the cashier. "We need a table for seven, in a quiet corner where we can talk undisturbed."

Servers quickly pushed two large rectangular tables together and covered them under one long tablecloth. It was in a secluded alcove away from the few other 3:30 afternoon lunchers. When the table was set, the cops seated themselves.

"People, this lunch is for planning Lieutenant Karl Schmidt's promotion party. Lieutenant Sean Gilhooley on my right will be picking up the check, so order whatever you like. I'm Sergeant van den Hoose, and this is officer Mahoney."

Amelia's guys gave her inquisitive looks, and she returned them with a silent command they understood. "I am Sergeant Youssef and these police officers are; Nabil, Ashraf, and Tariq. We are looking forward to planning this promotion party." After saying that, she winked at Luke.

Their server, a young African-American woman appeared at the table. "Hi, I'm Sarah may I get you something to drink?" Both Gilhooley and Mahoney ordered micro beer, while Luke requested an unsweetened ice tea. Amelia's men made disapproving faces when alcohol was ordered, until the server asked their boss if she wanted cardamom seeds in the hot tea she requested. Then they all ordered tea with cardamom.

The men settled into more friendly faces and casual conversations ran around the table. The group warmed to each other by degrees, having common work related adventure stories to share. When it came time to order food Gilhooley loudly spoke up. "This guy recommends your beer batter fried clams, are they good?"

Sarah the server said they were excellent, then picking up on the sudden drop in temperature, addressed Amelia's men. "Ted's is famous for its Mediterranean appetizer platter. Many people order it as a main course. It has a lot of tasty vegetarian foods and is not expensive for all you get. It is big enough to share."

On guard Ashraf asked, "What's on it, is the food fresh?"

Sarah didn't answer; she pivoted on her heels and was gone in the blink of an eye. Then she was back with a stout middle aged man wearing a long white apron and chef's hat. "I'm Ted this is my Diner, how may I help you?"

Amelia immediately picked up on Ted's Turkish accent and spoke to him in Turkish. After a brief animated friendly conversation, Ted hurriedly returned to his busy kitchen preparing for the evening rush.

Smiling addressing Amelia, Sarah said, "Ted doesn't get much chance to speak Turkish around here, and doesn't tell people I'm his niece unless he knows them, he must like you." Looking at Amelia's men she said, "Are you ready to order, or should I come back?"

Amelia turned to her guys after watching the server who she just realized understood Turkish. "Ted said he won't sell anything he doesn't eat himself, and he took offense at your suggestion his food wouldn't be fresh, Ashraf."

"Sorry, but I still don't know what's on the platter?"

Sarah rejoined the conversation. "It has hummus, babaganoush, falafels with tahini sauce, tabbouleh, stuffed grape leaves, Greek salad, and served with hot whole wheat or white pita bread. It's good, I like it." With Sarah's hardy recommendation all four anti-terror cops ordered an appetizer platter. The other three cops ordered the fried clams, onion rings and sweet potato fries. When the food arrived, it looked good, smelled great, and tasted even better. The meal went well with convivial conversations all around; nobody would have guessed these late lunchers were on their way to a gun fight.

10.

The two unmarked police cars drove up and parked on either side of the open auto repair shop rollup steel doors. It was a medium size prefab structure built on the back-left quadrant of a concrete pad just adequate for the large number of cars parked on it. Inside the building were two auto repair bays with enough unused open space to expand to a third, and a service desk. To the right of the repair work area was a small parts department's half door with counter top, and the worker's restroom was tucked behind it. On the opposite side of the building, were a glass enclosed office and open customer's waiting area with coffee service, bowls of snacks, and restrooms off to one side.

When they arrived, Amelia immediately had her men sign for assault rifles and ammo clips. She handed them out from the trunk of her car.

Rifle in hand Ashraf spotted the only van in the shop. He went directly to it with his colleagues in tow and the Lieutenant and his driver following. When the van's rear double doors were flung open, the five cops stepped back to stare at the bloody *Fairy Swatter* and gasoline powered chain saw. Lieutenant Gilhooley had Tim use a digital camera to take photos; Amelia's officers did the same with their cell phones.

Marco and Luke saw each other across the repair shop at the same time the other cops spotted the van. They walked to each other, Marco looking anxious.

"You brought a lot of people with big guns here."

"You said your grandfather was worried the bad guys would hurt your family."

"He is, but now he'll worry you will shoot holes in our computerized equipment and the customer's cars."

"Tell you what, let's meet with everyone and talk. Please call everybody to the open area?"

While Marco was assembling his family, Luke took a look inside the van, and then herded the cops together with the family. When everyone was assembled shoulder to shoulder, using his command voice he said, "Hello everybody my name is Luke van den Hoose. I came here today with my friends to look for new oversize high performance tires for my customized muscle car." Scanning his audience, he said in Spanish, "No *habla Ingles por favor arriba su mano.*" No hands went up so Luke continued. "My friends know a good tire deal when they see one, that's why I brought them. Also, rumor has it some bad men might be in your neighborhood today. So, we brought along some long guns to keep the peace, but we hope our shopping today won't require using guns."

Tariq snickered and Amelia gave him a look that shut him down fast and hard.

"While I'm tire shopping, it would be good if family members left and went somewhere safe. When the area is clear of bad men you can return, please leave right now."

There was grumbling, but most of the family collected their things and left.

"Ashraf, Nobile, Tariq, and Tim please move outside and take up hidden positions to cover the front and back doors. Lieutenant you take the parts department and Amelia occupies the office, and I'll cover the service desk."

"Who died and made you king?"

"Do you speak Spanish Lieutenant?"

"Fine, but why does she get the office?"

"That's where Marco's mother works. If the bad guys are halfway observant they expect to see a woman working there. And we don't have time to put you in drag, any other questions?"

Gilhooley didn't look happy but sauntered to the parts department. While the outside cops hid their cars then took concealed protected positions around the perimeter, Marco's father and grandfather marched up to Luke.

"We aren't leaving our business in the hands of complete strangers. Sending the rest of the family to safety, we appreciate that. But we aren't leaving."

"What are your names?"

"I'm Gabriel Sandoval and this is my father in law Paco Ayala. What exactly is going on?"

"I am a police officer, your son Marco telephoned me that Paco was concerned that the owner of that van might pay his bill with gunfire instead of money."

"How is it you know my son? I never saw you before in my life."

"Marco told me he came out as gay recently."

"That is none of your business; that is a family matter, and we are handling it as a family. That should not be any concern for you."

"It is my business; Marco and my nephew Dirk have pledged love for each other. That brings Marco and his family into my family."

"Dirk … I remember, yes, we met him. He seems like a nice boy, worked hard and wouldn't take any money. But I'm still not leaving my shop with strangers."

"For me to do my job I need to know you and yours are safe."

"Just how will you explain the work we did and answer any questions about it to those desperadoes? May I ask you that?"

"Oh, you're right, just get your family moving then come back to the service desk."

"I'm back, my family is unhappy about leaving me here with you. But I insisted so they are going home. Except Paco says no, he's half owner I can't order him what to do. He feels responsible because he spoke to Marco about guns."

"Guys, it's getting close to pick up time. Paco please go to the parts department with the Lieutenant. Gabriel if lead starts to fly hit the ground. Do you have the customer's bill ready?"

"Right here, look for yourself."

A bird started whistling right outside the garage front door then an Escalade pulled up and two men got out of the rear passenger door. Both men had gold tips and heavy gold spurs on their shiny black cowboy boots, and large gold nugget cinches on their braided black leather bolo ties. They wore wide brim high crown black cowboy hats and black tailored western style suits with gold embroidery accents on the shoulders, lapels, pockets, yoke, and at the cuffs.

The pox marked older uglier of the two men from the Escalade strode up to the service desk. The younger good looking man moved back and scoped out a field of fire like a trained body guard.

Gabriel Sandoval, eyes looking down, wordlessly handed the customer his copy of the bill for parts and labor totaling $436.25. The customer name at the top of the bill was Armando Pumarejo. After looking over the bill Armando Pumarejo, pulled a large wad of cash from his pants pocket and pushed two one hundred dollar bills at Gabriel. Mr. Sandoval looked down at the money but didn't move.

In a soft neutral voice, Luke said, *"Signor, mas dinero por favor."*

Armando Pumarejo took a step back lifted up the bottom of his fancy embroidered cowboy shirt to show the butts of two semi-automatic hand guns tucked in the waist band of his western slacks. They were stuck behind his thick black leather belt with large gold buckle. Pumarejo glared at Luke, daring him to start something.

Luke reached down into his open gym bag, brought up the Uzi and clicked off the safety. He rested the gun's barrel on top of the service desk counter aimed at the customer's midsection and met his glower, eye to eye, then with street authority loudly said, *"Signor, rapido, mas dinero por favor."*

The two men held eye contact in what could have turned into a long staring contest. At that close range, Luke figured he could cut Armando in half and still get his body guard before either fired a shot.

Mr. Pumarejo blinked, shrugged and then brought out his wad of bills again. He threw three more new one hundred dollar bills down on the first two. Hands shaking Gabriel stamped the receipt paid, handed the man his bill, the van keys and started to make change, when the Mexican gangster menacingly said in English loud enough for all to hear, "Keep it for now, I'll be back for my change when your whole family is here to give me gratification." Then he and his companion swaggered to the van.

Luke saw Pumarejo's words had a terrifying effect on Mr. Sandoval. His color drained to chalk white, so Luke put a reassuring hand on the man's shoulder. "I'm not letting anything bad happen to your family. But you and your father in law should lockup, and go home."

In the meantime, the two thugs climbed in the van, and Luke watched their faces as they turned the key in the ignition. The engine started instantly and ran smoothly. Judging from the list of parts the van must have been in sorry shape.

The van drove out with the Escalade following close behind. Luke said goodbye to Mr. Sandoval, and climbed in the back of Lieutenant Gilhooley's unmarked car. Officer Mahoney tailed the bad guys from a safe distance. From time to time he and Amelia switched off being the lead tail car. After about fifteen miles, the perpetrators drove into a new expensive looking housing subdivision. Many structures were still under construction. The big houses looked to sit on an acre of recently reclaimed and leveled land. The van and Escalade pulled in front of a Mansion style new house. There were four other big cars already parked in front, and two smaller cars off to the side.

II.

The two unmarked police cars drove past the house to a secluded dense forest area and pulled off the road for a huddle.

"Listen up everyone; we have no probable cause for backup. We are on our own," Gilhooley scowled at the cops before him.

"Amelia, are you up for a dangerous assignment?"

"I live for danger. What-cha-got sir?"

"The next chapter in tonight's story is my contribution. While shopping for tires, we noticed intimidating behavior from these bandito boyos. Rather than put civilians and their property at risk we followed these miscreants home to have a little confab about threatening law abiding taxpaying families, in front of off duty party planning tire shopping police officers."

"Is this where we get busy?" Luke asked anticipating the answer.

"Look at our options people; we could stake out the place and wait for who knows what for who knows how long, or we could leave and tell the feds what we know and hope it doesn't take them six months to follow-up. Or we can handle it ourselves, old school."

"Old school sir?"

"The squeamish here should bale now. If any of you are feeling the slightest urge to jump ship, please hurry and do it. I'll personally call you a cab, pay the fare and tip the driver."

Nobody moved.

"Give me a minute and then we'll start." The Lieutenant turned and walked off a short distance speaking into his cell phone.

When Gilhooley returned and faced the other cops, it was two phone conversations later. "Everyone synchronizes your watch to mine, this is critical. Do it now, everybody!" The other six cops put their wrists in and synced their wristwatches or cell phones to the Lieutenant's gold Rolex.

"Luke and Tim will leave when I say go. Take my car, drive past the perpetrator's house, and park out of sight. Use the back yards to hustle back, take up defendable positions at the rear of the hooligan's house, don't shoot unless fired upon. Any questions?"

"No sir, understood."

"Five minutes after they leave, we drive up near the front door, Amelia we need something to put over your guys squeezed low in the back seat."

"I have a tarpaulin in the trunk. Hey don't you men make faces, it is clean and fumigated since last time."

"When Amelia and I knock on the front door you three slip out on the opposite side of the car. Find hidden positions facing the front door. Tariq cover the upper floors, if they shoot you shoot back. If shots come from the front door, when Amelia and I go to either side answer them, return fire on full automatic."

"Do we identify ourselves and ask them to surrender first?"

"No, I only want a conversation with Mr. Pumarejo about the threats I heard him make against that family. After identifying myself, I intend to use my most convivial way of conversing with the King's English. If he is receptive to constructive criticism there will be no need for his surrender, now is there?"

"Oh okay, we don't identify ourselves."

"People relax; Amelia and I will show our badges at the front door that should be identification enough. *But everyone's number one rule today is* the perpetrators must fire first; the number two rule is you shoot to kill; the number three rule is none of us goes inside that house under any circumstances. We don't have a warrant and are not in hot pursuit. Let the uniforms and CSIs be the first inside. Let's keep this simple, I don't want a lot of he said she said nonsense clogging up the paperwork cesspool after the fact. Does everyone understand rules 1, 2, 3, any questions?"

"But if we are doing it by the book, can I get overtime pay?"

"Mary mother of God, patrolman, what's your Lieutenant's name?"

"For tonight you're my boss; I was just wondering."

"Look, boyo, do you really expect overtime for planning a party? How about some common sense, I bought you lunch? You people ready?"

The cops spoke in unison, "Yes sir."

"I am in charge, understand?"

"Yes sir."

"So, for the third time; they shoot first, we shoot to kill, and nobody goes inside the house for any reason."

As one voice, they loudly shouted, "Got it sir."

"Everybody listen up hard, if I'm dead or incapacitated at the half hour mark on your synchronized watch, leave me and get as far away from that house, as fast as you can."

"I just knew there would be more with someone else in charge." Luke muttered half under his breath while checking his weapons.

"If Lieutenant Leung doesn't hear from me at or before the half hour mark, he has two drone helicopters with programmed kill orders firing at the half hour mark plus two minutes. They are going airborne as I speak. His drones have the GPS coordinates I gave him to the house. Each drone is equipped with two Gatling machine guns and enough ammo to turn that building into a large pile of tiny splinters."

"Lieutenant Leung was Officer Robinson's boss, like you were Nestor's, right? Goodness you guys really know how to make a wrong right."

"Five cops were killed."

Half in jest Amelia said, "Where did he get killer drones, and may I have one?"

"His precinct has one of the police heliports. He usually has manned whirlybirds ready to fly for search and rescue or with sharpshooters. Unasked the military donated six of their older slower low flying drones to the police department."

"Lucky him."

"Lt. Leung received two of the six, and is replacing one machinegun with a high resolution aerial camera and long range infrared radiation detector. Tonight may make his point; two Gatling guns are unnecessary for local police work."

"I guess that means no killer drone for Amelia?"

"*Okay Tim and Luke, backyard, go now.* The rest of us leave in five minutes. Smoke if you got 'em. If you're religious say a little prayer about now.'"

"Overall, how much time do we have, sir?"

"A total of twenty-five minutes starting now. Everybody clear what happens? Check your weapons … let's go!" All heads nodded yes and moved at once.

The Lieutenant's plan worked precisely, Luke and Tim no sooner hiked in and took positions in the backyard then Amelia's car rolled up next to the front door. When she and Gilhooley knocked on it, her men rolled out from under the backseat tarp and took up firing positions behind the prep's cars opposite the entrance.

The front door was opened by the bodyguard they had seen at the repair shop. He'd changed into jeans a new white T-shirt and was barefoot. He looked agitated. "What do you want? This is not a good time. Go away, vamoose."

"We wish to speak with Mr. Pumarejo. We are with the police," and they flashed their gold badges.

Mr. Pumarejo, wearing the same clothes stepped forward opening the door to its full width. He stood shoulder to shoulder with his bodyguard. "If you don't have search warrants get the hell off my property. I have friends in very high places, and the *power* to make you disappear, so leave while you still can."

Lt. Gilhooley more sensed, than saw activity behind the two men blocking the wide-open doorway. He took a quick sidelong glance and saw Amelia had picked up the unseen movement too. So Gilhooley said, "My, boyo, are you threatening two of our City's finest police officers?"

Like a well-choreographed dance team, the two Mexican gangsters circumnavigated to either side on the inside of the open door, and Amelia and Gilhooley did the same outside. Gunfire erupted from the entrance hallway behind where the two thugs had been standing.

Two cartel men kneeling and two more standing let go with a long loud fusillade of high velocity rifle and 00-shotgun fire. Ashraf and Nabil waited for the shooters inside the house to reload. Then emptied their thirty round clips. Their fire was directed through the open doorway. It only took seconds for their hail storm of bullets to whiz in killing the men reloading. After that sporadic gun shots could be heard from the back of the house as Ashraf and Nabil reloaded their weapons. Then nothing, a palpable deathly quiet enveloped the night.

After several seconds of the unnerving silence Mr. Pumarejo's and his body guard's hand guns followed by their heads came around either side of the bullet splintered door frame for a look. Gilhooley and Amelia were waiting, and each took their man out with two head shots.

Then it was eerily quiet again. Catching his breath, looking at the dead, Gilhooley asked, "Amelia, you and your men all right?" She checked and nodded her head to the affirmative. With a booming Irish brogue Gilhooley shouted, "Tim, Luke, you okay back there?"

Both Tim and Luke yelled together, "All clear."

"Get your asses up here on the double." The Lieutenant turned walked a short distance and made three short cell phone calls.

When the two backyard cops jogged to the front Luke said, "You won't believe what they were doing in the kitchen."

"You went in the kitchen?!"

"No, we watched them through the window; they were repackaging a white powder. Some of your bullets tore into the packages and now there is a fine white dust on everything in the kitchen and all over the dead perps who ran out the back-door firing."

Back from his phone conversations Gilhooley said, "Good job people, it looks like no loose ends from here. If the white powder I overheard you mention is illicit drugs our little mission got a layer of legitimacy. Lt. Leung is returning his drones to base after their 'training exercises.' The uniform cops will be here shortly with bells and whistles. They will put yellow crime scene tape up, and check for wounded inside. They will be followed by the Crime Scene Investigators and pathologist. Next my boss Captain Jolly-Jones, accompanied by at least one assistant Commissioner if not the Commissioner herself will arrive to check out the scene.

"Amelia, you and your guys are welcome to stay and revel in the glory and paperwork from tonight's endeavor, or you can fade into the shadows if you weren't here. Tell me, what are your druthers? You get two minutes to decide."

Looking to her men, Amelia clearly received their nonverbal response. "For the sake of our ongoing undercover investigations, it would be better if we were never here."

"Then go with mine and the department's heartfelt but unofficial thanks. It was good working with all of you. Please leave the two assault rifles that fired, and your Beretta Amelia. Just so CSI doesn't go crazy trying to figure who shot what and where. I'll return them with fresh ammunition when the dust settles. I can loan you a Sig Sauer if you like, I always carry two."

Amelia handed Gilhooley her Beretta, and Ashraf's, and Nabil's rifles. "Thanks anyway, but I always carry a backup piece. We should all do lunch again sometime. It was tasty." Then she buzzed the Lieutenant's cheek and gave Luke a quick kiss too, waved goodbye, joined her men in the car and sped off.

"Luke what weapons did you discharge in back?"

"Just the Uzi Lieutenant, I emptied one magazine."

"Tim what are you using today?"

"My Glock, I went through two extended clips."

"Okay now for the official ending to Luke's little party planning lunch saga. None of us went to the auto repair shop today. Got it, Amelia and her boys weren't here, and we never went tire shopping."

"So, what's the story?"

"After lunch, I suggested we check out this neighborhood since it is new to me and I might be in the market for a new home."

"Sure you are."

"Through no fault of our own we were involved in a road rage incident when that van over there started tailgating us. Tim was going the speed limit when the van started riding our bumper, flashing its lights and blowing its horn. Tim sped up, and they continued road raging. So, at my direction we went off the road, let them pass, and followed them to here. A confrontation about road rage ensued and the end results you see before you."

"And you said my tall tale was blarney."

"Who's in charge Luke? Tim hand Luke your Glock and the magazines. Now Tim you take Amelia's Beretta."

"Now what?"

"Memorize what just happened; Tim you and I went up to the front door of this house for a powwow about traffic safety, and someone took a shot at us. We retreated to behind those cars, where all the empty rifle shells are and returned fire with these assault rifles we just happened to have handy in my car. Meanwhile Luke had been covering us from the car. I ordered him to go around back to secure the rear of the house. He was also was fired on and returned fire from two weapons to create the illusion of more than one officer on the scene. The reason his empty shell casing are spread out is he moved around returning fire to support the illusion of many cops. We did it by the book, any questions?"

"How do we explain having rifles and a sidearm belonging to Sergeant Youssef?"

"Oh, Luke, ye of little faith, Lieutenants have ways of explaining things Sergeants don't."

"Yeah well losing Nestor has shaken what little faith I had."

"If either of you are asked questions you don't have answers for, then the correct answer is 'God works in mysterious ways, or the Lieutenant may know.' Tim get my car and park it where Amelia's was."

Tim, who had not spoken more than ten words since Luke first met him, was muttering as he walked back for the car. "By the looks of this bullet riddled place, God also works in ungodly ways."

12.

After three hours of repeating Gilhooley's revision and addendum to Luke's original cover story, first to one then another high police official and then to lowly crime scene investigators, Tim Mahoney was finally behind the wheel of the Lieutenant's car. Gilhooley and van den Hoose were sitting in the back seat. The three men were talked out from being questioned over and over by bosses and colleagues. Following Sean Gilhooley's instructions Tim pulled up next to Luke's car in his precinct's employee parking lot. Three doors opened at once and they all exited the car glad to be finished working after a long night. Their story of events passed muster.

"Luke, tomorrow morning before you write up tonight's happenings, fill out and sign forms so that Uzi can be returned to your precinct's armory after CSI is finished with it. That will be one less loose end the new Captain Schmidt will have to deal with as he cleans out his desk, moves to headquarters, and names you acting Lieutenant to replace him."

"Damn, so he got his promotion after all that fretting, good for him."

"He was the only one who thought it might not happen. For God's sake, he was number one on the list. Now go open the trunk of your car and then come walk with me Lieutenant."

Speaking softly for only his driver to hear Gilhooley said, "Tim transfer that trophy from my car's trunk to his. Don't let him see you do it."

For several minutes, Sean and Luke walked aimlessly around the old red brick police station, sharing a silence. Both men were emotionally drained from the earlier combat. "Luke, it is none of my business and you certainly don't have to say anything. But does Amelia know you're a fag?"

"You're damn right it is none of your business, and is anyone going to even ask me if I want the desk job of acting lieutenant?"

"I only ask about Amelia because the way you two looked at each other tonight reminded me of my kids' teenage puppy love. But hey, like you say it's none of my business, and my kids survived it and are all grownup making me grandbabies." Changing his mood and making a show of looking serious Gilhooley said, "I am asking nicely lieutenant, Schmidt should have told you, and it's been a long night."

"What?"

"Encase you haven't noticed, I'm no desk jockey. The way I handle the job is to have very component well praised clericals handle the administrative bullshit with my cell phone number handy. I've been at this a long time, trust me, you'll make a good lieutenant. Schmidt said he told you as much. I wouldn't have spoken otherwise."

"Since you seem to want to get paternal with me, yeah, I told Amelia, but she knew already from before. When I told her about Nestor's death she was genuinely sympathetic."

"She's good people, I like her."

"She asked how my grieving was going, and I said it feels like I am all alone in the world, with a huge hollow space inside and no idea how to fill it."

"What did she say?"

"She asked if I would be excommunicated from gay life if she offered to help me through this time."

"Excommunicated, hell the Pope would do an Irish Jig in wooden clogs. What did you say?"

"I'm not available for anything much until I grieve Nestor, and I don't know how long that will take. But I got to tell you, the image of the Pope doing a jig in clogs will stay with me too long."

"I don't understand, so what was all that gushy looking at each other about tonight?"

"Amelia and I acknowledge a strong mutual attraction. I like how she looks, and how her mind works, and won't say no if she offers more. She wants to help me bury my dead, and I know I need help with that."

"It's smart to accept help when offered. Few of our new gung-ho officers seem to understand that. What would Nestor think about you with Amelia?"

"I don't think he'd want me to wear widower black the rest of my days. We were roommates, not married."

"You know what I mean, she's a girl and you're a fag."

"As near as I can tell she is a full grown, open minded woman. I think Nestor would like Amelia and she him. Anyway, that's what I think this minute, it's still early days."

"Can I dance at your wedding?"

"What wedding? You can dance at Captain Schmidt's coronation party."

"I wish you and Amelia the best. Let's get back to the cars; I need to get home for some overdue sleep."

The two men walked back to their autos in silence. Luke noticed his trunk lid still up and went to close it, looking in first. Then he faced the Lieutenant and shrugged his shoulders, his face showed the unasked question, *what do I do with this?*

"I thought you could clean up the *Fairy Swatter*, maybe even polish it real nice and pretty then donate it to the Gay Civil Rights Museum in Washington D.C. If it were me, I'd make the donation in the name of slain Police Officers Nestor Negron and Jamal Lawler, who died taking it out of commission. But hey that's just me, and you know how I feel about fags. Do with it what you think is right, Lieutenant."

RAPPER

Everett Crosland, a sixty-eight-year-old, balding African-American filmmaker, shed a good night's sleep for another placid day at Pristine Pond, a gated community for wealthy older persons. He had lived there one month. The resident's handbook, as much as he'd read so far said, "Expect three or four months to feel completely at home." The handbook had helpful suggestions to expedite the acclimation by utilizing staff, but he'd skipped most of that preferring to settle in on his own terms, at his own pace.

To celebrate his first month's snug-cozy feelings, instead of preparing breakfast as usual, Everett phoned the dining room and had a carafe of dark roast coffee, a toasted buttered English muffin, fresh fruit cup along with the day's newspapers sent to his apartment. It was another gesture toward accepting his new home. Pristine Pond had a four-star chef overseeing its food programs. Everett wasn't quite ready to take *that* next step, but the ordered breakfast was a step in that direction.

Residents could take their meals in the elegant dining room, have meals delivered to their apartment directly from the kitchen, or prepare meals themselves in their own apartment's fully equipped kitchen. Everett thought *so far so good preparing my own meals; I like to cook and am damn good at it. Although it seems magical how unasked, depleted or near depleted foodstuffs are replaced when I'm out.*

A knock at the door sounded just as Everett finished drying off from his morning shower. He slipped into his hooded floor length, thick pile burgundy colored bath robe and matching comfy slippers. Everett's medium dark African-American frame still stood ram rod straight at five feet eleven inches. He kept the same weight as in college and was in good physical shape from regular gym workouts, and weekend tennis. Though balding what hair remained was much darker than the creeping gray, he looked good for his age.

Everett answered the door to find a smiling young white person behind a rolling cart. "Good morning."

"Good morning to you sir, I have your breakfast, do you want me to set it up on the terrace or inside? -- Or okay then, I'll leave it for you to do as you wish, enjoy your meal Mr. Crosland."

"Thank you. Haven't I seen you around here?"

"I hope so I'm your floor's majordomo. Since you are a new resident and may not know, you can leave the cart outside your door and I'll have someone get it, or you can buzz me using the blue intercom button and I'll come and clear it away for you."

"Good to know, thanks."

"I'm Kevin by the way. I restock your kitchen as needed, if you want anything special please leave me a note. I also supervise your maid service; let me know if it's to your satisfaction. Oh no, we are not allowed to accept gratuities, but thank you all the same sir."

"It sounds like you are prepared to take care of all my needs."

"If I'm reading your innuendo and ogle correctly, I'd need to know more about those needs in order to provide the best possible service. Just between us, I like your work; you are the best in my opinion."

"What have you seen?"

"Your documentary on cotton production in the U.S. was required for my American History class in high school. When I saw you were moving to the Pond, I Googled you and watched many of your documentary films streaming online. Your work is amazing, easy to understand yet not dumbed down at all."

"That is nice of you to say."

"For me, your few Hip Hop music videos are absolutely wonderful. At least that's my opinion, bravo sir."

"Son flattery can get you a lot in life. How old are you Mister Flatterer? Sorry to be flippant, as you can see adulation embarrasses me. But I appreciate your sincerity, it is refreshing."

"I'll be thirty-one in May. I know I look much younger, and I still don't know what I want to be when I grow up."

"Many folks experience that. If you can be patient, the solution always presents itself. To make a not so subtle change of subject, would you mind explaining this intercom? There is a box in every room, including next to the toilets in the bathrooms."

"Sure, the blue is for me or whoever is covering for me, the yellow is for lobby reception, white is for food service, it's faster than telephoning and the red is for any kind of emergency. Push a button and talk into the box, someone will talk back, and for emergencies I'll appear first since I'm here. That's it in a nut shell; the residents' handbook has more detailed information, and I'm here to answer questions or go fetch, or whatever you need. I think I'm going to like you, I already like your creative video work a lot."

"Thank you, Kevin, I think I'm going to like you as well."

2.

Everett pushed his chair back, content after the tasty simple breakfast. It was perfectly presented; under a silver warming cover on regal china, with polished sterling silver flatware, cloth napkin, and fresh cut flowers artfully arranged in a silver vase on the tray. He finished reading the newspapers and stifled a strong urge to put the breakfast things back on the cart and roll it out into the hallway, then get dressed for a day of reading and exercise. Instead he poured the last of the coffee into his cup and leaned back taking in the view from his terrace. If ever there was a time to reflect on the fluke of him living at Pristine Pond, this was it.

A few months previous at a dinner party, not unlike the one described thousands of years ago, in Plato's *Symposium*, Everett told his friends he was split between starting work again after his last documentary's success, or retiring. He said, "I've flipped coins, tossed dice, cut cards, even consulted an astrologer and after all that I'm still stuck for what direction to take next. I'm retirement age but don't feel my age. Any suggestions old pals?"

A dear longtime friend, Sy Applebloom, a prominent entertainment lawyer responded. "Everett my good man, apply to buy an apartment at Pristine Pond, one just became available. If they accepted you, we all present here tonight can enjoy the amenities. If you're not accepted, go back to work, and work as long and hard as you want, with our blessings."

Other dinner guests knew of the Pond and demanded they get an up or down vote on acceptance, if he was selected to buy. They all concurred clapping their hands, stamping their feet and chanting vociferously, "Do it, do it, do it for us." The restaurant's manager rushed over and sternly asked the dinner party to quiet down so other diners could enjoy their meal.

Everett had never heard of Pristine Pond, to please his friends he took the prospective buyer's tour. His tour group of ten women and men was shown the elegantly furnished apartment for sale. Then the recreation rooms, the lobby and other common spaces, all furnished with expensive antiques, valuable art works on the walls and deep plush Oriental rugs under foot. The tour group was then shown the beautiful eighteen-hole golf course, eight tennis courts, Olympic size indoor swimming pool, two health spas separated by a modern exercise gym. They were given a calendar of regularly occurring cultural events held at the Pond, which included music programs by its resident string quartets bi-weekly cocktail hour recitals.

The tour group was then served an epicurean lunch in the Pond's dining room that had the ambiance of a chic restaurant. Over dessert and coffee, the tour group was given a talk explaining the complicate application process. The presenter said as an aside, "If the applicant's deep pockets are less than fifty million dollars, s/he should self-select out of the process. The top 100 of you from the expected 1,500 applications will be placed in a drum and one winner drawn. The other ninety-nine application finalists will be allowed to use the Pond's golf course, tennis courts and other common facilities at a nominal charge for one year." Diffidently the presenter said, "I've been told it is easier for a young person to get into an Ivy League University, than for a mature adult to buy into Pristine Pond Condominiums."

Normally Everett would not have bothered with such a haughty place. He hadn't seen any other African-Americans, except service workers and his gaydar didn't registering anyone of interest. But applying was part of a fun dinner party goofy game he'd instigated. His friends expected good laughs from each juncture of his Pristine Pond adventure. They also liked a good fight and were well lawyered for the faintest whiff of racial or other discrimination. So, he'd go along with applying to make his friends happy and prove to himself he could, even if he'd rather not be bothered. Nobody said so, but he knew it was a kind of therapy for his ambivalence. He knew his friends loved him and were giving him the help he asked for.

Everett already had a recent biography on a computer memory stick. At first the essay seemed daunting until he started. He wrote an 800-word essay in one sitting and felt it cathartic; getting his feelings about recent history out and on paper.

Everett's pockets were more than deep enough. The letters of reference were another matter; he was given two rights away. Since his documentary films had won two Academy Awards, and three others had been nominated over the years, the Academy was happy to give him a glowing letter which also mentioned international awards his work received. One of the day's super star actors had been encouraged by Everett when just a fledgling in the film industry. In those early days, Everett occasionally paid the actor's rent to prevent her becoming homeless during lean times. The super star was more than happy to provide him a reference letter full of glowing accolades.

But the Pond also wanted at least two letters from people with authority holding high office. Not having a clue where to turn Everett telephoned Sy and explained his application's deficit. "Hey old friend, I hit a wall I'm short three reference letters from power brokers holding high office. Sorry old chum, its game over, but I gave it my best shot."

"Wait, when do you need the letters?"

"Next week at the latest, everything else is a go."

"Email me the particulars and I'll have you sent copies. Busy, busy got to go, kiss, kiss bye."

Somehow Sy was able to get a United States Supreme Court Justice, the governor of their state, and the CEO of a major pharmaceutical corporation to send letters to Pristine Pond endorsing Everett's good character. Everett didn't know how Sy did it, and wasn't sure he wanted to know.

Even when he was informed he was included in the top 100 applicants, Everett was sure he didn't have a chance to win. He thought of a long-ago rap lyric *if you black go to the back, if you queer get out of here …* Remembering a lifetime of slights he skipped the drawing shindig. Pristine Pond had lost its allure at that point. He'd met his friend's obligation and life moved on, he was thinking about reading proposals for new film projects. If in his wildest dreams he won the right to buy a Pond apartment, he wasn't sure he wanted it. *Wouldn't that be sweet for such an arrogant drawn out selection process, to be turned down by an older queer black man?*

When the telephone call came announcing he won the right to buy the apartment at Pristine Pond, Everett suddenly had to fend off an urge to panic. In jest, not really expecting it to happen, he had given his friends the right of an up or down vote to buy. He couldn't beg-out without losing face. A short power nap helped, but didn't completely alleviate his building anxiety as he arranged a party for the original dinner guests to share the victory. Everett was so sure he wouldn't win; agreeing to pick up the check was part of the fun. After all he was a black gay republican and very out to the world.

He knew the party would be an outrageously raucous celebration at his expense. But had not anticipated the dinner party would be so boisterous, the group of over sixty year olds, would be permanently banned, '86ed' from their favorite restaurant. A restaurant anyone of the mixed-race group could have bought and sold without a thought. The management said they were unwelcome guests for the life of the restaurant, and added property damages, and the other customer's dinners, to Crosland's bill for food and drink.

Everett roused himself from his musings and placed the breakfast things on the rolling cart and pushed it out into the hallway.

3.

Just as he was about to go to the bedroom and dress the intercom softly chimed and the receptionist's button blinked. "Crosland here."

"Sir, there are four men here who asked to see you. They won't give me a name, should I send them up?"

"I'm not expecting anyone. Please ask them their business."

"... They only say they *will see you*." Then in a whisper she said, "They look ominous."

"Tell them to telephone for an appointment, I'm not seeing guests today, and I don't wish to be disturbed, thank you." Everett heard the receptionist repeating his words as she disconnected. Curious, he looked at his calendar, it was clear for the day, he *wasn't* expecting anyone. Maybe they were selling something, but four?

He headed to the bedroom to dress, when there was a loud banging on his door. Looking through the peephole he saw four large thuggish men. "Go away, no guests today."

They continued to bang loudly; Everett pushed all the colored buttons on his closest intercom box. Then he jumped back as he heard an ear-splitting shrieking, tearing splintering of wood as his front door violently sprung open. The solid wooden frame had been shredded away from the door's heavy metal lock mechanism by brute force applied to a jimmy-bar.

Four intruders rushed in the apartment guns drawn. They quickly ascertained Everett was alone, unarmed, and naked under his robe. They holstered their weapons.

"I don't keep much money in the apartment; take my ATM card and password."

"Don't insult me, nigga."

Just then a pale anxious Kevin pushed in the room and spoke in a shaky voice. "The police have been called and will arrive momentarily and all the exits are being locked by our armed security guards. You men must go down to reception and surrender to the police."

"Shut the fuck up."

"If you don't want money, what do you want? I don't know you, this is a mistake."

Puffing out his chest like a bantam roaster the shortest, stockiest intruder spoke loudly. "You just insulted me again. I'm Bloody Fangs, the best Hip Hop Rapper that ever was, or will be. You have been given the very great honor by the Hip Hop Council to make my next music video."

"Wait, what? Is this a publicity stunt?"

"No, the Council says the only way I can get back on the circuit is if you produce and direct my next rap video. But didn't you like my marvelous flamboyant entrance just now?"

"No, you've made a mistake hip-pity-hop, I'm retired."

"Get this pops; I can only work with you, got it? Word is you win big deal prizes. Win one for me or very bad things will happen to you. Have I gotten your attention old fart, do you understand American-English?"

"Give me the name of who sent you?"

Kevin turned to Crosland and spoke softly. "He just got out of jail for domestic violence. He beat his girlfriend into a vegetable, and now Hip Hop wants nothing to do with him."

"Rudy cuff and gag that babbling nuisance white bread punk. Then go wash your hands. These whites are so disgusting; you never know where they have been or what new disease they are spreading."

Bloody Fangs stood a foot shorter than his shortest heavily-muscled body guard, and outweighed the biggest by 100 flabby pounds. All Bloody Fangs' visible teeth were capped with gold inlays. His gold encrusted teeth clashed with heavy ropes of bling ornaments dragging down his neck. If the adornments were meant to distract from his roly-poly ugliness, they failed.

Everett could see from Kevin's eyes he knew Bloody Fangs raps. Crosland thought *typical white male adolescent grew up listening to violence glorifying rap believing it held secret messages to cure this sick racist sexist society.*

Everett had seen fleeting seconds of Fang's raps, while surfing music videos, but lying offered a measure of control. "I don't know you? Why would you think I'd come out of retirement for a rude, crude intruder?" He could see his words pierced the rapper's phony baloney bravado.

"Rudy cuff this Old Oreo Cracker and let's get them both out of here. We may have to make this white trash scream to get Old Black Joe to obey his betters."

"Randall get two pillow cases from the bedroom. Then pillow-top these two piles of shit."

Pulling out his cell phone, Bloody Fangs barked, "Jamell, bring the van around to the side entrance. We are coming out, shooting if necessary."

Hands cuffed behind his back and a pillow case over his head, the next thing Everett registered was being carried down the building's fire exit stairs. Then he could feel the cold outside air on his bare legs and butt. Finally, he was tossed like a sack of potatoes into what he assumed was the aforementioned van. He landed on something lumpy. "Kevin is that you?"

"Um hum."

"Mark my words there will be serious retribution for this outrage. These clowns have no idea who they are messing with."

4.

After a high speed bumpy ride, passing police sirens going in the opposite direction, the next thing Everett knew the van loudly skidded to a stop. He was dragged out of the vehicle, carried over someone's shoulder inside a building and up two flights of stairs. Next a door was noisily unlocked and he was carried into what he sensed was a large open space and roughly dumped in a wooden captain's chair.

"Welcome to my artist's luxurious loft home. Be impressed, I own this whole building, soon I'll own the whole block."

"I wish to go home, and take Kevin."

"No, you don't! Now, artist to artist we are going to discuss the prize-winning hip hop music video you are going to create for me. You will give me a time table and budget, right now."

"I'm retired and music videos were never my main activity."

"I want the most expensive red Italian sports car and lots of bling from Spliffiny Jewelers on top of big piles of $1000 bills, white furs and lots of naked women shot from every angle. And don't forget, plenty of close-ups of my face rapping. I want the best, but on the cheap. You can do that."

"I told you, I can't help you. Let us go home, you made a mistake. My lawyer will contact you."

"Everett Crosland old boy, I never make mistakes. We can do this easy or hard. If you chose hard your little pussy punk will suffer pain you can't imagine. If we find you like to watch suffering, then we'll find something you don't like so much, *after* you watch us have our fun making your boy-toy shriek to death. Got it, Uncle Tom?"

"Remove the pillow case and un-cuff my hands or I'm going to loudly sing every hymn I ever heard, and I can't sing."

"Well ain't you a tough old motherfucking bird. They told us you were a stubborn old fart. Kirk un-cuff him and toss his pillow case."

"Stand up Mr. Rich Black Guy, let me free your hands," that said he whipped the pillow case off.

After a long interval of fumbling with the plastic handcuffs Kirk finally stepped away. "Okay boss?"

"Now we'll call this a business meeting. Everett Crosland welcome to my artist's home, now tell me what you'll need, and how much, for my spectacular prize winning Retrograde Rap Video?"

"Mr. Bloody Fangs, if you are the greatest Hip Hop rapper since hot sliced brown bread, why aren't you signed with a major label? All the big recording studios have music video production departments; some are quite good using the best young artists today."

"Cut the shit, that's not your business, or why you are here, asshole. You are the one I'm required to use by the Hip Hop Council. So hurry up with the plan, we will start shooting video this afternoon, and the results must to be spectacular. No, how could you shake your head no at me?! Boy, you are going to be so sorry for bad manners!"

"I told you, I'm retired. Now stop this foolish nonsense and let us go home."

Everett Crosland and Bloody Fang began a circular conversation; Fang demanded the film maker commit to make his video, Crosland restated he was retired, and then Fang described escalating unspeakable horrors in store for Kevin. Crosland was convinced the threat of torture was a bluff. Fang became increasingly frustrated as the conversation went around, and around in circles.

"Randall, Jamell and Kirk strip the white cocksucker and tie him tight, spread eagle sunny side up on the long table. Then turn the table on end so we can watch him squirm upside down. Leave the gag in until just before we start cooking his eggs. No need to beg with your eyes fairy boy. Only Everett can stop what's coming to you."

"Why upside down?"

"We will squirt a lot of water inside him just before we cook his Quail egg sized balls. It'll be a big surprised when he shoots a big geyser out of his ass and the falling water sizzles on his smoldering nuts. It's something you'll want to see."

"Please, don't hurt him. There is no shortage of great young film artists making music videos. If you want, I'll make you a list of excellent guys and gals who are working right now."

The circular conversation began again going around and around but not going forward.

"Enough of this, men set the video camera on the tripod, turn it on and pour barbeque sauce on the boy's balls."

"Stop this charade and let us go!"

"All finished boss. He doesn't have much to roast down there, but his ass looks sweet. It's pretty enough to give us each a nice carnival ride before you start grilling."

"This is a business meeting, no carnival rides."

"Stop this stupid game."

"The best part is you get to see and hear *me rap*. I always do a rap in their face until the subject's screams become too loud to rap over and then I scream along and that is noisy fun. I really enjoy performing with human sacrifice. You'll get to see me have fun."

"Spare me your bullshit, I want to go home."

"Oh, wait I see the problem, I didn't explain the rap you will immortalize in video."

"I don't want to know."

"I'm the originator of retrograde rap, returning the art form back to its roots. The rap you are about to make a great video explains how all queers should be slaughtered, women used abused made into refuse, and the best cops are dead cops. Dynamite rap ideas, right?"

"Stop this nonsense, right now."

"Oh, look at pussy boy's eyes, so big with anticipation, or is it shame for having so little to show real men. Don't worry cunt-boy you can make up for your little crotch by screaming big as we turn you into a cunt."

"He hasn't offended you. If you have a beef settle it with me, Kevin is an innocent bystander."

"Not to worry Crosland, the whole building is empty except for this loft. You can scream with him and me it will be fun."

"Let me be absolutely clear, I'm not making any music video, so untie him and let us go."

"You kidding, we haven't started yet. Don't be a party pooper."

"Look, neither of us has done anything against you, let us go."

"For your information, Mr. Video maker; I make videos too. You are about to see the latest in my collection of barbequed butt boys getting their nuts charred. I draw inspiration for my raps from real life, like what's about to happen right here in front of your eyes will be a rap someday."

"Stop this madness."

"Crosland, at the least your toy boy's begging shrieks should make you reconsider making my video, before we have to extinguish him. Okay, if not we can play you the memory cards over there, of others screaming to death."

"The Hip Hop Council told you I was stubborn, right? Do you think what you are saying is getting results?"

"When the boy starts screaming that's a result. At the very least his anguish will be immortalized right to his last gasp?"

"What I think is you can't coerce me into working for you."

"Listen you shit for brains, you are going to make me a prize-winning music video and that is all there is to it. The sooner you get it through your thick skull the less your boy suffers."

"You can kill him, you can kill me, I'm stubborn remember?"

"How about I do my rap, and then you tell me how good it is?"

"Don't bother. I never liked patter songs."

"It will be the smell of his flesh frying that you'll remember longest. These Street Punks come in different savors."

"Just stop your bluster."

"I understand, we are having a battle of wills and butt boy is the sacrificial pawn."

"No, you are totally insane?"

"Not to worry, after we sacrifice this piece of white trash, if you still need convincing, we'll go out and grab another junky boy to grill. We'll do it until you get tired of seeing their noisy end of life spectacles. There is an endless supply of disposable boys selling themselves for drugs in this part of town."

"Stop it, stop your crazy talk." Several thoughts collided at once in Everett's head; *decades before Crosland had made successful rap videos for a young gay rapper intent on addressing rap's homophobia and misogyny. If Bloody fang was serious, Kevin was about to be tortured to death. And Crosland's integrity prevented him from making a video for Bloody fangs to stop it.*

"Last chance, you ready to talk rap video or do you wants to watch barbequed butt boy's balls twist and crinkle and char over an open blue flame?"

Looking around, desperate for something, anything, Everett noticed pistols lying out in the open, and strapped to the underside of the table top Kevin was tied to. There were many types and sizes of weapons. Crosland reached down under his wooden chair, and felt cold metal. "Do you collect hand gun replicas? They seem to be strewn all over your place, are they for decoration?"

"What a stupid question, I'm a gansta rapper; I have to be ready for a gun fight in an instant. Idiot, they are real loaded shooters. You are one dumb black wuss. Replicas, what would I want with replicas?"

Everett reached down and removed the piece strapped under his chair and stood up. "Oh, look you have a Desert Eagle Mark XIX .50 magnum, and with the ten-inch barrel too. I had one of these back in the day; mine was in the titanium finish with fine African ebony wood grips. I never saw one in flat black finish like this. I like the look, although mother of pearl grips are a bit ostentatious for my taste. Oh, yeah, the balance is still perfect, just as I remember. You know these little cannons have surprisingly small recoil for so much velocity."

"Put that gun down!"

"I'm just cracking the slide back to see if what you said is true. Oh yes, you keep a round in the chamber, ever ready like you said." A plan of necessity materialized as he handled the sidearm. So, Everett faked a sneeze to mask the sound of cocking the gun.

"I said put that down, I mean it now!"

"Just a second I want to release the clip and see if you keep it fully loaded like you say. Oh, yes there are eight big ones in here, you are a man of your word at least about this gun."

"Put the damn gun down before we come over there and break your fingers! One, two …"

Everett turned his head up toward the back corner of the room behind the five big men standing side by side ready to rush and overpower him. He sensed they were about to pounce. "Oh, are those bats up here?" The diversion gave him just enough time to take a shooter's stance, knees slightly bent, butt back. He swiftly brought the Desert Eagle up into firing position cup and saucer fashion, his left hand supported his right from underneath. Then he slid the trigger safety lock off, aimed the gun and started shooting the hand cannon from left to right.

In less time than it takes to tell, four bodyguards lay dead on the floor. Three had their guns out, and two discharged as the men fell with a hole centered in their forehead. The farthest right bodyguard had been turning drawing his pistol, so he was hit in the temple. That bullet exited above and behind his ear. Bloody Fang found himself standing in a large and growing pool of his men's blood and brains.

5.

"Shit, what did you do? You are a fucking insane person, you killed my men! I only wanted a lousy music video and now I have no protectors. We were only kidding about hurting your boy, can't you take a joke?"

"Your men shot first, it was self-defense." Crosland was struggling to accept reality when conflicting thoughts smashed together *I still got my aim, oh no I just killed four people, it was self-defense, they won't have breakfast tomorrow, how could I do that without considering consequences?* His worried fearful mood shifted to bleak black.

"You shot first."

"Shall we playback your video camera and see if it tells the tale? Oh, and if I view those memory cards, will they show you were just kidding around too."

"You're a fucking crazy man. This shouldn't have happen! It wasn't supposed to go this way."

"Did you know Kevin before today?"

"How could you think so low of me to even ask? He's common white trash."

"I'll take that as no."

"Listen, I'm famous and you're famous and as everyone knows famous people don't kill each other, it's a fact. Let's talk turkey, what do you want?"

"I guess you haven't seen the Hip-hop musical *Hamilton*."

"Rap has a lot to answer for trying to go colonial. Listen let's pretend you didn't just shoot my bodyguards, okay? Why don't you and your boy just leave? Have a nice lunch on me."

"*I'm retired,* retired people don't like lose ends. So, we have to decline your lunch offer to finish what you started. There are five more bullets in this gun, don't make me shoot you?"

"No wait, listen there is a garage under this building with eleven antique luxury cars. Why don't you pick out one, my gift to you? Hell, I like you, take two cars with my compliments. Your boy can drive one for you."

"Actually, I do want something from you."

"There is nothing wrong with those cars, they're legal. Hell, take three, I'll drive one for you."

"You didn't research me or you would know I don't drive, never did."

"Why not, what kind of Blackman doesn't enjoy driving a fine automobile?"

"I always did work while someone else was driving."

"Okay, look I have cash lots of cash and it is for you. No, you don't want money, what the fuck do you want?"

"I'm a film maker I like to know the whole story before *the end* flashes on screen."

Bloody Fangs held eye contact with Everett for a long silent interval as his face progressed from bargaining to anger. "I got nothing more to say then. You just jealous I threatened your boy toy. He ain't nothing."

"He's a human being you mistreated."

"Oh, here we go again, I told that judge she deserved what I gave her. She turned into a vegetable by herself. I just knocked her around a little." Then Fangs' face seemed to zoom into a deeper darker place.

Everett spoke up loudly to get Bloody Fangs' attention. "Fangs, reach for one of the pistols lying around here and I will shoot you in the wrist. Given the size of the .50 Magnum slug your hand will detach and I will have to tie a tourniquet around your stump to keep you around. The same is true if you try to run. If you question my marksmanship take a good look at your dead thugs."

Bloody Fangs face shifted to depressed, gazing at his fallen men. After another pause he muttered, "If you want me to beg, forget it, I don't beg fairy fruit flavored faggot maggots." Then he looked down at his dead men again, his face ashen.

"I need you to admit to your video camera you caused this mess. I only wanted to be left alone today."

"Fuck you pansy!"

Kevin made a muffled sound through his gag.

"Oh, let me get you untied. Fang, you move I cripple you."

Everett removed Kevin's gag, then untied his ankles and wrists, all the while keeping one eye on Bloody Fang and the hand cannon close to his mitt. As he released the five-foot seven-inch captive, he couldn't help appraising Kevin's well-proportioned swimmer's body. But the young man's genitals were trying to climb back inside his torso from terror threats. The young blond emerald green eyed man was easy to look at and imagine in a more tranquil tender scene.

"Kevin, go wash and get dressed."

"I am totally uncovered, everyone saw me naked. They said I look like a plucked chicken; they all laughed at my nakedness."

"Kevin that part of this fiasco is finished. For the record, I think you have an attractive body."

Turning his head to closely study his dead body guards, Fangs spoke to the room. "Randall is my third cousin and Rudy has been with me from the beginning. How could you heartlessly gun them down without a chance?" Bloody Fangs scowled different faces at Everett like an angry toddler having a silent tantrum.

"You caused this; we were minding our own business."

"It's my life, my career and my building, I paid these men they worked for me and knew the work was dangerous. What's it to you anyway, you queer son of a bitch? This is *your* fault, not mine."

"Answer me two questions and we'll be done."

"Tell you what; I can make you rich if you don't kill me. I have a drug business on the side, I'll cut you in. You won't believe the profits."

"Sit down on the floor, no not there, right over here where your video camera can see you."

"What questions?"

"Who told you to use me for your video, and who else knows about today's escapade?"

"Fuck you."

"Using your words, 'you can make this easy or hard.' I want you to meditate on that while I attend to Kevin now he's back. If you move, I'll remove extremities."

6.

"Kevin, how you doing?"

"They were serious about wanting to burn me alive."

"It didn't happen, calm down."

"But every one of you saw me naked and they made fun of my body. That was humiliating, how can I ever be all right again? What they wanted to do is unspeakable."

"Be with me in the here and now ... trust me you will get beyond this day."

"I'm a modest person; I make love with the lights off, even alone. You saw everything, everyone did ... I'm so ashamed. I know I'm no stud; I'm how I was born, that was okay before today."

"Kevin truth be told, I liked seeing you in the altogether you have a nice body. Everyone doesn't have to be a physique model."

"I know we agreed to be friends ... but I can't get past what they wanted to do? Watching me suffers, and laughing at the suffering they caused. I don't understand how could they enjoy that?"

"Kevin do me a favor; go collect all the guns you see lying around this loft. Put them in the bathroom you just used to wash off BBQ sauce."

"What about all these knives and truncheons?"

"Those too." That said Everett walked over to Fangs, the Desert Eagle in hand.

Alarm registering on his face; Bloody Fangs took a deep breath and then tried for an assuaging tone. "Tell you what let's be friends, I could be a valuable asset Crosland, you have no idea the people I know."

"No thank you."

"Okay, I take everything back. I'll beg if you want … how do you want? I'd like to be your buddy, really. I know how to be a good and generous friend."

"You need to tell me what I want to know. Who and who?"

"Today you were just lucky to get the jump on my boys. You got off a few lucky shots is all. My men were crack shots."

"Luck had nothing to do with it."

"What were you a military sharpshooter back in olden times or something?"

"Can't you tell I don't bond with sadistic bullies? Pay attention, who sent you and who knew?"

"Tell me; were you a soldier or something? I was almost in the Army; we may have that in common. If you tell me, I might tell you."

"Might?"

"Humor me."

"Okay fine I'll play along, no to the military, in my much younger days I belonged to the Lavender Pistols. It's a lesbian gay male shooting club. We competed all over the country and won trophies. From there I won a silver medal in pistol at the Olympics. Then my film making career took off."

His sham offer of friendship refused, and not expecting an Olympic medal, Fang's mood shifted to antagonistic again. "Lavender Pistols, what a twisted name, but that's okay I can use that in a rap. I will say the men all wore pink panties and the girls wore lavender combat boots and they all pranced and minced."

"Or you could tell me who sent you and who knew."

"Or not, did you enjoy slaughtering my men?"

"No, most of us have evolved to surmount our demons, not embody them."

"You know mister Lavender Pistol; you are a waste of space pink panty, limp wristed, minty menthol faggot."

"Kevin, you might find this elucidating, wherever there was a spate of queer bashing, the Lavender Pistols would show up and put on a fancy pistol shooting exhibition. Then after the show we'd signup members to start a local chapter. It was surprising how quickly the queer bashers found new hobbies. Giving it some thought I'd say today was a kind of queer bashing, wouldn't you Kevin?"

"Just wait the future I have planned for your sorry fairy asses is beyond nasty."

"Finally, you have reached acceptance in how today turned out. Now tell me who selected me, and who else is involved and we're done?"

"I'll tell you this; you only got lucky with my men because I ordered them not to hurt you until you made my video. They were eager to listen to you cry as they broke your old brittle bones."

"You going to answer my questions, or what?"

"No."

"Hey Kevin, get a grip. You look wobbly, green around the gills; nobody is going to hurt you, this gun in my hand won't allow it."

"I'm shaking like in an earth quake. I can't stop this trembling."

"What can I do to help?"

"God I hate violence."

"It was that, or watch you be burned alive. His men died instantly, they didn't suffer, stop shuddering."

"My brain is overloaded, I can't think. It would help if you held me for a minute? Just until I can still these shakes and clear my head?"

"No problem, but first cuff Bloody Fangs. Use the plastic handcuffs piled over there. Do it and then I'll give you as long a cuddle as you want?"

"The idea of touching that evil beast makes me nauseous. Hey wait, what are you doing?"

"I'm turning the sound off his video recorder and zooming in on his face for a close-up view."

"We were recorded the whole time?"

"Yes, you fucking fairy fag, and by all rights I should have recorded toasting your nuts."

"Kevin, I just flashed on an idea. Do you think his homophobia could be from self-hate? He definitely is not man enough to be gay."

"Dream on you Nancy queers, my magnificent masculinity is the most you ever saw."

"You look gay to me."

"I'm not a fag!"

"Let's keep this simple, you cooperate with Kevin cuffing you, or you experience your propane torch's blue flame applied to … I don't know say your toes or fingers. I think we can accommodate your choice?"

As Kevin approached Bloody Fangs awkwardly struggled to his feet and bowed his head in compliance. Then to a nonverbal head nod, he turned facing away from his captors. Kevin reached around and pulled one then the other of Fangs' hands behind his back and into the white plastic handcuffs and synched them tight. Then he spun fangs around to face Everett.

"He's tied tight sir, you want him standing or sitting?"

"Sit him back down in the muck for his camera to see."

"Okay, done sir, you can shoot him now."

"He may still talk. Do you still need a hug?"

Kevin rushed to Everett arms open. "Oh God, you make me feel safe. They really meant to castrate me with fire, ugh, that's beyond horrible." Kevin didn't appear feeling safe, he spoke looking terrified. He was visualizing images of how recent events could have turned out. Everett held the boy tightly to his chest and gently stroked Kevin's head, neck and shoulders.

Suddenly aware Bloody Fangs was staring hate at them, Crosland locked eyes with him. "Fangs, why don't you tell us who picked me to terrorize and who else knows? Or would you rather Kevin show you close-up, the business end of your Plumbers propane torch?" Kevin had snuggled against Everett's chest as he spoke. But recoiled and went ridged at the idea of using the propane torch.

"Fuck you queers, go on kill me get it over with. We'll meet again soon enough in hell."

"This can be over quick or turnabout and suffer like your victims?"

"Shit stink faggots go play with yourselves; nobody likes you or ever will."

"Fine if that's what you want, take a second to prepare yourself for a long slow hurt and complete loss of dignity. Oh right, you've seen this film before."

Fangs made a sour face then ejaculated loudly, "I'm a gansta rapper pain and death doesn't scare me. I am the greatest artist that ever lived. Killing me we'll only make me more famous, if that is even possible. My fame and glory will live after me forever, I'm better than Beethoven and all those other long hair freaks."

"And you believe that?"

"I can't understand how a Whiteman could get inside your Blackbody? You are such a waste compared to my greatness."

"What I know is an artist must have a fertile imagination, hard earned technique, and integrity. You Bloody Fang have a microscopic twisted imagination, feeble technique, and absolutely no integrity. In other words, you are worse than a pathetic dilettante. But hey enough truth telling, let's get this over with. Kevin, want to hear what I think caused today?"

"Sure Mr. Crosland, if you want me to know."

"It might focus your mind away from fear."

"See how your holding me has calmed me? I stopped shaking. Oh wait; I can feel you got hard holding me. May I take care of that for you sir?"

"Right now … here … how?"

"Please sir, may I suck your dick?"

"Won't we be on display with that depraved creature watching?"

"Before today I couldn't have done it. Now everyone has seen everything that is me. I was totally exposed; I might as well complete the picture. Sir, it is exactly what I need to do right this minute and your body wants it."

"Am I just an object or do I get a say in this?"

"Sorry sir, it's just your dick is so hard. I know you will enjoy my service. Let me reward you for saving my life. I know what I'm doing."

"Settle down young man; take a second to make sure you really want this and it's not just a response to what's happened today."

"I want to do you, unless you will feel uncomfortable with that monster watching? I could put pillow cases over his head."

"And you said you were modest. Let the villain watch, I don't mind showing off to a closet queen."

"For as long as I can remember people said I was bashful. Today everybody saw all there is of me and how afraid I can get."

"You survived and hopefully you will grow from the experience."

"When I was tied to that table upside down and all of you were looking, I wanted so badly to disappear, evaporate. And now I want to feel liberation from sucking your cock with the light on and someone watching. This is the next step, on my terms, and I'm not bashfulness anymore."

"Well then as long as you won't regret it."

"You won't be sorry, allow me this."

To move beyond the day's terrors Kevin opened Everett's bath robe then pulled it off his shoulders. He stood back and drank in the older man's attributes in heightened state of arousal. Everett wasn't monstrously large, but fully aroused he was more than average and very ready for lascivious attention after the day's discombobulated tumult. In an instant Kevin realized he'd been missing visual erotic pleasure by only permitting sex in the dark.

Kevin turned them sideways so they could see the bound virulent homophobe Bloody Fangs watching. His face was an omelet of envy mixed with hate, raw drooling lust, and anger overlaying fear, and remorse. Bloody Fangs' face was like a movie showing his paradoxes.

Going down to his knees, Kevin licked Everett's cock shaft up and down and around. When the entire shaft was glistening, Kevin began tickling below and around the rim of Everett's cockhead using the tip of his tongue in hot wet staccato caresses. When he sensed Everett was getting too close to the edge of blasting off. Kevin brought the older man back from the brink by licking, then sucking his balls. Finally, when the new teasing had gotten its desired effect, Kevin swoosh - swallowed Everett's purple dickhead and shaft down his throat as far as it would go.

The soft warm pulsating sheath of Kevin's throat sent subtle electric waves of pleasure through Crosland's body. He began slowly moving his head up and down, that action became increasingly inspired by the older man's sighs, soft growls, and accelerating breathing all indicative of his increasing sexual excitement rushing toward culmination. Paying close attention keeping the pace slow; until Everett was about to start to cum. Then Kevin rapidly bobbed his head up and down. His right hand massaged dick too long to swallow. To amplify Crosland's mounting pleasures, Kevin lovingly fondled Everett's balls and nether regions with his left hand. At the exact perfect moment while he bobbed and stroked, he began humming the National Anthem.

Everett's breathing stomp on passing gear, his cock expanded and nuts move up into firing position. That was Kevin's cue to move his left hand all the way back behind Everett's scrotum to finger the man's hypersensitive pucker. That pulled the trigger. Everett shut his eyes, and threw his head back in pure unadulterated ecstasy. His body went ridged then throbbed; finally, he purred then barked out copious amounts of man cream, pumping directly into Kevin's egger throat and mouth. At the completion of the act the two men held each other tight, savoring their shared euphoria.

Spontaneously the two fell into a deep kiss, locked in an embrace. Finally breaking for air, his average endowment's erection tenting out the front of his work slacks Kevin said, "Thank you sir, I really enjoyed that. Mind if I give myself a quick hand job while we kiss? It will be another first for me with the lights on, but as you can see much needed."

"Here, let me help you with that. Let's give Fangs a show he'll find inspiring?" Everett knelt and undid Kevin's belt and dress pants. Then he slowly pulled pants and snug bright white briefs down in one continuous motion. He studied the younger man's over eager masculine appendage drooling precum. Given the day he'd had so far, he knew he needed the blessing of a little dalliance.

"Sir if you don't mind, I'm beginning to feel bashful you checking me out that closely."

"You have nothing to be ashamed of down here. You have a lovely set of perfectly proportioned parts. I was just thinking I'm glad we could save your body from that monster. Close your eyes if you must, concentrate on what you feel." Then Everett took Kevin's cock in his mouth. After a small amount of bobbling back and forth with hot saliva's bubbling wet friction, the over stimulated young man came fast and hard. A sudden prolonged explosion of ecstatic bliss made Kevin's legs go rubbery; he had to hold tight to Everett's shoulders as his body convulsed blasting long strong jets of scorching spunk one after another until he was gratifyingly drained of the day's anxiety, and years of hidden shame.

Panting like a marathon winner after the final sprint Kevin sputtered, "Oh sir that's exactly what I needed; proof it still works down there, thank you, thank you so very much." The two men completed their short intimate exchange with another long impromptu soul kiss.

Breaking the lip lock for air Everett took another long appraising look at Kevin as the young man hastily pulled up and fastened his clothing. Then he took him in his arms for a hug that seemed to melt them into one.

7.

When they finally broke their clench, Everett and Kevin looked over to see a shame-faced Bloody Fangs. "You two disgust me." His words didn't quite fit his facial expression or the hard on showing a wet spot through his pants.

"We gave you a sex show you obviously enjoyed, why not return the favor and tell us who picked me today?"

"Fuck you fruit fairies."

"Interesting, you hate gays but your pants say you came watching gay sex."

"It wasn't on purpose; I'm not a sissy like you two."

"So, stud, what happened in your pants?"

"Not a big deal really, sometimes I cum for no reason like just now. It is perfectly normal and has nothing to do with the man on man porn I watch to get inspiration for rants against queers. I know I am not a faggot!"

"Really, you enjoy gay porn because it gets you off and you hate gay people? Kevin what do you think; he qualify as an evil closet queen?"

"I think so and for sure he is a self-centered sadistic brute. Who does he remind me of? Oh, I know those evangelical preachers who spew homosexual hatred all day Sunday then use their parishioners' contributions for the poor to hire male prostitutes."

"Not true, I'm a true artist and that's just how I work."

"Fangs, you wouldn't know a true artist if s/he bit your big butt."

"All you need to know is I'm bringing Hip-hop back to be Great Again. I'm done educating you fool."

"Kevin, I'm guessing the Hip-hop Governing Council permanently sanctioned Fang for domestic abuse, homophobia, racist hate speech and glorifying sadistic violence. Knowing my reputation for helping out before, the Council must have told Bloody Fang the only way back in for him was to hire me to make a G-rated music video. They knew I was retired, so it was easy to end his merciless bigotry without a lot of fuss and possible gun play. Am I right, Bloody Fangs? Did they give you catch-22?"

"Fuck you, Uncle Tom; you don't know the whole story. *And I am not a one hit wonder like they said! I'm a star, a major talent, not a fucking dilettant like you said. You hurt my feelings; I'm not a want to be I am already great!*" His out of control shouting rage caused him to temporarily blackout.

"Okay, that means I'm right." While saying that Everett went over and checked Fangs was still breathing, he was.

Everett turned to face Kevin and saw the young man looking distraught again. "Fang agrees with the gist of my story, and if others were involved we should have heard by now."

"What you say explains the cause, but now what? Do we tell the police we had sex, he will? Who tells the cops details of what they wanted to do to me? It's embarrassing and makes me sick to think I was almost a eunuch, neutered by fire or dead. I don't want to relive that by telling it to the police, maybe over and over."

"What happens next is I call my lawyer and let him take charge."

"I don't want to tell him either, it was so horrible."

"Do you see Fangs' video camera over there? Let it tell the tale after the abduction."

"Oh okay, then call him."

Everett Crosland borrowed Kevin's cell phone and called his lawyer, Lorenzo Ghirardelli. The attorney said he would be there in ten minutes, and Everett and Kevin should not speak to anyone until he arrived. Handing the cell phone back, Everett relayed the lawyer's instructions.

"How did you know this address? I have no idea where we are."

"I memorized it when they ordered pizza."

"What? Where was I?"

"When you were tied upside down, Fangs told one of his men to order pizza delivered for after they were through with you. That's why at first I didn't think they would hurt you. When I realized they would there was no choice but to take action."

"Unbelievable, a pizza is coming? Who's going to pay?"

"How is that your concern?"

"We've had a really bad day; there is no reason a pizza delivery guy has to share in it."

"You are sweet."

"If you say so, I know I'm a submissive. Since I was a little kid it's been important to me that people have what they need and are comfortable, which makes me happy. Everyone doesn't feel that way, I know."

8.

When Lorenzo Ghirardelli arrived his presence seemed to fill the loft. He was dressed in an expertly hand tailored three-piece dark blue suit and wearing a mauve silk tie. Somehow his presence projected authority and the clout he often wheeled arguing cases in Court and won. Everett addressed his attorney friend as Larry, and gave him a condensed scenario of recent events. The lawyer carefully perused the crime scene. Then with Kevin present the three watched the small screen on Bloody Fangs' video camera. Then Ghirardelli telephoned a high-up police official. Waiting for the cops to arrive Crosland showed his lawyer the stack of video camera memory cards Fangs indicated showed young men tortured to death. Lorenzo (Larry) Ghirardelli took custody of the cards on the oft chance they would be needed in court; copies would be supplied to the police.

Police Sargent Higgins arrived with three uniformed officers. Attorney Ghirardelli handed her his business card, explained his clients could only speak to her with him present. Then he explained the abduction and what transpired subsequently, had Everett hand her the gun he used in self-defense, and showed her the video with six distinct gun shots on the audio track.

Then the pizza delivery boy arrived and removed three large boxes from his thermal carry bag and the loft was engulfed with delicious aromas.

"Sargent, would you and your people like pizza or should I have him take them back?"

"If you are buying, we haven't had lunch. Officer Jenkins remove those cheap knock off cuffs from the perpetrator and use your metal ones." Turning to the attorney who had phoned her bosses, bosses boss, and sized him up and down. "Are there cold drinks?"

Taking a guess, Kevin pointed to the loft's oversized refrigerator.

Lorenzo paid the pizza boy and gave him a generous tip. When the kid tried to profusely thank him, he indicated the thanks go to Crosland, since it was going on his tab.

Officer Jenkins pulled Bloody Fangs to his feet and cut his plastic manacles off. But before he could attach both police issue metal handcuffs, Fangs dropped to one knee and grabbed one of his body guard's automatics. Standing again quickly he pointed the weapon at Patrolman Jenkins. The other cops drew their guns and pointed them at Fangs.

Sergeant Higgins loudly said, "Drop your weapon." Where upon Fangs pointed his gun at her and two officers shot and killed him.

After an appropriate pause for gun smoke to clear and nerves to settle, Lorenzo Ghirardelli handed Sargent Higgins another of his cards for the detectives. "If my clients' are not being charged, we'll be leaving now. As an Officer of the Court I guarantee to produce them and meet with detectives at a time and place convenient for all parties. I don't envy your paperwork describing this crime scene."

Sargent Higgins made a shooing motion toward the door.

Going down the stairs Everett said to his friend Larry, "Did you see that?"

"Yes, suicide by cop."

"What didn't I see?"

"Kevin, Fangs didn't release the gun's safety, the trigger lock was engaged. That gun couldn't fire, and with the number of handguns lying around that loft he had to know how they work."

"Oh boy, today just keeps going from bad to worse."

"Spit it all out young man."

"With violence and death happening before my eyes, part of me wants to scream and pull my hair out. And part of me feels like I'm in a grownup situation handling chaos like an adult."

"I vote for the later. Oh, here is my car. I need to rush to the office for a meeting. If you want to come along for the ride my driver will take you to Pristine Pond after he drops me off. Or you could take a cab?"

Sotto voce, without looking at each other both men concurrently said, "Cab."

Outside the loft building both men drew full breaths of cool fresh air, as the attorney's limousine sped off. Their heads cleared and nerves settled Kevin hailed a cab. "Driver, Pristine Pond please, back entrance and I'll need a recite."

"I need a long hot shower."

"Do you think I am permanently damaged after today?"

"No, why do you ask?"

"I've been nonviolent as long as I can remember and yet I'm hard again. You know I had a good long orgasm just minutes ago. I don't understand I shouldn't be horny. Usually I only want sex occasionally."

"I sincerely doubt you are permanently damaged."

"So then why am I hard? Here feel."

"Once upon a time long ago, I made a documentary film about the human brain. It seems sex and violence are small parts, next to each other in the Amygdule. That's the primitive part of the brain. Their proximity explains the sex and violence connection for some people. Personally, I prefer my sex without violence, but hey that's just me."

"Me too, but can I go back to how I was before this morning?"

"I don't know, today was an anomaly for both of us. Let's play it by ear, one day at a time with the lights on and no shame. If you like, I know a good shrink and could set up an appointment for you, I'll pay."

"That's okay, thanks anyway."

Settling into the cab's backseat and fully relaxing for the first time since breakfast Everett said, "It is sad, just as I was feeling at home in Pristine Pond; they will want to evict me."

"Why would they do that? You didn't do anything wrong."

"I can't imagine them letting me stay after today."

"Nobody is evicting you if I have anything to say about it."

"Thank you for saying that, but I expect to be held responsible for this whole gruesome catastrophe, complete with broken door."

"You really need to read your residents' handbook. It's difficult to get in Pristine Pond and harder to be kicked out. Think about it, you paid for your apartment all cash as require. The bylaws favor the owners."

"Oh really?"

"It makes sense."

"So, what happens now?"

"First thing I do when we get back is have maintenance repair your door, and then order new sheets and pillow cases. I'll have your whole entrance replaced later."

"So why are we using the back entrance?"

"Because you are wearing a robe and slippers and that is strictly verboten in the Pond's public areas."

"Oh, I'm bad. Is it a serious offense? Will you be affected?"

"It's more embarrassing than bad, if you are noticed?"

"Embarrassing how?"

"You'd be expected to appear before the residents' committee and explain your public undress and promise to follow the rules in the future, basically that's it, you're a new resident you'll get a free pass."

"You take good care of me Kevin."

"I'm submissive by nature. Taking care of you is my job and I take pride in my work."

"Thank you, Kevin, you're sweet."

"You are most welcome sir and if you don't mind my saying, you give good head sir."

"As do you, we should try doing it in tandem, with the lights on."

"I'd like that."

FORT GNATS

Fort General Sherman was originally a makeshift Army Base for killing Apaches. When the Apaches, nomadic tribes, finally agreed to stay on the Great White Father's Reservation, their slaughter was stopped, and the Federal Government gave the surplus Fort General Sherman to the Arizona Territory. The Territory turned it into a prison for bad boys not yet lynched. Overall the Fort looks austere, and is a hopeless place for inmate and staff alike.

The juvenile prison is located on an immense flat barren stretch of desert, surrounded by sulfur flats, many miles from water and civilization. Isolated, bad boys are easily forgotten, out of sight out of mind. But traditional Arizona values demand retribution be odious, thus the prison's nick name Fort Gnats, from the year-round swarms of pesky Gnats that swarmed over the open garbage pits, cesspool, and humans.

One condition of Arizona Statehood in 1913 was it stops lynching minors less than sixteen years of age. In compliance with federal mandates the new State made an indeterminate sentence to Fort Gnats abhorrent enough to be worse than death. In the context of the Fort's harsh physical conditions, being worked to physical exhaustion and little to distract from them, the message to inmates was reform. Annually there were a few unexplained accidental deaths of boys too incorrigible or mentally ill to adapt.

The Eugenics movement started in England to improve the human race. It caught on in the United States during 1905 to stop designated undesirables from breeding. It was especially popular in the South and Midwest. By the 1930s the Eugenics movement in Nazi Germany expanded its mission to include extermination of handicapped, Communists, Gypsies, Homosexuals, Jews and assorted non-Aryans in order to improve the Germanic Race.

A grant was given to Fort General Sherman by the American Eugenics Society, seven years after Arizona's Statehood to celebrate the Fallen of World War I. In part the grant was intended to expand Eugenics reach into the Southwest. The grant was large enough to require renaming The General Sherman Industrial School for boys, to the Eugenics School for Incorrigible boys and required Eugenicists sterilize the boys to improve society.

Legal battles were started by Do-gooders to prevent sterilizing boys under age eighteen. Given the publics' pro or con enthusiasm for Eugenics the court case was destined to last for years. However, it was expected to be settled in the Eugenics Society's favor by the U.S. Supreme Court. The majority of the renowned Supreme Court Justices of that day had written in favor of Eugenics' social purity mission.

But as the case reached the highest court, the Second World War intervened. After the war, it was revealed Nazi German Eugenics Theory was used to exterminate huge numbers of innocent people. Photographs of extermination camps seriously diminished the American public's interest in gene pool purification. As a result, for financial reasons, the American Eugenics Society had to abandon its court case to sterilize Arizona boys, and more ambitious goal to sterilize all Eastern European Jews and Southern Italians living in the United States. After all was said and done, the school continued to be called Fort Gnats, its new name was never used.

The only educational subject taught at the industrial school was the daily dawn to dusk building of a road to nowhere. It was a leftover artifact of the Eugenics program based on the death-march concept popular in Turkey and Japan at that time.

The school lesson at the end of each back breaking sweat soaked day in the baking hot sun was for the boys to stand at attention at dusk. Then watch the glorious sunset while their carefully measured, leveled and meticulously constructed day's accomplishment was bulldozed into ruble. Then they were marched double time to a short cold shower, a bland meal and to bed until sunrise and the process were repeated. To add to despondency, more often than not hot winds blew in off the nearby sulfur flats and through the Fort most evenings after sunset; as the inmates were eating their one hot meal. The cause of death for weak boys was always listed as consumption.

By the end of the first week new arrivals were stunned how abysmal their life had become. The toughest among them lost even residual rebellion against the daily hard road work in relentless bright sunlight's heat. If Fort Gnats failed its mission to reform, the adult prison system would in theory take custody of the Fort's convict before his eighteenth birthday. With their spirit broken the too few guards had little trouble controlling the many dangerous prisoners.

A boy's indeterminate sentence to the Fort was the same for greater or lesser crimes, no distinction was made. For the younger boys, a year or less was enough to break their spirit just short of complete infantile regression. For the older, more experienced, willful boys, it took eighteen months to two years to completely scrunch their sense of self. In Arizona children sixteen and older were tried for heinous crimes and incarcerated as adults.

No matter the age entering Fort Gnats, the inmates were always released before their eighteenth birthday a strict requirement of State and Federal law. Consequently, as required by that law the under eighteen-year-old must only be released to an adult, preferably a family member.

Over time Arizona Do Gooders put in place a system of less harsh group homes, halfway houses and therapeutic communities for rehabilitating young, often mentally ill or developmentally delayed law breakers. The new system differentiated between the child who stole bread to eat and young vandals looking for a thrill. Nevertheless, as society progressed, Fort Gnats and its draconian methods remained the last stop in Arizona's Juvenile Justice. It was supposed to be used only when all else failed to rehabilitate, or the child's crime was deemed too atrocious. Helping professionals, law enforcement, and young criminals alike knew the Fort should be avoided at all costs.

I.

In Fort Gnats' long history, Leighton Easley was one of a few inmates who refused to yield their will. When new to the Fort Leighton made a wrong turn running an errand for a guard and he ended up at the motor pool by mistake. As he arrived a guard had just pull down a hysterically protesting young inmate's pants. The guard bent the boy over with a hard punch to the stomach and started to sexually mount the boy. Without forethought Easley attacked the guard with flying fists and kicking feet. He was no match for the larger stronger adult, but the intended rape victim escaped during the fracas. Leighton's effort to protect the slight effeminate adolescent named Billings from rape earned him a reputation in an institution that didn't allow them.

Leighton's atypical behavior was brought to the school administrator's attention. Mr. Giles Tharp was headman at Ft. Gnats, a short roly-poly curmudgeon with a brittle personality. Mr. Tharp had to always be right, especially when he knew he was wrong. Since he'd never had any he openly expressed resentment toward people with friends or lovers. Whenever he met someone new he'd immediately become that person's best friend, until inevitably the friendship wouldn't work out, due to the unworthiness of the other.

Tharp had Leighton brought to his office, sat him down. With a sadistic look on his pinched face, Mr. Tharp said, "Boy be thankful, you get a free pass today. But the next time Mr. Leighton Easley, you will be crushed to death under the school's earthmover. You know the Fort's bulldozer you see it working at the end of every day. From this day start imagining yourself smashed into the dirt under it. As you probably heard this school has a fatal industrial accident every year or so, and I just put your name on the waiting list. So, you understand; look at these before and after photos of boys who didn't learn to behave."

The before photos showed terrified boys tied to steaks sunk deep in the ground, the after photos showed mangled bloody corpse smashed flat by the bulldozer. Seeing his future gruesome death graphically illustrated. Leighton resolved to keep his head down, mouth shut and to use breath and other mental control skills to stay alive.

Leighton was sentenced to Fort Gnats as a result of a high-profile murder and media circus trial. At the time of sentencing the scrawny teen stood a scraggly five foot one inch, and weighed slightly less than 100 pounds. He had long straight corn silk colored hair, and oversize brooding light brown eyes. Immediately after arriving at the Fort, his hair was sheared down to his scalp, as required of Fort Gnats' inmates. Like his fellow convicts, he was only allowed to wear the shapeless scratchy dull gray industrial school uniform.

During his time at the Fort Easley filled out and grew into a strong well-proportioned physique as a result of hard manual labor. But Leighton's eyes never took on the dull zombielike vacancy of the other boys. He'd learned to control his mind and find ways to keep it active before imprisonment.

Once a month on the first, Leighton allowed himself to brood over the injustice that superseded his incarceration and destroyed a family that tried to protect him. Reflecting on those events he had to keep his rage at a low simmer rather than let it boil over and cause his premeditated death by clanking giant earth moving machine, as promised. Easley figured out how to expend his anger constructively by volunteering to do extra hard labor rather than yield to his emotions, and that kept his eyes bright and alert for the sake of survival.

2.

On Leighton Easley's eighteenth birthday, Fort Gnats' administrator Mr. Tharp jubilantly contacted his superior at the State Capitol in Phoenix requesting a transfer to the State Penitentiary for one of his inmates. He expected a newfangled form would be faxed to the school, and with it to see the last of Mr. Easley. Truth be told in Mr. Tharp's long tenure as head man he'd never transferred an inmate to adult prison, and thinking back, his father his predecessor had never made a transfer either. But the threat was made so often it was assumed to be real.

No one in the chain of command he telephoned was aware of procedures for juveniles in custody to be transferred to the adult prison system. But they all mentioned it was a violation of State law and grounds for serious civil legal action for an inmate to be over eighteen and incarcerated by Juvenile Justice. His Central Office superiors made fun of him for waiting until Leighton's eighteenth birthday to start a transfer process, whatever it was? Tharp's usual ineptness made his bosses work harder than necessary and they never appreciate him for that.

With fear and loathing Tharp phoned the Commissioner Cyrus Amenders in the State Capitol building, and spoke out his transfer frustrations.

"Screw-ups are happening too frequently with you Tharp. I get a lot of complaints, a lot too many. Stop whining or I'll replace you with a computerized robot that will do the work. Don't bother me with details, just do your job and be quick about it."

"What about the protocol?"

"Protocol is overrated, be creative man, the agency doesn't want to be in violation of the law, and you don't want to be without a job, do you?"

Over fifty years old, Mr. Tharp lived at the Fort from meager paycheck to paycheck; he had never had any other employment. He'd grown up at the school with his father as administrator. His father hated paperwork as his predecessor had, so Gills Tharp hated paperwork too.

Gills knew he wasn't a creative person. In fact, he equated creativity with disorder and lack of discipline, things he detested as much as paperwork. Without protocol to guide him, he faxed a plain paper hand scrawled note to the warden at the Florence, Arizona prison, the closest penitentiary. The fax note said *this is an emergency; send someone quickly to pick up a transfer prisoner. It is very important this be done immediately, no later than sundown.*

An hour later the Prison Warden faxed, a typed response on official letterhead stationary stating, *the prison system does not have authorization to pick up teenagers from Juvenile Justice Custody. Furthermore, any prisoner destined for us will require documentation from at least four different State Agencies in agreement (good luck with that). Administrator Tharp I suggest you read your staff manual regarding this matter and get started on this long arduous and yes tedious chore dealing with Judges, Social Workers, physicians, Do Gooders, and Lawyers, all of whom have different vocabularies and none use fax machines. This communication should have been an email, and probably sent months ago. Yours truly, Warden Aidan Smelts.*

Not to be dissuaded by an uppity prison warden, Tharp though *those people are so full of themselves.* Administrator Tharp telephoned the Highway Patrol Barracks at Wilcox, Arizona. He knew they crossed county lines. "Hello this is Head Administrator Tharp at Fort Gnats may I speak to the person in charge?"

After plowing through computer menus like; *if this is an emergency hang up and dial 911, if you know your party's extension enter it now, otherwise stay on the line for assistance* and then long intervals of very bad elevator music warbled in his ear. Finally, Tharp was connected, first to a distracted operator, and then, "Hello, this is Captain Martinez, Wilcox Highway Patrol Eastern Command. How may I help you?"

"Good morning Captain, Fort Gnats needs the Highway Patrol to pick up and take one of our inmates to the closest Adult Penitentiary, probably Florence, and it must be done as soon as possible *today.*"

"You're kidding, right? Look at that; a little levity in my over worked under paid day, thank you Jesus. Now what can I do for you sir?"

"No, I'm serious; we need you to do a pickup and delivery today."

"Listen fella, we don't have authority to do that service, kids, pizzas, or whatever. We give out speeding tickets, investigate accidents and fastidiously stay out of intra agency squabbling, like this."

"You mean you won't help me?"

"So, your call wasn't completely a waste of my time, let me suggest several missing steps in what you think you're trying to do. But then hey, how would I know what those steps are, that's your job. I'm not sorry I can't be more help, nothing personal but you sound like a nincompoop, and I don't suffer fools and dolts well. Goodbye amigo and you have a nice day."

Insulted and frustrated, and running out of ideas the Administrator decided to send Leighton Easley to prison in the Fort's passenger van, and just leave him manacled to the prison front gate. He pondered *why hadn't I thought of this instead of wasting time with rude people?*

Mr. Tharp had several releases going to various Southern Arizona locations that day. So, he'd just put Easley in shackles. After the driver and guard dropped off the released convicts, they could take Leighton up to the adult prison, cuff his hands to the big gate, and let the prison do the paperwork. On their way back his workers would pick up the Fort's new batch of young felons in Tucson, Arizona. It wasn't an ideal plan, but he had no authorizations or warrants, or other bureaucratic nonsense to direct him.

Giles Tharp grimaced and swore when the copy machine broke down and couldn't be revived; he vigorously kicked the old white elephant, vehemently cursing it. He had just started to photo copy Leighton's Fort Gnats' file to accompany him to prison. Giles became furious at yet another problem that he alone must solve, because the secretary, who normally did photo copying and knew the copier best was busy filling out the boy's release forms by hand. Giles thought *I'll fix her for not being available when I need her, I will replace this old crappy copy machine with a box of carbon copy paper like the old days. Let's see how she likes that.*

Frustrated and fuming, Tharp stuffed all the paperwork he had at hand into an oversize manila envelope. Every scrap of official paper with Leighton's name on it went into the big envelope. Administrator Giles Tharp wrote Easley's name in big block angry letters on the outside of envelop, and a note it needed to be photo copied.

He was stressed more than usual, so he distracted himself with the budgetary issues; paying overtime for sending the van a good distance off its route. Then there was how to pay for fixing or replacing the copy machine. On its own, his mind drifted back to his ongoing battle with Central Office over his job becoming automated. He knew in his heart electronic technology was just a passing fad soon to be replace with some other newfangled nonsense on its way back to the good old days.

3.

Giles Tharp's problems just kept growing, the next occurred when the assigned van driver slipped in oil picking up the van to load with releases. He had to be air lifted to Tucson Medical School Hospital with serious head trauma sustained in the fall. When Mr. Tharp's secretary handed him the release forms she said, "I was so busy I forgot to tell you, six staff members called in sick with the flu. As I juggled staff you won't have anyone to ride shotgun guard on the van."

Undaunted as problems piled, Tharp telephoned Eldon Johnson, an as needed off the books, under the table per Diem worker. He offered Johnson van guard duty for the day. The man desperately wanted to be hired full time at Fort Gnat; he lived in the area and enjoyed boys. But Johnson was on the State's sex offender list, so he was not allowed to be around children. Nevertheless, Johnson took every opportunity to score points with Administrator Tharp who was known for bending rules. So, when Tharp was informed the van driver was injured and would be out on workmen's comp for the foreseeable future, Johnson volunteered to drive the van without a guard. Giles Tharp thought *maybe my luck has changed and finally something is going right.*

It was surprising that no one noticed the large motor oil puddle around the Fort's passenger van, or checked its unsecured oil pan plug after flushing it in preparation for the trip. When Johnson started the engine, the heat gage quickly shot into the red zone. First a burning smell quickly followed by dark smoke and then loud deconstructing metallic sounds which explained where the mystery oil the driver slipped in came from. Not yet at the end of his tether, but close, Administrator Tharp ordered the trip be done using the Fort's battered old school bus. "Dam it," Tharp said to Eldon Johnson, "I will be creative with this task, if it kills me or I have to kill someone trying. Only I don't know how in hell the school can pay for a new van engine and copy machine when I'm already over budget? Don't worry, that's not your problem."

Confronted with another moral-legal dilemma, as usual Johnson took the coward's way out. He justified it thinking *I do not want to upset Tharp more than he is. The administrator seems to be unraveling, my mentioning I never drove a bus could get him angrier and I might be sent home and lose a day's tax free pay and brownie points for more work.* Even though he didn't have a license to drive a school bus, Eldon felt he could. He thought *how different could it be from driving a car, really?*

"I appreciate you handling this run by yourself Johnson. You better wear a sidearm since you don't have a guard to assist with the boys. Do you have a handgun with you?"

"No I brought my shotgun, I was told I'd ride shotgun. But I don't expect any trouble. These boys are going home they should be happy."

Tharp's demeanor swiftly changed back to angry frustration. "Riding shotgun is an expression dim-wit! Leighton Easley isn't going home, and you have to pick up a new batch of ruthless thugs in Tucson on the way back."

"Sorry sir, I wasn't thinking. I didn't bring a pistol."

"It's against the law, but you'd better shackle the new ones' hands and feet to their seats. Take the box of wrist and ankle restraints from the van and for god's sake wear a sidearm for insurance. I'll get you a piece while you load the bus."

"I'm on it sir, thank you Mr. Tharp, thank you."

"Oh, board Leighton Easley last and chain him to the front seat opposite you. The safety laws be damned. If he gives you any troubles bash him over the head. It is important to Phoenix and yours and my prospects this transfer go smoothly and before sundown."

As instructed Johnson boarded the teens onto the rickety old bus. When Tharp returned, he saw all eight boys seated in their new bargain store cheap going home clothes. On each boy's lap was a green plastic trash bag containing the clothes he'd arrived at the Fort wearing.

Leighton Easley was shackled hands and feet to the front passenger seat. He was the only one who wore the shapeless scratchy Fort Gnats gray reformatory uniform.

Tharp handed Johnson a holstered large frame brushed stainless steel revolver, a document pouch holding the boys' release forms, the large manila envelope with Easley's name, and a manifest listing new prisoners to be picked up in Tucson. Eldon quickly scratched his signature on the clipboard for the hand gun and documents.

"Johnson, remember each boy must be turned over to an adult. The law states persons under eighteen must have adult supervision at all times. Drive safely, but be quick." Turning to Easley, Tharp said, "Don't make Johnson shoot you. Oh by the way happy birthday and good luck in adult prison. Who knows, you might like it. I've heard they even have television and three hot meals a day."

Leighton stared straight ahead breathing slowly and deeply, not acknowledging Tharp.

4.

Johnson half stood over the driver's seat to strap on the holstered pistol. Then he started the cranky old school bus without adjusting the mirrors or seat. At first, he drove very cautiously, but once past the Cochise exit, he carefully took the banged up old rattle trap bus up to highway I-10's speed limit.

With a little trepidation, Johnson dropped off the first returnee and his release form in Benson, Arizona. It didn't look like a happy reunion for either the boy or his parent. Eldon Johnson thought *I like to see boys happy, that boy looked so sad. I could have made him feel happy.* Heading toward the next drop at Fort Huachuca, Arizona, Johnson thoughtlessly took the old bus up to 82 mph, thinking *hell I can handle this old crate, I could get a license to drive one if I wasn't on that damn offender's list.*

All of a sudden, the exit off the highway appeared without his notice. Even when new the long bus wasn't designed to take sharp turns fast because of its high center of gravity. Eldon's abrupt high speed maneuver to catch the exit off the interstate caused the four fifths empty bus to tilt up on one side going into the sharp turn. That started the loss of equilibrium. All the right-side wheels lost contact with the asphalt road surface. Then turning inertia and gravity pulled the speeding bus all the way over onto its left side. It slid sideways off the paved surface, dropped on then off the road's shoulder and rolled tumbling sideways over and over. The growing crescendo of metal scream-scraping against asphalt then rocks suddenly ended in an ear-splitting boom when the bus plunged into a deep ravine hitting its bottom hard. The bus landed quite some distance from the highway, on its top, hidden in a deep arroyo. A dense wall of silence immediately followed the crash, and then was quickly covered in a thick cloud of dust.

Desperately gyrating to get control of an out of control bus, Johnson's neck snapped too far back and twisted to the right when the bus suddenly landed upside down in the gully. His body twitched violently then was still, his neck broken hanging upside down strapped into the driver's seat.

After a moment of terrified silence, the teens shouted and yelled as they scrambled to kick out the bus's one unbarred window. Freed at last, they fled up the dry wash's bank like Johnson's ghost was chasing them. The exception was Billings who ran forward to check on Leighton and the driver. Shaken and pale he yowled. "Easley, you Okay?"

"I think so. I'm all tangled up in this jumble of chains. I can't move enough to know if anything broke. I think I'm okay, nothing hurts everything works."

Billings' face flashed fear and he howled. "Oh shit, I smell gasoline? Hear that clicking, the electric fuel pump is still going. There could be a fire any second. Shit we got to get out of here quick." Billings reached up and after a moment groping found the keys in the bus's ignition, he turned off the stalled engine's electric power and the fuel pump stopped. He handed Leighton the ring of keys and in frenzy shouted, "Hurry we got to get out, the hot engine could start the gasoline on fire." While Easley desperately tried various keys to locks, Billings frantically tried to revive Johnson, but he was dead. So, Billings took Johnson's wallet, removed the money and tossed the billfold, then un-holstered the big revolver. As an afterthought, he looked in the paperwork pouch near Johnson's body, removed his release form, and the big brown envelop with Easley's name on it.

As Leighton freed himself, Billings said, "Quick, grab some of those trash bags. You might find clothes that fit. But hurry!"

Outside far enough away from the bus, Leighton quickly rummaged through the returnees' trash bags. He found a pair of old holey jeans that were too tight but would have to do. In another bag, he discovered a stretched out of shape too loose-fitting T-shirt and in still another bag too big worn-down sneakers. He stripped off his prison garb and hurried into returnees' out grown garments, then stuffed his prison uniform in a trash bag. In the three and a half years at Fort Gnats he had grown to six feet, and 178 pounds.

When Leighton was dressed, Billings said, "Here take the driver's money, gun, and this envelop with your name on it. But from here you are on your own, and I didn't help you, right?"

Taking what was offered Leighton exhaled a deep breath along with doom and gloom about going to adult prison on his birthday. "Right, I'm on my own now and you didn't help me. Thanks Billings."

"I owed you Leighton; I hope this evens us up. Now get out of here."

Billings ran in a different direction than the other boys' foot prints. If asked he'd claim he didn't know what happened in all the confusion after the crash? He knew how to survive in the desert. His father had taken him hunting more than a few times; it was supposed to butch-up his girly mannerisms. It hadn't worked, but he learned desert survival skills. If he hauled ass he would get back to Benson before the other boys, given the route they'd taken. The Sheriff's Deputies would use dogs to track Leighton. The more sets of tracks going in different directions the better Leighton's chance of escape.

Scrambling up the side of the arroyo Leighton spotted the tracks most of the other teens left, and saw Billings heading in a different direction. He followed the other returnees' tacks until they headed east, then he went south toward Mexico.

5.

Luck was with him, Leighton no sooner found a secondary road than a pickup truck came along. He put out his thumb, and got a ride in back. The native-American driver left him off just outside Sierra Vista, Arizona, at the Tombstone Highway junction. It should have been a perfect place to get another ride. It wasn't. So, he found some shade and used the time waiting for a ride to read the papers in the large manila envelope with his name. Then he tore each lying page into tiny bits and released them to float away on the hot dry wind.

Finally finished ripping up his Industrial School paperwork, he walked putting his thumb out at occasionally passing cars. He finally got a ride with a youngish guy, expensively dressed, in a new luxury car. After driving in silence for a while Leighton became aware the driver was studying him in long sidelong glances. Then the car turned onto a desolate side road, pulled over and stopped. The driver turned to Easley while unzipping his pants. "Suck my cock and I'll give you five dollars. You're not my type but will have to do."

Leighton was startled by the unexpected proposition. "I have money, see."

Ego hurt, the driver glared at Easley for a long moment; his erection deflating from rejection. "The way you are dressed? No blowjob no ride. Suck me off or get out of my car you stumble bum."

Disoriented from the bus crash, escape, reading his gibberish legal documents, then an offer of money for sex, Leighton mechanically exited the car.

With no traffic on the road, Easley hiked several scorching hot miles in the glaring sun, until he found a gas station-convince store. There was no other structure as far as the eye could see on the flat desolate road and surrounding landscape. An old beater car was parked behind the store and a new European SUV was fueling in front,

Leighton walked over to the older Asian man pumping self-service gasoline.

"Hi. Uh mister, any chance you are going to Mexico?"

The Asian glanced at Leighton for a second and then back at what he was doing. "Sorry, no. We're going east, that way. Then off road up into the Pedregosa Mountains, and if time permits over to the Swisshelm Mountains. We are doing scientific field work, and on a tight schedule."

"I have some money; I can pay for your gasoline to drive me across."

"Like I said we're on a tight schedule, maybe another time?"

Leighton lifted up the bottom of his purloined T-shirt so the man could see the black rubber grips of the bus driver's pistol. Just then another older Asian man came out of the store carrying two frosty plastic spring water bottles. He walked directly to them, and handed one of the bottles to the man fueling the SUV. Leighton felt the second man's eyes meticulously scrutinizing his too tight jeans, too baggy shirt and sock-less worn-out too big sneakers.

The first man replaced the gasoline nozzle, closed the car's gas cap and turned to his friend. "He has a very large pistol, and wants us to take him to Mexico." The two men exchanged a private look; the kind intimate couples cultivate over time.

The second guy looked directly into Leighton's big brown eyes and stonily said, "Why not just take the car? It'll be less fuss for everybody."

"I don't know how to drive. I need *you* to take me to Mexico."

Stalling, the first guy looked at his friend but spoke to Leighton. "What is the plan young man?"

Suddenly feeling lost, Leighton first looked glum then mumbled. "I don't have a plan." Then it just poured out of him in tears. "Look I need your help, why can't you just be decent and help me?"

The second Asian man held eye contact with his friend as he spoke. "How come you can't drive? Everybody drives in Arizona. This car is both automatic and manual shift. It's easy to drive."

"I just don't know how," said with a boyish shrug of shoulders, tears rolling down his cheeks.

Confused by the contradiction of a crying teenager attempting to car jack them, the second man said, "There is nothing wrong with our car. It's a good one, just take it and go. Why are you crying? We are not resisting." Getting more frustrated, the guy gave it another try to get the carjacker to leave. "There is food and camping supplies in the back, things you'll need in Mexico. Go, just go."

Feeling better after the short cry, Leighton figured out the impasse. "Look I've been in prison, they didn't teach us to drive, okay?"

The second guy was trying to come up with something beyond his just go. "What did you do to get into prison?"

"They said it was murder. But it was an accident."

"Accident, what kind of accident?"

Realizing what he'd said made things worse instead of better. Leighton decided to forge ahead and be honest anyway; he'd had enough deceptions trying to understand his file folder. "Television and the newspapers made such a big deal out of it, and things that were nobody's business. They had it all wrong and were so unfair."

The second Asian without realizing it slipped into falsetto voice sounding and fluttering his hands like dowager. "Oh, my goodness, what things beside murder did you do? I can't even imagine."

"I'm not saying another word! Look, you both get in the front. I don't want to hurt you. So, don't do anything dumb. On the count of three everyone opens his door. One - two - three, now get in the car."

The fueling man slid behind the steering wheel, and the second guy took the front passenger seat. Leighton jumped in and slid to the middle of the back seat.

"Good thing I paid at the pump with a credit card. Okay, where we going, Nogales, Aqua Prieta, or Noca?"

Not knowing Leighton gulped air. "Drive south, that way. Slow down, not so fast the police stop you. Now which place is best for me to cross?"

Nervously the second man started speaking too rapidly in his normal voice. "Don't tell him. If we help him, we are accomplices to his flight from justice. This is bad, very bad. Maybe we should teach him how to drive?"

The driver calmly gave his front seat passenger a sympathetic look and placed a hand on his thigh. "First of all, he has a pistol. If he doesn't shoot us, then we can discuss being accessories under duress, if it comes to that. Secondly, teaching him how to drive is helping him escape. Anyhow he doesn't seem interested in driving. Thirdly since I've never been in this situation, I have no clue which border crossing is best. Do you have an idea? None, right?"

"No, oh my gosh-oh-golly-mightily, none at all," spoken in a falsetto again.

The driver outlined the carjacker's choices to Mexico; Nogales being the biggest, and busiest crossing with the most Border Patrol Agents and lots of sniffer dogs. By process of elimination, Aqua Prieta might be his best. But the Douglas, Arizona, police could put up road blocks on the U.S. side, if they want him badly.

"Wait a minute," the second man said in his normal speaking voice. "Do you remember that night we watched those wet backs sneaking across? We were camping south of Patagonia, Arizona, right? Do you think you could find that place again?"

The driver gave his friend a curious look before speaking. "Yes, I can, but we couldn't take a car over the border there. That country is too rough for a horse. As I recall it looked like the illegals ran through a series of interconnecting dry wash beds. No way could this car go there."

"Right, I remember we watched them with field glasses, they'd seem to disappear, and then sometimes only their heads could be seen bobbing along. He'd have to wait till dark to cross there on foot. Well, what do you think of that idea Mr. Carjacker?"

"Hold on, you want to drive me out into the desert, and drop me off, at night? I don't think so! If that's the plan, forget it."

"Do you have a better suggestion, Buster?" The man in the passenger seat demanded speaking loudly in his normal voice.

Leighton's face crumpled up and tears poured from his eyes again. They flowed down his cheeks, and dripped onto his pilfered shirt. Face wet with tears the sobbing teenager said, "Stop the car let me out."

"What are you going to do?" The driver asked concern mixed with curiosity.

"I'll just kill myself. Sorry to have bothered you." With that said he drew the revolver and prepared to open the still moving, car's door.

"Hold on, let's talk. Maybe we can help. We know people, a few even in high places; we certainly could get you a decent lawyer. What do you call yourself?" The driver had slowed while speaking, but didn't stop as the Teen ordered.

"My name is Leighton Easley. You can call me Easley, or Leighton, or hay you, it never mattered."

"What happened to you, Easley?"

"I was serving a twenty-five to life sentence for murder. But now that I've escaped, I guess it's my whole life locked up. No lawyer can help me now. Let me out and I'll end this. Jeez, if you think about it, what's the point?"

The driver made eye contact with Easley through the inside rear view mirror. The boy's tearing eyes looked soft and unfocused fitting his emotional outburst. "I've heard the Israeli illegals come across the Canadian border in the Midwest. That might be doable for you. Don't give up so easily life is precious."

"I don't get it. He didn't want to help me at all. Then both of you decided to dump me in the desert at night. Now Canada, what's with you two? What are your names?"

The driver said, "I'm Dr. Ashton Tao, and my friend is Dr. Kou Xing."

"Doctors?"

"We are university professors half the year and desert rats the other half. He's a geologist, and I'm a geographer. When he finds water, I map the location. Do you like geography?"

"Not that I remember. Where do you live?"

"We have a small ranch outside of Bisbee, Arizona, which is usually our base when doing field work."

"That sounds nice and now for me it is check out time."

"I can speak for both of us when I say we don't want you to kill yourself. We value life, all life."

"I don't want to go to adult prison for the rest of my life, and I don't have a plan, and I can't drive a car, and my Spanish sucks. So, what's the point?"

"You asked for our help."

"I did, but before I get upset again and act likes a cry baby, let's talk about something else for a minute. I need to get in control with deep breathing."

"Okay, what would you like to talk about?"

"I don't know, we just met and you guys are much older than me?"

"Pick a topic, any subject; we'll try to keep up. Just so you know we do really well with maps and rocks? Just kidding, do you like football?"

"There was no TV or radio at Fort Gnats. Do you two live together when you're not in Bisbee?"

"Well if you must know, we own an apartment in New York City," Kou sarcastically spit out in his falsetto. "We both teach in Manhattan, but at different Universities. Mine is more prestigious than his."

"Let's just have a little conversation until I'm ready to talk about a plan of escape. Okay? You don't have to be so nasty Mr. Xing."

"Sorry to offend Mr. Carjacker and it is Doctor Xing to you."

"Have you two known each other long? Help me out here, how did you meet?"

Ashton kept the SUV moving below the speed limit. "Tell you what; I'll answer your questions, if you tell us what happened to get you a twenty-five to life prison sentence. Is that fair?"

"Okay deal," Easley responded guardedly.

"All right, Kou and I have been together for thirty years next September eighth."

"How did you meet?"

"We were both standing in a ticket holder's line outside a Manhattan theater. A friend of mine walked by with a friend of his. Then we were all introduced. After the show, Kou and I went for coffee, and discovered similar interests. After almost thirty years I'm afraid we mostly take each other for granted. Now your turn."

"Oh-my-God, you guys are gay, right?! I don't believe this. Holy shit! Gay! Arizona Desert Queers!"

"Ashton was that the reaction you were aiming for. You do know he is armed and dangerous, not to mention an escaped convict carjacker?"

"Sorry Kou, in this day and age of same sex marriage I didn't expect him to be shocked."

"I'm not shocked. Really, I'm not. That was the something else they made such a big deal about in the newspapers and television. Arnoldo and I were lovers. You must know how Anglo-Arizonians hate anyone who isn't just like them. Imagine what they thought about a white boy and a Mexican-American boy in love. They would have lynched us if they could have gotten away with it."

"Ashton, where are you driving us? It's almost lunch time."

"South toward the boarder, is lunch your priority right now?"

"Well excuse me, but when I'm upset, and *I am* upset by this situation, I want to eat. You *know* how I get."

"There is no place to eat around here. Do you expect us to unpack the car here on the road?"

"Let's go back to the ranch?"

"You can't be serious? We closed the house up this morning."

"Ashton, I'm very upset hungry. My low blood-sugar has me freaking out. It will take too long to unpack and find fire wood, and get lunch started. The closest, fastest food to right here, right now, is home, in our refrigerator and freezer. It's that way and not too far either."

"You *are* serious." Glancing over his shoulder, taking a good look, Ashton said, "Leighton you want lunch?"

"Sure okay, why not if you're offering? But right now, I'm very thirsty from walking in the sun."

Handing the teenager his spring water bottle, in a stern voice Kou said, "But you can't bring that gun into our house. Understood, that gun stays outside. Also, the Alvarados can't know about you. It is one thing to risk our futures, but it would be very wrong to get them involved in this debacle. Agreed?"

Bringing the SUV up to the speed limit, Ashton sighed. "You are both a couple of drama queens. It wasn't complicated enough before? Easley, do you agree to leave your gun outside?"

"I guess, maybe? What are Alvarados?"

"The Alvarados are the family that runs our ranch year-round. They live on the opposite end of our land. But if one of them comes to the house for any reason, you have to keep out of sight until we can figure out what's best for you."

Grinning ear to ear. Easley used facial muscles he'd forgotten he had. "Now this sounds like a plan. I'll leave the gun in the car, if you promise not to call the cops. Drama queen, me? Ha!"

"Mary if the shoe fits."

"What kind of ranch do you have?"

"We breed and board horses; the ranch is mostly self-sustaining. The Alvarados keep chickens, goats, and occasionally fatten a pig. The years the ranch shows profit, we all share it or make improvements. In some ways, we're like a big happy family."

"That sounds nice, but are they going to come around without warning?"

"Usually they don't just drop by, because we like to skinny dip and they are conservative about clothing being optional. But we leave the pool open in case they want to use it when we are away. In other words, they might drop in out of the blue for a swim, since we are supposed to be away."

"A cooling swim sounds *good* to me, and then a long glass of iced sun tea. Both would definitely help settle my frayed nerves."

"Am I invited to tea?"

"Yes, Easley you don't have to skinny dip if you're bashful. You can swim in your underpants."

"I'm not wearing underwear. I left all the prison clothes at the bus. But I don't think I'm bashful, at least no one ever said so?"

Ashton turned the SUV off the highway and onto a serpentine rutted dirt road that climbed steeply into the foothills and beyond. "Would it be easier to tell us what prison was like, since telling us how you got there seems difficult?"

It took a good ten minutes of rough jostling, and kicking up thick dust clouds to get to the high mesa where the ranch house was perched. Leighton Easley had time to tell about his Fort Gnats experience and the bus accident before they arrived.

The Spanish style white stucco covered adobe house had a red terracotta roof. It sprawled out with an Olympic size swimming pool and surrounding bluestone patio on one side. Lofty views of the valleys and nearby mountains were inspirational. Ashton parked on the circular cobblestone drive in front of the artfully landscaped dwelling.

Kou stared straight into Easley's eyes and sternly said, "All right young man, leave the gun on the car seat, and I'll rustle us up lunch after I cool off with a swim."

Easley could see Kou meant business, so he did as told and laid the revolver on the black leather car seat. Then they all climbed out of the vehicle and walked to the shimmering pool.

6.

Suddenly wary Easley half turned ready to run for his gun. "Who's that?"

"Relax Leighton that's only Gilberto Alvarado swimming."

"I thought you guys were away, your house is all closed up. You don't mind me swimming, do you?"

"Of course not, and you won't mind us swimming without suites, right?"

"I'm here alone so not wearing one either, please don't tell my mother."

Ashton and Kou immediately stripped down, garden hosed each other off, and then dove into the cool blue green water. Suddenly feeling self-conscious, Easley took a few moments to get nude, rinse off with the hose and jump in with the others. He was fascinated by and yet leery of the stranger about his age already in the pool. However, soon they were all vigorously splashing each other and swimming energetically. It was infectious fun and Leighton got into the spirit of it, cautiously at first.

Kou got out of the pool, shook water from his hair and said, "Everybody want iced tea?"

Ashton nodded yes.

"I'll try it," came from Leighton.

Gilberto said, "Sure, need help?"

"That's okay I got this."

"Your garden looked thirsty when I came over. I better go turn off the water. If you want I can get dressed and go home, I don't want to be any trouble."

"You're here now; would you like to eat with us? Are you hungry? It won't be fancy but should be nutritious."

"Thanks okay, I'm still a teenager I can always eat. Be back in five minutes." With that said the handsome buff Gilberto, slipped on his sandals and ran off to the garden.

"Just how old are you guys? Your bodies look younger than your faces. I hope you don't mind my asking?"

Half camping half serious Kou said, "If you have to know, we both exercise regularly. Didn't anyone tell you it's not proper to ask a lady her age?"

"I can see there are no ladies here. Why don't we have a contest to see who is the most unladylike?"

Flailing his hands about and in full camp falsetto voice Kou said, "Now he is impugning our femininity. Oh, youth today can be so cruel to their elders."

"Come on Kou, lighten up."

"Ashton and I are both sixty since you're so inquisitorial Mr. Easley. Actually, I'm three months older than him. And the better looking, if I say so myself."

"If you say so, and are not fishing for compliments."

"Fishing indeed, before you ask any more impertinent questions, I'll get our drinks and then scrounge us a lunch."

"I'm sorry if I offend him. I didn't mean to."

"Don't worry about it. When Kou's blood sugar goes out of whack so does he."

"How old is Gilberto? Is he gay too?"

"Let's see? Gilbert is nineteen last month, and my guess is he hasn't decided which team he bats for."

"Oh okay."

"For our edification please try to tell us the rest of your fascinating story, after lunch. It will help us formulate a plan."

Leighton mumbled, "Okay sure, if you want," and dove under the surface and swam the length of the pool and back underwater. The exercise made him feel alive. Swimming hard and splashing around the pool also allowed Easley to momentarily forget his predicament.

7.

After several minutes, Kou brought out a tray with a large pitcher of iced sun tea, a small plate with lemon wedges and fresh mint leaves, and four tall frosty glasses full of ice. "Ashton after you have some tea please help me prepare lunch."

Ashton stirred from his revere watching Easley's graceful underwater swimming. "Kou, you said you didn't want the Alvarado family to know about Leighton. Now Gilberto has met him, are you going to revise that?"

"I don't know, we couldn't very well tell Gilberto to avert his eyes and run home. That would be inhospitable even rude and call attention to Easley."

"Are we going to ask him to keep Leighton a secret from his family?"

"No, but for now let's play it as it lays. Our work plans for today are kaput, and if I don't eat soon I'll be very sick."

"What are we having?" That said he poured himself a glass of tea and crushed two mint leaves into it. After taking a sip of tea, he walked into the house through the sliding glass pocket patio doors following Kou.

"I thought we could wok some dry rice noodles with those defrosting vegetables and shrimp, and there are still fresh salad fixings in the fridge. Doesn't that sound like enough for lunch? If anyone is still hungry there's all that homemade ice cream in the freezer."

"What shall I do?"

"Hard boil some eggs for the salad and peel, clean, and butterfly the shrimp."

"Kou, I'm warming-up to Easley, he seems like a nice enough kid in need of a break. What are your thoughts?"

"This situation is very troublesome. Who knows how this will end? He might still murder us."

"He doesn't look like a killer."

"Let me hear the rest of his story, and then I'll decide."

Easley called from the patio, "Do you guys need help? Gilberto is back and we can set the table or do whatever."

"We'll be ready soon," Kou shouted back vigorously working cooking tools in the sauced wok. Pausing to taste his cooking he said, "Help is always appreciated, you could set the table out there. Wrap a towel around yourselves, like we have. We call it formal dress for meals; Gilberto knows where the extra towels are out there. The tablecloth, napkins, and things are in here."

The meal looked and tasted good, so Kou and Easley concentrated on eating their fill. Gilberto was on his best behavior, so he didn't ask for seconds even though normally he would have. Ashton picked at his food lost in thought. When the meal was over the younger men cleared it away and then returned. Ashton filled a meerschaum pipe with a strong English Latakia tobacco mixture, and put a ring of fire to it with a sterling silver pipe lighter. Meanwhile after closely examining the wrapper on a Cuban Churchill cigar, Kou sliced off the tip with a gold cigar cutter, and then carefully rotated the other end over a flame from a matching gold cigar lighter. Then both mature Asian gentlemen leaned back in their chairs. "What have you told Gilberto about your situation?"

"I asked him if he were gay and if he read about my story in the newspapers three and a half years ago. He thinks he might be gay but hasn't done anything about it, he remembers what was in the newspapers, and prefers to be called Gilbert. He'd like to stay when I tell my story, but he will go home if you want."

"Gilbert, you can stay or go as you wish. We would hope you will use discretion talking about this lunch, other than with those present. Leighton, why don't you bring us up to date on how you got into your present situation?"

"In the car, I told you about Fort Gnats and the bus accident. Now I suppose you want to know what happened before that."

Both smokers nodded yes, Gilbert watched with interest. He thought he should leave but wanted to stay, and did.

"When I was eight, my parents got divorced. I never saw my pop much; he worked on the railroad, and traveled a lot. I remember when he was around, he was sleeping or drunk or both. A year after the divorce we became homeless and had to live in the car. A few years after we got on our feet, mom married Whelan. I was 12 by then. He turned out to be a mean drunk like my pop. Whelan beat mom same as my pop did, and made life at home awful when he was around and awake."

Ashton met Easley's eyes and softly commented. "That must have been hard for a growing boy."

"I started spending as much time as I could with my best friend's family. Arnoldo Cruz was one and a half years older than me, but we were in the same grade because he got left back in school because Spanish was his first language. The Cruzes said they didn't mind having me around because I helped Arnoldo with English and school homework, and I'd be helpful in other ways when I could. Arnoldo was big for his age, and that helped when bullies picked on me at school."

"Didn't your mother worry where you were and what you were doing?" Kou asked showing an academic interest.

"I still had to show my face and sleep at home, but conditions there just kept getting worse. When mom cut Whelan off for sex, he started trying to get into my bed, and touch me in places where he shouldn't. He'd unzip and tell me to touch him. I never did or let him do anything to me. When I told my mother, she said I was making it up and lying, and beat me with the broomstick."

"Did you report it at school?"

"When I told Arnoldo's parents, they said social services would send me to a group home if I reported it at school. His parents said I could stay with them as long as Whelan or my mom didn't make trouble."

Ashton and Kou exchanged a couples' private look, and then turned back to Easley. Gilbert sat passively listening, hanging on every word with his hands folded on his lap.

"It was just after that, Arnoldo and I started to fool around. It was my idea. I was curious what Whelan was after from me. I told Arnoldo it was like an experiment. He said okay. But once we started messing around it felt good and we liked it, so we didn't want to stop. We even got into French kissing and other things from the movies. It was great, and then the trouble started.

"One afternoon Whelan walked in on us doing the nasty. It was after school, at my home. He and mom were supposed to be working. But Whelan got sent home for being drunk on the job. He went crazy seeing us doing sex, and called us all kinds of names. Whelan beat me and Arnoldo bad. Then he locked me in the storage shed out behind our mobile home. And he told Arnoldo if he ever saw him around me again he'd kill him." Easley sadly shook his head from side to side recalling the ugly scene.

During a long pause, Gilbert softly asked, "Then what happened to you guys?"

"When Arnoldo's dad came home from work and saw how beat-up and upset his son was. He came over to our trailer home and kicked the shit out of Whalen; he beat him up one side and down the other of our street. The neighbors called the police, and of course they believed white Whelan. He said we were little faggots and he was trying to straighten us out. You know how much the Arizona gringo police hate Chicanos, so they arrested Arnoldo's father, and took Whalen to the hospital."

"Geez even when it's good it's bad for you."

"Later that night, Arnoldo freed me from the shed. We were both scared and embarrassed about what had happened, but we didn't want to be split up. Its important you guys understand we were in love by then. It wasn't just sex anymore we really loved each other. He touched me in ways I don't even know how to say. Arnoldo said we had to run away because of all the trouble, and how Mexicans can never get an even break in Arizona. We figured with us gone his father would be let out of jail. My mom stayed at the hospital with Whalen. So, we packed up our Boy Scout camping gear, what portable food we could find in both our homes, and took Whalen's .22 rifle. We hitched rides up into the mountains. Then hiked until we found a spot where we thought no one could find us."

Ashton smiled gesturing with an open hand. "Sounds like modern day Tom Sawyer and Huckleberry Finn."

"Sure, just like them we were on our honeymoon."

"Mark Twain never mentioned Tom and Huck having sex." Kou said this with an edge to his voice.

Ashton dismissed Kou's comment with a look, and then thought better of it. "Everybody assumes they were. Just like everyone assumes they were jerking-off together before they started more intimate sex. Kou every single detail doesn't need to be graphically spelled out or it would be called pornography."

"I agree with Ashton, Kou, I always imagined Tom and Huck slept together, and shared sex. Easley, did you have a nice honeymoon?" After speaking up, Gilbert looked back down at his cradled hands.

"Yes, it was great, we got used to washing ourselves in the cold stream that ran near our camp. We shot rabbits and squirrels, snared quail, pheasant, a grouse once, and caught fish. For three weeks, it was wonderful, we slept every night holding each other with our sleeping bags zippered together. Then necessary supplies started running out. We decided to get more supplies, by hook or by crook, when only two bullets were left."

Kou was closely following the story until that point. "How exactly did you plan to hook and crook?"

"You two know I'm terrible making plans. So, Arnoldo decided we should hike down to the paved road, when we saw a car coming I'd lie in the roadway and pretend to be hurt. When the car stopped, Arnoldo would jump out of the bushes and say it was a stickup, and we'd take their money and car. His dad had taught him how to drive, and was going to teach me."

"Then what?"

"After the robbery, we were going to buy supplies; bullets, fish hooks, salt, flour, rice and you know whatever. So, we tried it, I lay down in the road, and Arnoldo puts a bandanna over his face like in the cowboy movies. You know he really looked like a movie desperado.

"Then this Army guy driving home from the mountaintop radar station stops, Arnoldo jumps out and sticks the rifle in the car window, and said, 'Get out of the car, this is a stickup.' The stupid driver grabbed the gun barrel and pulled it against Arnoldo's finger on the trigger and the rifle fired. The bullet went right into his head and he died. We panicked and ran away, not taking his money or car or anything."

Kou gave Leighton a disapproving look. "You just blamed your victim."

Not understanding Kou's comment, Leighton kept talking. "A posse on horsebacks captured us a day later. I thought we were going to get hanged on the spot. But they were pretending. I mean we didn't know the Army officer was some kind of war hero? We didn't mean to hurt anyone. The posse took us to jail, after scaring us with those nooses around our necks and pretending we were about to die.

"In jail, we found out that Whelan had died in the hospital. His health had been bad with all that nonstop alcohol drinking, and chain smoking cigarettes, they said the beating killed him."

Kou gave Ashton an indignant look anyone could read.

"Gilbert can tell you, the television and newspapers wouldn't leave us alone. They said father and son proved Mexicans are bad hombres by nature. That teenage queer sex played a big part in causing the crime, and proves queers are just as bad as Mexicans. They even said Arnoldo's father knew we were lovers, and didn't try to convert us to heterosexuality."

"Did he know?"

"No, we were very private. Anyway, he had to work all the time and do family stuff. The media made Whelan out to be a saint trying to make his queer stepson a righteous heterosexual. They actually wrote that, like it is possible to change how you are born."

"My dad said you were all assassinated by the press."

"That's how it felt Gilbert. But it was always drunk Whelan who started the trouble."

Ashton asked, "Where was your mother during this time?"

"She never visited me in jail. My free lawyer said mom moved out east after Whelan's funeral. She told my lawyer she never wanted to see me again; I was bad seed, from my father."

Ashton made eye contact his face expressing empathy. "Gosh that had to be hard to hear."

"It is okay, I've had time to think about what happened, why, and her feelings."

Kou scratched his head and said, "You told us but I forgot, how old you were?"

"I was fourteen and a half, that's why I had to go to Fort Gnat Industrial School until my 18th birthday. Today I'm eighteen."

"Happy Birthday, do you want us to sing the birthday song?" Gilbert said this with a goofy grin and just kidding shrug.

"Before we sing Happy Birthday, is there anything you left out of your story?" Kou asked leaning in to show interest.

Looking down, a sad expression wiped across his face. "Arnoldo, his father, and I were all serving twenty-five to life sentences for murder. Arnoldo was given a second twenty-five years for sodomy with a young minor because of my age when we started having sex. They even registered him as a sex offender. I told everyone it was my idea, but nobody cared.

"Arnoldo was sentenced as an adult because he had turned 16. They sent him to a different adult state prison than his father. The press said the public wanted all three of us executed together. But you know the Arizona's gas chamber can only seat two at a time."

With a dismissive hand gesture Ashton changed the subject. "People say all kinds of crazy things. Did you know you were born in the year of the Ram?"

"No, is that good?"

"Well, you are living up to the mythology ..."

Kou butted in cutting Ashton off. "Is that the whole story, and everything you said the truth?"

"I got a letter from my free lawyer. He said I might have a chance at an appeal since Arnoldo was killed in prison. But I'd need to pay a lawyer myself. I wrote back, *Sorry I have no money, what happened to Arnoldo?*

"After a long time waiting the lawyer answered my letter, *the prison is still conducting an investigation into Arnoldo's death. But one of my clients at that penitentiary said Arnoldo was supposed to be gang raped. When he fought back they killed him.* So, you guys see I have nothing left to live for."

"Unbelievable."

"You'll find out just how believable my story is as soon as the media discover I've escaped. Gilbert, did I tell the truth?"

"Yes, exactly how I remember it. One thing the press said was, 'none of you three would ever walk free again,' and yet here you are."

"I'm afraid my freedom is very temporary Gilbert."

"Still just between us, I'm glad you got away. My folks felt your case was more prejudice than justice, and I agree."

Judicially Kou inquired, "Leighton do you take responsibility for what you did?"

"Of course I do, it was all *my* fault. If I'd just let Whelan do what he wanted to me, none of the trouble would have happened. Arnoldo and the army guy and Whelan would all still be walking around. And the Cruz family would be happy together like before they met me. Instead the family is broken up and punished because I was selfish. I'm sure everybody hates me and who would blame them?"

Ashton gave Leighton a pedantic look with a bite. "As far as your stepfather's abusive behavior, you handled it appropriately. No one can fault you for self-protection. We could play what-ifs until the cows come home and it wouldn't change anything."

"Yeah sure but look at the mess I made. At least after I kill myself I won't cause any more trouble."

"Please don't kill yourself, we've just met, I want to get to know you better."

"Thank you, Gilbert, but I'm poison and I can't help it."

Ashton gave Kou one of their intense private looks. Then relaxed a bit and knocked tobacco ash out of his pipe. Watching the two young men exchanging keen looks, the two Asian men spontaneously asked Gilbert, "Do your parents know you are here today?"

"I got up early to finish my chores so I could have a swim. I saw your garden looked dry and watered it."

"Gilbert, you are always welcome at our house, but do your parents know you are here right now?"

"As long as all my chores are done, they don't care where I am."

"Oh really, I know your folks."

"When I was much younger I heard my mom ask my dad where my brother Carlos was. He told her, his chores are done so he's probably jacking off somewhere. My mom said better that than knocking up a neighbor girl. At the time, I was too young to know about jacking off."

"Then I stand corrected Gilbert." Ashton turned to the other young lunch guest making eye contact again. "Leighton no suicide allowed. Give Kou and me a chance to work on your predicament? Did you know it is bad luck to kill yourself on your birthday?"

"Bad luck is my middle name, always was, always will be."

First looking from one to another around the table Ashton spoke sternly. "Leighton I want you to promise everybody sitting here you won't suicide while we are trying to help. Don't waste our time. Will you give us your word?"

"All right, you have my word, so now what?"

Looking relieved, Ashton said, "Having a nap will help you digest lunch after swimming. How about a birthday nap? We'll call you when dinner is ready if you are still asleep. We like to eat at sunset. The sky view from our patio is a spectacular light show most nights."

"Geez, I don't know. They are probably already hunting me. But you know, a nap does sound awfully good."

"Go take a rest you'll feel better."

"I guess a nap makes sense."

"Aston and Kou, would it be all right if I took a nap with Leighton? My parents don't have to know about my visiting today, if that is okay with you?"

"You are both over eighteen; I say it's between you two adults. Leighton is his request agreeable? We have a second guestroom if it's not."

"Whatever?"

After Ashton left it up to the teens, Kou's face showed several conflicting thoughts in rapid succession, and then paused at neutral, and he finally pointed with the stub of his cigar. "Down the hall, the guest's bedroom on the left is all made-up; it has its own bathroom. You probably want to shower off the chlorine from the pool before you lay down. Bath stuff is in the cupboard under the sink."

Ashton turned to Kou and spoke loudly for Easley and Gilbert to hear. "Come on let's get the perishable food out of the car. Our field work is on hold for the time being."

7.

They opened a rear car door; Ashton took the heavy revolver off the back seat. It was almost too hot to handle from the bleaching southern Arizona sun flooding through the car windows. At first, figuring out how to get the gun's cylinder to open was a mystery, but persistence of purpose prevailed. The cylinder finally swung out from the big stainless steel frame and Ashton shook six long thick bullets into his hand.

"They look big. What size are they?"

"Must you always be such a size queen?"

"Be nice to me, it's been an upsetting day. How are they measured, in calibers or inches? I've read about sixteen inch guns on battle ships. How many inches are there?"

"Well let's see, stamped into the bottom of the cartridges is 357 magnums."

"See I knew in my bones that boy was dangerous. The bullets are not even in inches."

"He didn't choose the weapon; it was the bus driver's. He told us in the car, remember he was so shook-up after the bus accident he spilled his guts after that crying jag."

Not listening to Ashton, Kou put on a pout and stomped his foot like an angry little girl. Then in falsetto said, "I thought gun sizes in the United States were calibers, and the rest of the world was millimeters and blessedly only champagne comes in magnums."

Without giving it a thought, Ashton took on his usual conciliatory role in their relationship, pointing out they had two twelve gage shotguns for skeet shooting in their utility room."

"I completely forgot those big boy toys."

"Hospitality requires we help our house guest?"

Back to his imitation of a scolding little girl, Kou stamped his foot again. "There is only one thing to do; convince Leighton Easley to turn himself into the authorities. When he does, it will go easier for him. And we might not have too much trouble and hopefully little to none for Gilberto."

"Seriously, he doesn't want to surrender?"

"Well if he won't, we have to turn him in; it is the only right and proper solution." Then he stamped one then the other foot, kick at the driveway cobble stones and shook his fists.

To buy some cooling-off time in a conversation that was rapidly heating to a full boil, Ashton changed the subject. "Kou, since you are so interested in how bullets are hung, I mean measured in calibers and millimeters. Why don't I tell you the story of non-champagne magnum handgun cartridges? Then you can add Miss Bullet Size Queen to all your other prestigious titles."

Speaking in his normal range Kou said, "And you have the balls to ask me to be serious? You seem to forget I have two PhDs. and you have only one."

"You left out my Post-Doc-fellowship at Columbia and being a Rhodes Scholar at Oxford. Do you want to hear this or not?"

"Go ahead Miss. Know-it-all, enlighten me."

Early in the last century the .32 caliber was replaced by the .38 caliber for lawmen's sidearm in the United States. It was done to match greater criminal firepower. To keep up many police agencies requested bullet manufactures increase the power in their .38 caliber shells. At the same time, it was discovered bullet velocity needs of rural cops were different than for urban lawmen. Eventually the manufactures reached the maximum amount of gun powder a .38 special shell could hold. So, the 357 Magnum was born, it will shoot all the varieties of .38 caliber cartridges and their own longer most powerful bullets. The principle is; the same bullet diameter, but accommodating different cartridge lengths.

"Why not call it .38 extra-long or jumbo or supersized and leave champagne out of it?"

"I have no idea."

"Oh my, here we are still in a pickle with this boy and his big gun, and we quibble."

"It's not trivial nattering for gunsmiths and lawmen. Won't you at least consider offering Leighton something more than a life locked in a prison?"

"I'm not comfortable having a fugitive from justice sleeping under our roof with our neighbor boy."

"Oh, is that it?"

"No not just that, his plight and ours have become linked. I think he's bad news Miss. want-to-be-a-gunsmith. Right now, by association we and Gilberto are outlaws."

"He wants to be called Gilbert."

"Yes, well okay fine, Gilbert."

"You know that people born in the year of the ram have tempestuous lives, right?"

"You are obsessed! It is the same Chinese Character for Sheep or Goat no matter the gender. Anyway, it has nothing to do with Leighton or anything."

"It is the year of his birth."

"I've spoken my piece, he goes back to prison by his hand or ours, and let's hopes Gilberto; Gilbert isn't tainted by this misadventure."

"We have resources, we could change his plight."

"This is not a *moral imperative*, Ashton."

"Yes, it is!"

"There will probably be a reward for his capture. You've read how unscrupulous those bounty hunters are for a few dollars."

"Okay, fine we'll let him decide."

"Surely you jest!?"

"Then how else do we resolve this insurmountable difference?"

"Tell you what, after he's back in custody, I don't mind spending money to get him a decent lawyer."

Allowing his anger to get the better of him, Ashton did something uncharacteristic; he showed his frustration. "No, *we are* going to settle this here and now?"

"Ashton calm down, Leighton is a convicted murderer. We on the other hand are law-abiding academics who pay our bills on time."

"Always stating the obvious, tell me something I don't know!"

"We don't need to get deeper involved in a hopeless situation. It's our civic duty to call the authorities, and that is a nonnegotiable."

"Have you no empathy?"

"Don't you give me that gay pride hurrah; it doesn't apply to murder."

"This is a classic star crossed gay lovers' story, drunken abusive stepfather driving young innocents into each other's arms."

"Stop, many love stories end tragically that is why we have grand opera."

For several icy seconds, Ashton and Kou stared stone-faced at the other not speaking. Then with a completely flat affect Ashton said, "Kou you refuse to see anything beyond your closed mind's self-interest. Probity supersedes the Law in this case. After thirty years is this what ends it for us?"

"Don't be dramatic, you don't do drama as well as I!"

Arms angrily folded across his chest Ashton's face a severe mask. "We have the power to change a human life destined for despair. I will help him with or without you."

"Now you are getting overwrought and cranky. You need a nap Miss Thing."

"I thought I knew you better than anyone, but right now *I don't want to know you!*"

"How can you say that after all we have meant to each other?"

"*Why are you so obstinate?*"

"Leighton must be turned in. It is not an option. It is a responsibility."

"We have the power to change Leighton's destiny. *I can't let you rat him out.*"

"Ashton, I've never seen you like this. You must be ill? Do you have a fever?"

"Don't touch me."

"If I didn't know your tastes so well, I'd say you had the hots for that boy."

"Bosh!"

"After a nap, I know you will see I'm right, and stop your convoluted thinking."

"I feel fine. Don't baby me, it won't work."

"Hey, *why are you putting the bullets back in the gun?*"

"I give up; I vote you out of the next chapter in this tragedy."

"You can't be serious, I know you, I love you, and you couldn't kill me."

"Walk to the abandoned mine at the end of that trail."

"And if I won't?"

"I'll shoot you here and let the buzzards pick your bones."

"You wouldn't."

"Try me."

"Huh, now this is getting interesting, well okay I'll humor you. But you are being foolish; I know you can't shoot me."

The two older gentlemen silently climbed the half-hidden century old donkey trail to abandoned silver mine's entrance. While they ascended, Ashton tried to formulate a scheme to frighten Kou into helping Easley. He knew he couldn't hurt let alone kill Kou, no matter how great his anger. What he needed was a gimmick to open his spouse's mind. Gimmicks had worked in other situations.

It wasn't a long climb to the blasted rock entrance of the long ago depleted mine. It was hidden behind a jagged rocky outcropping. Its opening was obscured by generations of dried-up and tangled tumbleweeds.

"Here we are, let me help you with my murder." Saying that Kou moved some of the desiccated tumbleweeds away from the mine's entrance. Abruptly a huge flurry of bats burst from the opening as the pulled aside dried brush let harsh blazing sunlight explode inside.

The bat guano covered rock floor dropped precipitously twisting to the left at a steep angle into blackness. Another tunnel to the right had a less sever descent but had a cave-in just before shadows turned total black. The timbers framing the openings had dry rotted ready to collapse.

Motioning with the gun Ashton said, "Walk into the entrance and don't turn around."

Kou walked into the mine entrance, then turned and faced Ashton. "It smells like bat shit in here. I go no further and won't turn my back on you. I want to see your face when you can't shoot me."

For lack of a better idea, Ashton decided to fire a warning shot near Kou to scare him into changing his mind. "It will be easier on you to turn around."

"You actually sound like you know what you are doing. But then again why didn't you bring dynamite from the car to seal the entrance after your dastardly deed is done."

"It is not too late to change your mind about Leighton Easley's fate."

"No, go ahead and shoot me. Come on let's get this over with, *shoot me, Shoot Me, SHOOT ME!*"

Ashton robotically brought the revolver up using a two hands cup and saucer grip. He aimed above Kou's head. Functioning from almost forgotten Army training he cocked the revolver and squeezed off one round. The gun's powerful recoil forced Ashton's hands to involuntarily jump a foot just before the pistol's earsplitting report. The gun shot echoed away in several directions multiplying as it grew fainter, and then was lost into the mountains.

The bullet fired at an upward angle struck a flat rock surface several yards behind Kou in the mine. The projectile ricocheted downward to the left, and then re-ricocheted boomeranging back up off another flat rock surface. It nicked Kou's ear and whizzed over Ashton's head as it flew out of the mine and into the sky. Ashton rushed forward and grabbed Kou in his arms.

Full of remorse he cried, "Oh my God you are bleeding! I didn't mean to hurt you. I'm so sorry!"

"Ashton, you live with a geologist for thirty years and don't know bullets ricochet off rocks? Give me a break."

With barely contained fury Ashton threw the gun full force at the mine's left twisting black void tunnel. It made a loud clunk then diminishing softer clunks as it bounced off rocks spiraling into the silence of the old mine's depths. The double action revolver had cocked itself with the first discharge. It fired a second round bouncing off of rocks deep in the mine's bowels. The two older Chinese men could hear the muffled second pistol report and then louder sounds of interior rock walls collapsing deep in the innards of the earth.

Turning back to face Kou, Ashton froze. "I made you bleed, what a terrible mess I've made."

"No big deal, it only stings a little bit."

"Oh, my God you could have been killed. I love you so much I never intended for you to get hurt."

Kou looked lovingly at Ashton. "I accept blame for yelling at you to shoot me. You did exactly what I asked. I didn't think you could. Once again, I sold you short and for that I'm truly sorry. This was as much my fault as yours."

"I should have known better. How can you forgive me?"

"Ashton that's enough now, we'll learn from this. For now, let's move on."

"But this is the right time to talk it out."

"No, what happened was I became intractable about helping Leighton Easley."

"Now we're back to that, after I almost killed you."

"I suggest an arbiter for resolution."

"What are you talking about?"

"Tomorrow morning go talk to Ed, *he owes you* for helping his youngest get into the Ivy League. Explain our impasse as a hypothetical. He likes us and he loves puzzles. What do you say?"

"Huh, excellent idea, I should have thought of that. But a favor for a friend never incurs debt. What about us right now, I almost killed you?"

"Let's go home disinfect and bandage my ear. I guess looking like Van Gogh for a few days won't hurt my image too much."

"Do you realize you've gone from one extreme to another in scant minutes? What's next with you?"

"Well since you ask, we could have some you almost killed me but didn't celebratory sex and then take a well-earned nap."

"Outstanding suggestions, there's no objection from me."

"If we carry all the food from the SUV into the house, later we can make a semi fancy dinner with some of it and then watch TV."

"You hate TV."

"But you like it. How about tomorrow we ride out for a sunrise breakfast. We always enjoy them and don't do it often enough."

"What about talking to Ed?"

"After breakfast, you can ride into town and talk to Ed and I can show our house guest some local geological sites. A day on horse backs will do us all good."

"I can always count on you to save the day after I almost end your life. It must be why I love you so much."

8.

The two sexagenarians collected dry ice coolers from their SUV and transferred the contents to the house's refrigerator. Then after time honed well-choreographed noisy love making, the two older men dozed, holding each other as was their habit during afternoon siestas.

Kou the lighter sleeper had his reverie disturbed by the sound of automobile tires on the front drive's cobble stones. Suddenly alert, he disentangled from Ashton's extremities. He pulled on an old pair of red flannel workout shorts and went to investigate. Leighton wearing only his too tight jeans must have also heard the car and was precariously pacing in the hallway between the bedrooms. The boy looked frightened and that stirred paternal instincts Kou hadn't realized he had. "I'll see who it is, we aren't expecting anyone. Why don't you wait in your room?"

Kou walked to the front door and looked through a glass side panel. A Sheriffs car, with its engine off had coasted in and stopped close behind their SUV. Deputy Sherriff Redding got out of his car. He went over and peered into the SUV. Throwing the door open wide Kou said, "Hey Jonas come in and have a cold drink."

Deputy Jonas Redding turned and smiled at Kou. "I wish I could, but we're on alert. I'm tethered to my car's radio."

"I could bring an iced drink out to you if you like."

"Thanks, I just had coffee. I'm just checking, you and your mate are supposed to be away. Your property is on a list to keep an eye on until next month. Aviation spotted your car and I got the call. There must be a clerical error."

"No mistake. We left this morning all right, but had to come back unexpectedly. With luck, we should be gone in a day or two or three."

"Then you stay on the list."

"Why are you on alert, if you don't mind my being nosy?"

"We may have to go up to Tucson to help out. Some white-man's scandal is brewing. Fort Gnat's failed to pick up prisoners today. Tucson is reporting dangerous overcrowding."

"Goodness gracious we haven't had a white-man's scandal since the last one. I was hoping they'd keep all that twaddle up in Phoenix, any idea what's up this time?"

"No, but Fort Gnat is in lockdown. The State Police went in with helicopters and are running the place."

"Well that sounds serious, doesn't it?"

"Yeah they had a big fire and arrested some staff. Oh, there goes my radio. If I can I'll check back here day after tomorrow. But if you are still around give the office a call and save me a trip." With that said Deputy Redding gave a half salute and rushed to his patrol car. In response Kou waved his best girly goodbye as the cop sped away.

Closing the front door Kou saw Leighton hovering in the hallway. "How much of that did you hear?"

"I think I heard everything."

"What's happening at Fort Gnat?"

"Beats me, it looked the same as usual this morning."

Both Kou and Leighton turned simultaneously to see Ashton standing in the doorway to the master bedroom suite. "Are you two having a union meeting or can just anyone joins in?"

"Ashton, why don't you put some clothes on, you're still half hard?"

"I thought I'd take another dip, and then if you insist I'll dress. What are you two chattering about?"

"I think I'll join you for a swim. Leighton, would you like to come along? Oh, is Gilbert still sleeping?"

"He left a while ago, said he had afternoon chores. But he'd try to come over tomorrow if that is all right? Yes, I'd like another swim."

"What happened with you two, or can I ask?"

"Lighten up, Ashton; part of me wants to say it was private, but another part wants to share. I get how protective you guys are of Gilbert and his family from me the escaped convict bad influence. I get it."

"If it will help, I could flip a coin to help your two minds have a decision?"

"That's okay I can see you want to know, and I owe you."

Still energized from the unexpected Deputy Sherriff visit, Kou eagerly jumped into the new conversation. "I don't feel you owe us. How was your nap?"

"What happened was he only wanted to nap with me because he wasn't ready for anything else. I said all right as long as we snuggled a little. It's been almost four years since I touched anyone, or been touched without the intention of hurt. So, after a little smooching we dozed off spoon style, Gilbert behind me. Then less than half-awake I feel a hand go under my towel and touch then strokes my prick. At that point it grew a mind of its own getting extra hard. I didn't know what to do, so I didn't do anything, except pretend to be asleep. The next thing was Gilbert squirmed over top of me and slid down. Then he was teaching himself to give head, using me for learning. I'm sure it was his first time, but he is a fast learner and before I could even warn him, I shot … a lot. I really needed what he gave me."

"And there went his virginity."

"So, I scooted down the bed and gave him a big thank you kiss. The look on his face was priceless. It was a combination of being pleased with himself, maybe even feeling proud and guilty thinking he should have asked first. To make it easier for him, I scooted down further and got him off with my mouth. I'm pretty sure it was another first for him. Then we made out, cuddled and dozed, at some point he twisted around glanced at the bedside clock and said it was time to take care of the horses and left. When we lay down I didn't intend to make moves on him, honest. He said he wasn't ready for anything besides snuggling and that was okay with me. My life is complicated enough at the moment. Kou, you going to tell Ashton the police were just here?"

"What happened!?"

"We aren't supposed to be home, Jonas says we are on a homeowner away watch list. The cops in the sky saw our car and got suspicious. Mr. Alvarado must have informed the Sherriff's Department we'd be away."

"Did Jonas look like he was in man tracking mode?"

"No, it looked more like a perfunctory visit with his hand on his gun. According to his list we aren't due back until next month. Is that what you told Alvarado?"

"Probably, I don't remember, must have? That was our plan, wasn't it?"

"It was."

"I like Jonas and his older brother." After a thoughtful pause staring out at the horizon Ashton turned to Easley. "Leighton, I agree with you, more complication is the last thing you need right now and what you and Gilbert are up to *is* a private matter. But just now you also saw how interested we are hearing about you two taking care of each other. Until your situation is resolved, Kou and I need to know what's going on with you for all our sakes."

"I understand you're facing bad consequences for giving me a holiday from prison. I wouldn't have blamed you guys if you had left me by the side of the road when I asked you to."

"With luck, it may not be a short holiday. Kou came up with an idea I will explore tomorrow."

"What? Tell me."

"Let's not jinx it, I'll tell you afterwards."

Getting embarrassed by an erection stirring in his gym shorts, imagining Gilbert and Leighton being intimate, Kou purposely changed the subject. "I wonder how Jonas keeps his uniform so crisp in this heat."

"Why didn't you ask him?"

"He had to rush off before I could; he said a white man's scandal is brewing up at Fort Gnat. No offense intended Leighton; we nonwhites talk like that among ourselves, I forgot for a second."

"I don't mind. I never understood why Arizona minority whites are the majority-minority and control everything."

"Gosh Kou, don't they ever get tired of all these political brouhahas?"

"Apparently not, do you remember when Jonas transferred here from the Indian-Police up on the San Carlos Apache Reservation? He was all lean angles and only a few years older than Leighton."

"You are telling me this why?"

"I used to be his exact height. I remember talking to him eye to eye back then."

"And now?"

"He's taller than me; I have to look up at him. Am I shrinking? You and I still talk eye to eye."

"It's gravity pulling us down, and you're barefoot, and he wears cowboy boots. I still want that swim, you two coming?"

The after-nap pool play was exuberant. Kou and Ashton were happy Kou was alive after the shooting and energized from afternoon sex. They didn't have as much sex as in their early years, but the quality continued to improve from practice and deep emotional commitment. The shooting increased the depth of those feelings. Their jubilant mood was verified by enthusiastic swimming, splashing and raucous shouting.

Leighton found it hard to avoid the others' energetic noisy fun. Their joyous humor did not fit his troubled mind, so Leighton left the water and reclined on a lounge chair to sun dry and ruminate. It had been horrible enough to be sent to the adult prison where the love of his life was killed. But since meeting and sleeping with Gilbert, not having a future came with a new kind of pain for the eighteen-year-old. As hard as he tried otherwise, his mind continued to dwell on how Gilbert looked, smelled, felt in his arms, and tasted. Thinking about Gilbert made Leighton smile, and then frown remembering he was deadly trouble to all he'd gotten close to.

Soon Kou and Ashton took pool loungers themselves. Kou tried to be funny and raise Leighton's spirits. "Easley's jeans are so tight he can hardly draw a righteous Christian breath or even enjoy farting."

Ashton instantly shot back, "Or even toots a Buddhist fart."

Without missing a beat Kou said, "Or even produce rapid fire curry flavored Hindu farts."

Easley looked confused then petulant at their intrusion. "I was raised Christian, and I have never farted in front of you. Fart jokes really, what are you guys eleven, grow up."

"Oh gee, where did the idea of farting come from? Huh, oh I know we are a couple of old farts, it must be us."

"Leighton, we want to buy you some nondenominational roomy pants for your birthday farting."

"I don't have a future. I'm sure the prison or mortuary will provide clothing."

"You promised not to hurt yourself while we're trying to help you ..."

Kou chimed in cutting Ashton off. "Mr. Easley, you would feel so much better in some new birthday duds. After all we have seen your Christian birthday suite twice, it's a nice one, except not suitable for all occasions. If you don't mind, we'd like to dress you for a variety of occasions."

"Kou, are you trying to be funny? Just so you know I'm not wearing a dress, okay?"

"Yes of course, you're too tall for drag. But I am funny, just ask my Geology students at final grade time."

"Look, I grew up poor, so I hate waste. It would be a big waste of your money to buy me clothes I can't wear where I'm going."

"We'd like to help you stay free. To do that you need to look presentable, like say in a lawyer's office or courtroom."

"I don't get it; you're trying too hard to be nice after not being nice this morning. Look, I'm still on the run. What clothes I have will do until I get to Mexico or dead."

Ashton, who had been watching the two interacting, joined in their conversation. "Once Kou gets an idea there is no stopping him, Leighton." Turning to Kou, Ashton asked, "So are you planning a shopping trip with Leighton before dinner or buying online during?"

"No, no, I thought we all could go. That way Leighton can pick out what he likes. Then we can make snide remarks about his bad taste. It will be fun."

His mind temporally off his troubles Easley jumped into the tête-à-tête. "To really be nice you should help me by making suggestions about what looks good on me or fits well or whatever it is girls do when out shopping together."

Turning to Leighton, Kou asked, "When was the last time someone took your photo?"

"Let's see, I guess when they arrested me three and a half years ago. It was one of those full face and profile with numbers underneath pictures. We never got photographed at Fort Gnat."

"So, the only photos of our boy are when he was much younger, and shorter. According to Jonas Redding, local law enforcement has got its hands full with some kind of Phoenix, Tucson, and Fort Gnats triangulation scandal."

"And that affects us how?"

"During evening rush hour, we go to the Big Box Store over by Douglas, Arizona. Nobody knows us over there, and we wear cowboy hats."

Leighton caught the spirit of the good-natured kidding-around and it lifted his mood. "I don't have a cowboy hat, never did. But if you want to adopt me I could sure use a name change."

"That's okay, for now Ashton will lend you a hat until we buy you one. Let's put your adoption on hold for the moment."

"Sure, he'd never fit into one of your hats. You want to knock off a quickie before we go?"

Suddenly looking concerned Leighton asked, "Kou what happened to your ear, I just noticed the bandage?"

"Ashton shot me with your gun."

"Oh no, Ashton, why did you do that?"

"I wouldn't give him more sex. He's a sex obsessed beast. You heard him just now he never gets enough."

"Gilbert and I heard you guys going at it this afternoon. It sounded hot, but Gilbert looked embarrassed. He thinks of you guys as family."

"We didn't realize you could hear us through the thick adobe wall. Sorry, if I knew we would have toned it down."

"That's all right; I didn't mind. Who has that gun now?"

"I threw it away after I shot Kou. It's not retrievable."

"That's okay; I'm not a gun guy. I never even liked that heavy bulky old thing. But don't shoot Kou again?"

Ashton abruptly changed the subject. "Kou I could stay behind and get dinner started while you two go shopping?"

"No, like I said it will be fun to go shopping together. If it gets too late to cook, we could go to Molly's for chimichangas or green chili enchiladas or whatever you guys want. How's that sound?"

"Sounds great, let's get dressed and moving."

The three improbable characters actively took over the sparsely customer populated male young-adult department at the Big Box Store. They started with a dark brown extra wide flat brim, low crown sheep rancher hat Leighton fell in love with. The three went on to fill their shopping cart with everything from packages of socks, top and bottom colorful underwear, and footwear, shirts, jeans and jacket. Every time Easley tried to put an item back for economy sake, one or the others older man insisted it stay in the shopping cart. The two university professors watched contentedly as Leighton's mood lifted from down in the dumps to high voltage teenager.

"Do you always enjoy clothes shopping this much?"

"Kou, this is all the birthdays and Christmases I never had, rolled into one."

The three tired shoppers finished their outing with a superb meal at Molly's where the older gentlemen were liked and treated like royalty. After dinner, they returned home, Ashton telephoned the senior Alvarado letting him knows they'd be taking three horses out early the next morning. Then the Chinese men and their young ward settled down to carefully read the newspapers purchased after shopping. They also scanned the local TV news for mention of Leighton Easley's escape from custody. His name was not to be found anywhere.

9.

At 4:00 AM the next morning Kou, Ashton, and Leighton were up and out of the house while it was still dark. They ran into Gilbert just arriving at the horse barn. He showed Leighton how to saddle his horse, and agreed to join the three for breakfast after he finished doing his first chores of the day.

The two professors led Leighton up to a favorite spot high on a mountain ridge. Years before they had built a stone fire pit with a permanent heavy metal cooking grate over it, and a stone picnic table and benches. Leighton was treated to a beautiful pastel display of soft colors as the sun slowly peeked over the Eastern Horizon. The sun prodded the darkness away with gentle warming light in micro increments of subtle pale color to enliven the night's hard cold gray tones. By small degrees' pure daylight crept in to heralded the promise of another day.

The two Asian men functioned like a well-practiced team, preparing breakfast fast and effortlessly. First the coffee was ready a little before the well-used black cast iron Dutch oven biscuits, next the griddle bacon was finished just as the grits were done and ready to receive some bacon drippings, and finally the eggs were dropped onto the grease drained cast iron bacon griddle. The eggs cooked quickly on the hot surface.

Gilbert rode up just in time to say how he liked his eggs cooked. There was no chatter as the four men watched the sun put on a display of soft colors, while they enjoyed their breakfast. Leighton and Gilbert sat close knees touching as they ate. From time to time they exchanged small smiling glances that Kou and Ashton understood from their courting days.

10.

Ashton left the meal cleanup to Kou, and Leighton. He and Gilbert mounted their horses and rode side by side heading back toward the horse barn. After several minutes riding in silence Gilbert said, "I guess you aren't talking because Leighton told you I took advantage of him at your house?"

"He didn't say that."

"What did he say about our nap yesterday?"

"I asked him if you guys did anything besides nap, and he said that was a private matter. I agreed it was none of my business, but was curious."

"What did he say to that?"

"He said he could see Kou and I are protective of you and your family, and even though he is an escaped convict, he promised not to be a bad influence on you."

"That's it, all he said?"

"When I pressed him, he said you were both more asleep than awake, and exchanged mutually agreeable orgasms. Leighton thought it might have been your first time."

"I did take advantage of him in his sleep, but he was cool about it. I like how he looks, how he talks, and I feel sorry he got such a raw deal in life."

"From the way he looks at you, I suspect some of that is mutual."

"In the past, I've had chances to have sex with both females and males. I wanted my first time to be special because I've heard so much about it. Yesterday with Leighton was special, and he didn't pressure me like others have tried. I definitely know I have feelings for him, totally."

"Yesterday when Leighton and I were talking, the way he said his life is complicated enough without any new involvements, I got the impression he has the good sense to protect you from his troubles."

"I've wondered if part of my attraction is because he is a wanted outlaw. I don't think so; I think I just like him in special ways."

"If you want my two cents and I know you didn't ask; take it slow and easy and as much as possible keep your feelings on low simmer. Hopefully later today I'll know if there is a way to keep him out of prison. At the moment, he needs to be handled with care, and you need to be self-protective."

"You know what, since meeting Leighton I've been thinking about coming out to my parents. I should have done it years ago; now that I had sex I've no excuse not to tell them."

"What's the rush?"

"Since my brothers are married my folks want me married too. They keep pushing young church women at me to date. Would you and Kou mind being there when I tell them I'm gay?"

"Sure, if that's what you want. It might be easier for the family, if they have concerns? Tell us when you are ready; maybe we could have you all over for dinner."

"Thanks, I'd really like that."

"No problem. I've got to go, see you.""

"And I've got to go finish my morning chores. Then I promised to rejoin Leighton and Kou up on the ridge for a saunter. Kou is trying to talk me into changing my major to geology, I might actually."

Ashton headed his horse to town to see Sheriff Ed Bachman. He had called the day before and spoke to Bachman's clerk to setup an appointment. Since Ed's wife died, he arrived very early and usually stayed late at the office. The clerk told Ashton, "Get here as early as possible the Sheriff is looking at a busy day with the shenanigans coming out of Tucson and Phoenix about the Fort Gnat mess."

After hitching his horse in front of the Sheriff's office, Ashton bought a couple of containers of fresh brewed Mexican coffee from a small cafe across the street. Then Ashton went directly to Bachman's office, stuck his head in the door. "Ed, you still take your coffee black with two sugars?"

Ed looked up from his computer and smiled. "Most definitely Ashton, I was just thinking about you. It's been a long time no see old buddy. What can I do you for?"

Handing over a coffee Ashton said, "Kou and I have been arguing over a hypothetical situation and hit an impasse; we were hoping you could settle it for us before someone gets hurt. But if you are busy it can wait. It's not a matter of life and death."

"I'll make time; tell me. I could use a little diversion just about now, craziness abounds."

"What's going on?"

"It looks like the proverbial shit has hit the proverbial fan up at Fort Gnat, and you know how panicked State Officials get with scandals. What's your hypothetical?"

Ashton sketched out a bare bones chronological version of his and Kou's encounter with Leighton Easley, without giving the boy's name or any extraneous information like taking him home. But he did give all the particulars Kou and he had fought over. Sheriff Bachman tilted back in his big brown worn leather desk chair, sipping the rich Mexican coffee and listened to the deadlock Ashton outlined.

When Ashton finished, Ed informed him it wasn't possible to simply transfer a prisoner from a Juvenile Justice Facility to an adult Department of Corrections' prison. It required many intermediate steps to interface distinct bureaucracies which the judiciary and a trial judge wouldn't normally have the knowhow to do. The different bureaucracies are too territorial to let a transfer happen without specific instructions from the State legislature. The Governor would literally have to sign off on the paperwork. If the judge knew what he was doing, he would have declared the juvenile an adult and just sent him to adult prison.

The only legal problem in your hypothetical is leaving the scene of a fatal accident. But given the situation it would be surprising if the convict didn't run. Then claim trauma from the accident when caught and sue everyone in sight and win big bucks as an accident victim and probably receive a get out of jail free card as part of the settlement. He could also sue the State for even bigger bucks for being held in a juvey facility when over age eighteen."

"So basically, I'm right and Kou is wrong, and the escaped convict can be saved from a life in adult prison, one way or another."

"Um, well yes if there are no outstanding warrants for his arrest."

"Thank you so much for helping us out with this puzzle. How could someone find out about outstanding warrants? And if you don't mind my curiosity, what is going on with the Tucson, Phoenix and Fort Gnat's shit storm you mentioned?"

"I'll check warrants in a minute. Fort Gnat will be in the papers and on TV News later today *so I won't be disclosing confidential information* if I give you the official story now. That's all I know anywho."

"I don't want to cause you trouble, but I love political intrigue."

Ed told Ashton the previous morning a Highway Patrol officer in an unmarked car stopped for a teenage hitchhiker. He didn't have any identification. In Arizona, no identification means arrest and jail until there is documentation or deportation. When the officer put the handcuffs on the teen, he totally lost it begging and screaming not to go back to Fort Gnat. She said the kid went psychotic. She calmed him down promising not to take him to the Fort. Then he told her about a bus accident. On her way taking the hitchhiker to Tucson for processing she stopped to check his accident story.

Sure, enough just as the kid said, she found a one vehicle accident west of Benson, Arizona; it appeared the driver's neck snapped in the crash. She ascertained the bus was traveling too fast making a sharp turn and rolled off the road. She found a document pouch containing a release form with the name the hitchhiker had given. He also fit the physical description listed on the form. The Highway Patrolwoman immediately called for a supervisor.

To make a long story short Highway Patrol Command called Fort Gnats for information and to informed them of the fatality and discovered the driver, a Mr. Eldon Johnson, was not one of their employees. To complicate the situation more, the Fort's secretary said the Administrator was sick and gave instructions not to be disturbed. She said he was the only one who could answer the Highway Patrol's questions. But when threatened with arrest for obstruction, the secretary said the Administrator had just admitted during what looked like a mental breakdown most of his required paperwork never existed. He feared his incompetence was about to be reviled and he was sure to lose his job to a robot."

Meanwhile back at the crash scene it is discovered eight sets of footprints leading away from the bus, seven in one direction and one going off alone. Then after some distance another pair of footprints split off from the group going in a third direction. But there are only six release forms in the document pouch, and no bus manifest other than for pickups in Tucson. There was also an empty gun holster.

While this was happening outside Benson, up in Tucson they were going into a panic because the Fort reported nine open beds and then did not pick up nine incorrigible junior felons before lunch as promised. Tucson didn't have enough food to feed or space to house both the old and new young guests of the State. In addition, Tucson became increasingly frustrated trying to communicate with Administrator Tharp at the Fort, their only designated contact. Apparently, everything at Fort Gnat had to go through this one guy. Tucson reported to Phoenix they had a dangerous overcrowding situation. Phoenix tried to get clarification from the Fort using telephone, fax, and radio, all to no avail.

Nobody in high position in Phoenix wanted to know what was going on at Fort Gnat, out of sight out of mind, until this incident. The place is hard to reach, bleak and barren, stinks of sulfur when the Gnats aren't biting, and the kids all look like creepy zombies. Office holders quickly started pointing fingers at each other in circular firing squad formation. Naturally blaming each other is not helpful for problems in search of solutions, but it is traditional here in the old west. The Fort has a disgraceful history. But it did have beds, in a system always short of beds. Consequently, the authorities have been willing to look the other way and know nothing. Being isolated in the boondocks, with no one watching, the Fort has done whatever it wanted and gotten away with it, until yesterday. Demanding telephone calls and faxes from people in authority, made the Fort's Administrator, Giles Tharp go off the deep end.

When the State Police took over the Fort they found there was sexual abuse of inmates perpetrated by workers both State and Per Diem. Supposedly the Administrator knew what was going on, choosing to use it as leverage. All this came to a head because of the bus accident. Tharp was probably cracking up in slow motion before yesterday's events pushed him too far. Since he ran the Fort as a one-man band nobody liked, none of his staff noticed or cared until he flipped. Then when he snapped having a hysterical outburst ranting and raving incoherently, his office staff just left and went home. Further disturbed by the walkout, Tharp got a five-gallon jerry can of gasoline from the motor pool, locked and barracked the office doors, splashed the fuel over the offices, then started a fire and shot himself dead.

The fire burned the Fort's administration building and motor pool to the ground, and all records such as they were with it. Any chance of completely solving the mystery of who was on the bus and where the driver's gun went has gone up in smoke.

The Highway Patrol tracked down some individuals from the bus's release forms. But they won't talk even with a lawyer present. Tucson Juvenile Justice Officials are freaking out about overcrowding. So, the court ordered their overflow be sent to the adult County Jail for health and safety reasons. And child protective services are threatening mega legal actions for housing children with adult criminals in an adult jail.

When Phoenix heard about the fire from the Wilcox fire department, they dispatched two helicopters of State Troopers to take charge of the Fort. So now we have yet another State agency on the case putting Fort Gnat under a microscope and trying to solve puzzles while adding to the confusion. And Fort Gnat has nine empty beds that the State Police won't fill until their investigation is complete and that could take a very long time.

"Talk about a muddle. What's next do you suppose?"

"So far the State Police in Phoenix have discovered bank records showing lots of State money not dispersed as allocated. State Troopers found boxes of computers and other expensive new electronic gear left in a garbage dump, unopened and ruined by the elements."

"Damn Ed, and to think I only expected a typical small bureaucratic snarl-up."

"My guess is a more definitive ending will be coming after more is uncovered, stay tuned."

"Unbelievable, my tax dollars at work, and much more story than I expected on this otherwise fine morning."

"The coffee you brought was fresh and from my favorite café. I wanted the story to measure up. It's been too long since I saw you Ashton."

"It's true, we both work too much. So, tell me Ed, any sage insights into a scandal of this magnitude?"

"Don't quote me, but Fort Gnat should have been closed 150 years ago. It has been a mean malicious place without hope or even a gesture toward rehabilitation. It was a school in name only. I wish the fire had taken the whole place down."

"Anything I should tell Kou about outstanding warrants before I leave you to your work?"

"Tell Kou to get a hypothetical lawyer for the hypothetical boy."

"Thanks for giving me the time and sharing the news. Kou is not going to believe you have trumped our story with a much better one."

"No really, I'm serious, as your friend, please take my advice; get that boy a good lawyer post haste. Then after his lawyer starts requesting nonexistent official documents and filing law suits, you two disappear into the mountains with him. Let the lawyer make the kid's problem go away."

"How did you know it wasn't hypothetical?"

"When I got in this morning I found an email from my deputy who moonlights as security for the Douglas Big Box Store. The email was from last night, and said two older native-Americans with strange last names and a white teenager were shopping at her store. She wrote they were having too much fun to be from around here, and in fact they looked too happy not to be suspicious."

"She's astute, with their long history of bloody oppression; the Original American's have little to smile about."

"No argument from me. She asked me to check out yours and Kou's names for open warrants. She took your names from the store's credit card machine. Just as you arrived I also checked for outstanding warrants for any John Doe meeting the boy's description, there is nothing for any of you. Do you know the kid's date of birth perchance?"

"I do, eighteen years ago yesterday."

"Wait a second, -- nope still nothing, so tell Kou if he brought the kid in I couldn't arrest him without a warrant to hold him, unless Kou wanted to bring carjacking charges?"

"I sincerely doubt he would."

"Oh, does that teenager have the driver's hypothetical gun?"

"No, I threw it down an abandoned mine shaft. It would be a big and dangerous production to retrieve it. The mine wants to collapse; I should have dynamited the entrance years ago."

"What else do you know that I don't?"

"Yesterday morning the bus left Fort Gnats with nine teens, one driver, and no guard. One boy was released in Benson. After the bus crashed two of the boys had the presence of mind to take their paperwork. Our ward tore his documents up after disagreeing with the content. At the moment, he has no documentation or any ID. He says none of the boys liked the bus driver because of the way he gawked at them. But he only worked at the Fort once in a while."

"Well that fills in some blank spaces. I am glad you came in for this little chat today; it clears up my deputy's mystery. And to protect my job you made the situation hypothetical rather than ask a favor I would grant. I appreciate you my dear friend."

"Do you have any parting hypothetical advice for this loyal friend, before he leaves you to it?"

"Hold on a second, my center desk draw is such a catch all. Ah here is one, take this business card, and use my name. Call the hand-written number on the back, it's his direct line"

"Who is this?"

"Dave teaches at the University of Arizona Law School. One of his pets is an Innocents' Project and has made it his personal mission to close Fort Gnat. Your ward may be just who the University needs to shut it down once and for all, and in the process, get your boy right with the law. But if you and Kou take this route it will cramp your style in the short run."

"How's that?"

"You'll have to keep the kid close at hand. If he has a court appearance and doesn't show an arrest warrant will be issued and that could exacerbate his problems. On the other hand, if he does what the lawyers say, his record will be sealed since everything except the accident happened before his eighteenth birthday. If he behaves, and is punctual; with luck, he is looking at becoming wealthy after all the lawsuits are settled."

"Thank you, Ed, you really came through for us, you get two boxes of Moon Cakes this year."

"Let me know if there is anything else I can do, and tell Dave hi for me."

"Since you asked, our ward has no identification, any suggestions?"

The Sheriff ripped a form from a pad on his desk, scribbled on it then signed his name and handed it to Ashton. "Give this to my clerk on your way out. She will issue him a temporary driver's license while you wait."

"He doesn't know how to drive."

"Then teach him."

"Thanks Ed I appreciate your help. Let's get together soon."

Riding back to the ranch Ashton mulled over what Ed said about taking on the responsibilities that came with helping Easley. Ashton taught young people in college, knew well their boundless energy and rambunctious enthusiasm that could be trouble if not channeled constructively. At an indecisive moment, Ashton recalled the moral imperative he had preached to Kou; that settled it.

Ashton found Kou and the two young men where he expected; on a high bluff overlooking a vast gently sloping valley that seemed to go on forever. They were off their horses and meticulously inspecting an unusual mineral formation. "Greetings friends and lover, we need a POW WOW."

As Aston dismounted the others found rocks facing each other to sit on.

Aston gave an abbreviated rendition of what Ed had to say, then said, "Kou we will need to sacrifice to see Leighton's legal troubles to an end. I will only call the Lawyer if we three are in complete agreement to do what is necessary to get Leighton's juvenile record sealed."

"Wait up, how can I pay a lawyer? I already told the free lawyer I have nothing, and no hope of ever having anything."

"Don't worry about that, I got you covered."

Ashton's face showed surprise at Kou's uncharacteristic quick generosity. Kou saw the reaction and said, "Yesterday Ashton tried to convince me to help you Leighton, I was obstinate. My paying your legal fees is a way of atoning. I don't make many mistakes but I correct them when I do."

"Kou is this about wanting to drop me off in the desert at night? I don't blame you, you guys don't know me. I might have done the same thing in your place."

Ashton gave Kou one of their private looks and then jumped into the conversation to move it along. "Look you two, according to Ed the University Lawyers will either work pro-bono or take a percentage of Easley's law suit settlement money for their Innocents' Project. That is if you Leighton keep all your court appearances on time *and yourself out of trouble.*"

"Really? Wait! No oh no, it is happening again!? My God, the last people who tried to help me had their lives destroyed. I only know you guys twenty-four hours, *I told you, and I am trouble from bad seed*. Please, for your own protection don't do this. Don't put yourselves in danger and that includes you Gilbert. I've ruined good people's lives before!"

"Leighton Easley, I respectfully disagree with your conclusion. Let's see, you defended your honor from exploitation by a sexual predator stepfather. You were forced to run away from violence in the name of love. At Fort Gnat, your life was threatened because you rescued another inmate from rape. It appears you have been forthcoming and truthful telling us your life's story. Based on that, I could write you a good character endorsement letter."

"The judge said I am an incorrigible felon and should be neutered to protect the future."

"I disagree, you and Arnoldo made a mistake trying to rob people. Hungry people sometimes act unwisely, ask Kou? You have paid for your mistake serving a long sentence at Fort Gnat, and Arnoldo paid with his life. If I thought you were bad I wouldn't help you for Kou's sake. You can see I love him very much. We want what is best for you, and have the fire power to protect you."

"Ashton, geez I'm all choked up, I don't know what to say besides thank you. If you are willing to take a chance on me, how can I say no?"

Kou had been watching the verbal interaction with interest. "One way to express gratitude to us is when you meet with the lawyers see if they can link Mr. Cruz's case to yours. If they can't, see if they can get his sentence reviewed independently? After all they are called the Innocents' Project."

"Yes, I will do that. If I come into the money you mentioned I will make sure the Cruz family has a decent place to live and what they need."

"You ready to start a new chapter in your life?"

"Sure of course I am. What do you guys do on field research trips, maybe I can help out?"

"Ashton will probably teach you to draw maps. But if you stick with me kid, we can break open rocks to see what stories they tell."

"When I was young I liked to draw."

Walking over and taking his water canteen off his horse's saddle horn, Ashton heard paper crinkle in his shirt pocket. "Oh, and here is Leighton's temporary driver's license." Looking from Kou to Gilbert, Ashton said, "One of us has to teach Leighton to drive now that he has a temporary license, any volunteers? Ah, thank you for raising your hand Gilbert, use the old pickup, he should learn to drive a manual transmission first."

Beaming for the first time since the previous night's shopping excursion, Leighton felt his skin tingling. "Oh, my God, this is what good luck feels like?" Leighton Easley seemed to glow with a radiating heartfelt smile.

MATRICIDE

Docking

"Shlomo, do you need a ride home? This parking garage is deserted."

"No thank you. How do you know my name?"

"It looks like your mother and sisters asked you to park their shopping cart and then drove away as you did what they asked. Let me wish you a Happy Hanukkah."

"What business is it of yours if I got left as a joke? Happy Hanukkah and I asked how you know my name."

"I was behind the four of you in the cashier's checkout line upstairs."

"Mm yes, I remember, you were watching us. Why weren't you minding your own business?" This said squinting twinkly brown eyes through frameless eyeglasses. He'd switched to a challenging tone of voice, attempting to scold by putting his hands on hips like a chiding school teacher. The effort failed to succeed.

"What else was there to see waiting in the shortest of the long cashiers' lines, all of which moved at a snail's pace? I learned a lot about you and your sisters; home for winter break from school, and your poor much put upon overly price conscious mother, frazzled by her three adult misbehaving children."

Shlomo's attempt at a confrontational posture melted. He meekly said, "That *was* embarrassing; my sisters are not always that obnoxious. But they know exactly how to get my mother going and then push her more and more to escalate untypical behavior. They do it for amusement. Mother thinks she's playing with them but they are really being cruel. She doesn't see it or want to hear about it from me. You saw, was I wrong? They are her precious daughters who can do no wrong."

"Yes, I watched, and to this casual observer your assessment appears correct."

"Let me apologize for that disagreeable display and holding up the checkout line."

"You didn't do anything to apologize for, but someone should buy that cashier lunch. She more than earned her wages today. Do you need a ride?"

"No, they've done this before, and sooner or later will be back. They think stranding me like this is funny, but it's not!"

"Do your sisters know that?"

"If I complain they say; 'you could have hitched a ride, who would bother such an ordinary uninteresting looking Yeshiva University student. You're just a lazy bum. Being the youngest and male you think we're here to serve you. Wrong! Face it bro, you are female dependent in a male dominant culture.' So, I don't complain and accept their abuse. What else can I do?"

"Mind if I wait with you?"

Stiffening into defensive stance Shlomo said, "Why would a tall good looking man want to wait with, according to my sisters dull me?"

"Just in case someone wanted to give you trouble, two are better odds."

"Mm well, if you have nothing better to do *and* no ulterior motives."

"I have no hidden agenda, honest."

"Is it true blue eyed blondes have the most fun?" This said with a bold but playful half smile that quickly changed to unsure, and then slight trepidation flitted across his face.

"Absolutely, we have more fun than everyone. What is your major at the University?"

"Theology, I am expected to become a Rabi." Then with a wink Shlomo went on, "So it is true, you tall blondes get laid more than the rest of us. Mm, I suspected as much."

"Why did you choose Theology?"

"If you must know I'm doing a double major, Urban Anthropology and Jewish Theology."

"That's an interesting combination, what in anthropology are you mixing with theology?"

"You ask a lot of questions for a complete stranger … oh well. In general, I'm interested in minority group issues utilizing large hospitals, and specifically how well my minority group's genetic problems are treated. You don't have to stay. I'm an adult and can take care of myself."

"What genetic issues interest you?"

"You really do ask a lot of questions for someone I never met. Since you care enough to ask, I'll tell you. I'm not the only one in my community who can't pass the Department of Motor Vehicle Vision Test to have a driver's license."

"Can anything be done to fix that?"

"Nothing, don't worry I won't go blind. I just can't drive motor vehicles. And as you noticed my sisters exploit that and it's a bummer. What is your next topic?"

"What if your sisters forget they left you, and *you'd* rather not spend the night keeping company with those parked shopping carts?"

Eyeing me closely, a question formed on Shlomo's handsome young face before he spoke. "Mm well, is that your only reason?"

I was enthralled watching his pretty plump cherry red lips move. Then I stared into his warm milk-chocolate colored eyes, magnified by his eyeglass lens. Caught off guard I spoke without thinking. "No, I like talking with you and your ear curls are cute. I guess it is a weakness of mine, I love men dressed in black with scraggly facial hair wearing wide brim hats."

Stiffening on guard again, pursing his succulent looking lips ready for verbal combat. He moved his feet to an ersatz martial arts stance. "Yes, about that, I remember seeing the way you were looking at me in the checkout line. You have to know by my clothes I'm Hassidic, so not available for whatever it was you were thinking."

"Gosh and I thought you were Amish or Mennonite, ha, ha just kidding." To cover my faux pas, I made it worse. "In my travels, all religions have contradictions, and yours is no exception."

His body went ridged. Shlomo half pivoted sideways, hunched his shoulders ready to fight, his voice tight. "We have electricity and automobiles, except on Shabbos. I've heard Amish and Mennonite food is not kosher. *What contradictions?* Be careful, remember I study theology."

"Okay for instance in your religion all sex is *trey* called dirty, with the one exception of fucking your wife through a hole in a sheet for the sole purpose of making a baby. Yet all the Hassid guys I've been with whipped it out and shot a load, just like Amish and Mennonite guys and all the rest of us, just for fun."

"Sorry to disappoint you but that's not me. By the way you haven't introduced yourself. I don't know your name."

"Evan, Evan Burke, I hope I'm not making you uncomfortable with my frank talk? I will go if I am, but the offer of a ride still stands?" I said this in a conciliatory voice.

"Nice to meet you Evan, this *is* a longer wait than usual. But I'm not nervous about it; my sisters can be mean, well you saw upstairs." Shlomo said not nervous looking anxious.

"Nice to meet you too, did my blunt talk about sex with other guys offend you?"

"No, it doesn't bother me. You should hear some of the students at my Yeshiva talk dirty, I blush just thinking about things they say."

"Do you consider yourself a pious prude?"

"No, I am not! Why do you like Hassidic men? If I were you, I'd go for less complicated and restricted males. They'd be uninhibited fun."

After giving it a moment to digest *less complicated and uninhibited,* I thought, *well at least Shlomo is not restricted by dogma, he gets points for that.* "I don't know why I like what I like. But I'd be very bored only doing it with my clone that I know for sure."

"Maybe the law of attraction likes variety, and opposites do really attract. I used to be skeptical about that. In my community, we are similar."

"Or possibly I like how you dress; the 18th century may be underrated for male fashion. Seriously, I like facial hair and hats on men. My first man was Hassidic, maybe that's it."

"Oh, I see, maybe that *is* it and you are marked for life, poor fellow my condolences."

"Your ear curls and twinkly eyes really get my motor running. Sorry, I can't help it."

"Mm, this is interesting; I've never been talked to like this. So just for the sake of conversation mind you, what would you expect from me in return for a ride home?" Shlomo's face went into a playful lascivious grin, backing up his mischievousness expression with relaxed body language.

"Nothing, my offer is made with no conditions, promise."

"Come on, you just told me you get turned on by guys who look like me. Surely you would expect me to put out some way in exchange for a ride?"

"In my value system being a Good Samaritan is its own reward."

"Evan, before you spoke of contradictions, what you just said is an example of one? You could try and exploit my situation for your intents and purpose and you're not. In my experience, that is totally crazy."

"You are still in school. I graduated a few years ago, and since learned taking advantage of another's trouble offends the universe."

"Mm well, I can see you are serious, but I don't get why you forego your advantage?"

"Do you expect me to try an exploit you, if so, can't do. Sorry that's not my thing." I said this with gravity while trying to keep the conversation going.

"No, I don't want to be exploited. But it doesn't make sense not to use an advantage when you have one." His body language was still relaxed, but Shlomo's face matched his words attempting to figure out a problem's solution.

"Let me break it down; you need a ride and I represent a no strings attached ride. But in your imagination my speaking of preferring sex with guys who dress like you has the little wheels whirling in your head."

"You're right, that must be obvious, but what about you and your motives?" Shlomo threw out the challenge making direct eye contact and holding it for emphases.

"What may be confounding you is I'm not devious, and you are correctly on guard against devious."

"You can never be too careful around strangers especially accepting rides."

Resigned to being redundant I said, "For me you represent a fellow traveler in need of a good deed I can easily provide, that is all, nothing more."

"You already said that?"

"I know, and the ride has nothing to do with the fact I like talking with you and find you pleasing to look at. In your imagination, you may have us frolicking naked in tall summer wheat."

After shifting through conflicting thoughts, registering on his face, Shlomo came to a decision. "Mm, just for the sake of argument, if I insisted on paying you by barter, what would you consider a fair sexual exchange for driving me home?"

"Insisting to pay for something free is crazy in anyone's book. Okay, okay I can see I'm making you antsy. So, for the sake of your argument ... my car is paid for and relatively fuel efficient ... I guess a quick handjob should be more than adequate recompense."

Dropping his guard completely Shlomo revealed a startled open face. "I don't understand you would swap a hand-job for a ride. But you could do that for yourself, and probably better than me."

"Right, but some of my pleasure would come from watching you get me off, and even more pleasure would be feeling what you were doing while I watch you do it."

"Huh, so that's it? I wouldn't have to take my clothes off. No penetration, no exchange of body fluids, or something profound that I'd need to take responsibility for later or try to understand beyond you wants to get off looking at me getting you off?"

"You are making this too difficult. My wheels are right there, it is a luxury car less than a year old. We could just walk over and you get a lift home, no strings, no moral crisis, no messy body fluids, and no big deal."

Showing annoyance stamping his foot, Shlomo spoke with resolve. "Yes, big deal, if I accepted a ride, I'll pay for it on my own barter terms."

"Hey relax, whatever you say."

Shlomo's thoughts showed on his handsome face *I have options; could hitch a ride, call a cab, or accept this free ride.* His conclusion also registered; *this is too unusual an adventure and cock stirring interesting.* "All right, I'll jerk you off in exchange for a ride home. Where do we do it, in your car?"

"No, I have textured leather upholstery, stains would be a shame." Disappointment flitted across Shlomo's face, and his mood downshifted. "How about we go behind those rows of shopping carts? This basement parking garage is as huge as the mega store upstairs, and there aren't any customers coming or going at this hour."

"But what if someone does come and sees us?" He stiffened saying that with real concern showing.

"Standing behind push carts, no one can see us below the waist. If we hear the elevator or shopping carts coming down the ramp, we stop, I cover up and pretend to be talking until they leave."

Shlomo looked doubtful, probably reevaluating his plan for offbeat adventure. "Out in the open, -- in public, -- isn't that against the law?"

"Yes, and that makes it more exciting. Relax it won't take me long to cum being exposed in public. I've got more to lose than you."

Shlomo appeared not sure of what he'd started. And I was close to an arousal peak thinking about where this was going. He nonverbally indicated let's do it, and we walked wordlessly to behind rows of stowed shopping carts. We were completely hidden on two sides by the corner of the basement's poured concrete walls, and then half hidden by a wall of row after row of stacked together shopping carts. The total effect was a long narrow alley with a cart wide opening facing out to the vast parking area.

In back against the concrete corner, we turned to face each other. "Can I kiss you?"

Shlomo shook his head no. "I don't kiss boys. But show me your dick I want to feel it in my hand."

"If you are sure, here I am." I said this unhitching and zipping then pushing my pants and light blue briefs down to mid-thigh. My hard cock jumped out into the open-air swinging from side to side feeling enthusiastic and expectant with arousal.

A shocked look on Shlomo's face revealed his thoughts *Oh my God he isn't Jewish, but he wished me Happy Hanukkah, and knew about the chosen people's mating practice. What do I do now?*

"Is there a problem?"

"You're not Jewish. You're not circumcised; I never saw one of these up close before. Gosh you have a lot of foreskin. What do I do with it?"

"Actually, I am about average in the foreskin department. I have Amish and Mennonite friends with extended *lace curtains* that is what they call really long foreskins."

"Mm Lace curtains, that is a fascinating name for it. I guess I can see a connection. I heard those people are into handicrafts."

"If it matters, I was raised Presbyterian and according to the writings of Saint Paul, a Jew and one of Christ's apostles, Christians don't circumcise."

"What are those marks there, just above your pubic hair?"

"When I was in high school I was in the wrong place at the wrong time and got jumped. Thugs cut me up pretty bad; the scars have faded to only those marks. Do they bother you?"

"No, what do you want me to do with your dick?" Shlomo seemed to want to please me, and at the same time I felt his palpable apprehension.

"Firmly grasp my cock about halfway down the shaft, that's it. Now push your hand back toward my body." I was thinking *I'm not sure this was such a good idea -- but I couldn't just leave him here by himself.*

"Oh, I see, there is your dick head, it looks like mine only bigger. Okay now what should I do?" Shlomo visibly relaxed seeing a familiar sight in his hand. But I suspected his heart was pounding with excitement from being naughty in public, outside his usual comfort zone with a stranger's dick in hand.

"Work it back and forth just like you jack off." His fair skin cheeks blushed red at the forbidden suggestion he pleasured himself. Then his indignity was gone in a flash, accepting I knew his secret. "No, I'm sure you don't do it that slow – whoa, now you're going too fast -- do it like you're home alone with no distractions. No, come on show me how you enjoy yourself? Ah that's it; you found my rhythm, good man."

Smiling broadly already knowing the answer Shlomo asked, "Does this feel enjoyable?"

"Yes, it feels extra, extra nice … wait, stop! Isn't that your mother's car pulling into the parking garage?"

"I don't want to stop; I'm just getting into this. It is fun and we didn't finish."

"Then squat down, maybe they won't look back here."

"They're gone again, but your mother didn't look happy not finding you. Want to give her a call and say you are all right? Here, use my cell phone."

"I have my own cell phone. I turned it off when they left without me, I know my sisters' tricks, calling every few minutes saying they are on their way and then not showing up, over and over, running my phone battery down for no good reason."

"That sounds mean."

"Let them stew a little. I want to get back to what we were doing before we were disturbed."

"Sure, -- here, you can see I'm still hard. It won't take long to get me off the way you were working it."

"Could I ask you something before you cum?"

"Ask away, you're the one who's got me in hand. In case you were wondering; what you are doing feels amazing and watching you do it enhances that feeling by a factor of ten."

Obviously not sure if he was crossing a line or violating a scared rule, Shlomo spoke solemnly. "Would it be all right for me to slip your foreskin over my cock? I'm not too big and you have enough for us both."

"Sure of course you can, the technical term for that is docking. Lots of discordant couples do that playing bedroom games."

"What is a discordant couple? I know the words but not used together like you just did."

"Oh, like us, one natural one cut."

"Mm well, if it has a technical name it can't be that unusual. So, I won't be committing some kind of aberrant act; offending you or my God or your Universe, right?"

"Right, join me – join us together and see what you think."

Shlomo immediately unpacked his average size very excited looking cock; it was standing straight up stiff and proud pointing at the sky. It looked happy to be out in public. Precum was already dribbling from his piss slit. Fumbling at first, he joined our two slippery drooling dicks, cock-docked as one. Then he squeezed with his warm tentative hand, to make them drool precum over each other's dickheads.

I placed my hand over his and set them moving in a steady easy pace. We smoothly cantered short even strokes back and forth between our pubic bushes. The expression of being naughty and feeling nice on Shlomo's face was precious. We sped up evenly as nature dictated driving toward mutual pleasure climax.

"What do you think, how does this feel?"

"It feels amazing, in fact, your foreskin fits me perfectly. Can I have it?"

"I don't think transplant surgery has progressed that far."

"So, you know; it feels soft and snugly warm, my cock loves it. Holding hands, holding cocks is new for me. I like it."

"I can tell."

"Wait, stop, what are you doing now?"

"I'm stroking your balls with the fingers of my other hand so you will cum because I'm over ready."

"I'm holding back waiting for you. Let's finish, squeeze my hand tighter, oh that's it, yes, ah, ugh, oh Yes, YES!"

"Don't close your eyes; look at me looking at you. This is where kissing is really good."

Joined by our clasped hands holding our docked dicks, we shuddered and shook reaching pinnacles. Then after a few vibrating seconds; we shot strong jets of hot man juice onto each other's cocks, mingling copious amounts of cum to overflow dripping on fingers. Just as our orgasm's internal and external frenzies subsided Shlomo went up on tip toes and locked his pretty plump lips on my half open mouth. He slipped in some tongue and we relaxed into a soul kiss lasting until our breathing returned to pre-coital respiration. Then unclasping hands, in mirror image we took out clean white handkerchiefs and wiped up our mingled spunk, occasionally stopping to exchange another kiss. I thought *we will remember this; it was sweet and a first for him.*

Both of us got busy tucking ourselves away and putting our clothes back in order. "Evan, I don't want to seem pushy, but do you think we could do this again before my vacation is over? I liked what we did more than I thought I would. Thank you for such a unique Hanukkah gift."

"Sure, if you want."

"You made the holiday special this year. I wonder what gift I can give you in return."

"If you are feeling adventurous and are up for another escapade, a unique gift would be for us to try a different docking position for each day of Hanukkah left?"

"Cool, I like to be adventurous; I was just now with you. But we can't possibly improve on this awesome experience. I saw the pleasure in your eyes as I was enjoying my own. Who would have thought man to man sex *could feel that overwhelming times two?*"

"Docking has more possibilities without clothes, in a safe clean warm place. For right now though let's get you home before your mom sends out the Mounties to look for you."

ALS

Panting hard after a mind-expanding, spectacular orgasm Shlomo said, "Evan, you are a man of your word. Hanukkahs over and you keep improving our climaxes. I didn't believe it possible, but every time you make it better than the last. It is so totally amazing; you keep taking me to new places inside myself."

"We fit together well; I love holding you especially as you accelerate toward your precipice and then freeze just before flying off into ecstasy. It is an inimitable privilege to be included vicariously."

"Who knew sex could be this profound? With you it feels spiritual."

"Your nerves are wired better than most; even our after play is richer and longer than I've known." Kissing him passionately, I flutter finger touched all his sensitive post coital tingly places. "Are you looking sad because of a person, place, thing, or none of my business?"

Shlomo rolled on top of me, captured my hands and laced our fingers together. "Well let's see, I am feeling down my ride is taking me back to school in a couple of hours so this has to be our last time at least for now."

"Are you coming home for Purim?"

"No March is too close to midterms, we'll build huts on campus. But I wish I could be back to snuggle with you."

"I'll miss these afternoons too. Don't say goodbye, say Shalom."

"I'd like to talk before I go? We have such incredible sex, and so little conversation, what's up with that? Sometimes I feel like I'm in that movie about Mrs. Robinson."

"Do you mean *The Graduate*? I'm not *that* much older than you. If you think I'm a cougar you may be experiencing age and gender confusion."

"Whatever, nitpicker."

"Come on get dressed, I'll make tea and we can chat until it's time for you to go. Or we could sing that song *"Until It's time for you to go,"* over and over until you do go."

"You singing, country and western, who knew? I thought of you as more sophisticated and cosmopolitan than wearing cowboy boots."

"Guilty, come on, I have scones left. They're from that kosher bakery you like. How much time do we have for singing?"

"I'd rather use the time touching skin to skin, if that's all right cowpuncher?"

"What's on Mrs. Robinson's mind? Oh, wait I'm Mrs. Robinson and judging by your cock's alertness we could easily go for extra innings."

"Come on stop, hands off my thing, we never talk."

"Go for it."

"First off if you had told me you were going to shove fingers up inside me just now, I would have forbidden it as nasty dirty, *trey*. But you doing it at just that moment was a totally astonishing set of new sensations. It felt like your fingers were turbo boosting my orgasm from the inside. And if I'd known first, I would have said absolutely no way don't do that."

Smiling licentiously, I wiggled myself against Shlomo's luscious body lying on top of me. "I thought if I mentioned it you'd say no, not kosher, but knew you'd love having your orgasm heightened by inside stimulation."

"I've never been in touch with the erotic possibilities of that part. I was taught asses are dirty and to be avoided except to keep clean. Now I'm wondering what else I was taught that needs to be questioned. For instance; everything we do together, right?"

"Don't over analyze, just enjoy. You don't need to write a saga about it, nothing in life is static. Reserve your judgments for later, we aren't hurting anyone or stealing."

"But it felt so wonderful when you played back there before going inside. I don't want to deny myself new experiences based on fear or superstition or somebody else's prejudice."

"Hold on, we both know your instincts are good. You take smart risks with me, because you trust me. Trust yourself too, revelations will come with time."

"But I'm in a hurry now that I know what I've been missing."

"If I'd known I was opening Pandora's Box by putting a finger in. I wouldn't have."

Rolling off me and propping himself up on an elbow, our noses touched as we kissed. "When we first met, you settled a disagreement saying, 'you were educated and I was still a student.' At the time, I didn't want to be distracted from what we were talking about. But what I think is a person should never stop learning. Do you disagree? Because that's what we are really discussing, right, not butt fingering?"

"I remember that conversation about accepting a ride home from me a stranger. Cut to the chase; tell me what's bothering you."

"When we started, you said it was only about sex for fun and games and you wanted to be part of my sexual discovery. Nothing more, no strings attached, and no commitments. You said I shouldn't let my emotions get mixed up with physical stress release fun, remember?"

"And this chapter is ending with you going back to school. Let me guess; now you have these soft mushy feelings clogging up your objectivity. If we don't clear the pipes of your emotional sludge you won't be able to concentrate on your studies."

"Not exactly but sort of, when we *do* talk it is about intellectual things and I love that. We have never ever talked about feelings, mushy gushy or otherwise. How can we do what we do without feelings for each other?"

"For most people, peers, family, introspection, an enlightened rabbi in your case, plus challenging books are the best resources for making sense of feelings."

"Yeah, I know all that, and I know you have a preference for Hassidic or Amish guys past, present, and most likely future after present company is replaced. I wouldn't deny you and your next guy our amazing experiences."

"Very magnanimous of you, thanks muchly, and I wish you a full and rich future too. So, is this it, you ending our get-togethers for lack of mushy gushy gunk?"

"Heavens no, I'm not done with you. I want more sharing orgasms, and your schmaltzy tales from before."

"Then I'd say so far, your sexual exploration is a success, wouldn't you?"

"Yes, but I worry about *you*. You going from one to another of us black hat guys limit your prospects. I want you happy as a reward for expanding my world."

"I am happy, so happy I'm about to tickle your toes until you laugh out of control."

"Don't, don't do it, stop, STOP!"

"What are you being so serious about? We've only known each other a short time."

"You know Hassidic men are required to get married to a woman and produce lots of babies. So, then who is going to bring chicken soup if you catch a cold? Based on our original agreement am I even allowed to bring you soup after I'm reproducing?"

"You are sweet, but I know what I need and how to get it and do." With that said I started tickling the bottom of Shlomo's feet with ten busy fingers.

Giggling then laughing loudly Shlomo finally twisted free from the pretzel like configuration we had wriggled into. With a twinkle in his pretty eyes, he sat up cross legged on the bed. "Be serious a minute, wouldn't you like to settle down with a special someone and adopt children or raise poodles or ponies or something?"

I felt my countenance shift to business negotiations default neutral. "I discovered my freshmen year of college; I'm not a relationship kind of guy. I'm not like my friends and dorm mates with a constant need to be coupled up. I figured out, for me it is possible to be happy and fulfilled and know my life has meaning as a single entity. To be trite, I know what I like and how to get it. All my wants are fulfilled with little muss or fuss."

"That absolutely goes against everything I have been taught, and what the holy books say."

"Not everyone is programmed to be coupled into constant compromises and shared disappointment. You know me well enough; banging square pegs into round holes is not my style or good for pegs or holes."

"You are so tender and loving with me. I never experienced that. Wouldn't you like me to return that closeness 24/7? Whoops, I mean somebody; it can't be me the matchmaker is already looking for my future wife. But someone *like* me."

Reaching forward taking Shlomo by the shoulders and drawing him in close; I kissed his pretty plump lips. "In my way, I love you very much. If you like we can play house until you graduate and marry your future bride. I just can't tolerate whose turn was it to take out the trash or do the laundry, or any other this or that couples constantly fight about."

"It doesn't have to be like that if you make rules."

"Don't be presumptuous, I live by rules, and already told you I don't have unmet needs. One reason it is special for us; we aren't in each other's faces, good days and bad 24/7. When we get together, it is looked forward to exceptional, because we are at our best for each other."

"Mm sure that makes sense, but you deserve more. I want much more for you." With a pursed pout on Shlomo's lips, he briskly folded his arms tight across his hairless chest for emphasis.

"What's important to me is what enough *is*. I've doubled the number of buildings my father left me; I could have easily tripled them. My parents died too young in a plane crash. They would be proud if they lived; I have built a good life with everything I need and want included."

"Where am I in that?"

"Right now, you are who I want. Even though you are going back to school, I know how to wait for your return."

"For the record, if we were living together 24/7, I make a tasty chicken soup."

"Tell you what, how about for now we keep things the way they are, and make concentrating on your studies our number one priority. Let's deal with the future when it arrives."

"You are shutting down this conversation."

"Yes, for now, we can revisit it in the future. In the meantime, you have this safe sexual outlet."

"If you insist, just keep in mind I care about you."

We sat on the bed facing each other, my legs wrapped around him, our hands caressing each other in a long silence. I was lost in thoughts about his concerns; our cocks' half aroused nestled. They had become chums. "Shlomo is there more than my future weighing you down today."

"You really have my number, don't you?"

"If you want to get something else off your chest, do it now before I send your pretty little bubble butt back to academia?"

"You know me better than anyone ever has. I've been equivocating with this. I don't want to burden you with my problem; there is nothing anyone can do anyway?"

"Will you feel better telling me?"

"Of course, but you won't. I love you, *in my way,* why would I want to give you my grief?"

"See how broad my shoulders are, they are designed to carry heavy loads. *Tell me,* I want to know."

"Don't say I didn't warn you. At our final Hanukkah meal, my mom told us, she has been diagnosed with ALS. She has less than two years of rapidly declining health. Her primary care physician says she's been ignoring or hiding her symptoms for a long time. She doesn't deny it."

"I'm so sorry. That has to be hard for all of you."

"It gets worse; she wants me and my sisters to assist her suicide when the disease gets too much."

"Have you talked with you sisters? Can I assume you explored ALS and assisted suicide online?"

"Yes, and yes, I will join the ALS support organization and go to their meetings, but there is no way I can assist a suicide. That's impossible, no matter what."

"I'm here for you, any way I can help. How are your sisters handling the news?"

"My sisters are researching humane methods for killing our mother. Can you believe that? They want her involved in the process, since it was her idea. It is strange; they seem to be enjoying having her permission to kill her."

"It could be their way of handling the news."

"I don't know, maybe? I've tried but can't talk with them about this or anything else these days. I feel sorry for their future husbands."

"Besides each other and your mother are they talking to anyone for support?"

"Not that I know. But I talked with mother about what she asked. She said it was only a dramatic gesture to make sure she had our attention."

"You seem skeptical."

"I think she's afraid for when it gets too hard being trapped in her body, unable to move or communicate. I'm paraphrasing, but she said she doesn't expect us to actually kill her and go to prison for doing it, but it would be nice if she had an exit."

"Sounds like a double message?"

"I know what she says seems contradictory. I wonder if she even knows what she wants. ALS is a terrible disease."

"I wasn't much older than you when my dad and mom and sister died. My dad was teaching my sister to fly our private plane. For a time, I resented God for taking my family and abandoning me. How are you and God doing?"

"I'm sorry for your loss. God is one place I go and you are the other. Are you still fighting with God?"

"No, He and I worked it out."

"Good for both of you."

"I'll ask around about ALS and see what I can find. You won't be alone, call me if you want to talk."

"That means a lot, thanks."

"Is your whole family involved?"

"Not really, most of my living relatives are old. It would be a shame to burden them."

"I've wondered why you never mentioned your father."

"No, he's not that old, the others are. When I was born, my mom had female problems. The doctors had to do surgery to save her life. The results prevent her having more children."

"I didn't know."

"Mother says my father wanted a lot of kids like the Torah says, so he divorced her when she stopped producing. My sisters have vague recollections they have glorified bigger than life making our father into a super hero. They hate mother and me for depriving them of the father I never met."

"Your sisters' hero worship is why?"

"In Psych 101, we learned Freud had a lot to say about females and their real or imagined fathers. Neighborhood gossip has it my father's new wife has given him lots of babies."

"With ALS, you may want to mobilize all your resources. Could your Rabbi intervene with your dad for your mom's sake?"

"Huh, makes sense, I'll talk to Rabbi Abramowitz."

"Come on let's get you ready for your trip back to school. I'll pack up those orange cranberry scones you like. You can eat them on the trip."

Passover

"Happy Passover how was your journey home?"

"Shalom, the trip was uneventful. I snoozed mostly. How are you, besides missing me I mean?"

"Who says I missed you?"

"The hard on showing in your pants. Would you mind if we skipped this chitchat, got naked and did the deed? I am so horny I can hardly stand it. Come here big goy, I want you so much I could cum a gallon just thinking about us naked."

"Oh, wow so cool, that was incredibly awesome, you just keep doing that to me?"

"It *was* really good for me too."

"You constantly make my next orgasm better than the last. That is so amazing to anticipate."

A lascivious smile bloomed on my lips. "Okay then, let's make that our stated objective."

"Mm just a second Evan, so up to now it has been an arbitrary goal? Is it a stated long or short term objective? Um wait, if we want to quantify results correctly, we should use self sex as the null point. Mine is usually flat compared to what we do together."

"Don't get too formal; let's just use the empirical method?"

"No, I'd rather graph our orgasms together and then individually, to have cross references. What do you think I should measure; blood pressure, pulse, duration, or quantity of cum?"

"You want to plot our orgasms on a graph, and cross reference chart? Hold on a minute, how about you leave your academic tool box at school and we snuggle without hypothesis?"

"Without graphs and charts how can I possibly fathom your magical powers over my sexual response?"

"Oh, I see, you want insights into magic."

"I do, I might even write a book about it after graduation."

"Take notes, I see you have lead in your pencil again."

"*You* cause that reaction?"

"My magic power over you is simple. I know you and your hot body so well I can anticipate your wants; where and when, better than anyone could know those trigger points. And I love pulling the trigger."

"I really love you doing that, it is always thrilling. Just so you know being with you is all I think about at school."

"If your grades drop, fun time stops."

"My grades are fine. Tell me more about your magic."

"For me it's an uninhibited tactile experience, free of guilt and other distractions. It feels like we are intertwined alone in outer space. Plus, we magnify the experience through eye contact. Is that for your book?"

"You are too much. Did I ever mention under your ministrations I leave my body and go mind traveling in ecstasy, can you tell? I fly off during that long interval before I pump out gooey white cream and return back to your arms. When I'm at school I fantasize about not coming back from my mind trips with you. Is that crazy or what?"

"Geez I mind travel during sex too. I wonder if it's infectious, we usually cum together or damn close. Yup it must be catching; we should seek a vaccine?"

"Mm no, but you put your finger on something; when I'm at school I worry you will get horny and go looking for a Mennonite or Amish guy to replace me. I don't want to be jealous. Yet the green-eyed monster comes to visit me when I'm alone and feeling down."

"Hey, you are who I desire. I know how to wait, and you are worth waiting for."

Smirking Shlomo gave my ribs a tickle. "I guess there is no accounting for taste."

Caught off guard, giggling, without thinking I said, "Interesting, just now your facial expression reminded me of someone I knew when I was barely legal for sex. Whoops! Relax, I didn't mean for that to be a downer. The similarity is only slight, more mannerism than looks. You are my special person these days."

"You never mentioned him before, now I want to be jealous. Was he Hassidic, Mennonite, or Amish? Tell me all about him? Did you love him, live together?"

"Is it necessary to take a long boring trip down memory lane, right after talking about exciting sexual mind travel?"

"Tell me I want to know everything!"

"He was Hassidic, but wasn't special. He was my first."

"I want to be jealous?'"

"Be serious, jealous of a long-ago memory?"

"I can if I want."

"For your information, I haven't seen him in a decade or more. I wonder how he is aging; he was much older than me?"

"Mm, okay his old age lets me change the subject, if you don't mind? I'm just about ready to give you the special gift you've been wanting."

"Is this because I told you about your sort of doppelganger?" *I shouldn't have said anything. What was the point? Now I upset him for no reason.*

Indignation rising, showing bright pink colored splotches on each pale cheek, Shlomo's lips went into a tight pout. "No, it is not about him, it is about us. I gave this a lot of thought while at school missing you, and exploring my body like never before thinking about you."

Accepting I had unintentionally ruffled feathers, my tone of voice went to pacifying. "All right, what is this special gift from my randy soul mate?"

Calming down with pride in his voice he puffed out his chest. "I am just about ready … to let you fuck me for deeper docking. I already love docking with you our usual way. I'm sure deeper docking in back will be even better."

"*I never said I wanted to screw you*, where did you get that idea? There is a lot more to anal sex than the physical release. We haven't even started oral sex, and that will be a fun filled adventure for you. I expect you to love it like I do." This was said trying to thread a needle, not wanting to upset Shlomo again but expressing my determination not to skip important milestones on his journey.

"It's obvious to me you want to mount and fuck me, and I'm almost there for you."

"How's that?"

"The way you watch my ass walking when I get out of bed to pee or when we shower you spend extra tender, even adoring time lathering and massaging my Gluteus Maximums. And after Hanukkah you started slipping a finger or two up inside there just when I start to cum. I love the attention and how it feels. I'm ready to endure the pain involved to take us to a new deeper docking. I only need to get past a little psychological obstacle, my old idea of masculinity. I'm almost there."

"No wait, I am not on board with this, we're not ready. You're going too far ahead, slow down, we aren't there yet."

"Yes, I'm almost there."

"Shlomo, you said you like having each orgasm better than the last, why skip steps between. Be patient, at the right time we'll fulfill your wish."

"But I want to repay you right now with an amazing, totally remarkable orgasm docked deep inside me. I shiver just thinking about it."

"I didn't realize my appreciating your beautiful behind would cause a problem?" In an attempt to change direction, I said, "Why did you decide it had to hurt?"

"You are big, and my hole is small and tight. It takes a lot of lubrication for me to get two fingers in there. But I want to give it to you no matter the pain; you more than earned the gift."

"For your information, sex is never supposed to hurt unless you want it to."

"Who would want sex to hurt?"

"People who enjoy rough sex claim pain enhances their pleasure."

"Mm, I don't think so. Why would someone want to mix pain with pleasure, that doesn't make sense? Then again how can a big pole get shoved into a small hole without it hurting?"

"Were you snoozing in anatomy class, the anal muscles can change shape and stretch when persuaded nicely?"

"Show me?"

"Not yet. We'd miss the fun steps to arrive there. Remember the journey versus the destination. Be patient, we'll get there." I could see from his face he was heating to a full teenage boil. So I tried to turn the temperature down. "What about hygiene?"

Displaying righteous indignation Shlomo shouted, "You know I always keep myself impeccably clean."

"And I love you do, but inside too?"

Simmering down a notch he took paused. "Mm, how do you do that?" This said reeling back ire.

"Tell you what; let's wait until we're both ready for that level of commitment? Then I'll show you how to prepare. For now, we keep having safe sex through well timed attentive manipulations and then explore oral?"

"But I really want the experience of docking with my butt today. I'm more than curious how it will feel, and to please you that way."

"Sorry old pal not today, we'll know when the time is right, I promise."

"Admit it or not you want to take me in the ass. By myself, I imagine you bucking away and enjoying the ride, my gift to you."

"Why don't we grab a quick shower? I've bought some rare tea I want you to try. Also, I want to give you the number of a physician I've found who is an ALS specialist. You can bring me up to speed on what's happening with you at school and home."

"Okay, just know I'm serious. I want to feel your dick go deep inside, pump me, and cum buckets. I want that for us."

"Hold your horses; in due time. It's okay to wait; it makes the getting extra worth it."

"We will have to have a lot of extra sex over this Passover to complete your prerequisites for deeper docking. Hey wait up I want to shower with you."

Freshly showered, seated at my big antique mahogany dining table. A large plate of kosher bakery coconut macaroons, almond topped marzipan cookies, and chocolate covered matzos sat between us waiting for the tea to steep. Giving in to temptation, Shlomo picked up a chocolate covered matzo. "Tell me about the ALS specialist? I bet he's outrageously expensive. There are not many specialists and few accept new patients. See I did my homework."

"He is expensive, and doesn't take insurance, I can help you with his fee if you let me. He is in regular contact with the ALS medical team working with Steven Hawkins in England."

"That is impressive, and your *but* is?"

"Before he decides to accept a new patient he requires an extensive interview, then a lot of neurological tests done by his private lab. My guess is many tests will be repeats your mom already had. He sounds persnickety, but comes with the highest recommendations. Here is his telephone number. You can set up an initial appointment to get your mom started? Have his office send me the bills."

"Let me talk with mother first, she's funny about doctors. What do I tell her about how I found him and the bill?"

"I'll show you where I found him online. If she asks say she's received a scholarship from an anonymous source."

"She probably won't ask. I'm being a worry wart, after telling you about deeper docking, I feel oddly exposed."

"Don't be, if not me who?"

"I guess."

"What about tuition money, are you going to be all right with a sick mom?"

"My mother's parents invested school money for us when we were born. As far as I know everything is covered."

"Let me know if you need money, I don't mind helping."

"Has being a Good Samaritan ever gotten you in trouble?"

"You've seen the scars on my stomach."

"Mm right, do you still not want to talk about that? Okay, okay sorry I brought it up. So, I took your advice and defended my weak professor's stupid ideas in the mid-term paper and he brought my B- up to an A+. Thank you for the suggestion, but it felt dishonest not telling him what I really think about his convoluted, pathetic thinking."

"What is your overall grade point average this semester?"

"Four point zero, thanks to your help, and burning the midnight oil."

"You did the work; you get all the credit. Have you talked with your Rabbi about your mom?"

"Yes, he visited while my sisters and I were back at school. Apparently, it went well because he has been meeting with my mother and father for half an hour one evening every other week since."

"Sounds positive, what do you think?"

"I don't know yet. I heard my father has offered to help with home care when mother needs it. He knows someone in that field. These chocolate matzos are really delicious."

"They are good, but I love the marzipan."

"Mother says my father wants us to live with his new family after she is gone. She seemed relived telling us that. I never met the man; I will reserve judgment until he keeps his word about a home health aide or home attendant or whatever they are called."

"Are you looking forward to meeting your father and his new family?"

"It would be good if he helped out with mother's rent and medical expenses above and beyond her savings and insurance. Otherwise I don't expect much."

"When do you meet?"

"He's invited mother, the girls and me to one of his Passover Seders. We will meet his new family. I'll let you know what happens, but right now I got to go. Thanks for the tea and Matzos and awesome sex see yah, bye."

I walked Shlomo to the door and gave him a heartfelt mouth to mouth goodbye. "Good Shabbos don't be a stranger."

"Hey hi, it is good to see you, come in. I was just thinking about you and here you are."

"I hope you don't mind an unannounced visit. I've been missing you and Happy Easter."

"I'm always happy to see you, everything okay?"

"We're all walking on egg shells. Mother doesn't want us so protective of her."

"It sounds like she's still the matriarch. How was Passover Seder with your dad?"

"The Seder was interesting, though I'm still reserving judgment. Can I have a hug?"

"Come here, hugs and you go together with me." When I took Shlomo into my arms he felt taut, like he was tightly wound. "Were you and your mom comfortable meeting your half siblings and your dad's new wife?"

"No, I hate to think it, but she is preparing to die. Her withdrawing has to be from that. As is making sure her kids have a home after she's gone."

"Was she sociable at the Seder?"

"Mother tried, but it was forced. I don't know what I can do? She doesn't want to talk. I tell her I love her all the time, it doesn't seem to matter."

"You look uncomfortable telling me this. How about instead of asking questions, you say what you want, when you want, if you want? I'm fine with holding you being quiet."

Taking a deep breath Shlomo said, "You read me right, I don't want to be questioned about my family in turmoil."

"No pressure, someone said silence is golden."

"There isn't room for me and my sisters at my father's house. They hardly have room for themselves. His new wife doesn't like us, but said after we move in she will go back to work. Then my sisters and I can take over child care, maintaining her home, the shopping and the cooking. With her working, she's an accountant; they will have money for a bigger place."

"Sounds like something."

"Given half a reason my sisters will kill those wild half-sibling brats. They don't look or act anything like us."

"Oh dear, that bad?"

"Worse! Anyway, we want to complete school and go to work and have adult lives with our own homes and families. But we told mother what she wanted to hear about a future with the wild ill-mannered half breeds."

"Did you get face time with your dad? Oh damn, here I go interrogating you again, sorry."

"That's all right, I know you care. Dear old father and I are having lunch next week for what he calls the father son talk we never had."

"That sounds intriguing."

"Can you and I have some down and dirty sweaty intriguing sex right this instance?"

"Why not, that's what you came for?"

"Yes, to escape all my old and new family jumbles jamming my brain. I need you to keep holding me tight and make my worries disappear into panting blasts of steaming hot cum."

"What do you want to bet I can get those clothes off your body before we get to the shower and your pretty rocks off before we leave it?"

"Can I bet my hard cock on it?"

"Yes, you can because I really love that cock, along with all the accoutrements that comes with it."

"We never had sex in the shower as a main event before. How will you make me shoot my day's first load of spunk," panting for dramatic effect, "in that hot humid wet place," more panting for effect, "if I may be so horny to ask?"

"Be bold ask. After you're stripped, I will apply soft wet warm friction to all your parts using herb scented imported bath gel, and then rinse you off with a fine steamy hot spray. When your lovely hard on gets bigger from docking, just as you start to cum I will turn the shower spray full force ice cold to heightened our climaxes."

"Burr, what are we waiting for?"

Basking in the sweet afterglow of hot then suddenly freezing cold sex, we cuddled under a king-size comforter. "Did your mom contact that specialist?"

"You want to talk about my mother after you just made her pride and joy shake and shudder in unrestrained frigid pleasure?"

"That's me."

"She saw the specialist you found, with my father tagging along. The physician referred them to a neurologist who takes her insurance, but doesn't specialize in ALS. Apparently, there are even fewer physicians who specialize in ALS than I first found. She refused to let me go with them saying 'Of late you have become too clingy.' My guess is they made the doctor's visit about her insurance rather than what the doctor could do for mother's condition."

"Did you have lunch with your old man?"

"He wanted to know about my sex life, with a leer. So, I asked about his and he changed the subject. He said we will have lunch again and connect sharing family stories. All in all, I was uncomfortable, but he gets points for trying."

"There is a chamber music concert downtown at five. It's at an art gallery opening. I'm going, want to come?"

"Thanks, but I feel my clothes make me stick out like a sore thumb at the cultural events you've already taken me to. People stare at me."

"We are going for the music and art, not for what people think."

"I know you don't care. But I feel out of place, like a freak."

"If you'd like, leave some gentile clothes here for cultural events? I don't mind going shopping with you, my treat."

"Thanks, but I'll pass for now. But speaking of expanding my horizons, I should start research for my urban anthropology graduate school application essay. I just never seem to have enough time these days. I need an excellent essay. You and school are the only safe places I have left."

"So, what are you thinking?"

"I want my essay to be perfect because while nobody is noticing I'm dropping theology. I'd make a terrible rabbi; mother's illness has shown me that. Anyway, it was never my idea, that's what the family wanted."

"I won't ask about that. You will tell me if and when you want. Do you need help with the essay? I might have some ideas?"

"Sure, I'd appreciate essay assistance. Writing with you will increase our closeness, I'd like that. Do you know my topics?"

"Speaking memory from when we met, both your general and specific Urban Anthropology topics are too broad."

"What do you suggest?"

"For your master's theses; I'd identity and describe all fifty genetic diseases unique to the Hassidim. After the introduction overview, have a brief discussion of each, and after lots of background supported by citations, your conclusion will be; the gene pool is too small."

"Mm, interesting, simple but direct and covers all the bases. I like it."

"Your Ph.D. dissertation, huh, I'd pick one vision issue you are particularly interested in. Use the genome to support your genetics hypotheses, then after a lengthy discussion of available research and examples, make you conclusion brief and to the point. Include lots of those colored charts and graphs you do so well to illustrate your points. The more obscure your references the broader the speculation you can get away with. Be prepared to know everything there is to know about your subject for the oral defense."

"Dispassionate scientifically objective or personal, which do you think?"

"Do you want to write an autobiography? Besides the physical, there is a psych component when a teenager is denied a driver's license; it becomes a forbidden rite of passage. Back at you wants Anthropology or Psychology?"

"Wow what a question, let me think on it."

"With luck, we should be able to collect essay data quickly on line."

"I love how you show me love in different ways."

"It's an even exchange. Let's only deal with the Masters essay and worry about the Ph.D. another time? Do you have energy for this; given everything going on in your life?"

"It has to be done. What do you think if I changed topics and made ALS my Ph.D. dissertation subject?"

"I don't think it is unique to the Hassidim, is it?"

"I've been thinking the master's and Ph.D. don't have to be related."

"That means more work. But if you used your empirical ALS experiences in conjunction with whatever related data we can find, assuming your advisor and committee approves."

"You think we could find enough data to draw supportable conclusions about ALS?"

"For a master's theses, no doubt, but for a Ph.D. … you may have to change your major to neurology to defend it."

"Mm, I don't think so. I'm having a hard time between my mother's dying, my father trying to make up for lost time, and carrying a full double load of honors classes."

"It looks like your concentration is drifting. What would you rather talk about?"

"You got me; I need you to keep holding me, and hold me tight to keep the bad thoughts out of my head. Emotionally I'm feeling stretched to the limit."

"Let me shield you from your demons."

"Hi, shalom, goodness another week has gone by already? I'm so busy these days I hardly know if it is morning or night. How are you holding up?"

"I need something from you. But I hate to go back on my word."

"Shoot, how can I help?"

"What I need most, more than anything in the world is for you to fuck me, and fuck me hard and long and right now this minute."

"We already talked this over. Not now, not yet, be patient we'll get there when it's right."

"But I need it so bad. I desperately need to get out of my head, feeling you moving inside me will give me relief."

"We don't know that, anyway we're not ready, you promised to wait."

"I know, but I can't."

"Be realistic, for all we know fucking could make things worse? Now is not the time for something new, heavy, and emotional. Getting screwed the first time is a big deal. The last time you were here, you said you're emotionally fragile."

"Getting fucked is the only thing I think about twenty-four, seven. I imagine you mounting me, docking us like two spaceships in deep space. I need you to make it real."

"What's changed?"

"I need your strength to help me through what's happening at home. Mother's mobility has gotten very shaky; she falls down a lot, we'll have to feed her soon. Please fuck me, pump me full of your power, I need a transfusion."

"I'm so sorry, but no; going from fantasy to reality can produce unintended consequences. I know you; you are tough you'll get through this."

"Evan, I know you have the strength to take me out of my head. Just go deep inside my body and fill me with what I need."

"Okay tells you what old pal, when you graduate if we still have things to say to each other and your bottom is still virgin. I promise we will fuck, and make it a memorable fuck, whether I think we are ready or not. How is that for a compromise?"

I was dumbfounded when without warning Shlomo's open right hand flew out with vicious full force and slapped my face with a loud thwack. His stinging blow left a dark red hand imprint still visible in the mirror long after he left.

"How dare you suggest I'm some kind of slut that would give my virginity to anyone *but you*? Do you think I'm a cheap whore in heat?" He glared darts at me, his eyes on fire. "Do I mean so little to you? Why won't you help me?"

"OUT! Get Out; go before something really bad happens! I love you, and you hit me. Go on get out of here before I lose control and do something I'll regret."

Bursting into tears Shlomo sobbed, "Oh no, I'm so sorry I didn't mean to do that, oh my God forgive me."

"Hitting in anger has no place with us, get out of my house!"

"Please, please don't throw me out. I'm sorry; I don't know what came over me. I'll never do that again, promise."

"You mean until the next time, I know how domestic violence works. You think by hitting me you can manipulate me into doing what you want, after we kiss and make up. Forget that; the genie is out of the bottle and not going back. Stop crying;

get the hell out of here while you can still walk."

"I wasn't trying to manipulate you."

"Yes, you were!"

"OH NO, now I've ruined everything."

"Even preschool children know hitting is never acceptable. You know my history better than to try that; get out before I hurt you."

"Oh, my God, you are really throwing me out. Oaky I'm going don't get all threatening about it."

"It's for your protection. I don't trust myself, go. We'll talk when I've cooled down. I'll call you when I can be objective, now leave this instant."

Rosh Hashanah

"Happy New Year, I hoped I might see you for Shavuot. Why haven't you answered my phone messages and emails? Gosh do you realize it's been months."

"Mm, a lot has happened."

"Hey, don't look so angry, you are here now that's what matters. I've missed you."

"Mm yes, it is months since you threw me out for hitting you in the face. I remember it clearly."

"Correct, and that is what we need to clear the air about. Domestic violence is normally a terminal disease. But I think we can repair the damage and start fresh without escalating the violence. It's worth a try, don't you think?"

"No, I destroyed the one good thing in my life. The good news is I've learned to keep my hands to myself, it was a painful lesson."

"We can fix things. Let's give us another chance?"

"That's not why I'm here. I need a favor."

"Oh … okay, what favor?"

"For me to move on with life, I need to understand something. Tell me about your first time with a Hassidic man."

"Why, how could that be helpful? I just noticed, your underweight, you eating enough? Somehow your sparkle is gone too. What's happened?"

"Very perceptive as always, I've changed a lot in a short time. I couldn't go back to University this semester because I am now my mother's officially trained and certified primary home healthcare aid and care giver. Thanks to my father's friend."

"I wish you'd asked me, I could help."

"Mother's health failed faster than anyone expected. Now I take care of her every need, along with having a mind numbing part-time job to help cover day to day expenses, thanks again to my father."

"That wasn't the plan."

"Nothing has worked out according to *the plan*. A son shouldn't have to bathe his mother or change her diapers, but this son averts his eyes and does what is necessary, like it or not. I love my mother and suffer with her."

"I wish you had returned my calls, I can get you help."

"How could I return your calls, I struck you in the face after everything we shared. Anyway, that seems a lifetime ago, back when I was a fun-loving student. Then I lost my mind and got banished. I accept my punishment; I got what I deserved. What I did to you was unforgivable."

"I never banished you. We both needed time to cool off, I was afraid I might hurt you or worse. You know my history being attacked. If I knew it would take months to reconnect I would have handled it differently. If you want forgiveness, I forgive you. Now, let me help you."

"I'm sure you mean what you say, you always did. I didn't realize it at the time, but you were right. It was a manipulation to get what I wanted against your better judgment."

"All right, that's as good a place to start as any."

"No, just tell me what I need to know and I'll go for good, you deserve better than me."

"You have to know in my way I love you, present tense. I didn't use the words often enough, but I showed you love."

"Shall we not do this right now?"

"I was so angry you struck me, in that instant my love turned to hate. You know since I was knifed as a teenager being assaulted makes me go crazy."

"I remember, you told me. But what happened between us was my fault, don't make excuses for me."

"It isn't an excuse it's a fact. Anyway, I was worried what you wanted could make your situation worse not better. The last thing I wanted or want is to make your life harder than it is."

"Mm, it's interesting to hear you say those things. Just so you know I still love you. But a smart man knows when it is time to move on from what he wrecked."

"I'd like to give you an argument, but I can see your mind is made up."

"You're right, how about you make us some tea and tell me about your first man on man Hassidic sex. I need to know about something that's gnawing at me. Just tell me and I'm gone forever."

"If that's all you want, we can talk while I set the water to boil. What you are asking happened a long time ago, I was younger than you were when we met. I started college two years early due to AP classes."

"I read someplace people always remember their first time, even if it was horrible."

"Mine wasn't horrible. Since you insist … after my freshmen year at University my folks and sister picked me and my luggage up for summer break. I was sixteen going on seventeen. Driving home my dad felt sleepy and pulled into a rest area off the highway for a cat nap. The three of them went right to sleep. They had been driving since early morning. I'd slept late that day and couldn't doze off in the car. So, I went exploring and came across a public restroom. When I went in to pee I noticed there was this Hassid man at one of the two urinals. Both the booth stalls were vacant; I often wonder why I didn't use one of them. Instead I went to the other urinal and pissed, as I was about to tuck back in I notice the guy was playing with himself. He was hard and seeing that made me hard. When I looked over at his face to see what was going on, he took my right hand and put it on his cock. I was shocked and thrilled and confused and afraid all at once.

"Long story short I jerk him off with my right hand and myself with left. Just as he was about to blow his wad he took out a clean white handkerchief and dropped his load in it as I churned his cum out. Naturally that caused me to shoot into the urinal. When we finished adjusting our clothes, he asked for my phone number. I told him I didn't live around there and was a student. He insisted he wanted a phone number. I wasn't thinking and gave him my dorm's number. I was distracted, still trying to process what I'd just done with a complete stranger in a public toilet.

"I was surprised when he called the dorm phone next fall. Afraid others would find out what I'd done, I gave him my cell phone number, again without thinking what I was doing. At first, he just wanted to have telephone sex, which was okay when my roommate was out. Then he suggested we get together in a store after it was closed. I stalled him for a while, but he was very persuasive. He managed a small hardware store near campus and it had a cot in the office. Since that time, I find the smell of machine oil on metal a sexual turn on.

"For most of two years he sucked me off. He was an incredible cock sucker, I'm hard just thinking about his wonderful abilities. I'd cum two or three times while he took care of himself with his hand, shooting into a handkerchief. Then abruptly he said he had family trouble and no time for me, we said goodbye and that was that. I liked him; he sucked me off the best I've known. He would anticipate what I was feeling before I got there and knew how to make it last. I could cum right now, just thinking about how deliciously he got me off.

"But I didn't love him or feel he loved me. I was young, naïve and let him use me. I think we were a no strings attached convenience for each other. He had to have a wife and kids, and I was very serious about my studies. That is my story, is it what you wanted to hear?"

"Did he fuck you?"

"He wanted to, but I wasn't ready for that. The truth is I was conflicted about receiving his excellent blow jobs. I was still figuring out whom I was and if what I was doing was acceptable to my evolving college informed values."

"Did you let him screw you?"

"Yes, one night about two years into seeing him once a week, he was a little drunk and oh so needy. He was begging me more than usual. Finally, I thought what the hell let's see what the hype's all about. Truth is I was mostly ambivalent, and in the end yielded just to make the old guy happy. To answer your question, I'm not proud of it but I let him take me in the ass."

"Did it hurt?"

"No not at all, he sucked my toes and then rimmed me. It was my first time getting my toes shrimped and then he rimmed me for an extra-long time. His tongue wouldn't stop moving and went in deep loosening me. He got me so wet his cock just slid in."

"Mm, very interesting, yes very interesting indeed."

"When you give yourself to someone that way, it is a big deal. Afterward, it felt like we had made a commitment to each other, I gave him something special I'd never have again. At least that's how I thought about it. Is that what you wanted to know?"

"So, did you feel bad afterwards?"

"Yes, right after he fucked me he stopped having time for me. I felt maybe once he had had his way, I lost my allure and became just another notch on his belt. Just when I could have used some reassurance about what we did, if maybe it even meant something, he dumped me. It didn't help I was still sorting myself out about identity."

"At school the boys used to say, 'FFFF, find them, feel them up, fuck them, and forget them.'"

"For me, it's nicer to take my Hassid at his word. Pressing family matters took all his free time. I like to think we were both ready to move on anyway. To be honest, I wish I'd saved my virginity until I was ready to give it to someone special who would have appreciated it and cared about what it meant."

"Hind sight is always, you know."

"I'd almost forgotten him, until a gesture of yours brought him to mind."

"Did your deflowerer have a name? Here let me put out the tea service and things. Mm, these sticky bun honey cakes look scrumptious."

"Moshe, if I remember right? The hardware store is long gone. It has been years since I gave him any thought. Funny thing, it seemed to rain more often than not whenever he and I got together. I guess that was some kind of omen."

"What was his last name?"

"Levy, it's a common Jewish sir name, same as yours. Why? Wait, don't tell me what that look on your face says. I don't want to hear it."

"I discovered my father likes alcohol beyond a little ceremonial sweet wine. On our last father and son heart to heart talk, I brought a bottle of strong schnapps, his favorite kind. After he was lit up pretty good I asked him if he had ever done it with a man. He put his hand on my thigh and started kneading. I had to move across the room I got hard."

"I don't like where this is going. You sure you want to share this?"

"He said when he was very young and innocent an old lecherous goy seduced him. But they only did it one time. My sperm donor said it was wrong, he felt ashamed after, so never did anything like that again. He advised me to never try same-sex sex because it is *trey*."

"Sounds like what a father would tell his son."

"I've caught him in lies before. When he was even drunker, I asked him to describe this much older goy seducer of young Yeshiva boys, so I'd know what to lookout for. It seems the goy guy had scares on his lower abdomen from being mugged. This old goy guy was named, wait for it -- Evan."

"Can't be, no, he was at least ten years older than me. Damn, you must hate me?"

"How could I hate *you*? On the contrary, it helps me understand why you were so protective of me rushing into anal sex."

"I feel sorry for your troubles, and now this. Is there anything I can do to help?"

"In Psych-101 we learned about the Oedipal and Electra complexes. What is the name for the complex where your first lover's first lover was your father? I can't be the originator, can I?"

"I don't know? But if I were you, I wouldn't dwell on it. Don't make what happened long ago into a life defining Greek tragedy."

"I hear you, but it feels important."

"What happened was by happenstance long ago. Move on, don't get stuck."

"If you had known I was Moshe Levy's son when we met would you have had sex with me?

"No, I wouldn't, and you know me better than to ask."

"Would you have just left me alone like my sisters?"

"I couldn't have done that; I'd have driven you home or waited with you for your sisters."

"My life is such a mess these days, I need someone to blame."

"Blame never solved anything."

"I brought the strong schnapps and asked the questions, so finding out about you and my father must be on me. I'm guilty again."

"It happened; move beyond it. I doubt finding fault is making you feel better."

"This tea is excellent. But I've got to run; the woman looking after mother hates it when I'm late. Thank you for everything, I hope you understand why I can't contact you again. Just know I loved and love you and felt your love for me. You did not deserve to be hit or this Greek tragedy I brought you."

"We still can mend what we had."

"No, it's torn up, I destroyed it. You are much more than I deserved."

"Don't say that."

"Sorry, that's how it is. I have to atone for the wrong I've done you and my father has done before me."

"What we had was good. Here, let me pack up the honey buns for you to take."

"No thank you, I have to rush, bye."

I walked Shlomo to the front door, and gave him a heartfelt hug he returned stiffly. After closing the door behind him; I leaned back against it thinking. *Is it somehow possible, I am consciously culpable for having sex with father and son? They don't look alike. Moshe is almost as tall as I, speaks in a deep rough voice, when he talks at all. He isn't smart and doesn't wear glasses. Shlomo is shorter, speaks in a sweet lyric tenor tessitura, likes to showoff he is verbally astute and cognitively sharp and wears thick glasses. Thinking harder I had to admit there were subtle similarities when they climax, could that unconsciously be why I'd been putting off teaching Shlomo oral sex? Ugh, enough ruminating, I'll take the advice I gave him; there is no profit dwelling on what has happened if there is no lesson to learn. Since he refuses my help, I won't think further on the subject.*

Yom Kipper

Wrung out exhausted after a long hard successful day at work. I arrived home to find my telephone landline ringing. "Hello?"

"Is this 707-485-2882?"

"Who is calling?"

"I'm attempting to reach Evan Burke, are you Mr. Burke?"

"Who is speaking?"

"I'm Rabbi Abramowitz, trying to contact Mr. Burke about an important matter. Can you take a message?"

"I'm Evan, how did you get my private number?"

"I went through Shlomo Levy's school backpack and your number is in his contacts book. I'm calling all the names to seek help for him."

"What happened, is he all right?"

"He's in jail accused of murdering his mother. He won't talk to anyone, including me."

"Does he have a good lawyer?"

"His court appointed legal defense seems, how should I put this? Uh well, not up to the task. Excuse me for saying, he looks like a burned-out hulk. Because of the nature of this case none of the lawyers in our community will represent Shlomo. He may be sent to prison for life and he and his public defender won't talk to me."

"Do you think he did it?"

"*Absolutely not,* I've known him since he was nine days old; he is no killer. He loved his mother."

"Hold on let me get something to write on … okay give me the information my lawyers will need to get started?"

I walked through the offices of Reilly and associates; Napolitano, Friedberg, Zapata, Washington, and Chang as if I owned the firm. I don't, but I do own the building that houses them. Without waiting to be announced I entered my old high school classmate's office. "Liam, what can you tell me about the Levy case thus far?"

"Hey Evan nice to see you too, since you want to cut to the chase, this is not a case for us. Sorry, I'll have to turn you down old track chum. Why don't you use your own legal guys they're good?"

"They are real-estate lawyers. Why are you rejecting me, I always passed you the winning baton without dropping it in high school? As memory serves me I've gone to the mat for you on more than one occasion since then."

"You know my firm's reputation, we never lose a case and this one is iffy at best."

"I know you guys have won more challenging circumstantial cases than this. There are no witnesses or motive to talk about."

"If the local media gets hold of it … well let's just say nobody likes a mother murdered by her son on the local TV news during dinner. And especially if they are religious or vaguely religious or just happen to have a mother they like."

"Hold on, bring me up to speed. What have you found out so far?"

"As you please my dear landlord, Mr. Levy comes home to find his mother dead and the woman Mrs. Gold, who he pays a pittance to stay with her while he works part time, gone. Instead of calling 911, he calls his Rabbi to say Mrs. Gold is missing and oh by the way my mother's dead.

"This Rabbi Abramowitz tells him don't panic, he will take care of everything, and calls a Hasidic physician to go sign a death certificate. The doctor's answering service couldn't find the Hassidic practitioner so sent a physician just starting practice. As it turned out he was the only one available on short notice, but not Jewish or aware of Jewish traditions. The new doctor sees unexplained marks and bruises on the dead woman's body and refuses to sign the death certificate without an autopsy. An argument ensues with the Rabbi and mortician, who are now present to collect the body but require a death certificate to do so. Feeling threatened the physician calls the police. The first police on the scene see a distraught Mr. Levy and calls for supervision and when a Sergeant arrives she calls the medical examiner's office. They had a van nearby and came quickly to take the body to the morgue. As usual autopsies are backed up into the distant future.

"So, the Rabbi calls a Hasidic lawyer who immediately files papers to get the body released. He is thwarted and starts suing everyone in sight because Jewish dead are supposed to be buried by sundown and under no circumstances do they allow autopsies. Mrs. Gold is still missing, Mr. Levy is in custody for questioning but not talking to anyone so he is held on assorted charges mainly related to contempt of court, and basically that's the long and short of it.

"If Mr. Levy was talking, the DA might offer him a very sweet plea deal to avoid negative publicity, bad feelings with the Hassidic community and save everyone lots of time and money. But he is not talking, so no plea deals for him. What you need is a good Hassidic law firm. I'll have my office manager recommend some."

"I know you; you love a fight Liam Reilly. Over the years, we've had more than a few ourselves. Why won't you take my case as a favor for an old track and field high school relay team buddy?"

"Why, let's see why; none of my people have Hassidic cultural competence, there is already a Hassidic civil case tied to this criminal matter, on a slow news day this case could garner way too much negative publicity for me to get an impartial jury, and to tell the truth Evan, it feels icky to me. Just why didn't he call 911 as soon as he discovered his mother's body?"

"I know Shlomo Levy, he is no killer. Tell you what, we have an excellent Hassidic lawyer in my legal department, I could loan him to you for Hassidim oversight avoidance. But I want him back, he's good."

"Why didn't Mr. Levy call 911?"

"The Hassidim have issues with non-Jewish authority. It comes from thousands of years of Jewish persecution at the hands of non-Jews, not calling 911 was appropriate. Calling his Rabbi first was consistent with the authority he was taught to trust."

"Just between us, you are looking at spending a lot of green on legal fees whoever takes this case. I can't even begin to estimate the number of billable hours for such a high-profile mother murder with an uncommunicative defendant."

"Money is not a problem. Tell you what, how about I offer you a special reward above and beyond your usual fees for clearing Mr. Levy's name?"

"I'm listening."

"It is clear your firm needs more room, you guys are bursting this office suite at the seams. Does the Fire Department know about your gross overcrowding?"

"Play nice Evan."

"You get Shlomo cleared and his record expunged and I'll move whichever of your neighbors you say to expand your office space to legal occupancy, and I'll pay for the renovations, how about it?"

"Huh, it's a tempting offer, but I don't know? I'd have to clear it with my associates. Will you suck my dick as part of the deal?"

"No, we don't have that kind of friendship, and never did. But if you insist I could find someone who would be up to that little task, but only if you win this case."

"That's not important, and I'm not that little. You never saw it hard; I'm grower not a shower. What about the rent increase for expanding my office suite?"

"For the remainder of your lease no rent increase and we will negotiate the next lease using the lowest per square foot rate for this area. You won't get a better offer anywhere; otherwise expect a hefty rent increase for this grossly overcrowded space in two years. Oh, you'll need a Hassid investigator."

"You'll put all that in writing?"

"No problem."

"Cleared one way or another, we can more than likely do that. But expunged record will be another matter and possibly a lot of bother and much more cash."

"Without a Hassidic investigator, no one will talk to you."

"I heard you the first time. Don't worry I know a retired cop who is a private detective. We've worked with her before, she's Hassidic, and very thorough. I'll talk to her; most likely she'll be on board for this case."

"How soon can you get Mr. Levy bailed out of jail?"

"There is no bail if you kill your mother. But you could visit him while he's locked up; see if he is being treated fairly and needs anything. I'll have my people make sure he is not abused in there. Tell him it will save you mucho big bucks if he talks to my lawyers."

"When can you start working on this?"

"When do I get the written agreement to expand my office no rent increase and the loan of your Hassidic lawyer?"

"How's one hour or less, delivered by hand by him?"

"Then we start working as soon as your ass goes through that door."

"Goodbye and thank you."

I had never given the word incarceration much thought beyond it was the consequence of breaking rules or bad behavior and probably wasn't very nice but disserved. Standing in the visitor's line outside the entrance to the jail I though *this is true democracy. Rich and poor, celebrity or not we are all equal waiting with mixed anticipation to see our imprisoned loved one.* Then after passing through a metal detector, I was relieved of my 24K gold pen and matching money clip, keys, pocket change and solid gold Rolex watch. Then I was herded with the other visitors into a ten by ten foot, painted concrete-block pen. We were facing a ceiling to floor wall of thick greasy grimy dirt encrusted steel bars. Suddenly without warning another wall of steel bars behind us loudly slammed down then noisily locked. At that moment, I fully understood what the loss of freedom meant from a sudden claustrophobic bitter churning in the pit of my stomach. After a very long interval with no exits available the wall of steel bars in front of us was unlocked and slowly rose. Then our group was escorted to the visitor's room by sullen looking uniformed guards of both genders.

The captain of guards instructed us to find seats, keep our hands visible, and left the room. Moments later guards were back escorting prisoners wearing black and white striped baggy coveralls. Shlomo was the last in line; his head bowed looking at his shuffling shoes. His face was the embodiment of misery.

"Hi, do you need anything I am allowed to get you?"

Looking up after being roughly pushed into a seat across from me by a burly guard, Shlomo shook his head no.

"Are you all right, you getting kosher meals?"

Shlomo forlornly shook his head yes.

"I've got a problem only you can help me with. Don't give me that look, please say 'what?'"

Shlomo defiantly made fierce eye contact and vigorously shook his head no.

"Have it your way. I am out of here. You can expect to live the rest of your life in a place like this. Goodbye and good luck to you." With that said I pushed back and started to stand.

Eyes suddenly alarmed, his voice hoarse from disuse Shlomo said, "Wait, don't go. Problem, what can I do from here?"

"Your legal team can't find Mrs. Gold, and they need to talk with her. Why did you stop talking?"

"Everyone thinks I killed my mother, I didn't. When I was speaking people always asked one way or another, over and over, 'how could you kill your own mother?' When I stopped talking they stopped asking."

"I never thought that, nor does Rabbi Abramowitz."

"Did my mother get a proper burial?"

"The Rabbi is working on it. Very soon I hope. Where is Mrs. Gold?"

"I have been sitting Shiva as best I can in this place. I've been praying she was finally laid to rest."

"Mrs. Gold?"

"I have an address book in my school book bag, if it hasn't already been thrown away. Under Mrs. Gold's name there are several telephone numbers, they are for her daughters, the one with the Florida address is where she should be. She always goes there after Yom Kipper."

"Why do you think your belongings will be thrown away?"

"I was served an eviction notice here in jail. If the back rent isn't paid all my family's things will be carted off by the Sanitation Department. Then if uncollected they will be thrown into a landfill after thirty days."

"Does your legal team know about this?"

"No, no time, the Marshall's eviction is set for 7:30 tomorrow morning. It's too late for everything. Nothing matters anymore."

"Trust me, my tenants showed me how to block an eviction on short notice. But if that apartment holds bad memories for you, I could have your family's possessions put in storage until you are out of jail."

"*Get over yourself Evan*; I'm never going to be free again. The cops made that very clear."

"Help me out here, visiting hour is not really an hour in this place, back rent or storage, which?"

"Storage would be cheaper and easier in the long run, and give my sisters a chance to go through their stuff. That apartment was bad luck from the day my father rented it."

"Where is your father in this?"

"As usual the letch is among the missing."

"Geez, what was that awful noise?"

"Visiting hour is over, you have to go. Thank you for caring so much and coming, it means more than you can know."

"Please talk to your legal team; they are trying to get the charges dropped before there is a trail so your record can be clean. Don't make this harder than it has to be. Bye … okay I'm going, don't push me Officer Beal, you *don't* know who you are manhandling."

Less than a week after my jail visit, Liam Reilly, Esquire, stuck his head in my open office door, and said, "Knock, knock."

"Hey don't stand on ceremony, come right in and pull up a chair. Just a sec, let me save this document. So, to what do I owe this unscheduled interruption in my busy work day? Would you like some coffee or tea or other refreshment?"

"No thanks to a beverage, I've come to collect my reward. Are your architects on this floor or do you keep them elsewhere?" This was said as he flopped down in one of the soft taupe leather clients' chairs facing my father's large antique teakwood desk.

"Before we talk reward, tell me results."

With a self-satisfied broad smile, lightly grasping the chair arms, Liam tossed his head back in triumph. "If you have the time I have the requested outcome."

"I'll make the time. Talk to me old high school track star."

"I was a star wasn't I; hell, I'm still a star! Okay, ready or not here goes. We had Mrs. Levy's autopsy expedited by threatening the City with the biggest ever multibillion dollar law suit. She was suffocated; the official cause of death is murder. However, the unexplained marks and bruises on her body are consistent with her terminal illness.

"From contacts in the community the Hassidic investigator discovered where Mrs. Gold was and flew down to Orlando, Florida and interviewed her. Mrs. Levy was alive the last time Mrs. Gold saw her. The reason Mrs. Gold wasn't present when Mr. Levy returned home was his sisters arrived unexpectedly and told her they would take over their mother's care. They said Mrs. Gold should go home and prepare for her Florida trip. They all know each other since the sisters were children.

"When local police telephoned the sisters at their school to inform them their mother's death and their brother was under suspicion of murder, both said they hadn't been to the City since before the Jewish High Holidays. They were also positive their brother had nothing to do with their mother's death. As a matter of formality our police had the University police bring the sisters in to sign statements validating what they had said over the telephone. During their face to face with police the sisters appeared anxious and weren't so sure their brother was innocent after all. Based on that information and extensive unresponsive questioning, Shlomo Levy was held over pending further investigation and probable indictment for murder.

"My paralegal picked up on the girls' inconsistent statements, and checked the CCTV at the highway toll booths and the tunnel. Sure enough she found images of the Levy girls driving to the City and then immediately returning to school after an extremely short visit the day their mother died.

"What sealed the sisters' fate was Mrs. Gold is good at what she does. Mrs. Levy's physician instructed Mrs. Gold; her patient could easily choke to death on her own saliva, and needed to be watched closely."

"For safety sake Mrs. Gold put a baby video monitor on top of Mrs. Levy's dresser. She put it out of sight behind some framed photos, while dusting, so Mrs. Levy wouldn't feel uncomfortable being constantly watched. With the monitor, Mrs. Gold could use the bathroom or answer the door all the while keeping an eye on Mrs. Levy. But Mrs. Gold forgot to take her video monitor when the sisters made their surprise visit and hustled her away. When my people went to find the baby monitor, your folks had moved the contents of the Levy apartment into storage. But when asked one of your workers found the monitor, no problem. Unfortunately, the audio function was broken.

"I offered the District Attorney what we found, including a copy of the video recording showing the murder sans audio. It is horrific to watch; it shows Mrs. Levy awake and aware even feebly protesting. Terror was in her eyes at what her daughters told her they were about to do. She was clearly not ready to die but too incapacitated to defend herself. The video shows the daughters remove the pillow from behind their mother's head. Then each girl held one side of the pillow over their mother's face and pushed down, smothering her as she thrashed about. When their mother stopped moving they replaced the pillow back under her head. Then they shook hands, hugged and quickly left the room. In return for the evidence, Shlomo goes free and his record is expunged. Now where do you keep your architects?"

"When does Shlomo get out of jail?"

"One hour ago, he was met outside the jail by his Rabbi and some morticians. They went to the coroner's office to collect his mother's remains. The morticians will wash and box the body and a burial will be held at two o'clock this afternoon at Beth Israel Cemetery Section K. I'll send you an invoice, the total cost is a lot less than expected. Again, where can I find your architects?"

"Hold on a minute, if I move one of your neighbors to expand your current office, depending on other spaces available for them and length of negotiations, it could take six months to a year before the architects can go to work. However, I have a suite even larger than you need, on a higher floor in this building, it's vacant. Or I can offer you either of two nice suites the right size for your present needs, available very soon in a building nearby. You can have the deal we agreed to on any one of these office spaces, or you can wait to stay where you are. What do you like?"

"Can I see the suite upstairs, and have it at my old rent?"

"Sure, you earned it, let's go check it out. The views up there are great."

Commitment

I parked off the road, at the back of a short row of cars lined up behind a black hearse. A small burial service across the way was just dispersing when I exited my car and stood surveying the tranquil verdant interment place. I drew a deep breath of chilly fall scented air and said a silent prayer asking for Mrs. Levy to rest in peace. As the mourners straggled off after the service, I spotted Shlomo talking with a Rabbi at the grave side. When Shlomo noticed me watching, he disengaged and walked over. He had lost a lot of weight his clothes didn't fit.

"Shalom, I am sorry for your loss. Can I offer you a ride?"

"Hello Evan, you missed the service, thank you for coming anyway."

"I was sent to the wrong place, this isn't section K, and then I had trouble finding the right section. Want a ride home?"

"Thanks, but I longer have a home as you are aware."

"Then make my home yours, no strings attached."

"Generous as always, but I can't accept your offer. This homeless orphan jailbird with no prospects still has a little pride. Don't worry I learned how to survive on the street from the fellows in jail."

"How will you do that?"

"I'll collect discarded cans and bottles to redeem for their deposits. First, I will need to appropriate a shopping cart to carry them. The quantities necessary to survive in my new profession *can collector or canner* for short, requires a large cart."

"Are you sure that's what you want? The Hassidim is known for taking care of their own."

"Mm well yes, Rabbi Abramowitz offered to let me sleep on his living room sofa until something more permanent can be worked out. I've declined the offer. He's got a house full of noisy foster children and my nerves are frayed."

"Surely you have other prospects?"

"Not really, my community will forever associate my name with my mother's murder. Somehow fake news trumps real facts. Who would let their daughter marry someone accused of matricide?"

"Times and people change, nothing is constant. You told me in jail you'd never be a free man, and here you are. I think we should celebrate."

"Sorry, I'm not in a party mood."

"You have to eat you lost weight."

"Evan I never thought of you as being of the world, you know our laws and customs too well to be an outsider and yet you are not one of the chosen people."

Not sure where this was going I focused on the known. "I usually like what catches my attention, that's why I speak Yiddish and Pennsylvania Dutch."

"I don't get why you bother? I know our life is insanely difficult, I was born into it. From what I've read the Amish and Mennonites don't have it much better."

"One of my heroes is Moses. He spent a big portion of our old testament, fighting with God, while leading his people to the Promised Land and then wasn't allowed in."

Shlomo let his defensive shield slip, and with searching eye contact exposed I'd hit something. "Mm yes you identify with Moses; the orphan baby in the reed boat who wouldn't give back his foreskin. Before I was taken to the police station in handcuffs, then to jail in handcuffs and back and forth to court manacled hand and foot, I had been taught to be afraid of the outside world. With you I learned to thrive in it, even dock dicks and God didn't strike me dead."

"Yahweh gets points for that. Has your thinking about me changed since we talked on Rosh Hashanah?"

"No, you are still my special someone and the community wouldn't approve." This was spoken showing firm determination.

"Well I think a celebration is in order to mark an end to a grim episode. It doesn't have to be elaborate, but you'll feel better after some good food and drink."

Showing his old steadfastness Shlomo said, "I told you I have nothing to celebrate. My whole life I knew where I would lay my head to sleep, and when awake what was expected of me. Wait, wait just why am I burdening you with this? You must have spent a lot to get me out of jail? I don't know how I can ever repay you?"

"I don't expect repayment. Why did you decide your freedom was expensive?"

Shlomo looked at the horizon and then spoke evenly. "Those guys you sent don't buy their suits off the rack. I'm no expert but I know quality when I see it, I've been working part-time as a stock boy in a man's clothing shop. What can I do to express my gratitude?" The question spilled out of his pretty mouth, and was displayed frankly on an unguarded face.

I put a hand on his forearm. "Reilly is a friend from high school; we're used to exchanging favors. He billed me only for his expenses to get you cleared. In the grand scheme of things, it wasn't much."

"Still, I owe you and like to pay my debts."

"Do you remember when we first met and you were questioning my motives? I said being a Good Samaritan is its own reward. Trust me it's the gift giver that gets the better gift."

His face looked unsure, then serious, and then unsure again as he spoke softly. "Mm, yes I do remember you saying that. So then thank you for all your Good Samaritan help."

"You are more than welcome."

"Mm hmm, I'm not good with social cues; I'm afraid it's a deficit of my community. I wonder, isn't this where we shake hands and wish each other well and walk away in different directions? Am I correct about that? I think I am, so goodbye to you and thanks for everything. Have a great life, you deserve it," Shlomo turned about to walk away.

I increased my pressure on his forearm, holding him in place. "Wait, don't go, we can fix what broke and move forward together side by side in the same direction."

Turning at the waist to face me, he suddenly looked down at the ground in frustration. "How is that possible, I struck out in anger and destroyed something I treasured?" Shlomo turned away again, and looked over at his mother's grave. His face was a grieving mask.

With my hand still holding his arm I turned him back to face me and spoke firmly. "Give us a chance. You've heard if a bone is broken, it is stronger at the break after mending. We can get beyond what happened and be better for trying."

His spirit returned in a rush and he defiantly met my gaze. "I know you; you are not a relationship kind of guy. I struck you because I wanted more than you were willing to give? How could you trust me not to be an ingrate and want too much again?"

"Don't know, I guess it is a risk I need to take. Or just maybe I've grown more democratic since then? We will need trust and patience to find out."

Resolutely holding my gaze and speaking confidently Shlomo said, "What metamorphosed your M.O. being a fulfilled single unit? Where is the lone wolf with no deep emotional commitments, the guy I used to know and love? You look just the same."

Rather than acknowledge the sarcasm, I reminded myself Shlomo just buried his mother and went through a lot of pain to get here. "Hanukkah is coming and will mark the one year anniversary of our meeting; I've had time to do a serious rethink about commitment."

"What I wonder prompted that, surely not me and my despicable family?"

Letting go of his arm, I took a step back breaking what was feeling like a brittle connection. "Since you ask; visiting you in jail did it. The meaning of the word incarceration became graphically defined when I was locked between two huge doors made of filth covered steel bars, and no exit. It triggered some deep solemn soul searching about you and me and what matters."

"Mm yes, I know that scary confinement. A shudder went through me just now when you mentioned the place I passed through this morning. When I was locked up and not speaking I discovered something about myself. I'm queer, before meeting you I was afraid to open that door. Now I'm okay with it, thank you for that." Shlomo's mood mollified as he spoke.

"Will your community accept you as gay?"

"You know they can't. My choice is live a lie like my perverted father or be out in the world like you. And how is your life going, Evan?"

"You told me to get over myself, remember?"

"I do, have you?"

For some reason I don't know, I felt this was it; the moment we reconnected or walked away in different directions, forever. "I'm working on it. Watching you suffering put me in touch with feelings I didn't realize ran so deep for you." With the hand arm physical connection broken, I moved closer to him.

The air between us lightened perceptibly, my old loving Shlomo showed his sweet face speaking candidly. "In spite of hitting you, I never once stopped loving you. You taught me joy, I never knew it before. Thank you for that." Then his mood darkened again and he gloomily said, "But right now I just buried my murdered mother. My hateful sisters won't be out of prison for decades, my father couldn't be bothered to show his face at his first wife's funeral, and today I was released from jail schooled to be a homeless canner. To tell the truth, I feel like badly damaged goods unworthy of being with you or anyone. Sad to say, pushing a shopping cart full of discarded drink containers is my destiny. I was wrong to allow myself high expectations when so many I saw in jail were born to their fate."

"Shlomo, you are who I want to be with. If you can accept me with my faults, I can accept yours."

"Even me as a secular Jew? You think you will still want me after everything that has happened, and with a haircut and shave?"

"Yes."

"Dressed like everyone else? As the Amish say, 'Dressed like the English.' Mm, I guess that means tweeds and ascots for me? It could be worse."

"Ha levity Levy, okay I'll go with it. Have you considered what you will wear under your tweeds; bikini or regular briefs or are you a boxers' kind of guy?"

"I find thongs interesting to look at, though I wonder if they are comfortable."

"What about G-strings? Actually, have you ever worn any undergarment that didn't have tassels hanging over the top of your pants?"

"No. But how complicated can colorful goy underpants be? I've seen you get in and out of them with ease. What's a G-string?"

"Imagine a much-abbreviated thong. Humor, trying to be funny, you *must* be feeling better."

"Nothing gets by you."

"What lightened your mood?"

"It occurs to me, I tried to end this conversation and walk out of your life minutes ago. But you won't let me, for the first time in a long time; I'm feeling a twinge of hope."

"Then this hasn't been a waste of time."

"Except I know you, I won't be able to turn you on wearing secular clothing. I wish I could."

"When we met, it was your attire that attracted me, then undressed I learned to know and love you. Secular or religious is your call. But for your information there are gay orthodox synagogues, they may dress differently than the Hassidim but the practice of faith is similar."

"Good to know, thanks. I'm not sure what I want to believe after recent events. Evan, don't change the subject, I'm really afraid you won't find me attractive dressed like the English." This was said sincerely with Shlomo's emotions showing close to the surface. So, he pulled out and blew his nose on a white handkerchief.

"I've gotten way beyond what you wear. For me the best part of being with you is more than the sex act, or the fun foreplay and tender lingering after-play touching and holding."

"I won't dress up to turn you on, that would feel wrong."

"After what you said about me and your father I've done a deep think about being turned on by costume. I no longer want or need that fetish for stimulation. Seeing you in a tux or wearing nothing at all turn me on."

"I wish I believed that, and could be sure I won't hit you again."

"What do you require?"

"I don't know? I guess I could cut off my hand to guarantee it will never strike you."

Spontaneously I grabbed his hands. Squeezing them I drew him closer. "Don't you dare cut off your hand; I love this hand and this other hand and everything attached to them. I don't require proof."

"Look you mean well. I just don't believe we can put Humpty Dumpty back together, I wish we could."

"Have I ever lied to you or done anything that wasn't in your best interest?"

"No, you have been generous to a fault. That's why what I did was unforgivable."

"Maybe the proof you require is to trust yourself enough to trust me. I believe we can get back to building a relationship and get beyond what happened."

"I don't know, trust is so intangible, what if like before I lose control without meaning to? I can't let that happen again."

"You need tangible, how about this; you strike me again and I break your arm. Then I drive you to the hospital, and sit with you while the broken bone is set."

"Mm sounds like over kill, you think it would work?"

"I don't know. But we'd have the time it takes to heal the break to find strategies and tactics to prevent future broken arms."

"Huh, so how many times are you prepared to break my arms until you realize I sometimes can't help myself? I already told you, I am damaged."

"We're all damaged, nobody's perfect. If we discover hitting is outside your range of control, there are psychotropic medications. They help people control what is beyond their reach. I'd like to try managing hitting without drugs first."

"Mm yes, deterrence times two *that just might work.*"

BEBOP WRITERS

Support for the Second World War on the home front affected every U.S. citizens in the Country's forty-eight States, only some more than others. Rationing was imposed to back the war effort. Most folks made their own soap with kitchen fat scraps and lye, because everything from gasoline to soap required ration coupons to be purchased, when available. Individual family Victory Gardens produced more than thirty percent of all vegetables and fruit consumed during the war. Due to the shared effort at home and abroad, the homeland *had* been attacked, the racially, ethnically, religiously and culturally diverse people of the United States were never more unified for nationalism's singular focus; defeat the fascists.

Ration book counterfeiting and black-market trade in impossible to find items, like automobile batteries or tires, were perpetrated by organized crime. The authorities used well-publicized arrests for ration fraud to maintain control over its citizens during this period of national anxiety. By periodically parading greedy rent gauging landlords or small time black-marketers before the press, the government encouraged the public direct their anger over wartime hardships at the homegrown enemy. The public's outrage directed at cheaters helped quell governmental fear of domestic insurrection.

To escape the anxiety created by regular air raid warning drills, official blackout window curtain inspections, constant domestic media war propaganda, and the ration shortages. Many people turned to the new exciting Bebop music for relief. Bebop Jazz was not as emotionally transparent as other popular music. Many listeners found Bebop cognitively invigorating if not challenging and it helped assuage fears with diversion. Real fears of aerial or naval bombardment or invasion or poison gas attack of the homeland were distracted with a good beat, modern harmony, and intricate melodic lines.

2.

Aaron Gingersnap and Jay Kirack were undergraduate English Majors and budding writers when they met at Columbia University in the City of New York. The two men enjoyed spending time discussing what they were reading, writing, and the ways of the world at war. But most importantly they enjoyed listening to Bebop music on twelve-inch acetate 78rpm phonograph records or from live radio broadcasts. They were so passionate about the new exciting Bebop Jazz music they dubbed themselves the Bebop Writers.

When they met, Aaron was secretly making an effort to become heterosexual, even though his natural inclinations lay elsewhere. In the 1940's it was a serious crime requiring imprisonment to *identify or be identified* as homosexual. It was also a diagnosable chronic mental disease that required lifelong commitment to a psychiatric hospital to protect the public from homosexual contagion. The outlandish Bible thumpers of that day considered nothing less than an eternity of suffering hellfire's damnation adequate for those who engaged in same sex love.

It was only natural the dreaded homosexual contagion with its medical-legal-religious consequences was discussed by the two Bebop writers. Often it was discussed in the context of famous artists publicly shamed to suicide. The young writer's conclusion was the morality police were stifling creative voices and thwarting the art world's vitality.

One late night while listening to music and drinking alcohol to excess, Aaron confessed his avid wish to become heterosexual in spite of his natural desires elsewhere. Jay offered to help him anyway he could. Soon Aaron's trials and tribulations attempting to find a heterosexual life also became a regular topic for the two novice writer's late night music, boozy, bull-sessions.

Between high school and college Jay took two years off and worked as a merchant seaman. He knew intimately how sailors nurtured each other sexually on long lonely sea voyages. The only known alternative was not viable. At that time, it was a well-known fact that masturbation caused blindness and insanity.

Aaron often expounded on his many attempts at becoming a heterosexual. Jay told Aaron he'd rather provide him an emergency same sex outlet, rather than lose Aaron to the morals-vice police. Since Jay was often sleeping with a few different females at Columbia his masculinity was secure enough to allow for Aaron's slips while on his heterosexual quest.

Their idea was for Jay's abundant heterosexuality to rub off on Aaron by close association and when necessary ejaculate ingestion. Nevertheless, Jay only engaged in sex with Aaron as preventive therapy, for example when Aaron was tempted to cruise Mafia owned dangerous gay bars or to explore public parks for sexual encounters with men after midnight.

Another sure way to get Jay's preventive sex therapy aroused was for Aaron to talk about his observations of public toilet sex. He'd observed undercover police entrapment and been told by fellow travelers of unscrupulous persons engaged in blackmail and thuggery against innocent citizens with no other sexual outlet. Aaron reported what he'd read written on public bathroom walls about violent queer bashings, and he found in yellow tabloids about murders where the perpetrators got off free using a homosexual panic defense and so the victims were blamed for their own murder.

For his part, Jay viewed Aaron as a promising poet of great significance. So, he felt an obligation to keep Aaron away from homosexual contagion, even though he thought the idea was a hoax and enjoyed challenging authority. It probably never occurred to Jay; Aaron was in love with him. During that time the concept of romance between two men or two women was considered unnatural so impossible.

3.

Willis Brown became a mutual friend and classmate of Aaron and Jay when he registered late at Columbia University as an English major. He was also an aspiring writer and loved Bebop music almost as much as getting high. He was the precocious progeny of a wealthy Midwestern family, and had already graduated Harvard University's medical school. Willis had more than adequate discretionary funds to purchase the best legal and illicit drugs, in quantities large enough to share with his often financially challenged classmates. Willis like Jay was a few years older than Aaron but was taking the same classes.

The three English majors had common interests for long if not always meaningful philosophical conversations while getting high listening to the latest Bebop recordings. Willis like Aaron wanted to be heterosexual in spite of his natural disposition, but initially he kept that a secret from his friends.

Willis Brown had the resources to live alone off campus. He had an apartment down in Greenwich Village where he was often left to his own resources. He secretly experimented with identifying as bisexual; a new concept put forth by radical social scientists challenging the traditional medical, legal, and theological establishment's inflexible gloom to doom dogmas. But Willis became frightened during a disastrous same sex encounter with a rough-trade Marine Corporal on leave from the War.

Badly beaten during rough sex and emotionally devastated from trying something new, Willis spoke to Aaron in confidence. "How can I save myself from the dangers of bisexuality?" Staunching a bloody nose, he said, "I found out first hand for safety sake being bisexual is no better than being queer. A guy could get killed just trying to get a little physical relief."

After swearing Willis to secrecy, Aaron told him about the ongoing heterosexual conversion help he received from Jay. Although alcohol, drugs, music, and then sex were important for the three budding Bebop writers, their intellectual growth and development as writers were the stated heartfelt purpose for their irregular meetings.

4.

At the start of 1944, nineteen-year-old Lucas Carmel transferred to Columbia University from the University of Michigan as a second semester freshmen. He aspired to be a writer, was well read, intellectually astute, imaginative and handsome with a charismatic personality. He filled any room he entered with a magnetic presence that drew strangers to him. Lucas met Aaron while living in the same Columbia dormitory from their mutual love of the recordings of Franz Liszt's music. Liszt was the originator of the Tone Poem musical form, which both budding poetry writers were enthralled with. Aaron introduced Lucas to the New York Bebop music scene, and he was immediately captivated by the new exciting music.

Lucas was taking a class with one of Jay's girlfriends and they met through her. When Jay and Aaron introduced their friend Willis to Lucas, the two already knew each other from back in the Middle West, and were happy to renew their acquaintance.

Straightaway Lucas, the youngest of the group, became a catalyst that energized and empowered the four nascent authors. Individually each man showed great but dissimilar talent for using the written word to express ideas and emotions that were far out of the literary main stream. Just as Bebop music was far beyond its day's popular music norm. The four writers weren't in competition with each other, but rather could be objectively critical and at the same time learned from each other's point of view, technique, and style.

Soon Lucas was the adhesive that held, and then drove the group to regular productive meetings. Other Columbia student writers drifted into and out of the group, but the original four remained constant. They operated like Bebop jazz groups in after hour's jam sessions. They learned by hearing each other's solo work then discussed it in ensemble. The new students to the group never figured out how to mesh with the insights of the well-coordinated if far-out original quartet.

Shortly after arriving at Columbia University, Lucas found a beautiful girlfriend at Barnard, Columbia's Women's College. Megan Scone was his exact age and temperament and they enjoyed holding hands, cuddling and in time became intimates. When Lucas discovered the dangers homosexuals faced in New York, like Jay, he too unobtrusively allowed one sided sex with Aaron or Willis to keep them out of the murky dangerous underworld of perverts and all its dire consequences. To Lucas it was a small charity to allow a friend to go down on him, rather than lose that friend to police brutes, blackmailers, or sadistic queer bashers.

Lucas wasn't as secure in his masculinity as Jay, but was not struggling like Aaron and Willis. Nevertheless, Lucas had unresolved sexuality issues caused by a mentor. Still, his self-doubts did not block him from jerking Aaron or Willis off while they were blowing him. To his mind, it was an unasked for quirky therapeutic act of kindness to keep them safe.

5.

After completing his freshman year at Columbia and beginning his sophomore with a summer course. Lucas Carmel discovered his stalker, Dylan Krumburn, had followed him to New York. Back in the Middle West, Dylan had been Lucas's first Assistant Boy Scout Troop Leader, and later became his Boy Scout Master. After the Boy Scouts Dylan became an intellectual guide recommending and often giving books for Lucas to read and discuss with him. Dylan encouraged Lucas's creative writing, and regularly gave him constructive feedback and high praise.

Through smooth fast talking Dylan was given parental permission to be Lucas' mentor. Lucas did not object although part of him felt he should. But it wasn't in his nature to rebel against his strict parent's wishes. Dylan's obsession with Lucas caused confusion and even occasional alarm. On the one hand Lucas enjoyed the material and intellectual attention from the older man. On the other hand, with some trepidation he suspected Dylan wanted him sexually. His remedy was to block out impure thoughts when they popped up. Lucas decided he would address his fears if Dylan ever tried to put hands on him in a bad way. Otherwise he'd ignore the fears.

By 1944, Dylan's most recent employment had been as a Humanities professor at The American Midwestern University. But he had inherited wealth, so could resign his full professorship to follow Lucas to the University of Michigan. Then after searching the Country, he turned up in New York in pursuit of his fixation, Lucas.

Once they were brought up to speed about stalker Dylan, Aaron and Willis tried to run interference for Lucas. At that point Lucas was still nineteen and Dylan was forty years old. The other three Bebop writers were in their twenties. All four younger men thought Dylan a dirty old man for pestering Lucas. They often made mean jokes about him among themselves.

Ostensibly to protect Lucas, Aaron and Willis individually began regular mutually active oral sexual relations with Dylan. The three men were to greater or lesser degrees in love with Lucas. It was not a reach to use each other as sexual substitutes. However, it was done at the risk of slowing Aaron and Willis' heterosexual conversion. They soon discovered Dylan was crazy; obsessed beyond reason with Lucas. They had to listen to him go on and on about his Lucas lust.

Since Lucas refused to have anything to do with Dylan. Dylan temporarily settled for sexual favors from Aaron, who found he could avidly love more than one man at a time while striving to be straight. And Willis who was stoned more often than not, consequently not overly discerning when in the mood for and during drug distracted sex. Too soon the diversionary tactic lost power in the face of Dylan's compulsion to possess Lucas.

6.

To help Lucas get away from his stalker, Jay devised a scheme for the two of them to work as merchant seamen on an intercontinental cargo ship. Using previous experience, he handled the paperwork. The stated goal was to see German occupied Paris a free city. Their plan was also to retrace the steps of Arthur Rimbaud, one of their literary idols, who was shot by his lover Paul Verlaine.

Unfortunately, the four Columbia University fledgling authors drank too much alcohol during a farewell soirée the night before the working ocean voyage. When Jay and Lucas arrived at the ship's dock, along with Aaron and Willis helping carry their luggage, and to wave goodbye loudly wishing them bon voyage. The ship had sailed. The four friends disheartened, and badly hung over, wandered around Manhattan dragging baggage, going in and out of movie theaters, hydrating and consuming junk food. Aaron and then Willis had previous commitments that evening, but agreed to carry the luggage back up to Columbia.

By night fall, back up on Broadway and 116th Street Jay and Lucas had an impromptu dinner at the *Greasy Spoon*, a favorite eatery in their price range. Then they were drawn to another student hangout across from the University and began where they had left off the night before, consuming alcohol to excess. After several hours of elbow bending chit chat, and already three sheets to the wind, Jay told Lucas in strictest confidence the year before after his Columbia football scholarship ran out he joined the Navy. But he only stayed two days, before demanding to be released from his enlistment. He was given an immediate psychiatric discharge.

Jay explained he thought the Navy would be like his collegial experience in the merchant marine. He believed his prior experience at sea would help win the war. But it wasn't what he expected, they kept yelling at him and making him do stupid repetitive even ridiculous drills and they wouldn't leave him alone, so he quit. He gave this information on the off-chance Lucas was thinking of joining the Navy after their day's failed attempt to be merchant seamen. Jay felt guilty having built up their hopes and then missing the boat.

At midnight, feeling bad he had disclosed too much personal information, Jay abruptly said, "Got to go, see yah later," and left the saloon's huge ceiling fans, and walked out into the sweltering humid heat of the August night. Jay cut through campus on his way from Broadway to a girlfriend's apartment on Amsterdam Avenue. In front of Alma Mater's statue on campus walk, Jay ran into Dylan Krumburn going in the opposite direction. After a nodded greeting, "Have you seen Lucas tonight?"

Drunk and embarrassed at disclosing his wartime psychiatric discharge, without thinking Jay pointed and sputtered. "He's at our hangout."

Lucas was morosely sitting at the bar, pondering what Jay said before leaving. If Lucas had been asked which Bebop writer might have a psychiatric history his mind would have gone first to Willis' heavy drug and alcohol use and sexual identity confusion, then to Aaron's almost constant need for sex with men and women, and whose mother was in a psychiatric institution. He would not have picked Jay.

The nineteen-year-old Lucas brooded *what could it mean for Jay's future?* Of the four Jay seemed the best put together physically and mentally and the most down to earth and sane by 1944 standards. His writing was the least far-out and most accessible of the Bebopper four. Lucas wondered, *what does it say about mine and my other friends' sanity if Jay is the crazy one?*

Finding Lucas sitting alone brooding, Dylan climbed on the bar stool next to him. "Can I buy you a drink?"

Lucas ignored Dylan. So, he signaled the bartender and had them both served strong libations until two AM. "We are both drunk and need some air. Come on let's go for a walk."

Lucas hadn't spoken or acknowledged Dylan from when he sat down, but he drank the drinks the barman brought. Lucas left the saloon with Dylan out of habit; he was used to doing what Dylan said since his early Boy Scout days. They walked over to Riverside Park and 115th Street, no one was around. Both men lay on the grass for relief from the incessant dense humid heat, and gazed up at the moon in a cloudless star filled sky. Slowly at first Lucas realized Morpheus was gently nudging him into slumber.

The summer of 1944 was hotter and more humid than usual for a New York City heat wave. People often slept out on their apartment's fire escape or building's roof and even in public parks to get respite from the stuffy thick indoor air. It wasn't unusual for two men, like Lucas and Dylan, to lie on the grass in Riverside Park at two in the morning seeking heat relief.

Dylan ruminated about beautiful Lucas' successes and his contribution. It didn't make sense that Lucas could be sexual with a group of recent New York friends, and ignore Dylan's burning desire to consummate their undeclared love. Rage suddenly flared in him as he tried to reconcile his burning hot lust for the boy, with Lucas' cruel behavior ignoring him. He had given Lucas his time and energy and nurturance to success in the Midwest and now in New York the boy became a hoity-toity snob? Dylan lost control; something snapped in his alcohol addled brain.

Without warning Dylan rolled on top of and then had his hands and mouth all over Lucas' struggling body. When his hands were finally captured and stilled by Lucas, Dylan pleaded his voice dripping with lust. "Please, please let me make love to you. The stars need us joined as one."

Inebriated slurring Lucas protested. "No, no I don't want that. Stop touching me. Get off me!" Lucas twisted his body and tried to push Dylan off, but to no avail.

"I have loved you from the first time I saw you, an awkward eleven-year-old Tenderfoot Scout. Stop twisting."

"No, what are you doing?"

"Our love is predestined by the Greek Gods on Mount Olympus. Don't you understand? That is why I followed you from city to city. Let me show you all the love I have to give."

Lucas head spinning drunk, slurred with diminishing volume. "NO, No, no you can't, I don't want that. I'm all sweaty grimy and stinky? Stop It! STOP!"

Enraged, forcibly shaking Lucas. Dylan was drooling spittle like a turbulent wild beast. "You owe me. I've created your successes. It's time to pay up."

Twisting from side to side trying to escape a vice like grip Lucas pleaded. "Stop, your body smells, your breath stinks too, get off me Dylan!"

Controlling Lucas' body with his own, keeping him immobilized Dylan simpered, "What I want is such a small thing compared to all I've given to make you feel proud. Your bill is due scout."

Forcibly subdued, finally yielding, Lucas was torn. It was the first time Dylan spoke of a debt. Dylan's eyes had conveyed a want for years, starting too early for Lucas to understand the sexual implication. Now in an alcohol haze fighting to stay awake, Lucas suddenly grasped what he had chosen to ignore. Drunkenly confronted with a debt; he considered giving in to Dylan's want, to pay a fee for unasked attention. Intoxicated he thought *it has been most of my life with Dylan's flattery and tutoring. Now his stalking suddenly has a context, so what am I supposed to do? Should I pay this debt with my body like a prostitute? Is that right?*

"You owe me, and now is pay up time."

It would be so simple, Lucas thought, *yield to Dylan one time as payment in full and then forget it ever happened and go to sleep.*

"You are a good boy Lucas; I know you want to give me what is mine."

Already feeling shame for what he was about to allow, it further dawned on him *by running from city to city I avoided responsibility for owing Dylan and that provoked this violence. It is my fault, I am to blame.* Then like a lightning bolt sober clarity hit Lucas, *wait a minute shouldn't my parents pay Dylan what he is owed with their money, they gave him permission to be my mentor. They pay my Columbia tuition, isn't it all the same? How could I owe something and not know it?*

At that instant holding a sliver of sober thought Lucas hated Dylan for his repulsive lust, pathetic neediness, and stale body odor. But the clarity waned and Lucas was confused again, his conscious avoidance mind and his unconscious concrete mind melded in jumbled unfocused woozy inebriation. He was again teetering on the verge of drunkenly saying out loud, "Fuck it, have your way with me. Let's get this over and done, debt paid in full."

Roughly handled, Lucas' muddled mental processes were harshly supplanted by physical struggle again as the two men tussled and rolled drunkenly grappling on the grass. Then suddenly Dylan, less intoxicated and larger got the upper hand. The next thing Lucas knew for sure his pants and underwear were pulled down and Dylan was aggressively performing brutish oral sex on him in an abrasive hurtful hurry. Lucas was nineteen, hadn't seen his girlfriend in a few days nor recently serviced by Aaron or Willis. He came right away. It was an inebriated physical release from rough fast hurtful friction with no emotion or attachment.

Lucas struggled to regain his normal breathing and wrap his mind around what happened, how it happened, and *without the consent he was about to give*. Dylan rolled him over, and prided apart his tightly clenched butt cheeks. Then spit on Lucas' butt bottom button, and spat a gob onto his prick. Without further preparation or consent, Dylan stabbed his hard dick deep into Lucas's unready and unwilling rectum. Alcohol was not enough anesthesia; Lucas experienced extreme tearing bruising pain, and briefly blacked out from the ferocious anal bludgeoning.

After years of hot pursuit and masturbatory fixation, Dylan was out of his mind jackhammer battering and ripping Lucas's ass with unbridled lust. Brutishly Dylan climaxed quickly and mechanically. Then overcome emotionally, his eyes spilled tears of joy after the conquest of his long-coveted quarry. He was too drunk to fully grasp he'd just committed a vicious rape.

As consciousness returned, Lucas' survival instincts and pain sobered him enough to know he had just been brutally assaulted. His primal instincts took over and autonomously reached down and removed his Boy Scout folding knife from his pants' pocket and opened it. The knife had been a gift from Dylan when Lucas first joined his Scout Troop.

When Dylan rolled Lucas over to kiss him, Lucas stabbed Dylan twice, hard and fast in the center of the chest. Then quickly struggled to his feet and stood and watched open mouthed as Dylan's life bled out in spurts and flowed into the thirsty grass. Both men looked at each other dumbfounded. Lucas from what just happened. On some level, Dylan had to know he was dying, but having realized his long sought after fantasy mattered more. The two men held eye contact until the light faded and then was gone from Dylan Krumburn's gaze and life.

Lucas was still full of rage from being forcibly penetrated, and his manhood viciously taken. Then without warning he abruptly doubled over in extreme physical pain from a cramp. The cramp was made worse by an uncontrollable need to vomit. To add to the mishmash of his confused thinking and forceful physical reactions, like a bucket of ice water crashing down he realized what he had done. At the same time his conscious mind rebelled at the fact he had just taken a human life. Lucas desperately wanted denial of the truth lying before him. The anal cramp passed as quickly as it had grabbed his guts and he was able to half stand to finish upchucking and squirt out Dylan's ejaculate and blood.

Suddenly aware he was shaking with sobs the flood gates opened and he cried uncontrollably from grief, confusion and emotional and physical exhaustion. His crying stopped when waves of cold certainty washed over him. Glancing down he saw the look on Dylan face, it beamed sexually satisfied. Fighting nausea, and without forethought he reached down and closed the dead man's eyes and pulled up and fastened both their clothing. Then still on autopilot, his cognition overwhelmed by recent events, he rolled the lifeless body down the hill to the edge of the Hudson River. Like an automaton, he filled Dylan's pockets with rocks and shoved the cadaver over the river bank and into the swirling dark dank river. Rather than feel relief, he felt baffled as the dead man disappeared out of sight in the roiling river.

7.

Aching from internal and external abrasions, Lucas waddled back to his dorm room dazed. He collapsed on his bed and tried to sleep, but slumber wouldn't come and the heat and humidity seemed more oppressive than annoying irritants. Exhausted beyond reckoning yet too keyed up to rest. He thought *maybe if I told someone I just killed Dylan, sleep would come. But I can't talk to the authorities until I figure out what to say. Damn I have to track down my luggage from the aborted ocean voyage before I can change into clean clothes. Wait, I can still shower.*

Lucas searched for but couldn't find Jay or Aaron, so he took the subway down to Greenwich Village and found Willis stoned alone at home. Speaking with bravado his body language belied he said, "I'm finally free of my stalker; I killed the bastard before he could rape me. That creepy old man is dead and good riddance to bad rubbish." At the same time, he thought *may his ghost not haunt me and all the gods forgive what I've done.*

It didn't matter that Lucas' words did not fit his affect; Willis was so high he could barely nod his head in response to what Lucas was saying. Willis only fully grasped the seriousness of what was said when the police questioned him later. Nevertheless, with an arm around his shoulder in blurry speech Willis managed, "Turn yourself in before the cops come looking for you. I don't want the cops nosing around my apartment; who knows what they might find."

Unsatisfied telling Willis an abridged and fictionalized version of events in Riverside Park, Lucas went back uptown searching for Jay or Aaron. He finally found Jay at another of his girlfriends' apartment, and told him a better thought out but still fictionalized version of killing Dylan.

At the end of the tale Jay was quiet thinking for long seconds, then his face registered concern. "We need to call the police and tell them before they find the body."

"I'm not ready to talk to cops. What happened has to sink in, I'm still all discombobulated."

Hands on chin in a comical pose Jay sputtered, "Discombobulated eh, sorry to say you sound like English major. That is a sad state of affairs, but there may be an inexplicable cure, though it is reported to be worse than the malady." Then getting serious again, "Let's take a walk over to Morningside Park and clear our heads. We both need air; the muggy heat in this apartment makes breathing a hazard. Come on, a killing should be talked over."

"*I major in English,* and have the vocabulary to prove it. Just like you, a sad and sorry state indeed." That was said to Jay's back as he followed Jay out the door. While walking to the nearby park Lucas discovered Dylan's eyeglasses in his shirt pocket. Dylan must have put them there in the bar and Lucas was too drunk to notice. "Look what I found, Dylan's glasses; want a souvenir from his murder?"

"No, toss them, they're evidence against you. What did you do with the knife?"

"Here," and Lucas pulled it out of his pants' pocket. His trusty Boy Scout pocket knife was still sticky with blood, as was his pants pocket.

"Give me that and the glasses." Jay swiftly took them to the street corner and threw them down a sewer curb grate. Walking back, he said, "It will be much better if you turn yourself in before the police come calling."

But Lucas shook his head no. "I need to get my head organized, before I face them. Let me try to sleep first. Walk me back to the dorm?"

8.

Alone in his dorm room, Lucas struggled with which actual events to reveal. He was ashamed to tell anyone he *had* been savagely raped. Everybody knew men didn't get raped, it was a fact. Plus, his masculinity had been brutally stolen in a violent frenzy he hardly recalled. He thought *I'll be viewed as pathetic, weak, a victim who caused his own downfall by accepting Dylan's favors and gifts without realizing a price was attached. How stupid was I? Yet how is it I am a murderer when I am against all forms of violence?*

Like most rape victims he blamed himself. Shaking his fists and speaking out loud to the walls of his empty room. "If only I had been more forceful right away, or shouted louder. Geez how would I feel if I had given in to him? Why did I go with him?" But Lucas was smart, after catching his breath he again spoke out loud to his dorm room. "It wasn't my fault even if it feels that way, it just wasn't my fault. I didn't start what happened. I never asked for anything, so how could I owe anything."

Lurking right below his conscious thinking, Lucas's concrete unconscious couldn't shake off the adoring look on Dylan's face as he died. That image made him nauseous and wants to shout and break things because it was so incompatible with how he felt. But Lucas was disciplined and so he remained outwardly calm as his insides twisted in turmoil over the death he caused.

To quell internal agitation, he finally asserted full control by deciding to say he'd drunk too much alcohol, which *was* true, and didn't remember much of what happened. He would tell that lie, but remembered every detail of how it felt to stab the knife into Dylan twice. That information might slip out during coerced police interrogations like they showed in the movies; enhanced beatings with rubber hoses under glaring flood lights. After soul searching rumination Lucas decided *enough looking backward, I have to tell the same edited versions of events I told Willis and Jay, and stick to it no matter what is done to me. Or else everything will spin out of control again, like the rape and murder.*

If the police questioned his friends, they would corroborate the story he told. Parts of it would match what a police investigation would discover about Dylan Krumburn, stalking him from city to city. But he would have to be resolute and not say anything about anything beyond his official version of events. Lucas was a writer, it was his fictionalized story and he would have to make it believable.

He repeated his final version of the story to himself, in his head, and out loud to his empty room's wall mirror one hundred and fifty times, until he could say it without thinking and almost believe it. Then he telephoned his girlfriend Megan in her dorm at Barnard College. He told her the story, adding he was on his way to turn himself in to the authorities. Telling her was a test; she knew him intimately and said she could always tell if he lied. She became upset, believing his tale, and promised to stand by him no matter what.

9.

Lucas located his ocean voyage luggage, took another long hot shower, and slept like a log for six hours. Then he went to the District Attorney's Office, dressed in his summer suite, fresh white pressed shirt, and Columbia University school tie. He walked in and confessed to killing Dylan Krumburn in Riverside Park. The D.A. staff didn't believe him. First of all, none of the murderers the New York City District Attorney's office tried, voluntarily walked in and confessed. Secondly Lucas did not look like the usual 1940s' murder suspect the gritty District Attorney's staff regularly brought to justice in the electric chair at Sing-Sing State Prison.

Mr. Lucas Carmel looked like a stunningly handsome, well-dressed nineteen-year-old University English major. He was carrying a well-worn book of poetry, was polite, and said he wanted to cooperate fully. At each juncture when he was told to wait, he sat quietly and read poetry. The District Attorney did send the police out to look for a body, more as a formality rather than expecting one.

A police boat eventually found Dylan's corpse downstream, but the Hudson River had washed away any forensic evidence and the larger fish had started nibbling on his carcass. Since Lucas claimed he'd only been threatened with rape, it did not occur to the prosecutors to order a physician's examination of his body. If they had they would have found marks and bruises from scuffling, and bruising and tearing around and in his rectum; physical evidence of rape.

One day after Lucas confessed Willis Brown, Jay Kirack, and Megan Scone were arrested as material witnesses. Megan was released on her own recognizance.

Officially it was due to overcrowding at the Women's House of Detention. Unofficially it was because she couldn't have survived confinement with the older hardened female felons. Jay's family refused to post bail to get him out of jail. Then the judge required Jay to marry his girlfriend before she was allowed to post his bail. Willis's father insisted on coming to New York from the Middle West in his private train to bail his son out of jail personally. He also intended to throw his considerable wealth and power around in case his son was implicated in the murder. Precocious Willis had had brushes with the law earlier in life; his father was experienced coming to his son's rescue.

Aaron Gingersnap was the only one of the Bebop Writers not arrested; he had been attending a family gathering in Brooklyn and knew nothing of the killing until days later. He was in love with Lucas, and treasured their ongoing mostly one-sided sexual liaisons. But Aaron's most complicated grieving came from having developed a mutually satisfactory sexual friendship with the late Dylan Krumburn. Aaron went into intense mourning at losing his beautiful muse Lucas, and his crazy friend with benefits, naughty but often entertaining, and very smart Dylan.

10.

For months prior to Dylan's murder the Bebopper Writers had discussed taking their education into their own hands. The quartet's consensus was traditional college education smothered creativity with cookie cutter like standardization. They wanted to experience life in the first person rather than regurgitated from books. One exploit in that spirit would have been Lucas and Jay traveling to German Occupied France working on a cargo ship.

The other Bebop Writers also planned to quit school sooner or later as opportunity and circumstances dictated. The big sticking point for their educational liberation from standardized learning was their student deferments from the war time military draft. Aaron and Willis were afraid if drafted the induction center doctors would figure out they were queers, mark them 4-F and lock them away in a mental hospital to be experimented on for the rest of their lives.

Lucas was against all forms of violence, but not so much as to declare himself a conscientious objector. Staying in school was an expedient means to an end for three of the four. Consequently, all four directed much of their young male rebelliousness against authority to subvert the university. Boys usually need something to zealously despise as they develop, and though intellectually astute the quartet was young for their years in practical ways. They targeted Columbia University as their enemy; it was close at hand and safe. It was without any serious retaliation; if they were careful. Therefore, the quartet became conflicted when the full force of the Ivy League, directed from Columbia University's English Department, mobilized to support Lucas's murder defense. Suddenly the Bebop Writer's enemy was Lucas' most powerful ally.

To deal with the gravity of murder, the absurdity of dealing with the criminal justice system's bureaucracy, the intimidation of real or implied threats from the police and the enemy of choice now ally Columbia University. Aaron, Jay, Lucas and Willis decided to adopt new alter ego names for the duration of the trial and maybe beyond. If they couldn't change the system, they could change how the system knew them. By pretending to be powerful goofy oligarchs they shielded their identities as creative writers.

Pompous titles allowed acting out of character; using peculiar personalities and behaviors that fit their novel new identities. And most importantly it was good boyish fun in the face of serious adult consequences. The shocked confusion on the faces of bureaucrat drudges forced to deal with four unruly haughty Bebop jive talkers using decorative titles, putting on theatrical snooty aristocratic airs, was good boyish pranking at an otherwise gray-bleak time.

By consensus the Bebop Writers dubbed Lucas; Count Claude de Nobris, Willis became Vice Count Cecil de Nobris, Jay was named the Canadian Duke Conroy de Nobris, and finally after much haggling Aaron (of diminished status), became No-account Count Cornelius de Brisket. Aaron was the only member of the quartet not arrested as a material witness or perpetrator and jailed. Consequently, he was titled the no-account Count; he had no personal account prior to the official proceedings. Furthermore, he had been attending a family event where brisket was served when the others were jailed. Megan thought the boys were being silly, and refused to take a royal title no matter how hard they tried to convince her.

Lucas, aka the royal Count Claude de Nobris, was eventually charged with second degree murder. But the tale of the handsome teenager, fighting off a much older stalker, as conveyed by Willis, Jay, Megan and Lucas, allowed the prosecutors to readily accept a lesser plea of manslaughter.

Lucas' girlfriend Megan Scones testified, and attested to his character and guaranteed his heterosexual orientation with keenness yet modesty. Mark von Donets and Lionel Terming, two major stars of the Columbia English Department appeared as character witnesses for Lucas. They portrayed him as an Ivy League scholar and literary prodigy, claiming he was a one in a generation wunderkind.

Radio stations, newspapers, newsreels, and news magazines were captivated by Lucas, his witnesses, and the implied sexually tawdry nature of the case. They expressed their points of view loudly, often, and with editorial bias toward Lucas and the privileged Ivy League. It was a titillating diversion from the hardships due to a world war and the domestic war support rationing.

The full power and weight of the University, Willis's father's considerable influence behind the scenes, Lucas' sincere expression of remorse, and Megan's striking beauty and sweet personality encouraged the judge to sentence Lucas Carmel to eighteen months for the murder of Professor Dylan Krumburn. The judge sent Lucas to Elmira Reformatory for Young Felons. It was a prison for young adults over eighteen but under twenty-six year olds. A different Judge might have sent Lucas to a maximum-security Penitentiary for murderers like Sing-Sing Prison. At sentencing the judge called Dylan's murder an honor killing, and regretted press attention forced him to incarcerate Lucas.

If Lucas had admitted being raped, he knew he could have gotten off with self-defense or justifiable homicide and no incarceration. But he was too ashamed to admit what really happened. His boyish pride was often in conflict with his better self. It was his pride sending him to prison, and that was nothing to be proud of, and yet on a deep level he accepted it as just. He had taken a human life and that went against his core beliefs. To his unconscious mind eighteen months didn't seem an overly high price for such an unforgivable sin.

II.

At first Aaron, Jay, and Willis continued with their alter ego names for fun and as a reminder their friend Lucas was locked away in a cage. They also felt the melodramatic names gave them a Bebopper's view into unreality during the world at war. Initially due to Count Claude de Nobris' haughty arrogance in captivity it only seemed appropriate to multiply his aberrant conduct while visiting him. The quartet in spontaneous impulsive dramas spurred each other on like naughty children goading each other. The reaction from the guards and inmate trustees was shocked disapproval. It was a humorous diversion to an otherwise drab experience after the long tedious non-air-conditioned bus ride to the upstate Reformatory from Manhattan and back again.

By the sixth week of incarceration, Count Claude de Nobris was still not acclimated to prison life. Then without warning or explanation, Lucas told the other Bebop writers to stop calling him by his royal alter ego title in front of the guards and other prisoners. He refused to say why the abrupt change, but adamantly demanded they grant his wish. "You must only refer to me as Lucas Carmel or my convict number 982013. And please tone it down, what you do here; I live with after you leave. Prison is dangerous, not a place for fooling around."

Lucas refused to elaborate, but his three classmates found out by talking to other prison visitors on the bus back home. The three students acting like passive aggressive fools and then aggressively antagonizing prison officials and trustees, targeted Lucas for abuse beyond being a newbie. As a result, he was routinely punished for his visitors' behavior, and their gifts to him stolen immediately after visiting hours. Lucas' pride at being the Beboppers unofficial leader wouldn't let him tell his friends the reason he dropped his fun name, or his fears about escalating threats becoming living nightmares.

By his friends' next visit, the mistreatment from inmates and some guards had become so bad Lucas refused to speak beyond yes or no during their visit. Immediately after that visit, Lucas wrote his friends to stop visiting him and to stop sending gift packages especially books. He didn't tell them inmates had started forcing him to eat pages torn out of the books he received. At first the three Bebop writers didn't connect the request with Lucas' safety. They thought he was just going through some new jail house adaptation, by rejecting them and their gifts. Their consensus was he was having an obnoxious adjustment to prison life, and Lucas would be fine again after he settled in.

Because of his pretend titled aloofness, and many resenting his short sentence for murder, and others jealous of his previous privileged life, Lucas still hadn't made friends or allies in prison. A friend could have clued him in on the how's and why's and dangers. But people had always been drawn to Lucas, so he didn't know how to react when rejected for his fumbling attempts to reach out to others. He sensed his isolation was getting more dangerous, yet nothing he attempted to end it worked.

Prior to Count Claude de Nobris' imprisonment the quartet developed a written secret code expecting their letters to and from the reformatory to be censored. Because the Second World War continued to occupy the public's attention, newspapers from time to time had articles on codes that could be secretly used to transmit military intelligence if or when the country was invaded. The articles proved useful for the Bebop writers to build their own schoolboy like secret system that might slip past prison censors.

The Ivy League beboppers finally understood Lucas' need to be safe when he used their code to write each basically the same heartfelt letter. *The various vicissitudes I have been undergoing in this horrid putrid place have permanently changed me. Your dear friend is gone and can't be reconstituted. I have learned that the powers of intellect and nonconformity are much less important in my present circumstances than hard muscle and developed hand to hand combat skills. To a man my fellow convicts are complete imbeciles and most are illiterate or close to it and yet they hold immense power to physically harm me. This is my penance for what I did. Please cease and desist all contact with me since I am no longer the person you knew, and others here violently resent you because they do not have an equivalent in their pathetic little lives and punish me for that in horrible ways.*

Lucas wrote a similar message to Megan, but not in code. In her letter, he added, *you must start dating and it is my fervent wish you find someone to love you like I did. I am no longer who you knew. You wouldn't like who I have become, I don't.*

12.

Life in prison didn't improve as Lucas hoped after severing all ties with the people who cared about him. Threats and abuse continued and he was more alone than before with no visits to look forward to. Grasping at straws Lucas contacted the legal team that defended him. After making a pest of himself a new young attorney was sent up to Elmira Reformatory to meet with Lucas. With great trepidation Lucas confessed to the stranger, a man close to his own age. As he unburdened himself he felt the temperature between them drop and he harshly judged. "I was ashamed, so I lied about being raped. But now I need a new trial to escape the daily horrors in this terrible place."

The new young inexperienced attorney's attitude changed from open and friendly to hostile cold as Lucas confessed. "Without physical evidence or a witness there is no hope of getting you anything better than you got. You shouldn't have lied that was stupid; you put yourself in here by doing that."

Lucas listened in shocked disbelief; by swallowing his pride he only gained a disgusted look from an unsympathetic contemporary. Whimpering in a whisper Lucas said, "My life here is going from bad to worse. They hate me so much and I don't know why. Now they are threatening to gang rape me and a terrible death if I tell after. I just *can't get raped again, I'll go insane.*"

The lawyer shook his head not trying to hide revulsion on his face. "Look, you arrogant ungrateful son of a bitch, can't you see they hate you for looking down on them."

"But I don't look down on anybody."

"I had to work dirty jobs at night to pay for law school, while you partied at a fancy University. Your file says you want to be an author. Don't you know all artists consider themselves superior to the rest of us working stiffs? Hell, your privileged back ground even shows in how you walk and talk."

The young attorney's words struck Lucas like a hard punch to his testicles. He and his friends were only pretending to be arrogant aristocrats; they didn't mean anything by it. It was supposed to be a fun game to help him get through incarceration. "I'm sorry if I offended you somehow. Is there is anything you can do to help me; I'm at my wit's end; and expecting the worse."

"If I appealed your case right this minute, you would have already served out the sixteen months left on your sentence before my paperwork was processed into the system."

"Oh no, please don't tell me that!"

"Look, you aloof little prick, the war has backlogged everything for years to come. Climb down off your high horse and find a way to tolerate prison life like the rest of these punks. You're a smart boy, figure out something."

"I can't, I Don't Know How. NOTHING I TRY WORKS!" Taking a breath to settle his nerves Lucas said, "And that's why I'm desperate for your law firm to save my life."

"Don't be an idiot, it is simple really, give them what they want. You just told me you had queer sex before. Relax just take it, you will be out of here soon enough." Then the recent law school grad stood up, not making eye contact, a look of distaste on his fresh young face. He turned his back and left without offering the customary end of interview handshake.

The rapes started the day after his lawyer's visit. A trustee aimlessly pushing a broom around them purposely listened in on Lucas' conversation. He took what the lawyer said as an invitation, and spread the word. The first rape occurred when Lucas was sent to a storeroom on an errand for a guard. Five thuggish inmates waiting inside the storeroom quickly overpowered and stripped him, then took turns viciously violating him while he was roughly held down and slapped, punched or kicked as he struggled against the attack.

Lucas suffered the disintegration of his modesty as he was roughly undressed. It was the systematic disintegration of his dignity that hurt the most as he was raped by one after another hoodlum. Even more hellish was reliving Dylan's brutal rape, sober, repeated five times by out of control louts having a party abusing his body, psyche, and spirit.

The inmate's unwritten code was; if the rape victim didn't protest loudly throughout the attack, they liked it and should be rewarded with more of what they liked. Lucas' old harmful pride made shouting, yelling or any loud protest impossible while being savaged. No matter how bad it got he couldn't verbalize his anguish more than involuntary whimpers, or groans of pain. He hadn't protested Dylan's rape; he couldn't find a way to protest the inmates' rapes. His natural survival defenses shut down knowing the rapists expected him to scream every thrust of stabbing pain... As hard as he wanted to, nothing came from his mouth beyond a reflexive exhaled grunt or moan. After many failed attempts at self-preservation, Lucas finally came to the conclusion his inner self was complicit in the brutalization as punishment for the murder he committed. In his terror driven convoluted thinking he decided *by nature I can reach down and feel I am still a man. Screaming is unmanly even if I am brutally emasculated for not screaming. And all these violations make me even less a man than if I pleaded and begged and screamed for them to stop hurting me. If I could vocalize the pain to externalize it, my life would still be a paradox?*

With ongoing gang rapes, another reality forced Lucas to swallow his last tiny bit of vestigial self-respect. The prison doctor voiced concern. "Since you are no longer new here, I'm worried if they pass you down the food chain the anal assaults will become more often and much more vicious. The lower rungs like it rough, tough and bloody. I'm already sewing you up on top of previous stitches. If you don't find a way to spread out these injuries so they can heal, you may end up wearing a diaper for the rest of your days. You're a nice kid find someone to stand up for you."

Lucas didn't have a clue how to find a protector, the more he needed one. And what little was left of his pride recoiled at the idea of having to wash out a protector's dirty socks and underpants, service without question or limit a protector's sexual proclivities, and be pimped out to other inmates in exchange for cigarettes. His mind revolted at the prospects. Yet soon his ass would be a public convince, to be used and abused by anyone, free of charge just for the taking. Instead of random rapes it would be constant rapes, until his body gave out.

Seven days a week, the constant insults from inmates and guards for being one of the prison's designated free skank holes, forced Lucas down into a miserable dark place inside himself. He acknowledged with anxious terror, anything could be done to him on a whim that could maim or kill him. The hopelessness of his plight made the prospect of wearing diapers for life a best-case scenario.

Lucas went into prison stunningly handsome, an intellectually creative writer and natural leader of Bebop authors. After only a few months incarcerated he looked like a cringing dull eyed cur, slinking around quaking, often peeing on himself from real threats of torture for fun. He was regularly humiliated and beaten for no reason other than the sadistic amusement of hooligans who wanted to see the college kid writhe in degradation. Lucas was the only inmate with some college. And he was constantly reminded being different from the others was not acceptable in the reformatory.

Routinely Lucas felt himself teetering on the edge of madness, and was tempted to go over into an abyss of drooling, incoherent dithering to blot out escalating real or threatened agony for other's sick pleasure. But suicide was not an option; it would give his tormentors victory. What little residual pride he had couldn't allow them to win. They'd have to kill him and probably would.

Lucas could hear when other unprotected new inmates were being viciously ravaged; from their loud pleas or screams for help. He could even tell which were genuinely shrieking out a horrific unthinkable experience, and those who were just pretending to protest as an adaptation to what was expected. During other's violations, he felt ashamed and disappointed for being relieved it wasn't him. He knew too well the cramped musty storerooms and mildewed showers were the violence was happening. And he knew the lust dulled ugly faces of the rapists as they thrust mindlessly in a rush for momentary gratification and to maintain their pecking order place among outlaws.

It occurred to Lucas *the line between perpetrator and victim must be very thin for the younger rapists. How much more terrible was it for them to receive the same indignities they gave to others in order to belong.* Then he thought *wait, if I am going to have sympathy it should be for all of us victims no exceptions.*

Shame at being relived, *it's not me this time,* led him to total despair, Lucas literally felt the last vestiges of his arrogant pride wither and slink away from his bashed battered ill-used body. But it left behind a sense of clarity he hadn't known since killing Dylan. With clarity, his imagination had him rush down a long dark tunnel, and suddenly at the darkest point he groped around a corner and came out into bright light. He raised his head looked around and thought *oh I see, so prison is like living in a fish bowl, there is no privacy, everyone's story is common gossip, and no one is allowed an inner life. These ugly sullen faced angry young men are mean-spirited and cruel to me because they have no prospects for a meaningful future; these poor souls are destined from birth to be life's losers. Raping me may seem the highlight of their lives.*

Overhearing inmates' conversations while standing in lines, Lucas learned just how limited they were, few had known a positive opportunity or realizable dream. Most of the guards and all the convicts carried poverty's inescapable wounds from social deprivations, and many of both showed greater or lesser indicators of mental diseases. With his new clarity, Lucas felt profoundly sad for his unloved maybe even unlovable fellow inmates and their bleak existence.

Empathizing with his tormentors, Lucas felt humbled by their lot in life. In a flood of realizations, he understood why the inmates hated him and his past arrogant behavior. Why they called him their Fancy Count Cunt. He had squandered future opportunities they couldn't even imagine. For the first time in his life he had genuine cause to know humility, and it visibly affected his physical demeanor and ever so slightly resuscitated his spirit.

He felt deep shame for his insensitive even rude thoughtless past behaviors. He'd refused to believe the young lawyer; that arrogance was at the root of Lucas' maladaptation to prison life. But now he saw clearly it was behind why he hadn't made a friend since coming to prison, and was avoided except for abuse. He had to make amends or continue to pay too high price for his inconsiderateness.

After long hard soul searching, Lucas decided to give up writing. It was something he loved. He was good at it, and the only thing he had left to give up, short of a body part. He had been groomed to be a creative artist by Dylan, his parents and teachers and even classmates. Giving up what he loved was fair retribution, true reparation for his crime. The proof he made the right decision came that night. For the first time since coming to prison he slept thought the night without being constantly frightened awake by terrifying nightmares. Then the next morning he found an inner peace that let him shed his usual anxieties for the day.

With his humbled change in physical presence from a new improved attitude and good night's sleep; his dessert cup wasn't stolen as soon as he received it on the food line. Other prisoners, unasked and non-confrontationally, prevented the bullies from spitting in his food. He didn't have to eat alone any longer or forced to eat pages from books and his poems. By giving up the Count's aloofness, and making an ardent promise to self never to write again as atonement, he became just another numbered member in the prison population.

Lucas was still friendless but life was a smidgeon better with others unasked watching his back without risking their own. He accepted the charity as an unworthy beggar, knowing it could be snatched away any instant. Lucas understood he still needed a protector if the rapes were to completely stop. They had slowed considerably with his changed attitude. He wasn't fun to victimize any longer, plus there was a constant supply of fresh meat arriving weekly to be raped.

13.

Prisons are run like the United States Federal Government, which from its inception has practiced a divide and conquer approach for the rich and powerful well washed few to control the disadvantaged unwashed masses necessary for menial work and cannon fodder. The too few prison guards kept the too many prisoners controlled by dividing them according to race or ethnicity or religion and fermenting tensions between the fragmented groups. The inmates divided themselves similarly into the few ruthless brutalizers and the many frightened into complying victims, thus mimicking the larger society's power and control of its people. It isn't a healthy system but is a time honored American tradition that allows its citizens to discriminate one against the other as reward.

To keep their inadequate funding, the prison administration had to be sensitive to the shifting needs of the day's politics, and also the wants of the powerful oligarchs operating behind the scenes. Initially Lucas' high profile case with its Columbia University heavy hitter support made his safety a concern for individuals in high places. They were apprehensive about the effect of negative publicity on funding if he was killed or too badly maimed. The primary worry was after lights dimmed and prisoners were locked in their cells for the night. Bad things like death or dismemberment might befall the famous Ivy League student murderer if given the wrong cellmate. To protect its interest the prison administration housed Lucas alone. They didn't like giving him special treatment but the solution worked to keep him alive his first six months and negative attention was nil.

Then overcrowding occurred from too many new convict's violations of the war effort rationing laws. And terrible new bombs destroyed two Japanese cities so the war was drawing to an end consequently military service ceased to be an alternative to incarceration. To accommodate the changes Lucas could no longer be housed alone, every bed must be utilized. If Lucas was killed, overcrowding would be blamed.

Lucas' new cellmate was a dangerous killer, a potential cause of mayhem and chaos in the reformatory. By sacrificing Lucas, the administration hoped to eliminate two problems at once. They'd use Lucas to feed the new cellmate's raw meat blood lust. Then after he killed Lucas they could send the new inmate to adult prison where he belonged. Or at the very least the new man's raging hormones might be controlled through regular sexual exploitation of Lucas after lights out.

Just turned eighteen years old, Vito Cannoli, was six foot three inches of two hundred twenty-five hard muscle pounds, and completely unregulated when riled. He was big in every way compared to 1944's average height of five foot six inches, and 150 pounds. Vito had been a golden gloves champion boxer starting at age six, all of Vito's boxing victories came by way of knockout. But his successful undefeated amateur boxing career was cut short by incarcerations pending trial for alleged violent felonies committed while a child. He came to prison with a psychiatric diagnosis of

Explosive Personality Disorder with chronic homicidal features and was double red flagged as potentially dangerous to staff and inmates.

Vito was at Elmira due to his age, and the Bronx District Attorney's ineptness trying to get him tried and sentenced as an adult for multiple deaths during an attempted robbery. Vito and six neighborhood friends took the subway up to the Bronx from their homes in Bad News Brooklyn intending to rob a cock fight. Vito was fifteen and a half years old at the time and the suspected ringleader.

The cockfight promoters had hired members of a Bronx Street Gang the A&P - *Allsorts of Pain* to provide security for their event. The *Allsorts* came well equipped to protect the lucrative illegal bird fight. Since both groups were heavily armed, as were many of the fight spectators, a massive shootout ensued resulting in thousands of rounds of ammunition expended and a body count of seventeen dead and twenty-nine hospitalized with serious injuries. The police were wholly unhappy sorting out the bloody mess after the gun smoke cleared, and let their displeasure be known loudly to City Officials high and low. The cops wanted extra pay for such messy tedious work and Vito permanently off the street by any means possible. There were no funds available for police overtime work. The costly war was still on.

It was proven by ballistic tests that some of the dead and wounded had been shot by one or the other of the two large caliber handguns Vito was carrying when arrested at the scene. Vito claimed he was only holding the weapons for someone whose name and description he didn't remember. The City Fathers pressured the District Attorney to get Vito locked up for good because of his escalating violent mayhem and police protests. Vito scared everyone. So, in the name of protecting society the Bronx District Attorney tried some questionable legal manipulations.

Vito's family provided him an expert legal team and working in concert with a sympathetic well-greased judge who said he was scandalized by the District Attorney's bold extralegal shenanigans. After all was said and done, in the end Vito's debt to society for his underage circumstantial role in the cock ring massive gun fight, there were no witnesses willing to testify, was three and a half years. His sentence included time served in pretrial incarceration, two years six months to be exact, the one additional year was to be served at Elmira after he turned eighteen. Vito expressed no remorse other than he had run out of bullets during the shootout. Nevertheless, if he stayed out of trouble at Elmira, he was scheduled to be released, as the fates would have it, on or about the same time as Lucas his new cellmate.

Both privileged Ivy League killer Lucas, and bare knuckle brawler, gun fighter Vito would not fit comfortably into the regular population at Elmira Reformatory. The guards and inmates resented the ridiculously short sentences both men received for taking human life. The word was Lucas and Vito had gotten away with murder and other inmates begrudged that, since they were serving longer sentences most often for lesser crimes like small scale black-marketeering.

From the highest administrative level, Vito and Lucas were assigned to be cellmates in order to contain potential problems. It was hoped they would cancel each other out one way or another during the year they had to serve. Staff was instructed; hands off and look the other way if possible. It was imperative to keep a lid on potentially dangerous, explosive, even embarrassing situations.

While reposing on his lower bunk, reading poetry from the prison's anemic library, two guards and a very tall movie star good looking new prisoner stopped just outside Lucas' cell. The convict was holding the standard issue new prisoner kit.

On a gut level, Lucas wanted to jump with joy, finally getting a cellmate, a companion to talk with. Who knew; maybe the new cellie could be a protector? He was big enough. But on a cognitive level a dark thought took over *huh my first cellmate, I wonder how bad this will get. Given my experiences at Elmira, my money is on new awful ways to be hurt.*

For the first time since discovering the clarity of inner peace, Lucas felt conflicted. Rather than become immobilized by his clashing emotions, as in the past. He put his book aside and stripped the bunk he'd used since being assigned the cell. Action was an antidote, so he remade his bed on the top bunk. Then unasked and ignored, walked over and took what the new guy was holding and made up the lower bunk for him after putting his other items on the shelf over their sink. All done, Lucas stood in mixed anticipation while the guards completed reciting the prison dos and don'ts. Still ignoring him, the guards finished their recitation and left.

With eyes cast down like a supplicant, he put out his hand to the new man and said, "I'm Lucas."

His new cellmate coolly looked him up and down, then took the offered hand in a hard grip. "I'm Vito, I didn't tell you to make my bed. I've been in and out of these places my whole life, I know how they work. Just so we get off on the right foot, this cell will be run by me, if I don't tell you to do something don't do it, understand? I'll find us slaves, don't worry about that."

"Whatever you say, you're the boss."

"Unless you are dying to be my slave, know, I hate living with slaves. I prefer a little resistance when I push. You look to be a slave?"

"I'd rather not be a slave. I was just welcoming you to this dreadful place by making your bed. I didn't mean anything by it."

In a rush five hefty thuggish inmates pushed into the cell behind Vito's back. Vito had been facing a standing Lucas while they spoke. He watched as Lucas in a reflexive panic scurried up to the top bunk to cringe quivering in the corner. Vito couldn't know these were five of the many ruffians who regularly raped Lucas. Nevertheless, he didn't appreciate the unannounced interruption in his conversation or Lucas' reaction to it. He sized up the men behind his back, seeing their reflection in the sink's mirror he was facing. Vito figured the punks smelled fresh meat, namely his, and wanted to show who was top dog.

The largest of the five interlopers, with his first lieutenant standing shoulder to shoulder stood in front of three smaller hooligans. Interloper number one tried to give Vito's back a lecture on the pecking order at Elmira. He pointed at Lucas over Vito's shoulder and sneered, "Your cellmate is everyone's Fancy Count Cunt Lucy Lucas. He lives at the bottom of our butt fuck barrel. If you want to join our gang let us see you screw him hard. We'll make a circle so nobody else can see, then we'll each fuck him and that will be your initiation into our posse, easy enough? Otherwise you got big trouble."

One of the shorter men in the back row piped up. "Don't worry no matter how hard you ride Lucy she won't make a peep. She just loves to take it up the ass."

The lieutenant chimed in, "Yeah, expect to ride the slut really hard, lately her pussy has gotten floppy."

Lucas saw Vito's face change from relaxed good looking to angry ugly and his big hands clenched into balled up boxer's paws. In a flash, Vito pivoted one hundred and eighty degrees and using that momentum plus his well-developed arms and back drove his fists with fast uppercuts. First, he hit one then the other gang recruiter. The knockout punches connected loudly, hitting the arterial pressure points of the moving jaws of each man lecturing his back. Their heads flew back, knees buckled and then in slow motion they went down sprawled arms and legs all akimbo. They were unconscious on the floor, looking like life size rag dolls in the blink of an eye. No one would have guessed a man Vito's size could move that fast and skillfully use his pugilistic training with such pin point accuracy.

Then Vito proceeded to punch out the other three hoodlums falling over themselves trying to get out of the cell, all the while tripping over their leaders laying out cold splayed on the floor. Vito dislocated jaws, blackened eyes, broke noses, and bruised ribs amongst the damage inflicted with unimagined speed and precision. The three unwelcome visitors managed to crawl away bloody and groaning and not sure what happened. Vito angrily called after them, "You say I got trouble with you, maybe you got trouble with me. If you know what's good for you don't come around here."

Vito looked up at Lucas, who had watched, open mouthed, as the interlopers were trounced. "Lucas, it's best to get this kind of trash straightened out right off. Otherwise they can be annoying. My apologies, I know violence first thing can be unpleasant. Don't worry I'll have these two clean up the blood and gore when I wake them. You want to fuck them, hey you all right?"

Lucas mumbled, "I'm fine, but if it is okay I'd rather not fuck them." He didn't look okay; he looked ashen like he'd just witnessed a horrendous train wreck. He thought *I should be joyous over my rapists' getting their comeuppance. But seeing the beating up close, I can only feel their pain.*

Vito saw Lucas' face fleetingly gloat revenge, then quickly settle and hold a look of compassion for men who said they enjoyed humiliating him. Not knowing Lucas, Vito wasn't sure what to think. He preferred action when in doubt, so he grabbed the two unconscious men by the scruffs of their necks and dragged them to the cell's toilet bowl. He dunked one then the other's head into the cold toilet water and flushed for each pate. When they shook their heads into consciousness he said, "You boys ready for round two or did you have enough today?"

The two men slurred over each other, "Enough - I give – uncle - no more – my head hurts so bad – don't hit me again - my whole face aches you broke it."

"So, you understand, you don't threaten me again, got it? Now clean up this cell, and start with all that blood and mess over there and then scrub everything down. Starting tomorrow after breakfast you two *will come here* and do our laundry, make our beds and wipe everything down nice and clean, neat like we want it, understand? Otherwise you are dead."

"For how long do we have to?"

"Until I say stop or I kill you. You two are my slaves until I give you to the undertaker."

When the two rapists finished cleaning the cell, and stood waiting further instructions Vito said, "You must have jaw pain to go with those swollen discolored cheeks and black eyes, so I won't tell you to do it over again, but next time rub harder when you scrub. Now get out of here, before I make my cellmate fuck you until you sing soprano." The two interlopers couldn't have exited faster if the evil eye were chasing them.

Turning to Lucas who had been passively watching the cleaning Vito said, "I can't read you. When those five punks came in here I thought you were going to shit yourself. Then when I gave them what for, you looked sorry for them. Make up your mind, will yah. What's up with you?"

With effort Lucas made eye contact with Vito for the first time; he had big milk chocolate puppy eyes. "I appreciate you protecting me, and will do what is required for that protection, because I *hate* being raped."

"I could tell, nobody likes being raped, that's why I don't do it. But what's up with sympathizing with the bastards who so disrespected you?"

"Lately I've changed how I think about myself and others. You saw a little of the old me hating them and wanting you to do damage. Then you got a look at the new improved me. Do you really want to hear about this?"

"I asked, didn't I?"

"Okay, stop me if you get bored. I'm here because I killed someone, I acted without thinking. Since coming to prison I've offended almost everyone here, also by not considering consequences. My life at Elmira has been beyond horrible, but it has made me understand what I did to get here and the personal sacrifice needed for penance. Are you bored yet?"

"No, climb down and sit next to me. I'm a killer too. I want to watch you talk to me close up. I find you kind of handsome. I bet we are the same age."

Climbing down and sitting next to Vito, Lucas looked at him closely and asked, "Is this better?"

"Yes."

"The old *me* would have felt flattered you called me handsome. Now I'm just happy *you* find me attractive for you. If you thought me ugly it would be bad for both of us, right? I mean I can't change how I was born. So, I have changed my attitude, make any sense at all?"

"Huh yeah, that's oddly interesting."

"Look, I don't expect nothing for nothing, let me give you head for protecting me, would that be all right? I know you didn't ask."

"Knock yourself out if that's what you want. I'm guessing your butt hole is raw from use by those visiting vermin. Just so you know I prefer the top hole."

Without saying another word Lucas gently pushed Vito down flat on the bunk and undid his pants and pulled them and boxer shorts down. Taking a long look at Vito's half hard cock, Lucas acknowledged to himself *I didn't come to prison prepared to do what I'm doing. It would even have been against my values. Now after everything that's happened, I'm doing this of my own free will.* He was knowingly crossing another line there was no going back from, according to is new lawyer. But as he'd come to know prison culture he was adapting to survive.

Lucas had paid close attention when Aaron and Willis went down on him. It was to instruct Megan how to give head for maximum benefit. He hated she always finished him off with her hand, while the others eagerly swallowed his payload. Without self-admonishment, he skinned back Vito's cock and moved it into position, exactly as Aaron and Willis did him. Then following their technique, he licked around Vito's rim, licked his dick shaft and balls until they were wet. He always enjoyed how that preliminary action felt like an appetizer for the main course.

Then like his cock sucking mentors Lucas started swallowing dick, and when the big sausage wouldn't go down deeper, he slowly bobbed his head up and down. In a weird way, it was vicarious pleasure giving what he'd enjoyed receiving. He knew what he liked, so mirrored it on Vito. Sensing from Vito's side to side rocking motion then thrusting something grand was about to happen. Lucas pulled off cock and lightly swirled his tongue over Vito's balls. Then he very slowly flutter tongued up to and around Vito's golf ball size dickhead; until he felt ready to accept what he knew was coming. Vito had gradually calmed down and lay sensitized with anticipation, so Lucas went back to sword swallowing sausage. This time with resolve to see it to the end, determined Vito should have a satisfactory outcome. Lucas increased his head bobbin while figuring out how to give more throats and tongue frictions. Abruptly Vito was thrusting again, and then his large cock quickly expanded in Lucas' mouth. That gave Lucas an idea he started humming the Columbia University Football Fight Song.

He knew he had given a passable first blow job as he suddenly had to gulp down profuse cascades of hot Vito jizz. It tasted neutral; he'd been told his cum tasted salty. But it wasn't sweet like what flowed from between Megan's legs.

Finally wiping his mouth and with a self-satisfied sly smile Lucas asked smugly, "How was that?"

Vito liked to get off soon after combat; normally he used his right hand while replaying the fight action in his mind's eye. On this occasion, he replayed beating five against one into a stranger's mouth. He came just as, in his I mind, the last three interlopers staggered away and Lucas increased head bobbing friction the second time humming some old tune. He took a few moments to catch his breath. "You're straight, right? I can always tell when I get head from straight guys. Here sit closer; I want to touch you and watch your face as we talk. You are cute you know that? Your eyes are pretty too. Uh you were saying you had a bad time in this joint until you realized *what?*"

"How could you tell I'm straight? *You came a lot.*"

"Gays are more into it. I mean they get really spirited and keen sucking on my big boner. Cock sucking is probably something they're born to do. Don't get me wrong, there is nothing wrong with your technique that more practice can't fix. But face it; it's not a religious experience for you."

"Dam it; I wanted to give you a special thank you for protecting me from those savages."

"Hey take it easy, you did okay for a straight guy. Everybody can't be gay, there would be no one walking around. So, what changed for you in this reformatory, I want to find out?"

"So, that's it, my girlfriend Megan and I tried so many ways for her to give me good head and nothing we tried was as good as my gay friends. How about if you teach *me?* I will try hard to measure up."

"You'll learn what I like in the morning. I'm a morning person. I always wake up with wood that needs wet polishing. Now tell me how you changed in here, before I get pissed off asking. *You don't want to see me pissed off.*"

"Oh sorry, so I remembered this short skinny guy wearing a loincloth, from Newsreels. You know the short films between the movies. His thing is nonviolence and at the same time he demands England give India independence. Imagine nonviolent demands, crazy, right? Here we are having a world war, and everywhere you turn is pro-war propaganda, sacrifices, and invasion threats with poison gas. And this little skinny guy is talking nonviolence and making demands for independence with fighting and killing going on everywhere."

"I've seen that crazy nut in the Newsreels, Mat Candy, is his name. Whatever he thinks he's doing won't work with the British. You were saying?"

"That guy Gandhi got me thinking about the violence I've done, and the violence done to me, and all the violence in the world. I hit bottom one very bad day, then using the Indian guy's philosophy of selflessness I found a better way to be inside myself. I'm sure you know this prison runs on intimidation of victims by victimizers, everyone is one or the other, a few are both. Anyhow I don't know, I can't explain it any better, sorry. Do you mind I'm straight? I don't believe I'm contaminated by homosexual contagion from the rapes."

"In here it doesn't matter, we got no women to show off for, and I think homosexual contagion is bullshit."

"I miss my girlfriend Megan, but I told her to find someone else. Now I suppose I'll have to be your girlfriend substitute?"

"I get you want to know how to be my cellie sidekick, and if I'm straight or gay, like that mattered."

"True, I'd like to know what you expect."

"I've been locked up most of my life. I don't give a shit about monikers. At age ten, jailed in juvie, I came the first time down a punk kid's throat. He'd been trying hard to get me off for a month. Guess what, he turned out straight like you. I didn't know what the big deal was until he finally showed me. Then I stopped beating on him and began fucking his face every chance I got. He liked my behavior change."

"I don't like to be hit. I've been beaten a lot since coming here."

"You do what you're told and I won't have to smack you around. And anybody else tries to hurt you; they come through me first."

"Okay I understand … what do you want for my protection?"

"For right now I like how you look, and you are no lady, so don't start acting like one." That said Vito smiled his movie star smile and put an arm around Lucas's shoulders, then cradled his head to his chest and stroked his hair. "Don't worry my little bunny, anyone comes at you they'll be sorry, I enjoy physical exercise."

Seeing an irony, Lucas had an unexpected problem; protecting inmates who hurt him from Vito's killer fists. Speaking into his armpit Lucas asked, "Do you mind I'm into nonviolence?"

"No, but you gonna miss out on boxing lessons."

"Hope you don't mind, that's not something I wanted."

"Enough chit chat let's get down to business, everything has to be calm and peaceful in and around our cell. You can disagree with me, but only agreeably. As long as there are no hard feelings we'll be fine. I always get my way. That's how it has to work."

"Whatever you say, all I have to offer is correct spelling and grammar."

"That won't be necessary; I was born a math whiz among other things. There is something you *can* help me with. I don't handle being upset well and if I lose my temper, well it can be very, *very bad*."

"What can I do?"

"The way I'll keep predators off your back, I want you to help me stay out of trouble that could add time to my sentence. The reason I wanted to know how you changed is; my lawyers say the D.A. only needs a small excuse to send me to adult prison and keep me there."

"I'll do my best."

"Now that I'm eighteen I'd like to see how it feels to live on the outside, before I get sent to the big house for life or worse."

"I'll make it my mission for you to live outside captivity."

By the end of their first twenty-four hours the Count Claude de No-Bris had been renamed Snuggle Bunny by his new cellmate. Vito had had different experiences in life than Lucas. Yet after talking over their lives, they saw similar personality traits.

Lucas learned Vito could be passive as a drowsy puppy, when handled by someone who knew how to unwind him when he started to get wound-up too tight. At first it was for self-preservation. Then he learned to like the big guy, and became skillful at unwinding Vito for both their sakes. He learned by watching and listening, then using familiar Bebop Jazz techniques like riffing. Lucas' ace card was Vito's fervent wish to stay out of adult prison to experience adult freedoms. Lucas offered alternative techniques to violence for maintaining control in hot situations. What he did felt like theme and variation ad-libbing in a jazz.

14.

The first morning cohabitating Lucas became awake with Vito's huge hard dick gently pulsing on his face. They had slept spoon style on the lower bunk, Vito cradling Lucas from the back. More asleep than awake they had become naked by turns adjusting to their combined body heat. Then somehow by early morning they were in a sixty-nine head to crotch arrangement. Dawning into full conscious Lucas felt hot lips on his morning hard-on and smiled at what was happening. He followed Vito's lead, reproducing the hot wet mouth friction he was enjoying. It was a challenge not to cum right away from Vito's expert manipulations. But he gave it his best Ivy League effort, just in case his life depended on it. After a pleasurable time absorbed in mutual suckling, with Lucas holding back with all his might. The mutual act built up speed and friction enough to cross the demarcation of no return. It resulted in electric fireworks that ended with hard panting feeding each other hot spurts of morning cream directly from crotch spouts as the clouds of bliss drifted away. After the sex, they cuddled and dozed for an unhurried pre-breakfast snooze.

The cell doors opened with loud clangs letting the inmates know; fifteen minutes to breakfast. "You did morning mouth sex pretty good Lucas, I mean for a straight guy. But you didn't do the humming like yesterday that was an unusual treat. So, there's room for improvements, I'll give you a list over breakfast."

"I'll do better, promise."

"Let's wash up, get dressed and eat. Breakfast is usually the least bad meal in the pen." Vito gave instructions over their oatmeal for Lucas to improve his sixty-nine performance, for what became their daily wakeup routine. Lucas was a fast learner and highly motivated. The last item on Vito's list was; he liked lengthy cuddling after sex. Being held by the big man made Lucas feel safe.

Prisoners in neighboring cells were stimulated by the smooching slurping sounds first thing in the day and naturally joined in with their own copulating. That area of the cellblock went from fast furtive impersonal give or take sex, to leisurely mutually satisfying oral first thing in the day creamery. The others' proximity to the Vito-Lucas cell was too close for the guards to risk extra bothersome paperwork and possible punishment from supervision or administration.

Showing compassion, tenderness, or any kind of affection, especially kissing is strictly verboten in any penitentiary system anywhere. Rarely is laughing or smiling or any overt pleasantness allowed in the punishment place. Yet nobody in authority or out said boo about Vito's need to kiss and cuddle his snuggle bunny cellie and that allowed him to do whatever else he wanted as well. Which was consistent with how he'd lived most of his life; either he got his way or potentially all bloody hell had to pay for why not. Lucas had his work clearly defined.

One afternoon while sharing a grainy chocolate bar Vito purchased from the prison commissary, Lucas wistfully asked, "Have you ever tasted European Chocolate? It is so fine compared to this coarse American candy." With the war on, chocolate was not easy to get even with ration coupons in the outside world, and rarely available in the overpriced prison commissary.

Rather than smack Lucas for not appreciating the chocolate bar. Vito was learning self-control as tutored by Lucas. So, he only shook his head no in physical response. The next week a large carton of Swiss Chocolate bars arrived at the prison mailroom addressed to Lucas.

Not keen on trying new things, Lucas had to work to convince Vito to try a small piece of European chocolate.

"You're right this Swiss stuff is way better than our domestic crap. Let me get another piece."

"Since we have a lot of chocolate bars, thanks to you, we can either get fat or sponsor a taste test for the leaders of the different gangs. But only one gang at a time."

"Why do that?"

"So I can pay back your generosity."

"That's not how it works. Don't mention it again."

"Vito, it could be a fun way to keep busy. It would make me happy for us to have a little business on the side."

"If it'll make you happy, that's what we do snuggle bunny."

Before meeting Lucas, Vito's emotions were limited to close to the surface; weepy, pissed off simmering, or totally out of control homicidal tornado. All emotions were expressed externally. With Lucas' new unwinding skills, Vito was learning new mostly good Bebop boy emotions that seldom needed external expression other than head nodding or toe tapping to the beat of the music heard on the small radio in their cell.

The leaders of the different feuding prison factions often kept their minions in line with little rewards like sweet treats because sexual favors were a valuable commercial commodity. Vito's outside contacts using overseas connections could easily get imported candy from Switzerland, a neutral country during World War II. At that point in the war the Atlantic commercial sea lanes were kept open by the U.S. military. Soon Vito and Lucas were supplying a small niche market in the prison with quality imported candy at a lower price and more regular availability than the prison commissary's inferior overpriced products. The reformatory authorities choose to look the other way, and do nothing rather than start something that could result in injury or loss of life.

Lucas was adamant they avoid the prison drug and weapon commerce because the competition was great and profits small. Instead they had the chocolate candy market to themselves. From time to time Vito had to be reminded to stay on the straight and narrow, because he liked to fight and needed little provocation to go off the rails with both fists flying. Over time Lucas got good controlling him, but when all else failed, he unzipped Vito's pants and reached his hand inside to direct the subject away from violence.

Vito began experiencing new feelings; someone was looking out for him without being ordered to and without needing a gun or knife. He liked how that felt and made self-control sacrifices to hold on to his new experiences. When he also realized *he liked* to see Lucas happy, and that in turn made him happy too. He easily gave up the enormous pleasure of punching someone's lights out even when they truly needed a tune-up.

An inmate conversation in the recreation room during a card game, intruded on Lucas' reading. The card player's loud consensus was, "This prison food sucks, but wouldn't be as hard to swallow with decent condiments to hide the taste."

Then a Polish-American convict almost swooned saying, "Polish mustard makes everything taste great, even ice cream. I miss it a lot."

Lucas recalled from a radio news broadcast that since Germany swallowed what had been Poland the best Polish mustard was now made in Buffalo, NY. Vito had a case sent in addition to their regular supplies.

A prison administrator noticed and tracked a correlation between Vito or Lucas receiving packages, and an overall reduction in violent altercations. He sent a memo to staff reminding them, *hands off Vito and Lucas.*

Since they had no place to store inventory, when a package arrived the contents were already sold and only had to be distributed. For new items, they had free tastings which built a loyal customer base from the various segmented groups at Elmira.

In the course of human events glitches occur and Lucas was good at fair and reasonable mistake resolution. Vito liked to handle the problems requiring less reasonable more dynamic solutions. But was regularly reminded by Lucas; the customer may not always be right, but should be kept in one piece for future business.

With Lucas' organizing and record keeping talents and Vito's math skills and connections outside prison, it soon became possible for inmates and some guards to preorder items in Elmira Reformatory that were impossible to get anywhere in the U.S. during the war even with ration coupons.

With little effort, to complement their imported candy business, a new line of tasty condiments was added. Then jams, jellies, cookies and crackers from war neutral Ireland were discovered to be popular with their incarcerated clientele for midnight snacks, or whenever.

The quality of the free domestic labor from the two gang recruiters didn't improve even under close physical supervision. Vito unceremoniously fired the louts by physically tossing them out of the cell for limp wristed scrubbing. With money to burn, Lucas and Vito discussed hiring out their cell's cleaning chores, and day to day mundane business tasks. The question was how to conduct job interviews without creating a ruckus.

Later that day Lucas watched a guard instructs a new slightly built effeminate inmate to go to a storeroom on an errand. It was the same guard and same storeroom Lucas had first been gang raped. He knew too well what was waiting for the newbie named Hasper Bakalis. Lucas told Vito what was about to happen. Rushing over, Vito quickly pushed into the storeroom ahead of Hasper, with Lucas bringing up the rear. After Vito knocked rapists' heads together, Lucas nonviolently demanded they strip down to skin or face another round with Vito's fists. When Vito was finished thoroughly thrashing the hooligans, the three late arrivers left the storeroom with the thugs' clothes and shoes. They promptly dumped the items of clothing down the kitchen's garbage chute. Besides saving Hasper's honor and ass, it was a chance for Vito to bang heads, an activity he was growing beyond but still enjoyed.

Vito, Lucas with Hasper tagging behind went to their cell to watch as the good guards' humiliated, then parade the naked bloodied men from the storeroom back to their cells. There was no believable explanation how the men got so beat up in the course of losing their clothes that subsequently disappeared. The only story they could agree on was it was dark in the storeroom and Martians attacked stealing their clothes.

Hasper watched the shamed inmates' parade with intense interest. "I've been raped before. But those guys look more like skinny plucked chickens than rapists. Anyway, I want to pay you guys for the protection. Only my commissary account is zero. What can I do as payment?"

"Don't worry about it."

"Yeah, it's okay. You don't owe us anything. We enjoyed bringing some balance to the situation."

"But I need to show my appreciation. I know how things work; I've been locked up before you know." With that said Hasper stripped the blankets and sheets off their bunks and hung them from the bars so no one could see in. Then he pulled off his clothing and walked to Vito and undressed him.

Lucas started to feel left out as he watched, until he thought *if Hasper goes down on Vito maybe I can learn a thing or two about how fems suck cock. Anyway, I've never been a voyeur; it will be interesting to just watch and see.* Then to his surprise Hasper turned and stripped Lucas out of his clothing. All three of them had raging erections in anticipation of something. Vito's hard on was huge, as usual. Lucas' cock was larger than one would expect for his height, and weight. Hasper's dick looked big on his five-foot two-inch frame, but was average size for 1945.

Lucas was zoned out gawking at the two others when Hasper interrupted, "Grease?"

Lucas indicated with his eyes a tube of petroleum jelly they used for chapped lips. It was on the shelf next to the radio. Lucas thought *I never used anyone's back door before, and I'm not sure I want to start, after mine was so ruthlessly battered.* Then he glanced up and saw Vito watching him with interest. *Is he looking for approval, or reading my thoughts? Whatever, I'll go along to be one of the boys, and group sex with a stranger as third wheel is an exciting kinky idea.*

Hasper greased Lucas' cock, then bent over and put some petrol-jelly on and in his dark pink pucker. "Okay guys let me do all the moving, Vito stand here and Lucas stands over there, remember don't move. I'll do the moving." Then Hasper reached between his legs and took Lucas's cock and pulled it to his hole; then rode back onto it and Lucas easily slid inside. Next Hasper reached out and took Vito's cock into his hand and then mouth. Vito and Lucas watched astonishment on their faces as Hasper seemed to dislocate his jaw in order to swallow Vito's manhood all the way down his throat in one long smooth glide.

Using a seesaw motion Hasper rode back taking Lucas up to his pubic bush and letting Vito almost slip out, then he moved forward almost sliding off Lucas and downed Vito's whole big thick dick. A contortionist ballet dancer couldn't have created a more beautiful forward and back liquid motion of erotic stimulation. The only thing missing was Bebop music. Physical sensations and visuals were so stimulating Vito and Lucas leaned over Hasper's back, grasped each other's upper bodies and kissed open mouth which heightens their experience. That extra sensual aspect with the fluid motion between them took Vito over the top and that triggered Lucas. Soon they were filling Hasper top and bottom with steamy strong jets; thick ribbons of profuse man cream. Both men were surprised they had so much to give so soon after their regular morning milking.

When the excitement ebbed then flagged the three disconnected, and fell onto the lower bunk mattress. Lucas reached over to give Hasper a hand getting off, and found his softening dick sticky. "When did you cum?"

"Right along with you guys. You were poking me in just the right spot. I hardly touched myself to shoot, you throw an excellent fuck."

"That was my first time active in back, *and* in a threesome. But I used to do it with females."

Tensing up slightly, on guard for rejection Hasper asked, "I wonder if you guys would mind letting me wash all three of us together." Not getting an out of hand dismissal he cautiously went on talking. "What I'd like is to see our three cocks hanging over the sink basin. I'm kind of a clean freak about washing up after sex. I know it sounds like a freaky fetish, but would you mind terribly if I wash our dicks together?"

Lucas watched Vito's eyes light up at Hasper's clean freak comment. "No, we don't mind, come on Vito let's let Hasper play with our cocks in water. He made them messy he should clean the mess."

Smiling approval Vito nodded his head in agreement.

While washing their crotches, Hasper talked. "I learned how to separate my jaw to accommodate large cocks the first time I was sent to juvie jail. I was very young, and learned out of necessity. It was that or get my jaw broke. I was much smaller back then and easier to dominate. Okay all washed-up clean and dried off. Here let me take down the privacy sheets and blankets and remake your beds. I'll let you guys dress yourselves. You do remember how, right?" He dressed last allowing his hosts to enjoy looking at his tight hard compact body.

Lucas watched Vito inspect Hasper's bed making skills with approval. "Hasper would you like a job taking care of our cell, and delivering merchandise once a week or so. In total, it shouldn't take much time. We already agreed to pay someone a monthly deposit of ninety-nine dollars, and ninety-nine cents to their commissary account. That is the max allowed, but it isn't chump change. The money will be deposited anonymously from the outside. Also, Vito and I promise to watch out for your safety as a fringe benefit. Are you interested?"

"A job sure, but I need protection more than the money. You saw what almost happened. Then again having a few bucks in my commissary account would be a nice change."

As the end of his sentence drew near and his release date was set based on time off for good behavior due to overcrowding. Lucas wondered out loud to Vito. "What do you want when I get out of here? Just shake hands, goodbye kiss, and that will be that, or what?"

"I like being around you. You've kept me out of trouble, something my family said was impossible. The sex is perfect, exactly how I like it, with or without Hasper in the middle. I still find you attractive to look at and you are smart. It'll be hard to say goodbye."

"Yeah ditto for me."

"Working together we figured out how to make money in prison without getting busted. Few can say that."

"But wait, you said you wanted to try female companionship and sex."

"Yeah, I said that, but you know I hate to try new things. In truth, I like you in ways I never expected and you look out for me in ways that show it's mutual."

"Ditto here again."

"Are you going to finish your education?"

"No, I won't go back to Columbia or any University. I doubt they'd have me? It would be embarrassing to be known as the undergraduate murder. I have no future plans."

"Too bad, if you knew what you wanted; I could probably arrange it. As you know I have family connections."

"Funny thing is; I already know I'll miss feeling safe with you, crazy, right?"

"Why's that?

"I've suffered so much violence and sexual abused the scares run deep. But hey, like it or not I'm turning a corner and will need to find a job and start new."

"*Have you* ever thought about us together outside prison?"

"Would they allow that?"

"In my universe, I decide what is allowed."

"Yes, I fantasized about us working together outside prison; making money legally. You and I fit together well, and since we added Hasper as a third, I am getting as much quality sex as I want. My heterosexual identity seems secure. I don't need to prove anything to anybody even if I have feelings for you. I don't think I'm queer, but if I am so be it."

"Same with me, so why not see how we do as a couple on the outside. But let's go slow and easy. There are people outside who'd like to see me locked up permanently or dead."

15.

Cash continued to pile up, well beyond their expected, 1945 wealth from prison commercial enterprises. And as both their release dates loomed near, Vito made arrangements for them to purchase an apartment, sight unseen, to cohabitate after release. They got an astonishing good deal, all cash, through Vito's gay uncle a real-estate broker, amongst other endeavors. The apartment they bought was a large duplex penthouse with terraces and indoor swimming pool on Park Avenue. They were set to try life's new adventures outside the confines of the reformatory in high style.

Bored discussing the details he already knew by heart, about how he was to run their prison commercial venture after their release. Hasper consciously changed the subject. "What are you two going to do with six bedrooms? With your business savvy, you won't need roommates or boarders. Do they even allow boarders on Park Avenue?"

Glancing at each other the couple shrugged in unison and then Vito said, "It was a good deal and the maintenance is low; it's controlled by a cheapskate condo board. My uncle was owed an important favor is how we got it so cheap in what he says is an impossible real estate market."

"Did somebody get killed there? Is it haunted?"

"No, the apartment was held off the market to inflate high end housing costs, but now the war is over the Government is seriously going after war profiteer landlords. This apartment seller was one of those guys, so like I said a favor was owed to make his problem go away and we benefited."

"The reason I asked is two of my young cousins are war orphans in Czechoslovakia. If you'd sponsor them, I'd work for you after I'm released next spring. You know I'm a hard worker. They are good kids and wouldn't be any trouble. Plus, I could be there to help keep them in line if need be."

"Huh, we thought you were Greek-American."

"I am Greek-American and proud of it. My cousins are Greek-Czechoslovakians, the Russians took their country after the Germans had and their parents were killed in the fighting. If you adopt my cousins, we three can continue our trysts after prison. I'd like that; you two fit in me just right. And at the same time, we could make a difference for my aunt and uncle's kids."

"Actually, we talked about adopting an orphan from the war. Let's see how it goes on the outside first, and let you know."

16.

Lucas Carmel aka Snuggle Bunny aka Fancy Count Cunt Lucy aka Count Claude de No-Bris was released from prison a month early for overcrowded good behavior. No one came to welcome him to freedom. He had been discharged quickly having no outstanding warrants or other bureaucratic entanglements needing to cleared up before release. Standing outside the Reformatory, holding his official discharge paperwork clenched tightly, he stifled an urge to feel sorry for himself. He was looking at a very different life than he'd planned before killing Dylan.

The old Lucas would have indulged in self-pity no one came to greet him. The new Lucas recognized and accepted why his parents, ridged Midwesterners, had disowned him. He had committed an unforgivable sin against their values, beliefs, and reputation. Lucas had told his Columbia friends to treat him as dead and then made it impossible for them to communicate with him; sending their mail back unopened. Sometime later he would discover Jay was living in Colorado, Aaron in California and Willis was whereabouts unknown the day he was released from

Elmira. Geography prevented the other Bebop Writers welcoming him home from prison, even if they had known the date.

Lucas humbly accepted he was not greeted due to his own doing. He was a very different person coming out of Elmira Reformatory than going in. Adapting to survive he had given up his greatest source of purpose, pleasure and pride, writing, along with its aspirations, and dreams to express something unique.

To prevent potential problems, Vito's release date was administratively changed to coincide with Lucas'. The official justification was the reformatory was overcrowded.

When Vito walked outside to freedom, he leaned down and gave Lucas a long lingering open mouth to mouth kiss. "Smell that air, it is clean and fresh, like us, and free as the birds."

After catching his breath from the kiss Lucas asked, "Which way to the bus?"

"We have a ride."

"Where?" As he said the word a long sleek black Packard limousine pulled around the corner and stopped next to them. A uniformed chauffer got out came around; touched the bill of his cap with two fingers in salute then opened the back-passenger's door. Vito scooted right inside. Lucas was frozen until the chauffer indicated with a nod he should get in too, and then closed the door. The driver returned up front and drove the limo away from captivity.

There were two large men inside the limousine, both baring a family resemblance to Vito.

"Hi dad, how're you?" His father acknowledged the greeting with his eyes and a hand gesture. Turning to the other man Vito said, "Nice to see you Uncle Paulie. Thanks for picking us up."

Since Lucas wasn't expecting to meet Vito's family, he kept his face as neutral as possible while rapidly assessing the older men. Lucas' father bought their suites off the rack from a medium price Midwestern department store chain. Vito's father and Uncle wore expertly hand tailored suites that fit perfectly and were made of expensive looking fabric. Both big men seemed to exude power and authority, but in different undefined ways. Uncle Paulie appeared to be friendly and receptive but Lucas got a vibe he was a force not to be trifled with. Vito's father had the air of a man who wielded immense life and death power solemnly.

Speaking to his male relatives Vito said, "This is Lucas Carmel, the brains behind our legitimate business inside."

"Nice to meet you," Lucas checked himself just before putting his hand out for a shake. He remembered an old Midwestern adage; *don't show your ignorance, follow your hosts lead*. These men were not hand shakers.

Turning to Lucas Vito said, "This is my dad, Vito Cannoli, and my mother's brother, Paulie Gellato. Uncle Paulie and his lawyers arranged for the apartment we bought."

Uncle Paulie winked at Lucas then leaned forward and took him by the shoulders and buzzed each of his cheeks. Then leaned back and said, "You have any problem call me."

Vito immediately chimed in. "No disrespect Uncle Paulie, but if Lucas has a problem I'll take care of it. But thank you for offering."

Uncle Paulie smiled warmly. "Then I'll be *your* backup junior."

Vito's father spoke up for the first time his voice sounded like Vito's only pitched deeper. "What are your plans Vito?"

"Dad I want to stay out of jail. I mean it this time; Lucas and I were making pretty good dough inside. I want us to make it outside and live a regular square life for a change. I'm getting too old to be a jail bird."

Looking stern his father said, "With your uncontrollable killer's temper how are you going to stay out of that electric chair they got up in Sing-Sing Prison, tell me that?"

"Dad, Lucas has been helping me with my anger. He taught me a lot about nonviolent ways to settle things. And he knows how to stop me when I start to go off. I trust him; he blocks me before I get stupid."

Turning to Lucas and locking eyes, using paternal authority the Senior Cannoli said, "You think you can keep him out of trouble and sane?"

Maintaining unblinking eye contact Lucas took a short breath. He was out of his depth; he wasn't dealing with the Midwest or the Ivy League with these powerful men. Nevertheless, feeling but not showing trepidation he said evenly, "Sir I don't want to see Vito get electrified to death in the electric chair and I will do everything humanly possible to keep him safe."

After a long pregnant silence, Vito's father broke the unblinking eye contact with Lucas by giving his brother-in-law a long look Lucas couldn't read. "Normally I wouldn't approve, we saw how you two kissed just now. But if you can keep my boy sane, I give you both my blessing. I make you Lucas Carmel my adopted son for that purpose."

"Thank you, sir," out of the corner of his eye Lucas saw approval registers across the faces of his Vito and Uncle Paulie. Then all four men sat back on the plush leather seats retreating into their own thoughts.

After riding in silence for a while Lucas asked Vito *sotto voce,* "Where are we going?"

"They hired a restaurant to give us a welcome home party. If these big galoots aren't enough, you get to meet the rest of my oversize family."

"I'm honored, but we aren't dressed for a party." Lucas started to feel peeved that Vito hadn't given him a heads up about meeting his family and a party. Then the realization hit *he knows me too well. If he had told me ahead of time I would have worried and been nervous and his father and Uncle would have thought me a wimpy milquetoast.*

"That's okay they understand we didn't get party clothes in the joint. Dad's tailor will take our measurements at the party to get started on our new wardrobes."

"*Really?*"

"A word to the wise; only take a few bites of any food you are offered, that way you won't insult someone by being too full to sample their cooking. You are going to eat like there is no tomorrow, enjoy it. But don't drink too much; the adopted son will want to make a sober impression."

The party was like nothing Lucas had experienced; the food was astonishingly good, both what the restaurant provided and trays of homemade food relatives and friends brought. There was a sixteen-piece dance band with a female singer, and a clown magician for the children. Everyone treated Lucas royally, like he was in fact don Vito's adopted son. Lucas thought *if I was still writing I'd have material for several books just from how warmly these complete strangers have taken me in as one of their own.*

17.

With the end of WWII, the public's interest in Big Band Swing Jazz waned. To capitalize on changing times and tastes the music industry executives renamed Bebop; Modern Jazz. After much effort, the name Modern Jazz didn't sell any better than Bebop, but the word modern became associated with Aaron Gingersnaps' poetry. He became known as America's MMP (Most Modern Poet), indirectly benefiting from the music business's failed name change effort.

Renaming Bebop, Modern Jazz was less than successful. So, the music industry barons renamed it; Cool Jazz. Again, its listening audience wasn't increased much, but Jay Kirack's writings became labeled Cool. In the end, Bebop was accepted as one other dimension of the great American multidimensional art form known as jazz.

While the music industry was trying to remarket Bebop for a larger audience, Doo Wop and R&B caught the publics' ear. They had less complicated melodic lines and harmonies and were easier on dance shoes. By 1955 a decade after the end of World War II, and just after the Korean War; Rock and Roll was born. Rock was accessible for everyone; it was the perfect post wars music for a war weary country that needed to dance.

By the time Lucas had been release from prison, the other Bebop writers had used the murder of Professor Dylan Krumburn in their published writings. The killing initially propelled literary careers with unimagined velocity for such fledgling authors.

Willis Brown missed out on Bebop music's name changing fiascos because he was living in North Africa. His father was paying Willis to stay out of the U.S.A. until the elder Brown's death. Willis' father was embarrassed his son's writings were banned as obscene in the U.S. Not dishearten Willis made friends with a compatible group of expat artists living in Africa. Besides making art and discussing aesthetics, they

202 | PETER MELILLO

shared inexpensive readily available quality drugs and low-cost handsome young men and women selling sexual favors.

However small quantities of Willis' books were smuggled into the U.S.A. from Canada, Cuba, and Mexico, and passed around like forbidden writings always are. It took many years of fierce legal battles fighting all the way to the Supreme Court before Willis' and other banned authors' works were allowed to be sold in the U.S. The public's demand for the right to read what it wanted eventually caused Willis' legal book sales to surpass Jay and Aaron for a time.

Three of the original Bebop writers achieved notoriety, fame, and eventually celebrity status. Over time they garnered prominence as America's most controversial, then forward looking, and finally most significant modern authors. Their most famous works; Jay's *Off the Road,* Aaron's *Holler,* and Willis' *Undressed Brunch,* became modern classics.

Before committing murder, Lucas lived the Boy Scout motto; "Be Prepared." His life would have turned out differently if he had been less prepared, and left his Boy Scout pocket knife home one terrible summer night during an oppressive heat wave. Regrettably the reading public will never know what literary masterpieces it was denied because, Lucas, the best and brightest Bebop Writer had to give up his writing gifts to survive the horrors of a young adult reformatory.

RECALL

Bryce walked into my office without knocking. He was wearing a beaming smile. My boss Bryce never enters without stiffly knocking first and in all my years with the firm I'd never seen him smile. "Randy your work on the McGinty file has been noted by the big bosses as above and beyond expectations. The partners want to show their appreciation for excellence by sending you to Fifty-Seventh Street and Seventh Avenue for the afternoon. Here I'll just put the ticket on your desk, enjoy the concert." That said Bryce turned on his heels, still smiling from ear to ear, and was out the door. My finding one particular needle in a hay stack full of needles must have made him look good too.

I gingerly picked up my reward; it was for an afternoon performance at Carnegie Hall. The City of Amsterdam Concertgebouw Orchestra was performing an all Pyotr Illyich Tchaikovsky concert. Bryce had actually noticed the small bust of Tchaikovsky, the martyred gay composer, on my desk.

The Orchestra performed flawlessly, the program was an emotional rollercoaster ride; soaring beautiful melodies, joyous musical outbursts diving down to deep bleak brooding Russian depths and then flying back to glorious heights of musical euphoria. Naturally the orchestra closed with the *1812 Overture*, it was for an American audience after all. Everyone knows how we in the U.S. love the sound of canons.

The biggest jewel in the concert for me was Tchaikovsky's *Pathetique Symphony* named after his death by his gay brother Modest. The symphony expresses the torment felt by Pyotr Illyich driven by his homosexual-self-hatred, and fed by his homophobic friends' need to protect their reputations from Tchaikovsky's queerness. His friends feared the looming disclosure of Pyotr Illyich Tchaikovsky's love affair with the Duke's son and disgrace and ruin to follow. So, colleagues and friends convinced the great composer he must die to save their reputations and the legacy of his beloved music.

After the concert's standing ovations and encores, a quick subway ride home was in order. I was emotionally wrung out from savoring Russian musical genius performed perfectly by fine Dutch musicians. The audience is a passive but present part of any live performance. So afterwards I marched out of the concert hall with the French National Anthem still playing between our ears. I'm no ingrate; I acknowledge the significance of my boss's gift, even if it was tinged by the staid, stodgy fuddy-duddy firm.

One subway station entrance is at the front doors of Carnegie Hall. Going down into the station's depths I was surrounded by fellow homeward bound music lovers mixed in with office workers from the area. We arrived on the subterranean platform in a constant flow, and then stood eyes cast down patiently waiting for the next Q-train to whisk us away. Naturally no transit rider made eye contact or looked directly at another for more than an instant; out of subway courtesy. It is Darwinian adaptation to subway rush hour crowding infringement into personal space. In my case I was also totally zoned-out by beautiful Tchaikovsky melodies swirling in my head.

As luck would have it a train arrived right away. I was standing in front of subway car doors as a train screeched to a halt directly in front of me. The loud noise abruptly startled my reverie, and I saw a disheveled man standing opposite inside the train car. His faded thread bare shirt was shredded into ribbons; it looked more rag mop than garment. The button-less-shirt didn't hide his perky erect nickel size nipples, well-developed hairless chest, and impressive six-pack abs. The contrast of a well-developed mature body covered in rags was striking. Then it occurred to me a well-built-sturdy body covered in tatters was indicative of our nation's switch to oligarch control.

Glancing down I could see the man's pants held up by a length of clothesline rope. I looked up from his shabby clothes to see he was directing a blank stare in my direction, I think? The man was my age, with strong good looking masculine features. From the expression on his face he seemed oblivious to his surroundings. The other passengers in his subway car were jam-packed around the other three exit doors; not even one was near him. I thought *he must stink to high heavens to get that wide a berth in rush hour.*

There was something about this man's face? It held my attention beyond the unwritten subway rule to only take quick glances at other riders, or be rude. I couldn't put my finger on what it was about this guy, but something was teetering on the edge of recall. *Was he someone once famous, or a person I met years ago, or just a stranger who looked similar to someone else?*

When the doors finally opened, keeping to the rules I didn't make eye contact. Even though he now seemed to be looking at me. I looked down, I know people need eighteen inches of personal space, and gawking invades that. Rubbernecking homeless people, he definitely looked homeless, can lead to rambling unintelligible conversations about the imminent annihilation of the human race by death ray or the forthcoming Martian invasion to enslave mankind. Worse still was the unlikely possibility of a deranged dangerous individual violating my personal space intent on doing me physical harm for rudely staring?

Expecting a wave of pungent stale body odor, I took short breaths and continued to look down in preparation for stink assault as I stepped aside to let him off the train. He wasn't wearing shoes, and needed a foot bath and pedicure. *But there was no odor, no smell, nothing out of the ordinary. He wasn't talking or shouting to himself, or gesticulating wildly. Why were his fellow passengers avoiding him?*

Pleasantly startled not finding a cause and effect stench, I did a double take. *What the hell, his cock and balls are hanging out in the open. This guy's junk jiggled as he walked away. The front of his pants was a gaping V-shaped void; the fly zipper and its surrounding fabric, gone who knew where? He did have a nice looking larger than average set, and an abundant golden blonde pubic bush. Then I checked myself; mouth open staring stunned?*

I didn't know how to react seeing the unexpected forbidden. My mouth stayed open watching this stranger walk off that Q-subway-train. His fellow passengers exiting the other doors scattered in all directions. Only a few glanced back at the man. Those rushing to board the train didn't appear to notice the guy's clothing deficits revealing public nudity.

Part of me wanted to be offended by this man's lack of decorum, my staid stodgy part from work. I was even working-up getting peeved at his disregard for mass transit propriety. *We all must follow the rules; those rules are what keep us civilized.* But there was a shameful primal part of my reptilian-brain getting turned-on hard by this man's *in your face unconventional boldness and attractive big dick.* The turned-on part of me enjoyed surprised exciting diversion, but seldom got exercised since college. *Hey is he checking me out, checking him out? Hold on, how come I'm not getting on my train home?*

My jumbled thinking and turned on cock happened together in counterpoint, then another thought jolted me, *I know that dick and those big balls.* I'd known that cock intimately years ago in my youth. I knew that dick almost as well as my own, once. What cinched the memory was looking for and finding the interconnecting double triangle shaped birthmark at the base of his prick's shaft. I'd never seen another like it, and cock watching and bobbing is one of my hobbies. *So how is this possible?* But the man's face was still a mystery?

Soon all the discharged passengers had scurried away and the waiting people were boarded. Rather than get on the train, I stood and watched the homeless man's genitals disembark, turn right and walk toward the end of the station.

The back of his trousers were split open at the seam, waist to ass cheek bottom. The rope belt held up the pants but didn't cover exposure. Walking away his well-proportioned muscular butt cheeks looked like two melons doing a well-choreographed duet. Watching those faultlessly molded ass globes as they danced harmoniously down the platform, I became painfully aware my cock had grown to its fullest insistent arousal in appreciation. My erection was conspicuously tenting out the front of my pants with its enthusiasm and clearly wanted to get between those dancing checks and rumba. A recollection of my cock doing that came percolating over the edge into full conscious recall.

On auto pilot I followed transfixed the poetic ballet like ass movements. While my mature brain scolded me; *get laid more, milk yourself regularly, and better manage this underutilized libido.* Then a cold dose of reality swept in red flags flying *I am following that ass where, to what and why? Danger, this could end badly, blah, blah, blah...*

The overexposed man stopped at the end of the platform, turned and faced me. He looked forty to forty-five, slightly shorter than my five foot ten inches and probably weighed twenty to twenty-five pounds less than my middle-aged heft. At first glance he had the look of a much younger man, but his hard-lined face couldn't support the illusion close up. I viewed his well-remembered pretty cock in detail, I couldn't help myself, it was the one that partook in many happy memories. Then I made eye contact with his well-remembered pale-lavender (pale blue pink-amber), colored eyes. *I knew him long ago in the best biblical sense. Huh, how did we end up here?*

Locking eyes with my steel-gray eyed gawk he said, "You can give me a hand job for twenty dollars, or blow me for thirty, or I'll blow you for forty."

I recognized his voice before I completely discerned his older, hard lived face. It had grown tough looking. But his voice was the same and brought me back to our youth. "We knew each other. You are Kurt Klingermanz, right? Remember me?"

"I don't know you, why are you following me if not for sex?"

"I'm Randy Stone. We rode the school bus from junior through senior high school."

Kurt took a second to study my face. "No, no memory. Why did we ride a bus?"

"The schools were two villages away."

"I'll suck you off for thirty-five bucks, how about it? I'm a good cock sucker you'll love how I do it. I could give you a free sample if you want to close the deal right now?"

"Thanks, but that's okay."

"Usually I charge more, but you need it."

"Why is that?"

"You already have a hard on for me. See it's showing in your pants. But being horny, you should pay me more, say fifty bucks? I'm worth it, I give great head."

"My cock remembers how nice it felt inside your bottom drawer."

"That costs more."

"Remember, we jerked each other off in the back of the school bus first day of junior high?"

"No, I have no memory of that. But let's talk business. What do you consider a fair price for fucking my sweet ass? I'm not cheap."

"We were the first students picked up and the last dropped off each day. Remember now?"

"If you want to screw me it has to be one hundred bucks with a condom, or three hundred without *and* you promise to pull out before sperming."

"What happened to your memory? Back in the day you had a good one; you always got better grades than me and didn't study half as much."

Shuffling his feet, looking frustrated ready to leave, he licked his lips looking at my cock tented pants. "I guess one day I forgot to remember remembering. Those things can happen you know."

"If I tell you about us, will that help your memory? We were really close friends long ago."

"Are you going to fuck me for $100, or what? The price *will* go up the more you yap. Oh, see now it is $125."

"You used to sleep at my house when we were little and even as teenagers when my parents were away."

Turning to leave Kurt said, "I don't know you."

Is it I don't believe him or I don't want to believe him? "During our first year of high school we mastered sixty-nine in your bedroom when your mother had to work extra shifts on her job?"

"You got any spare change?"

Feeling discouraged raising my voice unintentionally I shouted, "What happened to you Kurt? The last time we spoke you were going to marry Jennifer-Ann?"

Kurt gave me a look I couldn't read. He was obviously ready to walk away. "Just be gone and leave me be if you don't want sex, or have change."

"What happened to you?"

His body language said he was leaving agitated. "Stop bugging me wills yuh? Just get the fuck out of my face!"

"I don't mean to upset you, I'm trying to help. *Here* take my pocket change." When we were kids Kurt was more of a trickster than me. *Was he pranking me?*

Settling down counting my coins and then taking a long slow disinterested breath Kurt said, "Not that I care or will remember, but what happened to you after high school? Why do you get to ask all the questions? I didn't invite you here?"

"I went to Cornell in Ithaca and was hired at graduation for my present job in this City. I'm a forensic accountant."

"Was it a yellow School bus? Did we live out in the sticks with wild animals?"

"It was yellow, and we lived in a farming village far from big towns. The only dangerous animals I remember were bears and poor people ate them for food. Looking back, I'd say we were innocents discovering sex with each other, and we were happy."

"They have big and small yellow school buses in my City. Isn't it crazy we ended up here after starting out with wild animals that eat people?"

"What *did you* do after we graduated high school?"

"Give it a rest will yah, isn't it enough we have different size school buses? Oh, look at your face shut down. Did I hurt your feelings?"

"It's okay."

"Tell you what, mister. Give me five dollars and I'll try real hard to remember something. Because you only got $1.63 in change, and that's like nothing."

Pulling out my wallet, disappointed, discouraged and yes maybe showing hurt feelings. I handed him a fiver.

"Fine, oh a clean new bill, that's good luck you know." He made a show of rubbing his head with his hands. "All right, I remember just a little about after high school, actually just about five dollars' worth. What happened was; I couldn't find a job, my pregnant girlfriend committed suicide, and I went to a house party and forgot everything."

"Could you be a little more specific?"

"No one at the party told me the punch was spiked with LSD. It's a kind of drug. Ever heard that old song 'Lucy in the Sky with Diamonds'? I understand if you can't remember, I have that problem myself."

"I've heard the song, so what happened?"

"I was told the punch tasted really good, and I drank a lot and danced a lot. What I sort of remember was everything went Plastic Man weird after a while. All the shapes of things stretched out and changed, and then stuff that doesn't move moved and got scary. Then somehow I didn't have any clothes on and the State Police took me to a hospital."

"That's your memory?"

"No not really, I know most of it because the guy whose party it was told me. He felt guilty about spiking the punch with too much LSD. He visited me and the others in the hospital."

"Do you have memories of your own?"

"I remember things went Alice in Wonderland strange, and the staff at the first hospital kept asking me questions same as you. See a blowjob would have been quicker than all this yammering and for only a few dollars more."

"How long were you in the hospital?"

"I don't know I got taken to different hospitals. Then I was discharged to the street. That's where I live, the street is my home it's not bad. I'm the King."

"I am sorry you've had a terrible time!"

"I'm homeless; *it is not terrible*; the President says it's an acceptable alternative life style. There are millions of us, I'm their King."

Running fingers through my hair, and then meeting his pretty lavender eyes I said, "If you want, I could find your mother?"

He was twisting at the waist from side to side, and then tilting side to side doing some kind of calisthenics while I spoke. "Don't bother unless you are connected to the spirit world. She's in the cemetery. When she died my health insurance disappeared. Maybe she took it with her?"

"Weren't you eligible for public health insurance?"

"I don't know about that, there was so much confusion about death certificates and other papers; I didn't understand it. Anyway the hospital gave up trying to get paid and released me. I'm fine how it turned out. How are your parents?"

"They both died, one shortly after the other ten years ago. It has to be illegal to turn you out with no after care."

"No, it was explained, they had budget cuts. Fixing my insurance mess was too much trouble for a short staffed mental hospital. They did offer to send me to a big State Hospital, I said no. Do you have *your own* place?"

I anticipated where this might be going and possible consequences. "No, I live with a roommate. It's a shame; I make a decent buck and can't afford to live alone in Manhattan anymore."

"Oh, I see, that's too bad, but can I come over to hang out anyway?"

"Sorry, my roommate has a strict rule, no guests ever for any reason."

"Okay I can respect that, but can I visit your home just for today?"

"My roommate is peculiar. I'm not the one saying no, my roommate is."

"But I never met your roommate. Do you think he'd like an excellent blow job? I'm good I'm the King of blow jobs"

"You wouldn't like him, and it would be mutual."

"So, look, if you want to screw me for old times' sake, fifty is my absolute lowest offer. I usually charge a lot more. I'm clean; I always keep myself clean; it is a habit from the hospitals and good for business."

"I'm sure you are."

"To prove how clean I am, you can take a sniff your finger test? I don't mind giving out free samples as long as we close the deal right this minute."

"Thanks, but I'll have to pass."

"Okay, okay you drive a hard bargain, I don't usually do half and half, but for you I'll make an old-timer's exception."

"What's half and half?"

"I'll blow you till you're almost ready then you can fuck to finish."

While staring at him I transposed his youthful face onto his present countenance, and was flooded with nostalgia recalling fun filled youth. "Right this second my cock would love nothing more than to see if your back-channel muscles remember it. But I don't have fifty bucks on me and if I did it wouldn't be right to take advantage of you."

"What advantage? I'm offering. How much do you have?"

"I don't know, maybe thirty dollars cash after the five I just gave you. But if I had fifty, it would feel like exploiting an old friend. I couldn't do that."

"Bosh, I have much more money in the bank than you probably do."

"We had a special friendship years past; I want to keep those sweet memories intact." Taking out my wallet again then the bills; two tens and two fives I said, "Here take this, and my business card. Call me; I might know someone who can find you subsidized housing and maybe other kinds of help."

Quickly snatching the cash, Kurt counted it, dropping my card to the floor in the process. "I'll take your money, but I'd like to earn it. I have high standards you know. I'm not a Communist. Do you want a blow job, or you could blow me? Or for this money we could do M&Ms, it melts in your hand not your mouth. You look confused, mutual hand jobs; they're completely safe if that's a concern?"

Remembering us growing up together as equals on the school bus, and now in a major power imbalance, I couldn't accept his offer as much as my libido wanted to dance. "That's okay, but thanks. Yours is the best offer I've had today."

"What's your problem?"

"Accepting wouldn't be right."

"Damn, you are a hard case. Okay, you can fuck me now and give me the rest of the money when you have it. I don't usually give credit, but you look so needy. Did we fuck a lot back in history?"

I was torn between lust and scruples, so I stalled to wrestle it out. "Senior year high school, when neither of our homes were available for fucking, we'd drive your old jalopy out into the boondocks and do it au natural in every kind of weather. Those were such glorious fun days of great sex, and freedom from responsibilities."

"At least someone around here has memories. Come on I'll give you an over forty discount."

"You are too generous."

"We can fuck behind those trash barrels. You'll be finished before anyone notices."

I felt a sharp twinge of self-deprecation for wanting to ride his butt. "Thank you but it wouldn't be right."

"It was my idea, I want to do it old school day's style, rah, rah, zip boom bah. Who knows you might even stir-up some memories thrusting around in my back seat?"

I was at an impasse so changed the subject. "I've got credit cards, let's buy you some new clothes before the police arrest you for indecent over exposure?"

Looking indignant putting hands on his hips Kurt snapped, "The police don't bother me and I don't bother them. It's called symbiotic."

"How's that work?"

"If I see them I disappear and if they see me first it's pretend they didn't. With no ID and not knowing for sure if my name *is* John Doe, I'm more trouble than cops want to spend writing about."

"I'd like to buy you new clothes. You'll feel like a million bucks all dressed up in new duds."

"Don't be silly, if I go to Goodwill they give me all the clothes I can wear out of the store."

At a loss what to suggest I said more to myself than Kurt, "You really have all the angles figured."

Kurt's mood changed from all business to a glimpse of my old friend as we exchanged a familiar conspiratorial smile. *Could he be faking memory loss or was the smile a reflex?*

"Sure, I have it covered; the drop-in centers let me take hot showers. They even let me sleep sitting in a chair, all night if I want. See, I don't need your charity old big yellow school bus fuck buddy."

Scoffing with a seldom used smile I snarked, "Why did you take my thirty-five dollars?"

His demeanor changed to ingratiating, like he used to get over on teachers or other adults back in the day. "Walking around money, I don't like to withdraw money from the bank."

"How's that working out?"

"It keeps the money in the bank silly. You know it's a sin to tell how much I have, but a lot. Did I always have a lot of pride back when?"

"As a teenager, you took more pride in your appearance than me. Who would've thought we'd end up the opposite of that?"

Putting his arms straight out and giving his wrists and fingers a jiggle then looking down, his mood seemed to drift to distracted. "Well it's good you still remember things, I guess? See yuh around old yellow school bus memory."

"Wait, I'm worried about you walking around with your private parts in public."

Hands on hips again, eyes blazing exasperation he raised his voice to a shout. "You don't get it; privacy is not for homeless." Then simmering down a tad, half smiling his old familiar naughty boy smile Kurt said, "But you should see the expressions when some see my crotch."

"I bet the reactions are fun, like streaking. Do you remember when we streaked that football half time show?"

"No, don't remember that."

"There must be an ATM around here, let's go and get you a cash advance?"

Raising his voice again and getting noticeably agitated, his pretty eyes slits. "Didn't I say I don't want your charity? Pay *attention for the god's sake* and stop staring unless you are planning to suck on my big banana."

"Sorry, I thought you liked the attention, you used to."

"I got to go; you are wasting my time."

I could always take Kurt in a tussle, so I blocked his exit with an outstretched arm and a look he seemed to remember. "So, your pride's walking around money isn't charity?"

Glaring at me, he stopped and drew a breath. "It was a business transaction, that's what people do; they exchange money for goods or services. You just got the thirty-five-dollar view of my cock and balls close-up. Oh, look at your face, am I confusing you, or just what is your fucking problem?"

Locking on his angry eyes I calmly said, "Kurt, I think I used to love you in my cock-crazy teenage way. At least it felt like I was making love when we shared orgasms. If you leave now I may never see you again, even if you are damaged."

"DAMAGED, you are the damaged one, not me! You live in the past. I'm the King of all I see."

"I want to reconnect with you, whatever I have to do."

Kurt was silent a moment as his demeanor changed from agitated to pensive or *conniving*. I could never tell pensive from conniving when we were young. "So, watching your eyes and face talk to my crotch has triggered something from before. It is foggy, but you know we can never go back to that, right?"

"What *can* I do to help you remember?"

"Your hair wasn't always gray, was it?"

"No, I used to be blonder than you; I went all gray at age thirty."

"I can almost recall you blond."

Hope was rising and I spoke too fast. "We were tight growing up."

"You need to know I won't recall you, as soon as you are out of sight, so it doesn't matter."

"That's terrible."

"No, not terrible, no memory is best."

"Let's go someplace, sit down have coffee and talk. You might remember better in a calm caffeine rich setting?"

"Where we going smarty-pants, you in expensive looking business drag, and I in my well ventilated casual togs? Dummy don't you get it, your reality and mine live on different astral plains."

Some of that sounded like my old friend Kurt. "I'm not ready to say goodbye. We had something special with lots of great fun sex. I miss that. Hell, we had more sex together than boys our age had alone."

"Sounds like we were horny little bastards."

"If your pride won't accept my help, such as it is? Then I'll accept a renewal of our friendship on your terms. Kurt, be my best friend again, little fingers shake on it, like old times?"

"Show me your cock."

'What!" Flabbergasted, I stared at him, *he was serious.*

"You heard me."

"Right here in the Carnegie Hall subway station during rush hour, with all these people around? Are you nuts?!"

"Forget you; I won't shake your finger. I don't want to be friends with a wuss."

"Wait don't go, here I'll show you." With that said I unzipped my suit pants and reached inside to navigate my extra hard dick out into public view.

Kurt turned back. He reached out and stopped my hand with his, and gave me his old bad boy smile. "Were you always such a pussy, even as a boy? You are way out of your league with me, you know that?"

"I want us to reconnect."

"Come on I know a place where you can have a smidgeon of precious privacy. But it doesn't look like you have anything to be embarrassed about, unless it's an ugly one."

Before I could say it looks like yours. He swiftly walked his two melons dancing ass over to a hidden gate at the end of the subway passenger's platform. The gate was behind and to the left of an unoccupied police observation booth. Moving fast Kurt reached the rusting gate and opened the latch. There was a sign, once white now dirty gray welded to it. *No Admittance* was written in big black block letters, in smaller red painted italic writing the sign read, *Employees Only*. Kurt swung the creaking gate open and walked down metal stairs to track level.

I don't like breaking rules, I'm an accountant; following rules is my job. After vacillating a second I cautiously descended the stairs in spite of my better self's punitive judgment. "You know we're trespassing, right?"

"You said you recognized my cock first? Your eyes and voice are getting me close to a fuzzy golden blonde youthful recollection. Seeing your dick may help me remember you."

"Oh, that's it, where do you want me to stand?"

"Over there, move into that space between the stairs and tunnel wall. Jeez, don't have apoplexy; take it easy will yah. I didn't say strip everything off, nobody can see you down here if you did."

"Sure, okay whatever you say." Was he having me on or actually trying to remember? I couldn't tell and that was gnawing at me. In our youth, I would have known.

"Come on hurry up; show me that hard cock with my name on it."

I moved to where he'd indicated. It was a space about four feet wide, the length of the metal steps, open above and facing the electrified tracks coming out of the tunnel. No one was looking down from the platform above. I checked. So, I unzipped my pants again, and reached inside feeling sexy, like a kid doing taboo self-discovery.

Kurt stopped me again. "If you want to help me, bring your whole business out where I can see. Push your pants and underwear down. Show me the works, everything."

Embarrassed, and yet feeling defiant like my old bad boy self. I pushed my clothing down to mid-thigh and fully exposed myself. Then I felt pleased when Kurt's face, real or pretend registered surprised recollection.

"Holy shit, yup I remember your cock and those dangly nuts. Right, no birth marks on your cock. Wait, shit I remember your cum face and even cum taste. Son of a bitch how can I know that?"

"Gosh-oh-golly, halleluiah, Houston we have recall!"

"Can I touch you?"

"Sure, knock yourself out. But be careful, if I get any more turned on I'll cream you good."

Kurt reached forward and lifted my ball sack with his left hand, and then slowly finger fondled each egg shape within. Memory satisfied, he grasped my cock in his right hand and stroked it back and forth. Still exploring he took my dick in both hands and rolled it side to side between them. He was bringing me up to the edge of blastoff; so I stilled his hands with mine. Kurt looked up making coveted eye contact. "Thanks for the memories. You are dredging up bits and pieces from touching your magic cock. I remember it like it was mine. Wonder if you meant something special to me in olden times, like you were saying about me."

"Growing up; you were the most important person in my life. We were there for each other through some tough times. My folks were so into each other they often forgot about me. Your mom seemed to work all the time she wasn't sleeping."

"Back then did we kiss and make out like lovers?"

"No, we saved kissing for girls? Boys kissing boys was too gay for us. We just liked having queer sex. That sounds funny now doesn't it?"

"Not at all, I hate fags and wish them dead."

I was startled how quickly his mood shifted, and stepped back, his hands still on my cock. "When we were kids, you liked everybody and they liked you. Where did you learn to hate?"

"Let's see, we have to sit through preaching before meals at soup kitchens. I learned that God hates homosexuals and lots of other kinds of mud people. It is in the Bible someplace; we should hate people who don't look like us and kill them."

"That's not in any Bible I read, and my guess is God doesn't appreciate homophobic mortals putting words in her mouth. It's hard to believe an all knowing, all powerful, loving God would have a problem with two of her creations lovingly taking care of each other."

"I don't know about all that. They say the new name of God is Great Grand Designer or GGD for short. Maybe they're different gods, one hates one doesn't?"

"Could it just be soup kitchen propaganda?"

"I also heard on the radio that GGD wants all nonwhite and debauchers to be burned in hell. But the last time I heard a radio was in the hospital and I was drugged up to the gills with zowie ideas."

"I used to have a lot of internalized homophobic rage, like the Russian composure Peter Tchaikovsky. Then a therapist helped me accept myself, just as I am."

"Wait, you got cured of hating fags, no shit? I'm not sure my GGD would approve."

"Think about it, how can anyone hate people they never met? That's crazy; Jesus and all the other deities wouldn't go for it."

"Don't tell me what to think or believe."

"What happened to your old live and let live philosophy?"

"Not hating fags … is that like being an atheist? I already told you how GGD hates fags."

"I'm no atheist, and okay being gay."

"Unbelievable, you got cured of hating queers by becoming queer! I know GGD won't approve."

"Nobody ever gets completely cured of homophobia, or racism or sexism or whatever ism the preachers' are pushing on Sunday. I'm not cured, but I am working at weeding out as much negativity as possible."

"I hate fags more than the other mud people, and yet mostly have queer sex for money? I wonder, was I like that at a young age?"

"I for one never paid you or anyone for sex. What difference does it make now anyway?"

"I didn't mean *you* paid me."

"Do you remember in early high school we discovered blowjobs, but from lack of trust we progressed quickly to sixty-nine?"

"No, not really, what am I supposed to remember?"

"It was from Queer fear we started chasing girls. Except we always ended up sucking each other off when the girls wouldn't put out."

"That sounds fucked up; I mean sick."

Momentarily lost in nostalgia I said, "Out of necessity we learned to cum at the same time. Those were the best days of my life."

"Do you know how gay you sound? No wonder I hate fags so much. You were a bad influence."

"I remember how terrified we were of turning queer. That's why we dated so many girls; to prove we weren't. It's funny though, we ended up screwing each other after those girl dates."

"Why was that?"

"For physical relief, of course; we were sexually frustrated with making out with girls who wouldn't put out. I can't begin to tell you how liberating it was when I finally came out and accepted myself, after trying so hard for so long to be someone else."

"I don't understand, didn't I mention I hate fags?"

"Yeah you told me you're just like my idol Tchaikovsky. He couldn't accept himself either."

"Are you calling me queer?"

"Did I hit a nerve? Do you think the world would have loved Tchaikovsky's music less if it knew he was homosexual? I doubt it."

"I think you wandered off track from whatever we were talking about? What were we talking about?"

"Your memory loss, our teen years, how you might have loved me once and now hate me for being gay."

"Oh okay, so back at that ranch then. Holding your throbbing cock makes me remember things. I wonder if you stuck it in me would more memories come."

"I am conflicted about having gay sex while you hate gays."

"Forget all that, I want you up my ass like old times. Top my bottom like you said we did as boys. Pretend we are still boys. No kissing and you have to pay me twenty dollars more, so it is not a sin."

I was at that moral cross road again, trying to keep my integrity and lust balanced while my cock was being held and enticed by a familiar hand, not mine. "Common sense says we don't rush recovering your memory. That way they can stick around, and maybe you will have time to dump your gay hate?"

In a tight stern voice, eyes wide open and blazing Kurt snapped, "Have you always been a namby-pamby wimp? Think about it; if my hand holding your dick makes me remember things. How much more memory can I get from taking it inside? This isn't my first Rodeo, I've been fucked before, and apparently by you. So, will you please give me a fucking break Miss. Contrarian?"

"I want to help, not hurt. You are telling me to do something you say you hate. I'm confused."

"Stop teasing me and do as you're told, fuck me!"

"If that's what you really want? Watching you walk away made me curious if your ass muscles still remembered my dick … like back in high school."

Calming down slightly Kurt met my gaze with a question. Then he spoke it. "What do you mean?"

"We screwed so much, our asses recognized each other's cocks and autonomously bloomed opened to provide excellent accommodations."

"You're kidding, right? I never heard of such a thing."

"As soon as my dickhead touched your bottom bud the door opened welcoming me to slide in. I don't know how? But the why has to be practice, practice, practice. I've never achieved that degree of muscle memory with anyone after you. In hind sight our hinnies were definitely well schooled for penetration by only one cock."

With another mood shift and all the pompous authority of a grand potentate Kurt proclaimed, "Enough talk suite up, get your condom on. The time for action is now, the back of my pants are open for the business with easy access."

"All right since you insists."

"Come-on let's see if my butt remembers your dick." He moved sideways then leaned forward to grip the metal stairs.

Condom rolled on with a gob of spit in the tip, more spit on the outside in case of muscle memory lapse, and a glob fingered into Kurt's tight bung hole for extra insurance.

"What are you waiting for, hurry up. I want to know if my muscles have memory my mind doesn't."

I moved forward getting in position and gave his dangling balls a friendly tug. Bending my knees slightly I placed the head of my cock against his hole, but before I could push, it blossomed open to receive me just like in years past. My dick slid forward going in its whole length until my balls nudged his nuts in friendly recognition. My suave entrance happened without any resistance. It was a forgotten luxury that welcomed me. I took a moment to savor his inside's sensations. "Kurt, you ready for a rump romp? I'm so turned on; I won't be bucking long bronco boy, be ready for a short bumpy ride?"

Kurt nodded his head yes mumbling, "Rump romp, yes I remember we made that up. Lots of memories are flooding in about us now."

"What memories?"

"I already remember how you will do a little dance shuffling your feet for more traction just before climaxing. Then you'll freeze, moan, shake and after seconds buck grunt out each cum blast. Lastly, you'll abruptly stop, finished out of breath. It's like watching an X-rated movie I'm in. This is so rad and right, you inside me and me remembering it."

"Shouldn't we stop now to hold on to this moment, reflect on it and how positive it feels?"

"Hell no, I want you to get moving. Fuck me; ride me hard like in olden times. See I remembered I used to say that, wow!"

"Okay fine, in for a penny in for a buck seventy-five, and if I feel guilty after I'll blame you."

"Come on stop fooling around, fuck me, fuck me hard."

"If that's what *you* want, that's what *you* get." I couldn't remember the last time I smiled that hard.

"Oh yes, uh um that's so good. You said my ass muscles remember you, now the rest of me do too. Uh, uh um, hum, that's it oh yeah, ride me cowboy!

"This happening how you want?"

"Yes, uh, uh, uh, you go cowpuncher, harder. Wow this is unbelievably good, go faster, oh yeah. After all these years, you still got it. Fuck me; fuck me harder, oh yeah yes!"

"Shut up I am working here." Pulling way out, sliding back in deep, I was performing an old familiar dance routine with a long absent dance partner. It didn't take long and the dance tempo increased itself; then the tingling started. Proceeding to full on automatic fuck jockey, my cock pulled out further and pushed back in deeper while my thrusting went into top gear going faster and faster. Based on the guttural sounds he made; I was doing what he wanted. I grabbed Kurt's waist for support and then remembered he liked to feel the small of his back rubbed during this part of receptive sex. I gave him what he liked. My fingertips drummed lightly on his sensitized skin just as I was swallowed into ecstasy. He went from vocalizing each thrust, to yelling oh yes, yes, yes.

All at once smiling big I imagined Tchaikovsky's music swelling in my head as the intensity of my fucking went totally off the charts. I fantasized loudly beating tympani swelling to cymbals clashing my big crescendo finish with the French National Anthem going at full symphonic forte fortissimo. Climaxing shot through me titillating every neurological fiber, and in my head spectacular fireworks exploded as my body shook with imagined cannons' reports blasting each cum discharge deep into my old fuck buddy Kurt. I came hard, and finished totally out of breath.

I had not tried to draw out my orgasm for increased pleasure. I'd been too turned on too long to even consider my usual enhancement. It was enough, more than enough actualizing tactile memory from youth with a full on dynamic reunion highpoint. In shadow awareness, I noticed my feet do a traction shuffle and I involuntarily grunted each cannon shot exploding hot man spunk into the condom. It happened as Kurt said, except I didn't hear any moans of ecstasy. Maybe I was too busy to hear it.

I didn't feel middle aged self-conscious like I thought I might. It was what it was, decades past reconnection to our halcyon history. Still and all, I did think *my orgasm worthy of Pyotr Illyich Tchaikovsky's 1812 Overture. It was an orgasm even worthy of the famous composer and his lover, the Duke's son.*

My reverie was interrupted when Kurt said, "My GGD, I remembered all your moves just before you made them. That's called forecasting or stereo, or something? Shit whatever it's called it was much better than what I usually get."

"I haven't cum like that in years, maybe not since with you." This was said smiling ear to ears and hand on his back for support, as I slipped my cock out.

"It was more than just sex, but I don't want to talk about it."

Getting my breath back, I went up on the balls of my feet and stretched to limber up still smiling broadly. "Right, you're right, it was a lot more than just sex after all these years. Turnabout fair play; now you fuck me. I'm out of practice being anal receptive so go slow if my back door doesn't have yours' memory."

"Sorry I'm done, I came when you did. You rubbing the small of my back felt so, so hot, I went bluey it was great, like I haven't felt in years. Maybe like you said, not since the last time we were together."

"What's the big smile for?"

His mood sharply shifted almost like he felt criticized, his smile disappeared. "Huh, so how come you didn't feel me squeeze your cock when you made me come from the inside out? See there, I came a lot; my milk is all over those steps?"

"Maybe I was blissed out."

He seemed to calm down a smidgen. "Oh wait, yeah I remember, we often came together back in olden days."

"We did … whether hand jobs or sixty-nine or ass fucking we worked for a simultaneous team outcome."

I couldn't tell if Kurt suddenly got paranoid, but his tone changed to defensive. "That's not normal these days, how'd we do that?"

"By rushing ahead or holding back, we didn't want the other to cum first and then lose interest, remember?"

"But how did we do that?"

I rolled my head around on my shoulders to keep my body language open.

"Paying attention and talking during sex. Simultaneously shooting cum was the aim, it made sex better with less gay. No guilt having to service a late comer."

"Huh, so we hated fags back then and didn't even know it."

"No, remember the birthday blow jobs. You always gave me the best sloppy wet birthday gift by loudly humming the happy birthday song to finish me off."

His mood shifted to angry paranoid. "Who taught us that? I bet it was the devil."

"It did feel devilishly good when you went down on me."

"See, like I said."

"Back in the day we could be ready for round two and three right away. At my age, I'll need time to recharge."

Rubbing his head in contemplation, he made a series of faces. Then noticing my watching said, "Saying the sex just now was good is true, but business is business, I still expect you to pay me an additional twenty dollars for the fuck, otherwise it was a sin. The money makes it commercial and not gay okay."

"Whatever floats your boat to make you happy? This whole day has been unique, what's twenty dollars more or less? Want to talk about how it felt to be together again?"

Kurt said our fuck brought up memories of deep feelings for me as a teenager and then hate for having those feelings when alone. He believed my going away to college freed him of his self-hate. Since becoming homeless his sex life has been queer for money without any feeling. His face said it before his mouth did. "After this fuck, I don't know for sure where I am. You have to leave now so I can get myself back."

"I don't want to lose you again. Meeting like this has to be a once in a lifetime thing. We should parlay it."

Kurt looked less agitated, but still confused. His pretty lavender eyes seemed to cloud. "What was, was, what is, is and there is nothing anyone can do about it, least of all us living on different planets."

"Change is good, with change comes growth."

"No, you're wrong, change is an illusion. The Great Grand Designer says the unknown is unknowable, so no change for us. What's the matter with you anyway? Don't you believe in the power of the supernatural … everyone else does?"

"Supernatural?"

"You must know the saying, 'Things and people are never what they appear to be.' Many times, what I thought was solid wasn't and the other way around. I could tell you stories about supernatural goings on I've seen right here in the subway. But I won't."

"Hold on a minute, we have history."

"Maybe our meeting today was a cosmic joke. The GGD was playing with us. Ha, ha, now the joke is over and we must return to our different illusions?"

"But I don't want to go back. I'm enjoying rediscovering you."

"You owe me money. Until you pay up I'll be saying; good fuck, take care, be well, so long, don't let the bedbugs bite, adios, and all that other goodbye shit. Don't be a scofflaw you owe me for the sex."

"Hey you okay, why'd you doubled over like that?"

"A cramp grabbed my gut, I need to sit and fart. You must have pumped a lot of air up my ass pulling out and slamming back in the way you did. That air wants out in the worst way. I need to waddle up to the platform and grab a bench."

It dawned on me my pants were still down, feeling exposed I quickly pulled the full rubber off my well satisfied flagging cock, and tossed it into a corner where I noticed mounds of its brothers of various ages. I pulled up, tucked in, zipped up, brushed off, and straightened my clothes. Then I hurried after scrunched over Kurt, crab walking up the clanky metal stairs. On topside Kurt took a seat, and contentedly farted long, loud bursts of ass gas, just as I arrived. His raucous farting drove the nearby transit riders toward the other end of the station platform.

After he stopped releasing gas, I waited a full minute to let the air clear and then sat down.

"My memories are trickling in faster, mostly sketchy out of focus, except for you and me having great sex and later me feeling guilty."

"What do you think?"

"I was okay before you came nosing around. You need to go, get out of here before something bad happens. We shouldn't have feelings for each other."

"I'm not leaving."

"Why are you still bothering me? You got your rocks off, now get lost."

"You said you have money in the bank, is that an illusion? What kinds of work besides sex have you done to bank money?"

"Work, not me, I watch how you people are herded off to work in the morning crush-hour, all bleary eyed, freshly washed and unrumpled. Then in reverse during evening rush-hour you all look wrung out exhausted, sad or pissed-off and very rumpled in need of a good long wash. My banked money and how I got it is none of your goddamn business."

"I guess from your point of view work looks onerous, but there are benefits too."

"You folks don't look happy going and even less coming back. I know for sure I don't want that cliché life. I'm free as smoke in the wind. At least was before you came around.

"I'm not ready to say goodbye!"

"Don't ruin it -- it's been nostalgic visiting with your memory of us. Now go about your life and make some new memories with new people and leave me and my feelings the fuck back in your history. That way you won't be annoying."

I didn't intend to ruin anything, but wasn't ready to never see him again. "What are your plans for after this minute?"

"You got a hearing problem, or what? I told you I don't make plans. Now you get lost."

"No, I want to stick around with you for a while."

Kurt's face showed shuffling moods, he wanted me gone, and I refused to leave. Unable to find a solution to the problem a resigned look settles over him. "There is a so-so soup kitchen near here, the evening meal is soon. The food isn't too bad, as these slop shops go."

After glum silent seconds studying my shoeshine, I looked over at Kurt's crotch. "Is there any way we could meet up for a friendly fuck, say once a month? I'll pay for a hotel room. We could shower together like the old days. You always liked that."

"I won't remember once a month. Listen; as soon as you leave I won't remember you were here. You got what you came for, be nice like in the past and disappear. I don't want to make threats."

Down to my bones I wasn't ready to give up Kurt again. My life hadn't measured up as I'd hoped, even though today's concert seemed to have me on track for bigger bonuses. My position and material things didn't make me happy. I felt alive during the concert, and was happy with Kurt, as fucked up as he seemed. My face muscles smiled more since running into Kurt today than they had in years. *I was at a crossroad.*

"What if I stayed with you all the time? Would you be all right with being homeless boyfriends?"

"No, I don't know? Probably not, maybe, I hate fags. Wonder what's for dinner?"

"Sex just now gave you a peak at how good it was in our youth."

"Why would you give up your world to join mine? It makes no kind of sense."

"Be open to having new experiences with me, they will enrich your life?"

"Before you came around, every once in a while, I had flashes of memory, they were never good."

"We were boyfriends once. We just didn't call it that."

"Boyfriend sounds like a commitment, I don't do commitments. You just proved you can't afford my time, you owe me money big spender."

"There must be a cash machine around here."

"Look, I live a feral life; eat, sleep, shit, and have sex for money, that's it. No complications, no need for change. I'm good, you go away."

"Not so fast, you might like having an asshole buddy at your side when the urge strikes?"

"I get it; you don't understand living feral, because you are domesticated. You are about things, status, and being social. You care what other people think; I don't give a shit about anything."

"Do you remember being a part of my world?"

"All is predestined by the Great Grand Designer who appointed me the greatest of the greats, but of course no one is allowed to know that, even though so many are jealous of me."

"Kurt, I want to stay with you."

"My hobo life is not byzantine or dependent on your judgment. My life is perfect as is without you."

Taking time to make sense of what he said and I was thinking the silence was heavy. Finally, I came to a difficult but heartfelt scary decision. "In spite of what you said *I've decided* I will stay with you and see if together we can make a life we both enjoy, just like the old days. I'll look out for and protect you."

"You are certifiably crazy, you know that? Go see a shrink; your medication isn't working."

"Show me how to live a feral life? I promise I won't be a burden or expect a commitment or take anything you don't want to give."

"No, no you don't want that. Why can't you just go away?"

"If after a trial period you still want to be a loner, we'll both know it and I'll leave quietly no hard feelings."

Looking startled; his eyes grew big and dark again. Kurt's face showed his anger before he spoke it. "Son of a bitch, you really can't take a hint. What's the fuck wrong with you Randy? Damn it, nobody leaves quietly."

"I'm only suggesting a short trial, just a test."

"I don't want to go on trial, why can't you understand? *You crazy fucked-up fucker, be gone with you!*"

After his raging subsided I said, "Maybe we can create something new, feral for two. Who knows we could start a trend?"

"You just hold on one minute fancy pants cock sucker. Ugh, wait, Umm I know this won't work? Why are you mixing me up? Get behind me devil, be gone demon!"

"You know me, once we had something good going on. Just now we had great sex, where's the problem?"

"All right then what's the problem, let's see, okay, no not that, well maybe okay, no, yes, have to see I guess. Shit I don't know, come along let's at least get on line to eat."

"I'll follow you lead."

"If you won't leave then ditch the suit jacket and tie. Throw them over there. Now unbutton and pull the shirt out of your pants. Here I'll muss up your hair and rub some subway soot in it, on your face, shirt and hands. There, now you look presentable, but I'm doing this against my better judgment. Just follow the other bums and don't act fancy. If you stick out, I won't know you. I live in this world don't embarrass me."

Wearing gritty grimy subway muck made me feel uncomfortable, but invisible. No doubt having just had sex in a public place contributed to my feeling like an invisible degenerate, and at the same times a sexually liberated rascal. My mind's disorder must have showed, because I was admitted to be fed unchallenged. We sang a long slow groaning hymn and then saying grace seemed to go on much longer than necessary to smell the fire and brimstone of hell if we didn't change our evil ways and give up demon rum.

Looking down at the food I was handed I wondered out loud, "What kind of meat is this?"

"They call it mystery meat; it's made from road kill all pressed into a long roll and sliced up. Some homeless wiseasses claim it's not meat at all, rather something made in a chemistry lab from toxic waste. I doubt that, toxic anything would taste better. You'll get used to it; it's served in a lot of these places, it's donated by whoever collects road kill. Some say it is a government conspiracy to get rid of surplus war materials by grinding them up and sticking the mess together to look like meat. I don't pay attention to that kind of talk. When you're hungry it tastes fine."

"I just thought of something I'll need your guidance on, how to instantly vanish into your world without leaving a big hole in mine."

Eyes big, looking alarmed, lips in a frown Kurt admonished me. "No, no you can't vanish too quickly. There is a method that must be followed if you want to disappear without trouble. Otherwise the police can be a big bother and *they will* look for you for years, trust me I know of what I speak."

"All right, old friend, tell me how to vanish properly so no one gets upset?"

Head down facing his food, Kurt hungrily scarfed down his meal. I nibbled at tepid apple sauce; despite its tinny aftertaste. Finishing the last morsel on his tray, Kurt looked up in surprise. "You are not eating; they get mad if you don't finish all your food and fast. They watch us constantly you know. Give me your tray and take mine. Make small talk while I eat, maybe they won't notice and make a big stink."

I didn't see any mandatory clean plate rules posted. Nevertheless, I tried to explain my breaking the real or imagined rubrics. "I'm used to having wine with my evening meal and eating later."

"Oh, you don't like the food, don't let them see that, it hurts their feelings and they take revenge."

He knew me from our youth. "When I am hungry I'm sure this food will be delicious. I've had a lot of excitement today."

"Randy, you asked and I told you about me after high school. What's your story after I saw you last? Tell me while I eat your food."

"I told you I went up to Cornell University. I'm sorry we didn't keep in touch. I got busy with studies, working part-time jobs to pay for school, and chasing after unfulfilling sex."

With the sleight of hand of a magician Kurt switched our food trays. Then rapidly eating he talked with his mouth full. "Weren't there colleges closer to home?"

"I got a scholarship; fifty percent off the tuition. It turned out cheaper than the nearest public college, and Cornell is excellent."

"I never went to college, but everybody knows college warps your mind. So, aren't all colleges just the same? School is school, warping is warping; only some old buildings have ivy growing on them."

"There was no warping that I noticed. There are good to excellent Universities, so-so ones and some are only about their sports teams." Kurt looked up confused. "Let me give you an example, after graduation most professions require a certification, or some other licensing examination. The good schools teach beyond the test so their graduates pass easily first try. But graduates from weak or bad schools often can't pass the exams even after several tries. Does that help you understand?"

"No not really, I thought if everybody studied the same thing they'd know it the same? What is the point of going to college if you can't pass a test?"

"To charge tuition, so the State can collect licensing fees to verify minimum standards? What were you telling me about the right way to disappear?"

"Okay *that* I do understand."

"What's first?"

"Rent a post office box for six months. Give the P.O. a bogus physical address when they ask. Direct all your current mail to the P.O. Box."

"Sounds easy enough, and then what?"

"Resign from your job, have them hand you your final pay or if that isn't possible have them send it direct deposit to an existing bank account. Wait until all checks have cleared then empty all your accounts. Use that cash to open a new bank account under another name using a fake social security number. I can help you with that number; or the IRS issues tax payer numbers that look just like a social security number, but aren't. Or you could use my name and S.S. number. Wait at least a week and then sell everything of value on line and have that money sent to the new bank account."

"Fascinating, you have this all worked out, very thorough."

"You must make sure the new bank doesn't know who you were. Sometimes they ask sneaky questions to trick you. When you open the new bank account, rent their biggest safe deposit box at the same time. Put most of your money, jewelry and any small valuables in the safe box. Give me the second key to the bank box; I'll also need to sign cards for access in case you are too busy being homeless."

"No problem old buddy, I always trust you one hundred percent."

"Next go to your apartment, save valuable things like artwork or antiques you can't sell quickly and put them in a storage unit. Then give away what you can't sell or want to keep."

"What about clothes and shoes?"

"When the time is right, after a month or so, we'll take the clothes you don't want to put in your storage locker to the Good Will Store. At that same time, we'll have them give you suitable homeless clothes. I find it's best to wear the Goodwill clothes in layers for fall, winter, and spring. That way you keep warm and a change of clothes is always with you, in case someone is chasing you. Let me have an extra key and sign a card for your storage unit, in case you want me to get something for you."

"So far it sounds doable with your help and my ivy league MBA."

"It should take around thirty days to do everything. Then tell your roommate and friends and family you are going to northern Canada to pan for gold and go spelunking. Have them forward any first-class mail to your post office box."

"Bills too?"

"Especially bills, say you will send a permanent address when you have one. Then your job and home, friends and family have a reason why they don't see you."

"Jeepers, you covered all the details, and well thought-out plausible."

The light behind Kurt's eyes increased, I remembered its intensity as kids. "Randy, remember when I said touching your dick started my memories coming? Now I don't want to remember some of the stuff flickering in my mind; the images are all mixed-up with a lot of terrible things. Was I a bad person when we were young?"

"No, we were good kids who sometimes made stupid choices."

"I'm really getting scared."

"Slow down breathe normally, focus on your breathing. That's better; it looked like you were going to hyperventilate. Okay good, keep breathing like that slow and steady, that's it. Tell me what frightened you?"

"Okay I know, no, right, well maybe, fine we need to have a conversation about, what, something important, if I remember what it was? If it pops up again truth is best. There is so much confusion going on in my brain, it's all jumbled."

"What truth is best?"

Finished eating then pushing the food tray away, Kurt stood. "Let's get out of here so they can clean up for the next seating. Come on, I'll show you where to dump that tray. We can do our talking walking before I have a full-blown killer memory attack."

"Okay, lead me to my new feral life. This is exciting," *and nuts!*

Kurt steered us a couple of blocks south to a sliver of a private park wedged between two huge office towers. I remember the developer got generous tax abatements for donating the park as public space. We lay down on wooden park benches facing each other. "Before, you asked what scary things were swirling in my head."

"I'm curious, maybe can I help."

"There are random images of you and me at different ages all mixed-up mostly having sex and sharing emotions. There are songs that keep going round and round and run together and over and under each other with images of dying people."

"Can you be more specific?"

In quick mood shifts, Kurt went from looking frightened, confused, intense, and then stone cold somber. "You want us to be homeless non-fag boyfriends, right? Well you need to know in my world there are rules; the feral life has very strict rules. Being sexually exclusive is not allowed. In your old domesticated realm people pretend to be monogamous, but everybody knows that's a joke. In the feral world, we don't approve failed systems. Got it?"

"I suppose, in a way that makes some sense, I guess?"

"We have to be practical; do you remember what Darwin said about Intelligent Design's adaptability coming from supernatural belief in science?"

"Gosh no, what *did* he say about that?"

"He said the design must adapt or die for the sake of higher numerical powers."

"Oh, he did, did he? I missed that."

"Then let me explain it to you, there are these rich people who come around every so often. They like to have sex and be shamed by homeless folks, even high and mighty ones like me."

"No shit?"

"Yup, sometimes they just want us to fuck them while their chauffer drives around busy streets with the tinted windows down so any passersby can look in and watch."

"No bullshit, why do they do that?"

"I don't know why. Sometimes they send their limos to take us to parties in big empty warehouses, piers, or other abandoned places they own. They outfit the spaces with black leather fun stuff; fuck slings and things, and other kinds of kinky sex toys you don't see that often."

"I wouldn't have guessed?"

"These people tip much more than our usual sex tricks and their catered party food is always tasty and abundant. You can even fill your pockets and take doggy bags, they encourage it. So, if you're my non-gay boyfriend you will have to participate with the rich snobs when they come round."

"I don't get why rich people want to socialize with homeless?"

Adjusting his body to get more comfortable, Kurt's face looked like he was searching for an answer. "How am I supposed to know … well wait, no, I guess … I don't know the answer to that, because they don't come around that often."

"I was just wondering."

"I've heard gossip some of these rich ones caused homelessness in the 1980s, by grabbing tax breaks to turn SRO residential hotel flop houses into luxury buildings. I think they call that gender-fucking the neighborhood."

"You probably mean gentrifying?"

"Maybe I do and maybe I don't, that's what I heard, gentrifying."

"It seems strange for the high and low classes to mix. But hey, what do I know?"

"Well maybe from time to time they want variety in who fucks them?"

"Huh, you think so?"

"What I know is they're sick fucks who enjoy being spit on by the likes of me the king. For all I know it is a rare acquired taste to bow down and be shamed into remembering they're rich and powerful. Isn't that why you are here?"

"Do you believe any of what you just said?"

"How could I believe what I don't know? I can't remember my name most the time."

"You are Kurt Klingermanz, I'm Randy Stone, and we grew up together."

"So, you say, but what I *do* know is I'm very popular with the hoy-palloi because I can keep my cock hard all night long if I don't cum too often. They like that and to treat me as the royal king, so whatever they like, I do. I don't mind being as kinky as the grand dames and dandies as long as they pay extra for kink. And some of these old farts are twisted as all hell Just wait you'll see."

"Kinky like how, tell me what to expect?"

"Some want me to call them names, be rough, and even threaten them. Others want me to do stuff on them; like spitting and pissing. One time a group fed me by hand to over full. Then they had me take a crap on top of a big glass table. I could see all these faces looking up, watching my asshole open and dump. They clapped when I was finished and wiped my ass with 100 dollar bills. Ugh, it was strange, but they liked it."

"Sorry, I couldn't do anything like that. I'd be embarrassed."

"After they gave me twenty-five new crisp clean 100 dollar bills and a pat on the back for the good show. Maybe you aren't cut out to be feral and should go?"

"What happened to the shit dirtied money?"

"They took it as souvenirs or party favors or whatever the hell the sick fucks do. Who cares?"

"Did any of these rich people try to hurt you?"

"You shouldn't listen to rumors."

"What rumors?"

"You know; about the snuff parties."

"I didn't hear any rumor, tell me."

"I don't know why I bother; you're just a tourist soon to be gone?"

"Tell me."

"Supposedly some of the younger rich have exclusive parties for only one homeless guy. Rumor has it they pick a really young one with strong lungs. They call him the guest of honor."

"What gift does the guest of honor receive?"

"I've heard at first the honored guest is treated royally. All the party goers must do whatever he asks. Then about halfway through the party; bit by bit he is drugged with food and drink. Then all his clothes are auctioned off him while he is too ossified to object. I've heard as the party gets later and wilder, pieces of the guest's flesh are auctioned off, cut off and cuts cauterized. At the end of the party whatever is left of the guest of honor is slaughtered by highest bidder. Then all the money raised is given to charity. That's the rumor I heard, don't believe it."

"That sounds horrifying, could it be true?"

"No one I know went. It's probably another street life myth. We have a lot of those."

"You don't sound convinced."

"Listen folks around here disappear all the time just like in the world you come from. Some get hit by buses or trains and many die in their sleep. If you didn't see it, it didn't happen."

"Tell me more about the rich patrons *you* like to please?"

"I don't know if I like to please them so much as their money and food are plentiful. For the most part they are older than us, with more money than good sense. Sometimes they stare at you in creepy ways. I don't think they can help themselves from doing that. They enjoy seeing us stuff our faces and even provide thermal doggy bags to take away."

Covering my face with my hands I wondered *why wealthy folks would want homeless people to abuse and degrade them, and pay for the humiliation. Is there some ulterior motive I'm missing? If it is only fort denigration, they could have their own class do that with less bother, and risk. Could Kurt be making this up along with everything else?* I pulled my hands down and said, "Let me see if I understand, you want us to be not-queer but sexual boyfriends living together on the street, except when the rich come calling and we drop everything to have sex or otherwise please them, is that right?"

"Basically, oh wait actually there are others that aren't so rich or kinky who come around wanting sex."

"Sorry, I don't get the attraction? Why?"

"Okay to be clear, what I mean is they want sex with homeless men who can still get hard and stay hard. There are not a lot of us left; between illness, addiction and old age. I guess if it is a problem for you with these *other* people, you don't have to put out. They don't have any fancy party foods, or pay much above scale for sex. In fact, some actually want frequent flyer discounts, can you believe that?"

When I came out I stopped having anonymous sex. Now I prefer knowing something about who I'm being sexual with. It makes for better sex even if it is only a casual hookup. "So, give me a reason why I would want to have sex with these other strangers?"

"You and I are the same age; you also have a big dick. Working together could be a money maker; two dicks are worth a lot more money than one, with me negotiating."

"I still can't wrap my head around the attraction for non-homeless people to want sex with homeless folks?"

"You are really thick headed, you know that? You are not cut out for my kind of life ... Okay, okay fine, and think of it like renting a car. You can get a rent a wreck or tiny economy car, except very few people want those. Most renters want cars their neighbors would envy or at least not look down on. Or if they can afford flamboyance, and willing to pay the ninety percent more to go first class, rent a glamorous luxury racing car."

"And where are the homeless on that scale, rent a wreck?"

"No, there are people I've not mentioned yet. They want to rent the esoteric; drag queens, trannies, whips and chains and pain, or dirty disgusting foul mouth crazy homeless with big hard dicks ready to fulfill down and dirty fantasies. Now do you understand?"

"Have you ever rented a car?"

"No, but I know about renting out my body. I do it regularly, I'm sure it's the same. Have you heard there is no accounting for taste?"

Needing time to think about what was going over my head, I changed the subject. "You were going to tell me about living the feral life. Are there real dangers I need to watch for, beyond what you already mentioned?"

"Trust your instincts, if something doesn't feel, or look, or smell safe, run fast."

"That's it, all you got, nothing more?"

"Okay, sleep with one eye open? At the moment, we have teenagers from the suburbs, pouring gasoline on sleeping hobos and lightening them on fire. Just for the fun of watching them dance burning to death."

"Now that sounds scary, have you lost many friends?"

"A few, but the gossip is nonstop. You have to be careful sleeping is what I'm saying?"

"How could anyone protect themselves sleeping?"

"Burning bums is a fad, it will pass they always do. A few years back we had some holier-than-though pious bitches poisoning street folks. They claimed we were evil vermin and they were improving society by speeding us along to hell. These nut jobs made tasty treats out of rat poison then handed it out to hungry bums. I didn't see any improvements to society afterward, except the pious poisoners were in prison."

"So, your advice is I shouldn't sleep or eat? Great and probably drinking is also out."

"Don't drink from any container that is already open. I take cat naps during the day but always with one eye open. And like your mother used to tell us, 'don't take anything from strangers,' remember?"

We exchanged head nods with small wry smiles like long ago. He seemed to have forgotten about me having to have sex with strangers. I needed to define my feral limits once he accepted me as a companion, or was it if he accepted me as a companion? And I needed to figure out if going feral was really what I first imagined.

The little smiles brought to mind all the big conspiratorial, gleeful, even tummy tickling smiles we had exchanged in past years. Feeling nostalgic for our youth, I had to fill the void with chatter or get depressed. "You were going to tell me how you learned to vanish without a trace, I'm still wondering?"

Looking troubled, Kurt scratched his head, stalling. "I vanished the usual way, discharged from mental health confinement. I already told you. Good question though, I'll think on it?"

"Could it be you read about disappearing or someone told you?"

"I can't concentrate long enough to read anymore. But I should know how I know?"

"Don't force it; it'll come back."

"Maybe ... my memories are coming in fits and starts. ... I told you that ... Oh wait, there it is ... I know now."

"Tell me."

"Marvin, there was this guy Marvin Zukowskely. He dressed a lot like you. He started coming around more often for sex. Somehow, he could almost always find me. That's unusual; I never go back the way I came and change my location often. It's an old Native-American trick to avoid ambush."

"I remember that from Boy Scouts, what about Marvin?"

"He had a baby dick."

"Baby dick, poor bastard, I've only heard about them. Was he self-conscious?"

"No, he owned it, so it didn't bring him down. I liked that about him. Come to think about it, he was a sweet guy."

"Life isn't fair, one way or another. Peter I. Tchaikovsky's friends made him drink cholera water and die rather than face scandal for being homosexual. Oops I digress, going off on a tirade again. Did you love Marvin?"

"He loved to get fucked and gave good head. Sometimes he'd bliss-out chowing down on my dick, like you did to make my birthdays special."

"Sounds like you handle sexual dysfunction pretty well. Ha, ha, ha. I bet you could work as a sex surrogate."

"I never liked the four-letter word work. You're thinking like a domesticated drudge again. Get over your old wage-slave-self and go feral, rah, rah, rah, zip boom bah, or be gone apparition from the past."

"Okay old friend, what was it about vanishing that brought Marvin to mind?"

"A stray memory about him just floated to the top of a shit pile of memories. Marvin said life's pressures were too much."

"I can relate to that, I'm a forensic accountant at a prestigious old firm. You wouldn't believe how mundane and stressful my life is."

"He was an accountant too, I think, maybe?"

"What is it about Marvin's disappearing?"

"Good question, what's the answer? Oh, wait yes, I do know, out of the blue Marvin decided to leave his wife and four kids and come live on the street with me, just like you did today. That must be why I remembered him, he dressed like you."

"Did he start out as one of those not-rich regular sex clients you mentioned?"

"Oh, you're paying attention to something besides my dick. I remember you swinging on it hard for special occasions."

Blushing, I chalked up his comment to my wayward lip-smacking youth. "You were telling me about Marvin, not your dick. I know your dick; I grew up with it and remember just how to make dicky spit."

"Marvin missed finding me a few times he really wanted to get fucked and that decided him to go feral."

"Gees it must be hard to leave a wife and kids."

A sinister look passed over Kurt's face, as if storm was coming. "He never mentioned that. Why do you want to know so much about Marvin?"

"Is he the one who told you how to disappear without a trace?"

"Not exactly, well yes somewhat I guess. Honestly, I didn't mind him that much at first. The reason we figured out how to make him vanish without a trace was to avoid child support alimony and all that dust. Wait I remember, he was my first feral boyfriend to disappear. We learned together. Is that's what you asked?"

"Fortunately, or unfortunately, I don't have a wife and kids. Where is Marvin now?"

"Eventually his snoring became too much."

"What happened?"

"He snored something awful is what was happening. He sounded like a chain saw chewing on aged hard wood. Just now I recalled that sound from cutting firewood for money. That's how he sounded snoring."

"I remember you used to shovel snow, mow grass, wash cars, and cut wood for pocket money. Did you love Marvin?"

"What I recall is I couldn't get any sleep with Marvin around. We talked about it and he tried this and that to stop the noise, nothing worked. I had to put an end to that ruckus."

Suddenly an unwelcome insight struck and made me sit straight up on my bench. "How did you put an end to Marvin's snoring?"

"Why are you asking so many questions? I think some information is too personal, don't you?"

"Tell me, I want to know all about your feral life, so I can be feral with you."

"Okay but only because you're insisting. One night while Marvin was snoring away crazy loud, I couldn't stand it anymore and pinched his nose and covered his mouth with the palm of my other hand. It was only to keep him quiet for a minute. I desperately needed sleep, I was oh so, so tired. He didn't struggle much. I'd say he passed away peacefully in his sleep before I realized what happened. It was his gift to me so I could get some sleep. He was very generous and I still appreciated his sacrifice."

Thinking *that's it, enough is enough, I'm done here, AND, No, I want more adventure, onward and upward.* My conscious mind split, fifty percent wanted to run not walk back to my old safe predicable, stuffy staid life, and fifty percent wanted more feral ecosphere.

At the point, I realized indecision immobilized me; a physical phenomenon arose from within and shook me. I felt a forceful invisible power leave my body and take up a protective stance between Kurt and me. It felt like, I imagine a defensive force field activated would. I don't believe in supernatural anything, other than weather. So, I'm not calling it a guardian angel, or any other religious portent, and Freud certainly never mentioned the unconscious mind expending energy to get-up-and-go defensive. But whatever it was unified my mind and gave my thinking clarity. I stood, stretched feeling empowered.

"Why didn't you just ask Marvin to leave?"

Surprised then confused looking, Kurt was quiet. "Okay well, that didn't seem right. He left his wife and kids to be feral with me. How could I just abandon him back to his old life? No, that would have been wrong. I'm a superior being according to the Great Grand Designer. I couldn't just discard Marvin. I sent him to his celestial rewards."

"You said Marvin was your first feral boyfriend. Were there others?"

Looking thoughtful scratching his head, it occurred to me he must have head lice. After a minute's concentration Kurt faced me wearing a completely flat affect like when I first encountered him today. "Well since you want to know I'll have to tell you, won't I. There were Albert, Ryan, Bert, Harry and some guys who weren't my non-gay boyfriend long enough to remember their names. One nameless Joe I called slugger because he liked to hit people with his fists. He only tried that once with me. You see the truth is; many of these non-gay boyfriends were actually gay."

"Did they all snore?"

"Oh no, but in the end, they all had annoying habits. Slugger for instance would walk up to strangers, hit them in the face with both fists and then laugh his head off pointing his finger when they looked shocked. You know that's just not right!"

"Did you put an end to all your previous boyfriends?

"Randy, you know I had to I'm the king, it was my duty, and the right feral thing for the public good. You understand we live by different rules than your old wage slave's world."

"So I'm learning."

"Feral can mean many different things, like Darwin said about Intelligent Designers changing their message to fit in."

Staring into his pretty lavender eyes; I dubiously thought *I used to love the man with these eyes.* Then I felt my stomach twist as I mused *but the man I loved had all his marbles and was not a killer. I'm not a cock crazy kid anymore.* "You must have many storage lockers and safe deposit boxes?"

"That isn't practical; I consolidated to a few big ones. It is lots cheaper and easier to manage. Why do you ask?"

"How does it feel to kill someone?"

"I suppose you really want to know? It got easier each time, but I didn't set out to kill anyone. Things just went that way; I was more asleep than awake when Marin went to his reward. I'm sure he didn't mind."

I stood, feeling protected by an invisible force. Then I turned around to get my bearings and headed out, keeping Kurt in my peripheral vision.

Kurt's eyes opened wide and went bright like car headlights shifting to high beams. He snarled his lips back and angrily shouted. "Randy, where do you think you're going? You can't just walk off like that; the King has to digest dinner."

"Changed my mind, see you around old buddy."

"Hey wait, you agreed to be my not-gay boyfriend." He jumped to his feet while shouting, trying for a mollified tone but failing. "Stop don't go, don't leave me. I confided in you. You saw, we are good together. Damn it all, *you promised* to go feral!"

After two beats when I didn't respond to his shouting, he yelled full volume; out of control. "SHIT WHATEVER YOU DO DON'T TELL ANYONE WHAT I SAID. BOYFRIENDS DON'T SQUEAL ON EACH OTHER, don't be a dirty rat fink tattletale. WE HAVE HISTORY!"

I paused and gave Kurt a goodbye hand to forehead salute. "You know I have to tell the authorities your body count. That is what *you* expect; serial killers always want to be stopped. Isn't that why you told me?

"NO!"

"The Q-train is back this way, right?"

Quick as a flash Kurt ran toward me at full speed. I saw when he pulled a gray, thin metal box cutter from his pocket and push out the shiny silver cutting blade. When he reached me, I felt my inner-now-outer force's protection take over. My body drew a full breath and side stepped pivoting a quarter turn and grabbed his wrist holding the blade. Then with a hard-sweeping kick my shoe slammed into his bare ankle as my grip pulled and twisted the box cutter forward against his full force resistance. An instant after the kick registered pain on his face, my wrist strength reversed, pushing in the direction of his resistance. Using his and my force against him, he went flying backwards off balance. With gravity's help, he landed hard on his bare butt.

Then he sprawled out on the pavement, arms and legs all this way and that. His scratched-up box cutter remained in my hand. I unlocked and retracted its blade, and slipped it into my pocket. Kurt's all grownup hard lined face wore the exact stunned facial expression as when we were kids and he'd started something with me and I'd kicked his ass to the ground. His visible shrinking prick had shriveled to thumb thimble size in defeat. I guess something's never do change.

Addressing my bewildered looking old friend prone on the pavement, I felt a pang of pity for both our middle-aged selves. "Were you faking not knowing me earlier?"

"No, but I got a familiar feeling from the way you ogled my cock and ass the more you did it. Then after we had sex you drifted in and out, but I didn't know how to stop pretending without looking the fool."

"You had me guessing, until you fondly mentioned my excellent birthday blow jobs."

"Look you said you loved me once, and maybe I loved you back. I told you things I've never spoken of. You should respect the feral tradition and not squeal on me."

"You have it wrong; feral means not knowing where or when or if a next meal comes. Safe Deposit Boxes full of dead boyfriends' ill-gotten treasures is domesticated *criminal activity*."

No doubt for my benefit, while Kurt laid prone on the ground he distractedly manipulated his cock back to maximum flaccid protrusion. "Don't be a squealer, everyone hates stoolpigeons. How about I share some of my wealth and big cock with you?"

"No thanks."

"What are you going to do?"

"If you were smart, you'd turn yourself in. If the police have to hunt you down, they will beat you for giving them extra work."

"They won't; I already told you they ignore me."

"Serial killers make cops look bad; they don't appreciate it."

"Are you going to squeal to the police right this minute?"

"No, I'm going home. I need to delouse and shower. Then I'll pour a generous glass of single malt scotch whiskey over ice and write up our encounter. After emailing my write-up to this police precinct, I expect to sleep well."

"What about for old times' sake; give me a couple of days to get out of town?"

"Sorry, I could see from your body language you felt better unburdening about your murders. So while it is fresh, I expect to feel catharsis writing it all down and sending it on. It is what old friends do to stop serial killings."

"Damn it, Randy. All these years later and you would fink me out? Remember we once had something special going on, we could have that again. You know I only hate fags half the time."

"If your assessment of the police is correct, they won't be bothered with my write-up. It's the luck of the draw for you, old chum. But if the policeperson who receives my account of your crimes is having a slow day or is looking for a challenge, it would be best if you go confess."

"Bastard, you are playing Russian Roulette with my life. All this time and you haven't changed one bit."

"Did you suffocate them all in their sleep?"

"Of course, you know how I hate a mess. Why do you care? You never met them."

"I'm sure the cops can find you if they want."

"Randy, are you enjoying bringing me down after we shared our bodies and a meal? What happened to your fidelity?"

"Listen closely Kurt, I won't repeat myself. As far as we know there are no witnesses to sign complains, or bloody DNA covered weapons, and most likely all your bodies are buried in Pauper's Field. My guess is your victims were listed as homeless John Does who died of unspecified natural causes."

"Aha, so it comes down to your word against mine? I can handle that."

"Not exactly, everywhere you signed for access to someone's safe deposit box or storage locker your photo exists alongside theirs for security. Turn yourself in and save everyone unnecessary trouble, including you."

"Still, it comes down to your word against mine. There must be millions of those photos; nobody will look."

"It can't be my word against you. I work for a centuries old white glove accounting firm. They wouldn't relish finding out I screwed a homeless serial killer in public after the expensive concert they paid for me to attend, while drawing wages. If I want to keep my job, the report to the police will have to be from anonymous routed through encrypted hacker web sites. It's your word against anonymous. Unless the cops are already suspicious and have something linking you to one or more of your victims' morgue photos."

"Like what?"

"I don't know, say opening and closing security photos from storage lockers and bank safe deposit boxes linking your face and the victims. I suggest you stop killing people even if they are annoying and go confess to the police."

"Fuck you! I bet you're sorry you spent so much time studying my cock, instead of getting on the Q train?"

"No regrets. All in all it has been an unusual day."

"Just saying; if I turn myself in, will you visit me in prison?"

"Depends."

"On?

"Whether they allow conjugal visits?"

www.ingramcontent.com/pod-product-compliance
Lightning Source LLC
Chambersburg PA
CBHW022014010726
47494CB00003B/1031